"Diane Zinna carves her sentences on the page. This book is compulsively readable because no scene or paragraph goes to waste; each nuance of thought and feeling gets traced with generous intensity. Zinna renders all the vivid saturations of grief, but not just that: She also traces the complicated fretwork of young friendship. This book shows how coming-of-age and elegy can be the same story."

—EMILY FRIDLUND, author of the Booker Prize finalist *History of Wolves*

"This stunning debut novel explores the space between dreams and nightmares, life and death, the brilliance of the midnight sun and the darkness when you shut your eyes. Diane Zinna has given us a tender, aching, and unforgettable story."

—JULIA PHILLIPS, author of the National Book Award finalist *Disappearing Earth*

"Sensuous and hypnotic, *The All-Night Sun* reveals the many ways in which grief can distort one's judgment and even one's allegiance to the truth. Diane Zinna has gifted an empathic prose-poem to anyone who has felt displaced by loss and in search of a path out of the stalemate of memory."

—PAMELA ERENS, author of *Eleven Hours*

"*The All-Night Sun* illuminates the unwieldy paths the human mind will follow when chased by grief, loneliness, and the failure of memory. In lyrical, dreamlike prose, Diane Zinna's *mångata* leads her characters from profound loss to the promise of wounds healed. . . . An impressive debut by a gifted writer."

—CHRIS CANDER, author of *The Weight of a Piano*

"*The All-Night Sun* is a provocative examination of the often-blurred boundaries between teacher and student as well as the disorienting effects of grief. Using language so suffused with light and color that it's hard to look away from her words, Diane Zinna writes movingly about family, friendship, psychic black holes, and the ways in which art and writing can ameliorate the damage life etches on us all."

—JENNIFER STEIL, author of *The Ambassador's Wife*

"*The All-Night Sun* is about loss, guilt, faith, friendship, and, as the title also suggests, the human ability to go on. Zinna offers everything I come to a novel hoping for—a compelling protagonist, graceful prose, first-rate storytelling, and deep compassion for her characters."

—LORI OSTLUND, author of *After the Parade*

"A mesmerizing, disturbing, and heart-wrenching read about loneliness and grief . . . Diane Zinna writes sentences that will break you, and then suddenly everything on the page lights up again, and you go on the roller coaster that is love, and loss, and life. With poetic and hypnotic prose, *The All-Night Sun* is an essential addition to fiction on grief and a compelling story about female friendship, its limits and constraints, and the surprising ways it can make us whole."

—NATALIE JENNER, author of *The Jane Austen Society*

"*The All-Night Sun* is a testament to the power of storytelling. In much the same way that she pursues her emptiness across an ocean, the rawness of Lauren's pain will have readers chasing her through the pages. The lies she tells herself—and others—about her past become the ghosts that simultaneously accuse and exonerate her. As she unravels and cuts through the tangles of her experience, we can't help but cheer."

—BENJAMIN LUDWIG, author of *Ginny Moon*

"In *The All-Night Sun,* author Diane Zinna displays her deep understanding of the writing craft. . . . Her stunning debut novel is a twisting tale of grief, hope and self-deceit, a story as mesmerizing as the young women at its heart."

—*BookPage* (starred review)

"Inventive and luminous . . . Zinna's intimate debut dazzles with original language, emotional sentience, and Swedish folklore as it plumbs the depths of grief, loss, and friendship. . . . Zinna reaches an inspired emotional depth that, as the title signifies, never stops blazing."

—*Publishers Weekly* (starred review)

"At its core, this debut novel is about well-lighted grief, inescapable grief, swimmable grief. . . . Zinna's skilled writing and the world she has conjured are rich, textured, and vulnerable, exactly like the art that gains importance in the novel. To live is art, with darkness and light enfolded together."

—*Booklist*

"Diane Zinna's *The All-Night Sun* is an unexpected love story—about rebirth after loss, about the human connections that art and literature enable, about the adventures we undertake and the tales we tell ourselves to get by. It's also about risk and sorrow, about how our stories can fatefully mask reality. This is a memorable and meaningful novel."

—CLAIRE MESSUD, *New York Times* bestselling author of *The Burning Girl*

"Diane Zinna has written a mesmerizing story of how grief can pull us together while pulling us under. She is a writer deft with a paintbrush of words illustrating the dark hues of the deepest emotions. Her brilliant story is the heartfelt tale of Lauren and Siri, both orphans with pain shadowing their futures, which sends them on a journey together. Throughout the novel, we never quit wondering if they or their friendship will survive. *The All-Night Sun* is a gorgeous tribute to grief in all its forms and how we have to go through it to get to the other side—there's no way around it."

—AMY E. WALLEN, author of *When We Were Ghouls*

∴

The
ALL-NIGHT SUN

The
ALL-NIGHT SUN

a novel

Diane Zinna

RANDOM HOUSE
NEW YORK

2021 Random House Trade Paperback Edition

Copyright © 2020 by Diane Zinna
Reading group guide copyright © 2021 by Penguin Random House LLC

Published in the United States by Random House, an imprint and division of Penguin Random House LLC, New York.

RANDOM HOUSE and the HOUSE colophon are registered trademarks of Penguin Random House LLC. RANDOM HOUSE BOOK CLUB and colophon are trademarks of Penguin Random House LLC.

Originally published in hardcover in the United States by Random House, an imprint and division of Penguin Random House LLC, in 2020.

"If My Book" originally appeared in *Monkeybicycle*. Reprinted with permission.

Library of Congress Cataloguing-in-Publication Data
Names: Zinna, Diane, author.
Title: The all-night sun: a novel / Diane Zinna.
Description: First edition. | New York: Random House, [2020]
Identifiers: LCCN 2019037495 | LCCN 2019037496 (ebook) | ISBN 9781984854186 (trade paperback) | ISBN 9781984854179 (ebook)
Classification: LCC PS3626.I56 A75 2020 (print) | LCC PS3626.I56 (ebook) | DDC 813/.6—dc23
LC record available at https://lccn.loc.gov/2019037495
LC ebook record available at https://lccn.loc.gov/2019037496

Printed in the United States of America on acid-free paper

randomhousebooks.com
randomhousebookclub.com

1 2 3 4 5 6 7 8 9

Book design by Diane Hobbing

THIS BOOK IS DEDICATED
WITH LOVE
TO
MY MOTHER AND FATHER,
TO
BLAIR, AND TO SARAH.

The
ALL-NIGHT SUN

WHEN I ACCEPTED Siri's invitation to travel home with her for the summer, it was like taking her up on a beautiful dare. I can still see her with her backpack, eighteen years old, lightly crossing transoms of age and language to make me feel comfortable among her teenage friends. In dreams Siri leads the way through Gamla Stan's crowded caramel streets, turning to smile at me as I follow behind. Back in the United States, before I impulsively accepted her invitation, I had been Siri's teacher. Like the midnight sun that does not set, my decision to go to Sweden with her spread its undying light over everything. My grief was like that, too. I fell asleep to it. I awakened to it.

In essays, Siri had written about this place imbued with magic: trolls; water spirits; the holiday called Midsommar, when everyone flees the cities for the countryside, when everyone turns young again. Midsommar, when the sun didn't set and night's torments didn't come. Really? She'd agreed, yes, it was that green, that fresh, that new—everything would be just thawing out.

She wrote about her home back in Sweden. She was an art student. I asked her questions to color in her descriptions of the people she knew, of her country home in Olofstorp, of the traditions she kept with her family. She had a sister with long hair who worked at an airport, cleaning planes. She had a brother. She shrugged through a description of her town. It's not like here, she said. She missed home, but she didn't know why. I said, put down your pen. Just tell me about it. What colors do you see when you think of home?

And then we were there. Lush canvases of wet meadow opened

one upon the other, bright green oceans that undulated and tipped
with the wind like liquid. Did we create that place with our words?
I could barely remember the words she used to ask me to come
home with her for the summer break. It doesn't seem possible that
there were words enough to make me risk the job I loved. Teaching gave my life some aspect of normalcy, and I thought then that
it was normalcy I craved. But there was no hesitation. I bought my
ticket that very day. Maybe all those years alone were building to
that moment, that invitation to somewhere else.

I grasp at early memories of our trip now, and they are otherworldly, other-sensory. The purple door of her family's country
house—did it really smell of lavender? I remember our three days
in Stockholm as sticky and sweet, maybe because we got ice creams
from vendors on three different corners, one right after the other.
I remember sitting there beside the water, trying to talk through
bites, laughing because our lips were numb. We shielded our eyes
and watched tourists taking banana-boat rides out beyond the
Viking-style, curl-prowed ships in the harbor. And when I think
of our talks there, they can sometimes feel like sun in my eyes.

We visited many beautiful towns there. I could never pronounce
their names right. I couldn't grab hold of the sounds to remember
them. With so little English around me, I had the feeling of being
half-awake the whole time. In some ways, it was like being a child,
when you could just close your eyes during a conversation, slide
down under the table, and run around. But I was not a child. I was
almost thirty then.

For weeks we zoomed through storybook towns with square-
cobbled streets and curved one-lane roads barely able to accommodate Siri's tiny car. In the countryside, there were dark red
farmhouses with white frames around their windows. We jumped
from barn lofts, laughing so hard strands of hay got caught in our
teeth. We laughed as though we were both children.

And on the last day of our trip, she arranged for a group of us to
drive to Öland, an island off of Sweden's eastern coast, where we
would camp and celebrate the holiday. She said that at Midsom-

mar it would even be warm enough to swim, but I could see my breath when her brother, Magnus, helped us load the car that morning. And I could see his breath when he stooped to check the air pressure in the tires, and when, after all the other girls had gone inside, he stood to face me for the first time in days and mutter a goodbye.

"Goodbye," I repeated softly, unable to match his emotionless tone.

As he walked back into the house, I stepped into the place where I'd seen his breath in the air and willed myself to feel the warmth he'd shown me a week earlier, before he'd grown cold. I wasn't just going away for two days—these were the last days. Didn't he feel time running out like I did?

I suppose all those sunlit nights and long twilights had made it feel like we had enough time to work everything through.

All of Sweden was intoxicated with the endless June sun. The animals, too, seemed dopey and confused. That day in Kalmar, right before we started across the great Öland bridge to the island, a moose walked slowly across the road, blocking traffic for a while and blinking peacefully at the honking cars.

And then we were crossing the bridge, four high miles. Siri squinted hard at the white lines through the clouds that kept touching down. Her friends slumbered in the backseat, a mash of black clothes, smeary eyeliner, and punk-rock hair. They were tentative to use the English they'd learned in school even though they spoke it fine. Sometimes, when they were drinking, they tried more. I sat in the passenger seat, a crate of beer like insurance on the floor between my feet.

I had been looking forward to this trip being just us, but at the last minute, Siri had invited the other girls.

"The day is going to warm up," Siri whispered, trying not to wake her friends.

I was grateful that she was whispering. I thought it meant she was ready to talk to me about all that had happened, with her, with her brother. Through the fog, I could just glimpse the water beyond the bridge. There were promises of waves, but they gathered no energy.

"Kalmarsund," Siri said.

"It feels like we're flying," I said.

"I don't know if you can see it, but there's a castle on that shore called Kalmar Slott. It's from medieval times. People sometimes get married there. It's very beautiful at night. They light it up."

I tried to see, but when there were breaks in the fog, all I could make out was the glitter of the sound. I turned to look behind us, but there was a yellow inner tube pressed against the window of the hatchback.

"You're still going to swim with me, right?" she asked.

I shook my head, but I expected I'd cave to her and be swimming soon. Over those weeks, I'd let Siri dye my hair blond, then blacken the ends. We'd gone shopping for new clothes. I'd cut up the T-shirts I'd brought to make them look punk rock, crimped my hair with an actual iron, and skinny-dipped for the first time in my life. Afterward, in a woodsy bar, with my head still wet and with damp clothes, I shouted "*Skål!*" and danced with my eyes closed—not to keep the room from spinning, but because I couldn't bear to see all of that reflected back at me in the mirror above the bar. Siri had liked it—that I was trying, that I was shaking off the shell of grief I'd worn so long.

"There is an old legend. It says you *mustn't* go swimming on Midsommar because an evil spirit named Näcken waits out there in the water, sitting on a rock, playing a fiddle. He is waiting to pull you down. In the story, a maiden stabbed herself in the heart rather than go with him, and white water lilies turned red with her blood. If he gets you, he'll make you live under the water with him forever." Siri smiled mischievously. "You see? We have to swim."

She laughed, but I shushed her, afraid that her friends would awaken and commandeer the conversation and bring it back to Swedish. I was grateful for her smile, her playfulness now. I missed the first part of the trip, when we traded stories and taught each other what we felt were beautiful words in our languages. I had taught her *languid, gloaming,* and *verdant,* which remain charged with memory even now.

We were halfway across the bridge when another car pulled ahead of us and Siri stopped short.

She looked over at me with concern. "You okay, Lauren?"

I unclenched my fingers and rested them flat against the seat. I wanted to appear calm. I told myself the white fog was sealing us in.

I saw her mouth moving silently. She knew I was afraid of bridges. Maybe she was praying for me. Siri prayed a lot for a young person, in a manner less contemplative than compulsive. She said it helped her to feel closer to her mother, who had died when she was five. She'd never shared how her mother passed, only that her death had been hard on her and her siblings and it was the reason for the rift between her and her brother.

Before this trip, she'd told me some other things about Magnus: that he didn't want her to go to college, that he was too critical, an artist himself and disdainful of her desire to study art in school. For these reasons, I had disliked Magnus before I met him. I had disliked the sounds I first associated with him: keys dropped on the dining table, the loud slam of his door, the way he talked to himself on the other side of our shared wall. When Siri had asked me to stay away from him, it had been easy to promise. Now all I could do was think of him.

"If I swim, will you swim, too?" Siri asked now, slowing behind a car, its taillights glowing ruby through the thinning fog. A group of gulls floated beside the bridge and then disappeared above us.

"You know I will," I said. "But I might be the one Näcken pulls down."

"At least then you wouldn't have to go home."

I smiled and looked over at her. The last few days had been hard. I wanted to be going back to the United States, but I wanted to be going back with her, where it could be just the two of us again.

Siri was staying in Sweden until the start of the new semester. Though she had assured me that she was planning to return for her second year at Stella Maris, I kept worrying that she wouldn't actually come back to school. It was hard enough for me to imagine my classroom without her in the front row.

The girls in the backseat stirred and rearranged themselves, a bundle of limbs and blankets. They were Siri's age, and they brought the teenager out in her. I never felt the difference in our ages until I spent time with them. The awkward, motherly conversations I attempted with Siri's friends made them self-conscious. I tried to fit in, but the whole stretch of irresponsible summer, I was going around like Alice, dumbly drinking potions because they were marked "Drink Me." And then, I was Alice in the tiny house, barely able to fit inside, my legs scrunched underneath my giant body. What a lifetime you can live—or not live—in ten years' space.

There was the hush of the waves so close. We were coming down out of the clouds and land was again beneath us, a straight two-lane road. My guidebook had said that this island ground was a mosaic of blanched shells and fossils. I could hear the water and its rush, rush. The girls in the backseat started to stretch and talk, and their Swedish made me drowsy.

Siri announced that we were going swimming first thing. We drove through a tunnellike stretch of woods, the branches of trees knitting together over the road. It was like waking up when we saw the sky again. We parked alongside a rugged beach. The terrain reminded me of a beach on the north shore of Long Island I had often walked as a child with my mother and father, only the slope that the girls ran down was shining blue and green in the sun. Fringy ropes of what looked like blue algae swung lazily in the gentle waves, and the rocks were fuzzy with it underfoot. The beach was called Neptuni Åkrar—Neptune's Fields.

"You said you would swim!" Siri yelled, rushing down ahead of me.

Clutching the yellow inner tube, I picked my way down the

rocks. Bright blue flowers grew all along the shoreline. We were the only people as far as I could see, and the coastline stretched long and curved, changing from otherworldly blue beach to stark white in the distance. Three maroon sea huts stood at the top of the ridge and a thin string of cloud line ran parallel to the shore. I sat down upon the inner tube while the girls splashed in the sea. They had an easy, loving way among themselves. They were close in the way only childhood friends can be.

"Come in with us, Lauren!" Siri yelled.

I waved but didn't get up to join them. Suddenly they were running toward me with big, splashing strides, hanging on to one another, their hair wet and pressing against their cheeks. They each grabbed hold of the inner tube and pulled me into the ocean. I went under smiling and got a mouthful of water.

We couldn't stay in for long. The water was cold. When we came out, our skin was tinged blue from the algae. We wrung out our clothes to dry and sunned ourselves on the azure, blooming rocks. I loved that afternoon. There was no English, no Swedish, just sun on our bodies and sleep.

When afternoon came and the clothes were dry, we drove to the campsite. The girls in the backseat kept looking at themselves in a little mirror, their teeth shining stark white in contrast to their bluish skin. I rested my head against the passenger-side window, and my breath made a fog on the glass. I found myself thinking of Magnus's goodbye that morning, and in the condensation, I lazily traced a letter M. Sunlight streamed through the trees overhead, turning to clicks of light when I closed my eyes. I rubbed the wetness from my fingers against my thigh.

"Lauren," Siri said, soft and low.

I opened my eyes and wiped away the M on the glass.

"Can you help me?" She unfolded a map of the island against the steering wheel as she drove.

I smiled. Whispering. English. Things that made it just us again.

Spring

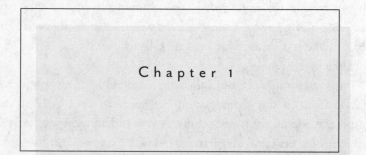

Chapter 1

I TAUGHT ENGLISH composition in the international program at Stella Maris, a small Catholic college outside of Washington, D.C. I was a popular teacher. When class started, my show started. I led with a gentle authority I never quite exacted in real life. The students all wanted to be my favorite. No one was ever disrespectful or unprepared. The other professors complained about their problem students, about how out-of-control some of them were, but I never had behavior issues in my classroom. I loved my students. They participated, and I graded hard, so they worked hard. They didn't skip my class. Their writing improved.

It was the first job I ever loved. In front of the class, I was always in the moment, fully theirs and full of movement, completely in my body, hands chalky, sitting atop my desk, laughing at their jokes. Students didn't depart when I dismissed them. They stayed after to tell me about their childhood bedrooms turned into walk-in closets, the jobs waiting for them in their family businesses. They would bring me candy from their home countries and want me to try everything right then. They would tell me how empty an accomplishment could feel when those you love aren't there to see it, to say *well done*. I knew what they meant by that. A check mark in the margin of their paper, a nod, a smile.

Many of them would write about being new to the country and all the ways they were struggling to fit in. They didn't realize how much I connected with them, how keenly I felt their descriptions of not having the right words, of not being in on the jokes, of laughing along to something you didn't understand when laughter was the last thing your homesick heart could bear. Grief can feel like homesickness.

I was just an adjunct, but I thought that having a few hours each day in front of the room, having the students' rapt interest and respect, made up for some things. I wasn't liked by several of the other professors in my department. Maybe they thought I was too young, or that I talked too softly, or too fast. I started out liking them very much. The first semester, some would ask me an occasional question, dropping breadcrumbs because they knew I was hungry for conversation. Weren't you working in the college library before this? How is it that you're now teaching in the international program? I'd realize, too late, that I was confessing to them parts meant for friends—a glimmer of connection with a student, a better way to teach something. They brooded. They didn't like any of my ideas. They didn't like that I'd never completed my thesis, that I taught at Stella Maris without a PhD.

Was that applause coming from your classroom, Lauren?

Yes, but it wasn't for me. Someone shared their paper and it moved the others.

Well, of course it wasn't for you. Do you hear that? She thinks we thought the students were applauding for her. Just close your door, will you? It's a distraction.

I could have borne it all more easily with one good friend.

It was a wintry January morning when Siri Bergström first came to class early with steaming coffee, one cup in each hand, her portfolio case slung across her back.

I'd noticed her in class. She always sat in the front row, off to my right. When students came in, she would acknowledge each one, sharing a sigh with a girl who also had a long walk from the dormitory, quickly trading notes from a math class with another, always smiling, telling them *hej,* the other students waving at her, the whole classroom gently tipping in her direction.

"You are so young to be a teacher, right?"

We sat opposite each other in the stillness of my first-floor classroom. Bright, floor-to-ceiling windows met behind her at a sharp glass angle, striped with condensation. We were alone, with just the hum of the radiator and the heat coming off my coffee cup.

"People think that," I said.

"You write a lot on our essays."

I looked down at the paper I was grading, at my skinny trail of words winding down the margin. I felt embarrassed.

"I like to read them. They are like whole letters you're taking time to write," she continued. "When this class is over, I'm going to save them. Just for what you've written down the sides."

She smiled. I realized she was being earnest. She shook out her hair with her hand and a sprinkle of glitter fell and dusted her desk.

I motioned toward her portfolio case. "What kind of art do you do?"

From her bag, she drew out her compositions: neon paint, glued-down metal grommets, glitter, and brads. They were sparkling multicolored ovals, like geodes, with enough depth that they looked heavy, about to drop through the desk to the floor. I couldn't think of the words to convey how their complexity startled me. I noticed a tear toward the bottom of one of the canvases that was filled in with gold.

"Some Japanese artists repair broken pottery with liquid gold. It's a way to highlight what went wrong, to say a break can make something more valuable or more precious." She ran her fingertip along the sparkling seam. "It's the same with people, right?"

I smiled. "Right."

"This is just very, very fine gold glitter. But I use it whenever I make a mistake now."

She stared at my face intently, like she was listening more to the curve of my mouth than my reply.

"You're wonderful," I said, and her face lit up.

That's how it started. In the beginning, that was all it was. She would come to class early and share her compositions with me. I'd fumble for words to compliment them, but mostly I could sense she just wanted me to tell her that *she* was good. Then she'd slide them back in her big flat bag, and we'd sit together in silence, attending to our work.

It wasn't much, but I came to look forward to those quiet half-hour intervals. She seemed to like being around me even when I wasn't on. And I started to feel, when the others filed in and filled the seats, when the bell rang and I took my position at the front of the room, that Siri was a friend in my corner, rooting for me to do well.

Siri was a sprite. She was freckled, small and thin, with a pair of skinny jeans in every color of the rainbow. Little accent—she could have been from anywhere. She wore her blond hair short and sometimes dyed it to match her bright pants, but it seemed to me that the way she cared about people made her an old soul. Like she had come from somewhere with the authority to discern goodness in people and had decided there was some in me. I don't think people knew that I doubted that about myself. I think I appeared like I had it all together. I didn't.

Siri turned out to be a good writer, though mostly she didn't understand the purpose of personal essays. None of them did. Often, if my students didn't know a word in English, they would just write the word in their own language. Siri did it, too. In one of her first essays, she used the word *ensam* for "lonely," over and over, as though no English speakers had ever had to express that feeling.

"It may mean the same thing technically," she said. "But it seems to be missing something. Doesn't it?"

We started to talk about that word like we were talking about something else. It was all the ways *ensam* had been defined for her in her lifetime, from her childhood, with her family, and now in the United States without them. For people she had lost, she seemed to want an English word that bore *ensam*'s same lonesome sound, its own turning-in, serious-mouthed hum. I pulled out a thesaurus and read her every English synonym, but it was the sound of her word she wanted, the right to use it and keep it. She told me *ensam* was the loss of her mother, and that's when I told her to leave it in.

"How did your mother die?" I asked.

"Nobody knows for sure," she said with a wave of her hand, a smile again. I knew that gesture, that means of waving things away, that smile to put another person at ease. I nodded. She had found a word that held something for her. I could see why she was protective of it. Both my parents died when I was eighteen. I was an only child without any other family. Without language for it, I'd floated a long time.

No. I'd white-knuckled it. And scrambled, and cried, and ruined my chances, and lost myself. But when I look back, it felt like floating, because before then I'd been so rooted.

Siri didn't seem to be floating. She seemed to know exactly who she was. Teaching gave me a sense of who I was supposed to be at twenty-eight. But there was something of Siri's earnestness that was my should-have-been younger self, the person I might have been at eighteen. I remember thinking, looking at her, *I could have worn my hair that way*.

Me, at eighteen: It was the end of August, when all my friends were going off to college for the first time in faraway towns. It was the dwindling end of summer. One by one they left in roof-packed cars, me helping to tighten their bungee cables, kissing them on their cheeks. Some remarked that I should have been the one to go away, that I was too smart not to go, that I would love their school. Others admired me for my resolve to stay back, work, and save for a year. I put on smiles and told them my plan—I'd spend the year reading all of Shakespeare and teaching myself Latin. I'd publish a short story before I even applied to school. The truth was that we didn't have the money for me to go.

The days grew short so fast, the community pool too cold to swim in, no one left in town to go with anymore.

In our house it was a September of tears and one-sided arguments. Stupid things. Me slamming the door. *Me* slamming the door, never my parents. *Me* losing my temper because the town was too small, because I got passed over for a promotion at the supermarket when the managers knew I needed it more than any of the others. Because I was talking again with my parents at dinner while my friends were in college cafeterias. Because even after I slammed the door, they opened it softly and told me they understood what I was feeling, but they couldn't help but feel glad to have me at home with them for another year.

So I felt, when it happened, that I'd brought it on myself.

At the hospital, I was shepherded into a little green room. The yellow-haired counselor asked if I could call another family member to come get me. But there was no one else. It had only ever been the three of us. Dancing on the linoleum, cooking beneath the open window of the kitchen, looking at the stars while lying on our backs on the patio table. There was no one else. A family of three is like a bet.

I was too old to be an orphan. Old enough to drive. Too young to know I wouldn't be able to make things work alone. They had been driving on the harbor bridge, on their way home from dinner in Port Llewelyn, from a restaurant I could never remember their going to without me. There had been a young college student on a bike. His girlfriend was sitting on his handlebars, and my father swerved, but he lost control of the car and it went off the bridge into the water, just before the posts where the ferries came in. I grew up watching those ferries from my bedroom window, their faraway lights like stars to wish on.

The story was in all of the papers. And then it wasn't. People could not understand that I had no other relatives. The people in town who knew my introverted parents were first sympathetic to me, then more and more started to become curious, demanding details. *We drive that bridge every day,* they'd say. *How could that have happened?*

When I met new people, I did not tell them about it. The nature of my parents' deaths made it hard for me to talk about. The idea of their drowning in a car—I feared that by sharing it, the image would continue to live in other people's minds. And they'd want to say something, but what can someone say? The car would just rev and dive in the strangers' thoughts, and they'd be left on the bridge without a clue how to respond to me. I came to believe the most polite thing to do was let the memory of it die inside me. And part of me started to die away with it.

I was too young to go through that alone. But I was old enough to balance a checkbook. Too young, perhaps, to anticipate the predatory instincts of some men. Old enough to know how to assuage a social worker's fears. I learned to lie. The years passed. I stayed adrift. I floated. I turned inward, my whole life a serious-mouthed hum.

Ensam. Loneliness.

After that conversation with Siri, I grew more hesitant to correct the first-language words in my students' essays, afraid I would tread on something important and untranslatable. I made a list of them. I related to the way any topic I assigned could become, for them, an essay on homesickness. For all of us, the college was a planet far away, and our growing index of untouchable words a language by which to navigate it.

"Why are we learning personal essays?" one of my students asked. They always wanted to tie what they learned to the real world. "Do you ever write such essays for pay?"

Hesitantly, I told them that outside of school I was a technical writer. Manuals. Warranty guides. Contracts and operating instructions and warnings in big letters appearing prior to the step to which they applied.

My students were all intrigued by this, and one girl asked, "How does one break into such a field?"

That girl was an expressive, beautiful writer. I told her she should never aspire to do that kind of work.

"Why not?" she asked. "People need safety instructions."

It compromises you, I wanted to say, feeling the layers of that word inside of me.

"How do you find such work?" *Word of mouth.* "Where do you do this work?" *In my bed.* "Where did you learn how to do this?" *I always knew how to do this.* "How do you get paid?" *By the hour.*

"Well, what *did* you want to be?" a boy asked, and I was caught off guard.

The students in my classes had traveled on their own from far away. For so long, I'd lived within myself, growing smaller and smaller—but they were bold, adventurous. I didn't know how they managed, but I admired them. I loved drawing out their stories. And I enjoyed being with them, something I learned early on not to share with the other professors.

"I've always just wanted to be here," I told them. "With you all."

I somehow sensed in Siri's gaze that she knew the parts I'd left unsaid. Hers was a gaze that always waited an extra moment, should you want to say something more.

"Besides, this kind of writing is important," I said. "Knowing how to express yourself to one another in real ways . . . it can help with loneliness and distance. It can help when you are feeling *ensam.*"

I saw Siri sit up straight in her chair like I'd called her name.

Chapter 2

I WORKED MY first year at Stella Maris at the campus library, checking out A/V equipment and helping professors pull books for their courses and unlocking the shredder cabinet when Secure-Shred came once a week, and repairing microfiche, and emptying wastebaskets. And reading, my ankles wrapped around the legs of a stool late nights when it was just me and a hive of students, with their headphones like blinders and gigantic 7-Eleven Slurpees.

I loved Stella Maris even then. It was nothing like the nondescript university I had eventually attended in New York, with its lecture halls designed by the same people who planned state prisons. My old college was better known for the force of its wind than anything else. There was a rumor that petite women had to wear weight belts there in the winter lest they be blown from campus. That fable was the most magic the place afforded me, but without anywhere else to go, I did graduate work there, too.

The wind that would carry me away came in the form of a boyfriend who was leaving town for Washington, D.C. Going with him meant leaving an opportunity to continue on for a PhD. I worried I was making a mistake, but I was more afraid of being alone. I got a decent-paying job at Stella Maris's library, which felt familiar and safe.

I was not unhappy. I'd always longed for the elegance of a pretty school like Stella Maris, its alcoves filled with art, bronze plaques fastened to the corners of white buildings, hedges cut into the shapes of animals. There was a lovely path on the west side of campus strung with one hundred rose plants, set in the ground by the graduating class during the school's centennial summer. All in a line, equidistant from one another, each bearing a black and white laminated tag with its name: *Sonja, Red Planet, Mr. Lincoln, Diana, Peace*.

I would bring my dog, Annie, with me for walks along this beaded fringe of campus nearly every morning. In time I memorized the name of each plant. Country Music was neon pink with petals that looked like plastic. Tropicana was my favorite, with bursting orange flowers the size of my hand. Having their names inside me made it easier when that boyfriend moved on again in three months' time.

Some people on campus knew me from the roses—I was the girl with the dog. Others knew me from the elegant library with its four white columns out front, its atrium of pink marble, its lonely reading rooms. Both places full of scent and color, both mine in ways that no one else seemed to want. The half mile of a Rose Walk morning was as compulsive and solitary as my movement through the library stacks. Just as I knew the names of all the plants, when someone came asking for a text, I knew exactly where it lived. I knew all the titles on the professors' book lists and thought that if I wanted to, I had a road map to take every class on my own, late nights, knowing everything they knew, filling up all the space in my head.

I had gone from one school to another, like a girl who marries up and moves into her in-laws' home. I liked to think that at some point Stella Maris could feel like a family. The older professors I worked for could be aunts and uncles. My co-workers like a group of siblings. They knew I was steady and dependable. But mostly, people kept to themselves.

I was soon able to take on the role of teaching assistant for extra money. The students were not standoffish like the professors. They let themselves feel. They read the assignments through the prisms of being young, bold, afraid—and my job let me talk back to them in their essay margins. I had been let inside. I loved it.

And I'd grown privy to the conversations of the professors. In the faculty lounge, seated with my grading, I felt almost invisible among them, and I heard the rumors of male teachers who had eyes for female students, and women who graded easy, too desperate to be liked. I learned the hierarchy of the school, the unspoken rules. It seemed they had a loyalty not to their work but to this place, this body of bronze plaques and rose gardens, and they sought to pluck out anyone who'd tarnish it with something as lowly as a need for connection.

I could have taken my grading to the library or done it at home. But I kept going back to the faculty lounge, simultaneously detesting their gossip and craving it. Listening. Invisible.

I was there one day, making my way through a high stack of essays, when some of the English professors started discussing a half-erased sentence of Latin on a rolling blackboard.

Prope sine ture.

I still recite the words like they bear magic. I sifted through the papers while people guessed at the translation. The clap-back academics, the too-loud-then-look-around laughers, so many degrees on their walls; Latin to them was a secret clubhouse language.

"It means 'to come near, to come beside'—"

"*Ture.* Without *ture.* What is that? *Smoke?* Someone look it up."

But they just kept throwing out their guesses, laughing, congratulating one another on being in this secret circle, where it didn't matter if they were right, only that they'd been the types who studied it once.

Quietly, me, the paper-ruffler: "In that context, it means something more like 'close but no cigar.'"

They all looked at the blackboard like the words were coming into focus. "Of course. From Erasmus's *Adagia,*" one of the men said. It was likely not from the *Adagia,* but they all responded: of course, of course.

I felt Latin belonged to me. It was my middle-of-the-night language. I'd learned it on my own after my parents died, to distract myself, to fill the quiet in my head. To those professors, the sound of it, the syntax, the rhythms, were a distant memory, a friend they'd all known once. It seemed to me that was also how other people experienced grief. They would have an acute, complete understanding of it for days or weeks, whatever it took, and then it would be over, and their minds were washed out like split gourds and they just went on with their lives, went to their neighbors' barbecues, chatted and laughed. I couldn't fathom this, how people could so easily move on.

"How did you know that?" Dorothy Wisch asked me that day. She was the head of the international program. She'd never noticed me much before.

Looking back, I don't think I was right—*prope sine ture*? Sometimes I would lie in bed worrying that I'd gotten it wrong, that everything good that came after that moment was based on a stupid mistranslation and I'd be found out, and the bubble would be popped. But it was a moment of magic. The next thing I knew, I was being encouraged to interview for part-time work as an adjunct, one precious class of my own, teaching comp. When I got it, I was so grateful for the chance, I told myself I'd never take it for granted. I was always early to department meetings, always looking to take on extra work. After the first set of student evaluations Dorothy Wisch received on me, she shook me by the shoulders and hugged me.

When my new colleagues heard how I'd gotten the position, they all smiled politely and asked the same questions: Where did you go to school again? You got the position in the international program *just like that*?

Yes, I thought. I know on the outside it all must have seemed so easy to them.

Though I was only an adjunct and skirting the place—one class, the outer rim of the Rose Walk, off-hours at the library—I felt I was finally living some semblance of the life I'd hoped for long ago. I would embrace whatever small part of it that could be mine.

I came to know the other adjuncts best by the bright concert flyers and lecture notices they tacked to the walls of our shared office. I'd try to start conversations. I'd ask them about their classes, but immediately their talk would turn to deconstruction or Derrida, recycled stuff from their grad school days, as though they wanted to prove that they should be teaching in the more academically prestigious English department, and not just giving comp lessons. I longed for a friend who loved teaching in the international program as much as I did. I once told one of the women how much I loved teaching, and she asked me, "Do you want someone to videotape your classes? Maybe then you could show everyone how it's done."

That was Hortense Ryan. She was a longtime adjunct who taught as many sections as they'd give her. She insisted on our calling her Tenny, a name that suggested youthfulness, though she was gray and slow, her thick legs a topography of dark veins. She wore sparkling hairpins, bright brooches placed just so, skirts that never wrinkled down the front. But the smiles that creased her face were more like a gritting of teeth. Her expressions of interest lifted her brows so high they became looks that asked, *What are you doing? Why are you doing it?*

At my first department meeting, she thought I was a student and told me I was in the wrong room.

But when she saw that Dorothy Wisch treated me like a friend, Tenny cleaved herself to me. She was the kind who aligned herself with people she thought could advance her. She got my mail for me from the department office, laughed when I laughed, was always lending me a pencil before I could reach into my bag for my own.

I felt she was taking me under her wing to smother me. "You laugh too fast at their jokes," Tenny would say. "You write too much on their papers. How much could you possibly have to say?"

But I wouldn't let her get to me; if the school was my new family, she was just a haughty aunt.

I told her that in Latin, *Stella Maris* means "Star of the Sea," a term used in seafaring to denote the star that guided wayward sailors home. Over time the star was called the protector of travelers.

I asked her, "Isn't that so apt for the students here?"

Tenny said, "Don't tell them that, dear. You'll be eaten alive."

Part of me once thought that she and I could be friends. She was an eccentric, obsessed with the life of Emily Dickinson. I learned that on the day she swept into the adjunct office wearing a gauzy black gown with a clutch of fresh flowers in her too-low décolletage.

"It's her death day tomorrow, you know," she told me, seeming defensive. "Emily wanted to be buried with heliotrope. They put it in her casket. She held a bouquet in her folded hands. I always wear white on her birthday and black on her death day."

"There's nothing wrong with that," I said. "Your students will remember the seasons. They'll remember the name of that flower. Aren't all our favorite teachers the ones who make things come alive?"

"Is that what you aim to be, Lauren? Their favorite?"

With Tenny, I grew careful not to share too much of what was going right.

I tried to stagger my office hours to work with my students in private, but it seemed no matter when I arrived, Tenny would be there, often sitting in my chair. She would fan herself, indicate the open window, say that she'd needed the breeze. The office had one window, which rose above my desk and framed the campus like a picture.

And my window also looked out upon the front steps of Bisson Hall, where Siri took her math class in the afternoons. I had a beautiful view of the blue-slate path that led from that building to my own, and of the willow trees that flanked it, expanding and contracting like sea anemones.

One day I saw Siri coming, carrying a little white bag with tissue paper poking out of the top. Behind me, Tenny was at her own desk, shaking the ice at the bottom of a soda cup.

When Siri came into the office—the way she always entered rooms, smiling: *Hello, hej, is this okay?*—I sensed the other teachers stop their work. My desk felt suddenly suspended, the air sucked into all their ears.

"I brought you something," Siri said, setting the bag upon my desk. "A very small thank-you."

I opened it.

It was a yellow bud vase, the shape of a lemon, its finish that of a lemon rind.

"They keep the international students rather separate," she said. "I live on the international floor of my dorm. I feel like you are my first real American friend."

She couldn't stay. I watched out the window to see her walk away. "Lauren," Tenny said. The little vase suddenly felt heavy as a paperweight, portentous as a bomb.

I looked up. Her mouth looked swollen on one side, and I could tell it was because she was sucking on an ice cube from her soda cup. Slowly she slit an envelope with a long-handled letter opener.

"What are you *doing*?" she said.

It was a teaching day. I returned to my apartment full of joy from it, an exhausted, adrenaline joy, a heart-racing, no-one-to-share-it-with joy.

I walked Annie. After, when we were heading back up the stairs, I let her leash fall and watched from beneath as her little white feet climbed the open-backed steps. Inside, I flipped through the stations and saw a yogi on TV. I tried to do all the moves. Annie kept crawling beneath me when I was in downward-facing dog to lick my face. When I collapsed laughing on the floor, she snuffled around my hair and ears. I wondered how the laughing sounded to my neighbors through the walls.

Many immigrant families lived in my apartment complex, and groups of their children played in the road until dark. I could hear my next-door neighbor, Mrs. Vallapil, calling to her son and daughter to come inside. In the evenings, she would sometimes knock on my door and hand me a fragrant plate of food, put her hands up, smiling, and say, "Just try. You might not like it." It was always delicious. I think she worried about my living alone. I gave her my extra key, and during the day her son, Ravi, would come in to feed my fish and walk Annie, but it was a comfort, really, to know that someone was thinking of me from time to time.

I knew her children's bedtime from the sounds through my wall, their muffled voices after their TV was turned off, the sound of their bathtub filling with water, then draining out. I waited for the splish-splosh-whoosh of their mother starting the dishwasher, then the sound of her sliding open the patio door to sit by herself in the dark and wait for her husband to return home from work.

The walls in our apartment building were thin. My bed was next to the window, so at night I could look through the slats of my blinds and see the other three apartment buildings that bordered the grass courtyard and small playground. Sometimes I could see someone cooking in her kitchen or someone smiling to himself in the glow of a computer screen. Though I watched and listened, I didn't really know why the young ROTC student in the window across the way was often taken away from his apartment by ambulance. I didn't know why the woman downstairs didn't say hello at the mailboxes anymore, like she used to. But what I did was imagine different stories for her in my head until I found one that helped me feel compassion for her, and when I did, and I was compelled to make her cookies, I did it, though she never really knew why.

In my loneliness, I had learned to string the smallest details into a story of how we were all very much the same: We all had dishwashers, and thin walls that nearly allowed conversation, and troubles that prevented us from ever slowing down, but we were all friends.

What did my neighbors think of me? Did they think of me at all? These were just-hanging-on years in every aspect of my life. The years of credit management. Of paying down debt. Of faraway friends breezing through for a visit and being surprised to see their old pictures on my refrigerator, commenting on my freezer full of vegetable potpies.

I visited all of the D.C. historic spots. I went to Mount Vernon and bought a box of flash cards in the gift shop that helped you learn the names of all the presidents and their VPs. There was a small black-box theater where they replayed George Washington's death with animatronics, black ribbons tied to the ends of the empty pews. Upon leaving, I started to cry hysterically, and later I came to on a riverbank as a dinner cruise sailed past on the Potomac. I felt a police officer's hand on my shoulder. He asked me if I had anywhere else I could go.

I always kept HGTV on. The calmness of the shows, the predictability, the excitement of choosing a new home, of decorating so that it is fresh, clean, and new. All night long. Did I ever sleep with all the lights out? My life was a back-and-forth, a blur, the comings and goings of work and classes and errands and then back to my apartment, where I'd turn on one of the home-buying shows and imagine my life in three other houses—one, two, or three?

Sometimes I was so tired I couldn't remember the drive to and from campus. I'd come home exhausted and let Annie go pee on the balcony. Once the German shepherd downstairs attacked Annie and nearly killed her, a bite across her stomach that required twenty stitches. I think I remember that my downstairs neighbor gave me her old mountain bike after that as a way of apologizing. I think I remember that I brought it to pawn when I needed extra cash.

Nighttime. I was in my bed, and Annie lay in her bed across the room. There was a flash of light outside, and I worried that it was an ambulance coming for the ROTC boy again. I drew up the cord of my blinds. As soon as I did, another flash, green, right beside my window. Then suddenly there were a dozen watery-green balls of light in the courtyard. They bounced from the grass to the tops of the buildings, then off of the sides and down again.

I scanned the courtyard. No one with a laser pointer. No one on the playground. All the other apartments were dark.

I wondered if they were balls of gas, and one splashed against my window like water. Maybe they were balloons, but one by one they hit the branches of a tree without popping. I saw them shimmering, saw the luminous outline of them.

I wasn't afraid. I felt they were for me. It was like watching children playing. Tears were streaming down my face. *Happy tears,* my mother would have said.

After about a minute it was over.

I looked over at Annie, sleeping soundly in her puff bed.

There were moments of living there that I was not depressed. But I was depressed.

I wanted to tell someone what I'd just seen. And that I had memorized the names of all the roses. And taught myself Latin. That I knew the names of all the presidents and their VPs. That the teaching job made my life mean something again. Each pretty hard to believe. Each, said aloud, sounding crazy.

I kept HGTV on to make sure that the sadness didn't creep in too hard. The stacks of frozen potpies for the days I didn't leave my apartment, so I had food. The debt management, watching the other windows in the apartment complex—I was trying. The beautiful green lights bouncing that night. The downstairs neighbor, the balcony, the German shepherd, the bike.

The next day in class, Siri came in smiling, a look to ask, *Hello, hej, is this okay?*

"The strangest thing happened to me," I said, a little breathless.

"Tell me," she said.

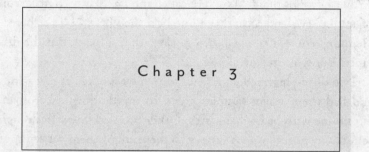

Chapter 3

THIS IS WHAT I wanted to tell her. Eighteen years old. I returned to the house of my childhood that was so empty, with all its things changed after the estate sale, all those strangers' grubby finger pads touching and rejecting, touching and commenting, laughing, making small talk while the green and red grapes that my mother and I had bought the last time we went to the farmers' market shriveled smaller and smaller in the refrigerator.

There was a funeral. I called the friends I thought would come. They were my first calls. My friend Dahlia—we grew up together—was the first person I phoned. She was at her college in upstate New York. She said she had a test, and she was so, so sorry. My friend Nicki from high school spent some time bitching about Dahlia with me, and it felt good for a few minutes, to hear her outrage that Dahlia would not see the gravity of this situation. "Dahlia has always been selfish," she said. Then: Wait? You want *me* to come down there? She kept asking me why I had no family, and I kept answering her questions like I was supposed to explain myself. *My parents were older. Their siblings were gone before I was born.* No cousins? *I have two. But I've never met them.* Her silence blamed me for not knowing them. Where are your grandparents? As though I had simply forgotten all the many loving family members who would help me.

An ex-boyfriend, the one who took me to my high school prom, heard about the accident from his parents and phoned me late at night. "Why didn't you call me?" he asked, sounding hurt. "You can count on me, Lo." He called me *Lo*. A way to make fun of my Long Island accent, the one he'd shed first. "I'll be there." He didn't come. *Oh, my God, I'm sorry,* they all said. But the distance. But why are you alone?

Two of my high school friends who now worked at nail salons and had their design samples glued to upside-down Styrofoam cups came with black manicures. Other people I knew from high school, my experience a mystery to them, all of them yet without an understanding of loss—they came, going through the motions. Their Italian parents prepared them before they arrived—go up two at a time, you kneel at the caskets and pray, cross yourself as you walk away. They came in suits and dark clothes and stood in groups like they did in my high school's hallways. I can see them so clearly, but there are times I cannot remember my mother's voice, my father's hands. They all took the laminated prayer cards emblazoned with pictures of outside-hearted Mary and Saint Jude. Did they still have them, somewhere in their homes? Or did they throw them away, my parents' typeset names too eerie to keep, and then forgotten?

I still have the black dress I wore to my parents' funeral. So many things could have happened to it in the years that passed. It hung in a cardboard wardrobe box, crushed against my mother's old clothes, for years.

When my college boyfriend wanted to move to D.C., I thought maybe it was time for me to start over someplace new. Nighttime in the Salvation Army parking lot: The store was closed. I'd emptied my dank storage unit and was trying to find a place to leave the boxes. My mother's suede coat, my father's books, all those boxes labeled so carefully—I could not even look at them as I unloaded the car. We'd been in the empty parking lot for an hour as I tried to decide what to take, what to leave. My boyfriend was saying, *Now, Lauren, if you want to come with me, let's go, otherwise, I'll be seeing you.* The furniture they used to love—the old patio table we used to lie upon, staring at the stars. How did I even transport it to the Salvation Army parking lot? That table was what my eyes caught as the U-Haul hummed up the entrance ramp to the long, black highway. I saved the wardrobe box. That came.

When we got to D.C., the black dress looked so wrinkled. I had it cleaned four or five times but could not get it to lie right. I left it in plastic, pressed against the back of my boyfriend's closet. When that relationship ended, I folded the dress over my arm and carried it to the apartment of another man, this one much older, where I didn't have much reason to stay dressed, much less wear dresses. I remember telling him how I wanted, just once, to go someplace in my life where I could wear a ball gown. He took to calling me high-maintenance, nothing's-ever-good-enough-for-you, snobby bitch, and when that relationship ended, he put all my clothes in a white garbage bag outside his door, the satiny collar of the black dress peeking through its neck.

With those bags, and with the furniture from my childhood home, too long in storage but still bearing the smells of the things we cooked there, the stains, the dust and creases we'd made there, I moved into my first real apartment on my own.

And I remember that with all the white, white walls, the clean kitchen, the new carpeting, it felt alive and like it wanted to know me. That first night I ate pizza off a moving box while the walls swam around me. The apartment wanted to know my business. Who was I to be there? How had I arrived there? I went to the garbage bag full of old dresses and pulled out the black one with the satin collar. I opened the closet door fast and hung it up in the apartment's mouth, shut the door again. Immediately, I felt more at ease. Now I could hang up my art prints and stick pretty shelf liner inside the kitchen cabinets. Now I could unpack the dishes. I carried grief like that black dress, and there were days that it was pressed into the back of the closet, and there were times I wore it many days in a row.

In that dress, I'd stood next to the twin closed caskets at the front of the room. There were no flowers. I couldn't afford anything extra. My name had not been on their bank account. The small amount of money I would eventually inherit, the money that would keep me going, was tied up in probate. Their insurance was enough to cover plain coffins and cremation. The caskets didn't need to be closed; I could not afford to line them. I was ashamed.

I didn't put an obituary in the paper, but people came anyway. A co-worker of mine named Jessica stood next to me, trying to make me laugh the whole time, and the other people who were there looked at her disgustedly. The director of the funeral home told me where to position myself so that I could shake the hands of those who came offering sympathy, but thank God for Jessica and her jokes! When the director was not looking, we left the room and explored the funeral home. I tried the knob of the basement room where the director had showcased the coffins to me. I showed her the others I'd had to choose from. "You should have gotten pink ones with pink satin inside," she said with a laugh, and rubbed her palm against them like she was a car model. She opened a drawer in a little side table and it was full of straight pins. She said, "They use these to pin the eyes closed!" And I laughed. My stomach muscles stretched and burned. It felt good to laugh. She had offered to take me out to eat sometime, but it never came to pass.

When all the people I worked with at the supermarket were gone, when my third-grade teacher, Ms. Roofson, who lived on the same street, was walking back home with her white pocketbook clutched against her hip, I went back into the viewing room alone.

It was a different place. There were suddenly flowers everywhere. The florist must have owed a favor to the funeral director.

Or maybe he brought flowers over from the other viewing rooms, those services long done, those visitors already at their grave sites. One arrangement between the two coffins reminded me of the horseshoe of red roses presented at the end of a derby.

When the director came in to sit beside me, I went weak. I cried and shook my head and told him everything. I told him how I didn't have any family. How I didn't know what I was going to do. I didn't know anything about money, about the house or the assets they had or did not have. I showed him an index card I'd been carrying with me—it was full of phone numbers of people others said I should call for help, and checked-off tasks, and tasks still to do, and ideas about next steps, the phone number for the morgue, where their bodies had stayed too long. The little card was soft from so many erasures and rubbing, and I told him that the morning after I got the call I was crying and suddenly felt my mother's hand rubbing the back of my hand. And I got very still and didn't open my eyes because I didn't want to know I was just imagining it.

He was kind and put his hand on my shoulder. He smelled of the Vaseline in his hair. He told me I should bring some flowers home, so I did, walking mechanically back and forth from the room to my car, loading them up to the ceiling. When he told me to take one chrysanthemum from the top of each coffin to press into a Bible, I did exactly that. I was so grateful for someone telling me what I should do—I would have done anything he said.

When I couldn't fit any more flowers into my car, I went back into the funeral home, and the director told me I should say goodbye to my parents. He left me alone. I felt like that was it, and I was running out of time. The white chrysanthemums spilling over their wooden caskets were already starting to brown around the edges.

I told them I loved them and not to worry about me, that I would find a way—like we were all in it together. I thanked them for sending me to that funeral home, for I felt that I had been sent there, and that the show of flowers and the funeral director's kindness were proof that everything was going to work out, somehow. People would help me. I would get by on their kindness until I could find a way to get by on my own.

It wasn't enough. I loved them so deeply. There was something else I needed to say to them, but I couldn't figure it out. All the tasks listed on my index card—there hadn't been time enough to prepare for this moment. As I stood there, I imagined my parents were flowers, growing in the direction of the light coming through the slits in their caskets, growing toward me as they waited for me to say the right words.

I couldn't breathe. The scent of the flowers made the air so thin. I went into the hallway to catch my breath and found myself standing outside the funeral director's office. He was on the telephone. He didn't know I was there.

"She's pitiful, really," he said to his wife. And he said it was pathetic my mother and father had not planned for this eventuality. What eventuality? For this? He told her that he didn't think I was ever going to make it. He told his wife that they had to do a better job by their daughter. I turned back to the viewing room and hurried to their caskets. I was shaking all over and put a hand on each one. The director had called me pitiful, and he'd blamed my parents for what had happened. Suddenly I couldn't bear to leave their bodies in the director's keeping. I wanted to see their faces. I thought if I could just see them again, maybe the words I needed to say would come spilling forth. If I'd had more time, I wouldn't have been scared. I would have opened those coffins and gathered them up in my arms. But I heard the director coming, and I could not face him.

I said the only thing I could think in the moment. "I'll come back."

I rushed from the funeral home after that, not even remembering my sweater, where it was slung on a chair in the front row. I drove to our old house and cried.

I never went back. I never even drove past the funeral home

again. A promise made to flowers, to wooden boxes. Sometimes I let myself believe the funeral director never put their bodies inside the caskets to begin with. And so, they could have been anyplace. I imagined one day I would open my bedroom door and their bodies would be laid out side by side upon my bed—oh, here they are, misplaced after all this time. My grief then felt like waiting, like it was just a matter of time before I found what had been lost.

I imagined Jessica telling the other supermarket cashiers about our jaunt through the basement of the funeral parlor, how weird it had been. I never returned to work there. I imagined my old teacher rooting through her white purse for a mint, telling people on a bus how strange it was that the coffins had been closed. Yes, how strange.

I WAS TERRIFIED someone would find out that I was living in the house alone. My parents didn't have a will. Maybe they thought they didn't need one because it was just us. I was eighteen. I didn't know if I would be considered an adult or a child, and I didn't trust anyone enough to ask. I lied to the neighbors. I said I had family taking care of me. I grew secretive about everything so I could keep living in the house.

I had their bodies cremated. Two weeks later, the director's secretary came by my house with the urns tucked under her arms. As I struggled with bills and sold off more and more, I feared I'd soon be homeless and left carrying these heavy urns with me, that I'd never be free of their weight, that weight so great, heavier than I ever thought, not furniture, not comfort.

After the accident, people in the town started to talk about our house, about how it was starting to look disheveled. I heard they said, "It was a shame about those people, but the woman used to plant annuals, do you remember? It just brightened up the whole corner." So I started planting my mother's old palette of flowers, clouds and clouds of them. I painted the porch and repaired the gutter, which had been leaning from the house ever since a bad storm, when we lost power and a swarm of stinkbugs flew through the house like they were charged with lightning.

I started dating to fill the house. I hung a set of wind chimes that one man, so tall, walked into on the porch. They never sounded right again. Another sat in my father's favorite chair and broke it, just like that.

Annie couldn't stand the men. I would put her outside my bedroom, but she would just bark and bark. When they went through the hall to use the bathroom, she nipped at their feet. They would leave articles behind so often—a cap, a matchbook, a comb—and in the mornings, I'd go about looking for them, for if I saw them later in the day, if they caught me off guard, a man's sock in Annie's mouth, my heart would race with the panic of having been burglarized.

I had a game I always played with men. Tell me the first memory you think of when I say the word (*blank*). We'd go back and forth, trading words, sharing stories, and sooner or later they'd hit on a word that opened up a door in me and I'd be telling them something about my childhood. Never the accident. Never that I had no family now, but a release of small, honest pieces. And it would catch me off guard, how badly I wanted to be known.

A word can be like a cellar door. Just a few steps and you're in a dark place. Some men quickly thought they loved me. I would start to care about them, too, but I knew I was engineering these bonds, and I felt guilty about it, weak and needy and dishonest. I wanted someone to hold me and to touch me, but so often I'd find myself frightened, in up to my neck with someone I hardly knew. They were often the ones who would not leave.

At night my hometown felt so large, so many people, so many men I'd never seen before, such a very good chance that this one, finally, hadn't heard of the old people who'd drowned at Port Llewelyn, and maybe he'd just see me as a cool, kind girl. But during the day, the town felt oppressively small, the neighbors like zombies standing on my lawn, watching my house.

IT WENT ON that way for about a year. Then I found a Realtor to help me sell the house. I'd just sold my mother's pretty copper pans, and the outlines of where they'd hung my entire life patterned the kitchen walls around us. She wanted to talk about nothing but the accident, and each time my answers to her questions were briefer, quieter, until the spool I was turning, turning, turning gathered up all the words into a tight, compact thing that I stuck away. She sold the house and some of its furnishings for me. I felt both grateful and unmoored.

When I finally went away to college, advisors asked how they could best support me, and I told them that I wanted to move into the family housing they reserved for graduate students. They all nodded and said, "Of course, of course," like they would understand that I'd want to—what? Be close to any family? Even families that were not my own? I just wanted a place I could keep Annie with me. She and I moved onto the campus in what felt like a permanent way.

It was the sale of the house that made college possible. I went to the same school I had planned to attend before my parents' accident, as though they could someday visit me there. I remember telling them how I had heard there were wind tunnels between the buildings and girls could just get whisked up by a gust.

Finally there, I would walk the campus longing to be caught adrift and sail away. But grief is a weight belt. I dedicated myself to my studies, taking summer sessions, multiple internships, extra jobs. I never went anywhere for holidays. I didn't have any close friends then. I read so much.

I saw a psychologist at school. I knew I needed help. He said he was working on his thesis and had this idea that helping others could soothe one's own grief, and he asked if I was open to meeting with people who had been in my situation. I said okay, and I had this private wish that the people he found for me would turn into friends. But when I went back, he said he couldn't find anyone like me. He said, well, what good advice *would* you have given, if there had been someone else like you? He sat there staring at me with his fingers on his computer keys.

You leave the television on all the time to keep the ghosts from talking to you; you all stare at the set. You give things away and live in the smallest space possible to prevent memories from taking over. Whatever you do, don't have a funeral. The people who come will remember the other people who came and assume that one of them is taking care of you, when they're not. Everyone will remember the people in that room as close, when they're not. They're somewhere else tonight; their life has gone on, and yours has not. When holidays come, you date or you drink.

Before I left for school, I tried to open my parents' urns. I banged on their lids like they were pickle jars, ran them under hot water, looked for seams in the brass. They were sealed shut.

I dropped the urns in a lake near my old high school.

When I let them go, and the urns left my hands, I felt like I would follow. I watched the shadow of the urns disappear under the muck. It was a mistake, returning them to water. Here on land, on a mantel, they could breathe. I imagined their lips up near the unopenable lids.

Some days I still fear a child will find them and roll them up onto the sand. Other times I imagine they are still falling, that the water was that deep.

Mine was still-falling grief, a sea with no floor. After ten years, I was still falling, feeling for the bottom with my feet.

What did my parents do in their last minute underwater? Did they hold hands? Position their mouths up to the ceiling of the car, for the last inch of air?

I tried to take solace in the idea that at least they were together when it happened. They loved each other so deeply. They never yelled at each other, and I hoped they didn't blame each other at the end. What was that rule we always recited crossing bridges? If the car goes into the water, do we open the windows—yes or no? Did they wait to hit the bottom before deciding, realizing that they'd always expected the water to be shallower near the harbor? Did they watch fish go past?

They would never get to fade away. Even after I died, they would be on the bottom of that lake, brass ghosts. Pennies tossed in a deep, deep well, their end a plink and a reverb below the water.

The sound—the rush—of water folding over ears. No one left to listen. The grapes in the refrigerator, green and red—like shriveled finger pads in a white bowl. The fingers of strangers as they touched my parents' things at the estate sale. A man, arguing with me that we should do it in my parents' bed, me saying no, that we stay on the floor, the carpet burn against my back as he pushed into me, the four circular scars it left on my skin. That man, the first one, smoked in my parents' bed while I stuffed my bloodstained underwear into the bottom of the garbage can and twisted in front of the mirror to see where my back was scraped—he terrified me, and though I asked him again and again, he did not leave until morning.

These are the things I wanted to tell Siri that day. Instead, I told her about the green, splashy lights in the courtyard of my apartment building.

But the way she listened, I knew it would only be a matter of time before it all came out.

Chapter 4

ONCE, A VIETNAMESE hairdresser who spoke choppy English asked me where my parents lived. Were they local? I told her that they were, and that Christmas with them had been great. I even made up a story about the presents I bought for them that year. My mother loved Chanel perfume. We got my father a shirt. The bright, generous lies were born to fill the space, then floated away with my hair trimmings to the floor. The nice hairdresser was no worse for not knowing, and I'd been able to exit the conversation without having to describe their deaths and how devastating it had been. I lied to avoid questions that were only ever asked in pity or out of obligation. Sometimes people just open the wrong door without realizing they are in a scary funhouse at all.

There were lies like the ones I told to hairdressers, but there were others. Testing-the-water, cautious lies. There was a hot pipe of grief that jutted from my chest, and there were lies like light twists on its release valve. Early on in the semester when Siri was a student in my class, I used a story of my parents' deaths to demonstrate how a comparison-and-contrast structure could be applied to a personal essay format. A-B, A-B, A-B.

My mother was A. Pacing in front of the room, I explained

how she had died quickly: A. My father, on the other hand, had suffered over many years: B. My mother, sweet but obdurate, shunned doctors: A. My father was hospitalized all the final months of his life, and had even participated in a clinical trial: B. I hadn't been able to say goodbye to my mother: A. I had been able to say goodbye to my father: B. Tack a hook onto the opening paragraph. In the conclusion, say something interesting about how A and B, though different, are really very similar. There—you have yourself an essay.

On the board, it looked like algebra. It was a good structure for the nonnative speakers to hang their new vocabulary upon. But in the front row, Siri sat with her mouth slightly agape and her pencil poised over the blank whiteness of her paper. I felt that she knew even then that it wasn't the truth. But she saw through it, too, and knew that there was something I was trying to get out.

I had used it as an example, but some of the students didn't understand the assignment. At midterm time, three ambassadors' daughters submitted moving, well-organized essays that compared and contrasted their parents' deaths. All the midterm essays were graded by the program head, Dorothy Wisch. She just assumed the girls had copied one another's papers. In their poor English, they each wrote out my own fabricated story about my parents, and its starkness shocked and upset me. They showed me the skeleton of my lie in three mirrors, but not the grief—the flesh.

Dorothy left it to me to address. In the department, she was my strongest advocate. To her, I could do no wrong. She never even asked me about it again.

It was a good thing, too. I didn't handle it right. The girls were all tall and thin, like high-fashion models. They came to my office hours and insisted they hadn't understood the assignment, they hadn't meant to offend me. I liked those girls so much, and I wasn't used to conflict with my students. They spoke with their long-fingered hands, widening their kohl-rimmed eyes as I tried to stand my ground.

"Why did you give us that example if we were not supposed to use it?"

"It was an example. That's the nature of an example."

"I will call my father," one of them threatened.

"That's my point. Your father is not dead. The nature of the assignment was to write a *personal* essay. Come on, now. You are smart girls."

"But you shouldn't grade us on whether it was real. This is a writing class. What does it matter if it was real?"

"That's right. You should grade us on whether we used the right format."

I saw then that Siri was hovering in the doorway of my office, listening.

"We are sorry that your parents are dead," another said.

They were the first students who ever challenged me on anything.

"C's. Would you girls do with C's?"

Siri came in right as the girls were leaving with their reassigned grades.

"What they did was wrong," she whispered. "They stole your story. That was a personal story."

"Maybe they did misunderstand the assignment," I said, and she eyed me with disappointment.

"They missed the whole point. People want to connect. You need to let people in and let them connect. That's what the writing is for, isn't it? That's what you said."

I looked out the window.

"You give so much of yourself when you talk, and they didn't give anything of themselves. They stole your sad story and claimed it for themselves."

"It wasn't my story, Siri."

"It had part of you in it. The part you wanted to share with us."

I looked at her. She hadn't hesitated at all. She didn't think it was peculiar that I had lied. She skipped right to understanding that—

what? That there are sometimes reasons we don't tell the whole truth.

"I didn't lose my parents like that. The way I described."

She pulled over a chair and sat down.

A clutch of students was laughing outside the open window above my desk. Siri rose to shut it, then went and closed my office door, too. Privacy. She returned to her chair and stared at the tattered corner of my desk blotter. She was waiting.

But when you don't share your stories, you eventually lose their normal starting places. How would I remember where to pause and how to pace it? I was afraid of the quiet, of her, of privacy, even though her face was full of kindness. There was a broken piece of tile beneath my desk chair, and I scraped at it with the heel of my shoe.

A bridge, a skid, the funeral, the way people talked. I chewed on the inside of my cheek. In the morgue, my father's hand was open and reaching toward my mother's, I said. I'd laid my hands upon my mother's stomach. Her face was gray and pressed in on one side, I said. Her whole body was rigid, but her belly was still soft. I remember loving her, the way her belly felt under my hands.

"I have my mother's same stomach shape," I said to Siri, pushing away from my desk slightly and looking down at my own body.

How long had I been speaking?

In the basement office, she tried to meet my eyes. I was suddenly ashamed of my hands on my own stomach. I dropped them into my lap.

She didn't rush to fill the silence. She didn't tell me she was sorry or change the subject in embarrassment. Instead, she reached for my hand. Her fingers were warm from holding her coffee.

She leaned forward and asked me, "What were they like?"

I hadn't told anyone that story in years. Her question meant everything to me. For so long I had felt physically unable to speak about my past. I wanted to travel with one of those small chalkboards people use when they have no voice. I wanted to write the word *pain* on it, string it around my neck, and keep people away.

But Siri really wanted to hear. What were they like? She gave me time to find the words I needed.

"Sometimes I can't remember their faces. Or I see them only the way they look in old photos, like statues. Often, I know I'm remembering things wrong, but I don't know where things are getting muddled. And there's no one to tell me what mistakes I'm making."

My parents look like movie stars in their old photos. I have hundreds of them from before I was born, all out of order, like a book with its pages torn out. I tried many times to arrange them by year, as though if I could just get the order right, I'd have a narrative that would last, a linear story that would make sense and always matter. A box less likely to wind up in a dumpster after I was gone.

I kept salvaged memories in the dream journal beside my bed: That my mother used to be a model, wore a clip with a white flower behind her ear, and she got so tan each summer, people would ask her if she was Hawaiian. That my father had once been a beatnik, was able to swan dive, able to do a backflip off the front stoop of his childhood home in Queens.

They were often mistaken for my grandparents. When I came home from school with my friends, my father would be there in his knit cap, squatting to water the grass with the hose and its long shot of water that reached all the way to the other end of the lawn. He would always have this huge smile whenever he saw me.

In my hometown, there was a deserted motel with a playground. It had a structure that looked like a squashed metal hamburger. You could climb up a ladder and slither on your stomach onto a circular platform that was enclosed by bars. I only tried to get inside of it once, when I was about ten. It was night, and I was with my friends. I was wearing this big coat, and there wasn't enough space for me. I was trying to back down out of it when the streetlights came on, which was always the cue for us to go home.

I could hear my friends running back in the direction of our street, but my puffy coat had bunched up, making it hard for me to get out. I tried to take off my coat, thinking that might help me fit back through the opening, but my arms got caught behind me in the sleeves. I was terrified. I just lay on the platform and screamed.

And then, there he was. He talked me through coming down. He caught hold of my heels and pulled me out so that my chin accidentally went bang-bang-bang against each of the metal rungs. The sweet tobacco smell of his coat as he carried me home.

These were the things I remembered easily. But I had blacked out the memory of the accident with a ferocious growth of neural vines that changed my mind, I said, my brain, the very structure of it—now the shape of my brain is a heart, now a horseshoe, now a—

"Did you say it has been ten years?" Siri asked.

"Yes."

I found myself wanting to add *I'm sorry*.

Ten years: by everyone else's account, more than enough time to get myself together.

She was counting on her fingers. "The pain never really goes away. I lost my father . . . fourteen years ago now?"

"Your father?"

"Yes."

"I'm sorry, Siri. I thought you said it was your mother—"

"Both. My father first."

Is this what had drawn us together, then? I couldn't believe it. This girl in front of me was so full of joy and lightness. She seemed so giving, outward looking. It didn't make sense to me that she could have also experienced such loss.

"I don't have many memories of him," Siri said. "But he used to do this thing, after my bath—he would take this big purple comb and comb my hair straight back from my forehead, over and over in the quiet. One night I asked him why he liked to do it and he said, 'Because I love to see your beautiful face.' That night I snuck scissors to my bedroom and cut off almost all my hair. When he came in to check on me, he saw the pile of hair on the floor and me looking like a hedgehog. He asked me if I did it because I didn't want him to comb my hair anymore, and I said, 'No, Pappa, it is so you can more easily see my beautiful face all the time.' "

She brushed her hair back with her hand and we laughed. She had told me the story to make me laugh. I was grateful for it.

"So my dad first. And then my mom, soon after." She shook her head. "But I have my sister and brother. Lots of cousins and aunts. I don't mean to suggest it's anything like your story."

When I first lost my parents, I used to go out at night and sit on the back lawn of our old house with Annie, the gentle, then-mourning dog that had been so devoted to my mother. I'd look up at the night sky and talk to them, and every so often, I'd see a plane or a satellite drifting by. I tried to imagine my parents as rocket people, living on another world for a while, and that one day, they'd come back for me.

My favorite story was Ray Bradbury's "All Summer in a Day." He described Venus as a planet of perpetual rain, where the sun only came out for one hour every seven years. I loved his nine-year-old Margot, who had moved to Venus from Earth. Her gray-uniformed classmates were jealous when she insisted that she remembered how the sun felt on her skin. They were too young to remember it themselves. I loved her poem in front of her class: *I think the sun is a flower / That blooms for just one hour.*

In the story, her classmates lock her in a closet, and when the sun arrives, they are so excited that they forget her there and run out to play. They only remember Margot when the sun has disappeared again into the mist for another seven years.

Since my parents' deaths, there had been so much rain. How had he put it? *A thousand forests had crushed under the rain and grown up a thousand times to be crushed again.* Living felt that way to me: a crushed and crushed and growing-again forest. But grief was also the painful memory of the sun. That yellow coin big enough to buy the world with.

The day I told Siri my story, something inside me clicked open.

It was as though I were eighteen again, and the years—all those bad, rounded-back years—thawed. And it was only the too-young, wet-faced me sitting, finally, beside a friend.

"I understand what you mean about forgetting a person's face," she said. "Ten years—it's not really that long, is it? Sadness is long. It's always long. A long string from a big ball that you roll and roll."

She said she understood. And for a time, I was better.

SIRI TOLD ME about stables within walking distance of the college. I'd seen people beyond my classroom windows riding on a trail shielded by trees but had never thought about where they'd started from.

I began to meet Siri there. We'd both grown up loving horses. The way she described her time in the countryside of Sweden, it sounded like she and her friends had trained as bareback riders in a circus. She told stories of learning to stand up on a horse's back, riding backward, riding three at a time, riding as toddlers bundled up in snowsuits, their snowshoes making the horses look like they had wings.

I remember the first morning we went to the stables together. "Here," she said, and she handed me some sugar cubes she'd brought to feed the horses.

It was March, and still cold. I could see her breath when she made a clicking sound with her mouth and the two horses in the ring ambled toward us. From her pocket, she drew out carrots and placed them along the top of the fence.

"You've been here before," I said. "They know you."

"This brown one is named Rockabye. The white is Irish Cloud. The first day I saw people riding I knew I had to find the stables. I needed something that felt like home."

"Are you homesick?"

"No. I mean, I don't know. I needed to get away from there."

"Why?"

"So many reasons."

"Tell me one."

She smiled. "Did I ever tell you that my brother is an artist?"

"No."

"His name is Magnus. He's good. He's even kind of successful. He said he'd help me. But I just needed to make my own way, you know?"

"Do you like his work?"

She paused for a moment. "No."

I laughed. I wasn't expecting her to say that, but she stayed serious.

"Why don't you like it?" I asked.

"I hate talking about Magnus," she said quietly.

"It's okay," I said. "We don't have to."

She emptied her pockets and seemed to be gathering her thoughts together as she lined up more carrots, small apples, and sugar cubes along the fence rail. The two horses watched her without taking any, like they were waiting for her to continue, too.

"Every painting he does seems to tell a story about me doing something wrong."

"He paints you?"

"He mostly paints my mother, but he makes her look frightening. When I was small, right after she died, I found all these sketches he'd done of her where each one was scarier than the last. When I was in Sweden, all I could do was paint beautiful pictures of my mother. And self-portraits where I looked like a perfect version of me, and landscapes with our house glowing as with a halo around it. All I was doing there was trying to tell my own version of things, fix what he did. I needed to get away to get him out of my head."

"And now? Your work? Is it more you?"

"Not yet. My work is still where I meet all my ghosts. And I still see a lot of argument in the things I do. Like I'm trying too hard. But this is only my first year. I'll find my way."

The horses had eaten their treats and were now staring at me.

"Give them your sugar," Siri laughed. "I think they saw me give you some."

The sugar had crumbled in my hand as she'd been talking. She'd had me entranced. I wanted to remember her in that moment, sounding so confident, so unlike me at her age. I wanted to remember her hair just so, the puffs of dust around the horses' hooves, their smell, her smile. I loved the way she spoke about art like it was her way to work through grief. I remember thinking, *How convenient to compartmentalize that way, to only meet your ghosts when you work.* She exerted control over them and met them where they lived, in her netherworld of geode paintings, mosaics, trompe l'oeil, plaster, glitter—unlike me, who lived at their mercy, memorizing a dead language so as not to meet them in the language they spoke.

I felt she had something she could teach me, and I loved being with her. Soon we were going to the stables most mornings. And soon, the pockets of all my coats were sticky with sugar.

THE SEMESTER SIRI came into my life, I was doing a lot of technical-writing work. Companies would host happy hours in D.C., and I'd often be invited and pass around my business card to the people there. My card had a logo like a feather pen. I still don't know why I thought that would be a good visual for that crowd of military contractors and tech people. Maybe to set myself apart from them.

"What do you do with feathers?" one of them asked.

I tried to make a joke, but it got swallowed up in the din of the place, and the man who had said it just turned back around to the bar. He was all shoulders, that man. The way he hunched, I imagined it was from the weight of his shoulders in that too-tight suit. I remember thinking that, too, when he was shrugging off his jacket in my apartment that night. In my bedroom, a red light glowed from the numbers on my digital clock radio. His back shone red in that light, his broad shoulders slick with sweat.

When I was depressed, or even when I was happy and had no

one to share it with, or when I was bored, I reverted to some of the same behaviors from the New York house, bringing home strange men. But here, the rubbing together of my beloved days at Stella Maris and my midnight life made me feel there was more at risk.

The red-backed man in my bed was a rectangle. He was a sponge. My blinds were closed. One by one, I leveled the slats closest to my eyes and looked out upon the playground and the swings, where a woman sat talking on her cellphone. I tried to imagine she was talking with me until I fell asleep.

In the morning, the man was a damp depression on the pillow. I thought he'd gone, but he was another thirty minutes in my bathroom. Finally, when I opened the front door for him to leave, there was Siri with a bag of scones from the corner bakery.

Fog hovered over the man-made lake behind her like paint. We'd had plans to go to the stables that morning, and I'd forgotten. She had never come to my apartment before. It was alarming to see her there, so out of context. Her hair was in short pigtails, and she was wearing a puffy coat and an off-the-shoulder sweatshirt that said *Casablanca* across the front in glitter.

"What's your shirt?" the man said.

She looked down at the front of her shirt.

"Siri, come in," I said.

"What's it say? I can't read it. It's all stretched out."

"You don't have to answer him," I said.

Siri smiled politely and sidestepped him, came through the door by ducking underneath my arm, and I shut it before he could say anything else. He may have thought he knew something about me, but I didn't want him knowing anything about her.

We stood awkwardly in my foyer. The walls suddenly felt whiter and blanker.

Her hands were clasped before her. She politely made notice of the things nearest her: "I like your mirror. I like your lamp." There was a stack of books on the coffee table, Asian American writers, the pages stuck with neon Post-its. A stack of blue notecards I sometimes laid out upon my carpet showing a timeline of Chinese writers in America: *Sui Sin Far. Onoto Watanna.*

"Are you enjoying all these books?" she asked.

She was avoiding asking me about the man.

"I heard there's a full-time job coming open at Stella Maris next year," I said. "Professor Trela is retiring, and she teaches a section of Asian American literature."

"You're going to apply? They will hire you. I just know it."

"I'm going to try."

I felt unsettled. I looked around my apartment. I was afraid of what she'd think of the dust, the childish items on the bookshelves, my old friends' teenage pictures on my refrigerator, the stains on the carpet. She stepped out of her shoes and put them by the door. "I don't know anything about Asian American literature, but I'll sign up for your classes. You're the only teacher who makes anything interesting. Is that your bedroom?"

Before I could answer, she was walking down the hall to my bedroom door and going in. I felt out of control. I hurried to follow her. I feared the room still smelled of that man, of sex. She went to the window and knelt on my rumpled bed to raise the blinds. I felt tears in my eyes. I was sure my apartment was about to come alive, my closet again a mouth, to swallow her up. I remembered all the men who had been in the bed she now knelt upon. She had pom-poms on the backs of her socks.

"Your view," she said softly.

"What?"

"You can see into all the other apartments. No wonder you care about all these people." She waved to someone.

I went to the window to see the ROTC boy was waving back at her.

"Where did you see the lights?" she asked.

"What?"

"The green bouncing lights. You told me that first day."

It hadn't been the first day. Only the first day I'd shared something of myself with her. But she thought of that day as the first day, too.

"Out there," I said, and we both watched, like they might materialize again in the daylight.

BACK IN THE living room, we ate the scones she'd brought. She sat on the edge of my couch and leaned forward, waiting for me, maybe, to say something about the man, but I felt that was an impossible conversation and avoided her gaze.

"I wanted to take some pictures of the horses today for a project. Remember?"

"Of course." I got up to take our dishes to the sink.

She grabbed my wrist. "No, let's go now. Before the fog clears. Let's see them in the fog."

"All right," I said, pulling away from her. "I'll just do these dishes."

She widened her eyes with impatience.

"Just *this* dish!" I laughed. I put the plates in the sink, beside two wineglasses from the night before. She was suddenly beside me, reaching for the glasses to scrub them out.

We stood shoulder to shoulder, me washing her plate, she washing the man's glass. She dried it with a towel and pushed it into the back of my cabinet.

We bundled up and went down the stairs and got in my car. When I started the engine, the radio blasted loud and she shut it off, ready to continue our conversation.

"So who was that?" she asked.

"I don't know. Just a person."

"What drew you to someone like that?" she asked, and her question stung me with its earnestness. I was reminded suddenly we were at different stages of our lives. I think she felt it, too, the coming and going of ourselves. I felt so protective of her in that moment, like if I didn't tell her about him, a man like that would never happen to her. I never wanted her to give any part of herself away.

"It's okay if you don't want to talk about it," she said. "I see you're just going through things. You need to go through things to come out the other side."

She was talking so quickly, and her words seemed rehearsed. Did she fear that she'd end up like me? When she spoke to me this way, was she also talking to herself?

We drove in silence to the stables and found the two horses we loved standing together in their ring, no one else around. Rock-abye and Irish Cloud. In our hearts, they were ours, they were us.

She wanted to take photos of the horses for her art project. We climbed to sit atop the ring rails and they ambled over to us. I looked at Irish Cloud's snowy face, the gray patches showing through on her muzzle.

Siri adjusted her camera and took a picture of me looking back at her. Then she climbed over the fence and approached Rock-abye, who was snorting and waving her chestnut head back and forth. Siri had a leftover scone in the pocket of her coat, and she fed some to the horse.

"Is that man your boyfriend?" she asked. She put her head against the horse's body as though listening for a heartbeat.

I pretended not to hear her.

"Does he stay with you a lot?"

"No. It was just the one time."

She nodded, pretending to look intently at her camera.

"I tricked him into staying with me, Siri. I play a game. I do it all the time."

"What kind of game?"

"I start conversations. I listen. I talk."

"That doesn't sound like a game."

"It is. It's all made up."

"You lie to them?"

"No. It's not like that. I just know how to talk to men in a way that makes them think they like me."

"I don't understand."

"It's just hard for me to be alone all the time."

I think that was the first moment I thought of the coming summer, of being without her for weeks on end.

"Here. Take my picture." She handed me her Polaroid camera, and I did. When the photograph developed, she gave it to me so I could keep it.

"You're not alone, you know," she'd said.

She meant her, of course. But had I tricked her, too, into becoming my friend with the words we traded, the words leading to stories, openings, words that took us down the stairs of a dark cellar? Just two people grabbing for each other's hand to hold, only thinking themselves friends?

There was a man we always saw mending the same foot of fence across the way whenever we visited the stables. He usually kept his distance and never said anything about our being there or petting the horses. But that day he dropped his gear and called out *hey* to us. I thought we were in trouble for climbing over the fence and getting into the riding ring, but as he approached, I saw how his eyes were fixed on Siri like a dart thrown from one side of the ring to the other.

"Hello," Siri said when he came close. "I just wanted to pet them. I'm sorry."

"I'm Jason."

"I'm Siri. This is Lauren."

The young man nodded. I don't think he expected Siri to be so beautiful up close, for her voice to be that high and silky. He'd lost his confidence. He reached out and pet Rockabye in a rhythmic way, something to do until he could think of something to say.

"You take good care of the horses," Siri said, climbing back over the fence. "I can tell that they are happy."

Jason squinted at her like he was looking into the sun. "You don't have to leave."

"We'll come back," Siri said, looping her arm through mine. "Take a picture of us, will you?"

He took a picture with her camera, but I saw her discard it after it processed. He'd only taken it of her, and she was a blur because of the way his hands were shaking.

SIRI STARTED COMING to my office hours more and more. Tenny Ryan would raise her eyebrows at me, and there was something in her disapproval that spoke of a usurped state. Tenny had imagined us to be close, allies, and here there was this girl.

But it wasn't just Tenny. Stella Maris was provincial. The other professors had inordinate standards of propriety. There were no desks arranged in circles in their classrooms. Everything was kept exacting. As long as they could keep everyone in line, they saw their classes as successful. In the café of the student union, afraid of their seeing Siri and me together as friends, I would keep a textbook open on the table between us.

Even when Siri started coming to my apartment, I made sure my grading book was out on the dining room table, as though my colleagues could see us there. I knew they would disapprove of the friendship. They'd say worse things about me than they did about those teachers who graded too easily, to be liked. But when you are suddenly given everything you think you need, how do you turn away from it?

I could see Bisson's doors from the window above my desk in the adjunct office. When it hit four o'clock, I would gather my things and run up the stairs to meet Siri as she came down the blue-slate path. Then we'd walk to my apartment, which wasn't far from the school. She made my walk home different. For two years they'd been doing construction on the road between the school and my apartment building, and though the same orange barrels and debris lined the curb every day, she made it feel like things were finally improving.

The Vallapil children loved her. She taught Ravi Swedish words, and he'd recite with enthusiasm the ones he remembered from days before. Khushi would tug at Siri's shirt, hold out her arms, and ask Siri to pick her up.

She made my apartment different. The things that belonged to my family were no longer souvenirs of grief but the beginnings of stories. They no longer spoke at me; I spoke of them. And when Mrs. Vallapil came to my door with food, she came with two heaped plates.

I would sit on my broken-down couch, drinking tea with honey-sticky fingers. Siri would sit on my mother's old velveteen chair, under the orange light of the standing lamp. We shared the ottoman and contemplated little Annie as she padded back and forth between us. She was fourteen now, a deep sleeper, with the gait of an old woman and white in her expressive Toto face. Siri would stroke Annie's ears and coo to her in Swedish. Annie would listen intently, like it was her first love language come back to life, then clamber up to lay her fluffy head in Siri's lap.

The room smelled too much of coconut lime verbena—the close scent of the candles I burned—Spot Shot rug cleaner, and the Vallapils' curry-strong dinners cooking on the other side of the wall. I was self-conscious of these things, but Siri just turned the pages of her magazine, comfortable and still. When she wanted something more to drink, she got up and poured it for herself without asking. And she'd bring me another cup, too. I could set aside all my papers and just be.

When we were together, I didn't need to read something to have a place to lay my eyes, and she didn't need to say anything to justify staying later than she'd planned. When she was done with her magazine, she would rinse both our mugs in the sink and dry her hands on my dish towel.

"All right then," she'd say. "I'll see you soon. *Hej hej.*"

Hej can mean both "hello" and "goodbye" in Swedish. We would be finishing up a telephone conversation, but then she'd say, "*hej,*" and I thought she wanted to tell me something else. I couldn't get used to it. For what felt like the first time in my life, it seemed there was always something more to say.

In her essays, too, she found ways to just keep talking to me. At Midsommar, everyone closes their shops, she wrote, and they go out to the countryside to be young again. That's just how she said it—*to be young again*. In my office hours, I sat with her, circling the many untenable phrases on her papers. Round and round went my pen, softly asking more of her: "What do you mean it never gets dark?"

"There is the *midnattssol*—the midnight sun. Have you heard of that?"

"Yes," I said.

"Come with me to Sweden this summer."

"What?"

How had we come to this point so fast? She offered the invitation so easily, like we could just walk out of that basement office and up the stairs and be somewhere else in the world together, right now.

"Really," Siri said.

A noise in the hall. Tenny Ryan was approaching. Soon she would be in the shared adjunct office, filling it with her smell—heliotrope, flowers meant for a casket. I felt our hourglass running out even then.

I'd had to put all of my energy into fending for myself for so long. I'd grown up fast and withdrawn so small. I'd never been Siri's age, that sparkling and confident eighteen. To be young again? She beckoned me back into the world of the living. *It really is that green, that lush,* she said. *It will all be just thawing out.*

I was suddenly overcome with a rhythm in my mind, a beat, the name of a childhood game played by girls on the edge of adolescence: Truth or Dare, Double Dare, Triple Dare. Consequences. Promise and Repeat. I found myself saying it over and over in my mind as she waited for me to answer. What I'd forgotten from having girl friends was that our games always turned darker.

When I accepted her invitation to travel home with her for the summer, I took Siri up on a double dare. That this place I had been reading about all semester was real; that our friendship was real.

Summer

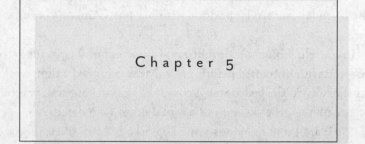

Chapter 5

RIGHT BEFORE WE left, I found a copy of *Per Vikander's Guide to Sweden* on the remainders shelf of my local bookstore. It was a couple of years old but beautiful, with pictures so glossy they appeared wet. I read that people called Stockholm's subway system the world's longest art gallery, with paintings on the subterranean walls of most of its stations. I told myself I had to *see* that. And each time I dog-eared a page in that guidebook I convinced myself that this park, this boulevard, this Viking rune was the real reason I was going to Sweden. Once there, I made detailed notes and drawings beside all the places we went, determined not to forget a thing. In the beginning, how I wanted to remember.

We arrived on a Saturday. Siri's sister, Birgit, greeted us from the balcony of their cottage among so many pots of yellow flowers their home appeared top-heavy. Birgit was six years older than Siri, and beautiful like her, but with dark hair she wore in a long ponytail that fell like a rope. She leaned over the metal balcony railing, reaching out her arms to me giddily, then rushed down and through the front door to clasp my hands in hers like she'd always known me.

"*Var är Magnus?*" Siri asked her.

Birgit looked between Siri and me, smiling. "You said no Swedish, Siri! She's been preparing me for weeks, saying that when Lauren is here, everyone must speak in English out of courtesy for you. And here she is talking in Swedish first thing!"

"Is he here?" Siri asked again.

"He's at work." Birgit grabbed my suitcases and pushed open the lavender-painted front door with her hip. "And he's been better."

Inside, the house was bright and full of color. The walls were covered with unframed paintings, and as we climbed a tight circular stairway to the bedrooms, I could see the curving wall was full of pencil lines, the skeleton of a mural never completed.

"Siri, are these drawings yours?" I asked. They filled the wall from the second-story ceiling to the light hardwood floor below. Flowers, faces. Intricate patterns, diamonds and vines, women with faraway expressions.

We passed a darkened bedroom. I could see an easel in each corner, rumpled sheets pulled back from the mattress, blankets draped in lieu of curtains, a pile of records upon a black dresser.

"Our brother, Magnus," Birgit explained. "He comes in late because of work."

Siri stared inside his room until Birgit put her arm around Siri's shoulder and led her away from the door. "Siri and my brother have a love . . . hate thing," she said. Light poured through a square window at the end of the hall, making the two girls silhouettes, black and cut out against the light.

They still referred to their home as their father's house, and I came to understand that was because he'd built it himself a long time before he died, too young, when Siri was just four. Their mother died when she was five.

There had been a series of grandparents and aunts who floated in to help them over the years. "We're really glad to know you," Birgit said, as though she were speaking for all the people who might have greeted me for the house in different times, when it was not just the three of them.

In the space of an afternoon, the house felt a part of me, more than my white-walled, white-mouthed apartment of two years ever had. I learned which of the floorboards creaked, found the rhythm for navigating their tight circular stairway, memorized the inlaid floral patterns in the landing step, knew the scent of that bright purple front door. Gravel drive, sloping-down hill, then green fields and no neighbors nearby. It was a dream. No matter which way you looked, the sun was on everything. I kept checking my watch to marvel at the sunlight, the late hour. It was squinty eyes and the feeling that you want to run, to move, to spring; the reminder that your body has parts that need watering.

Her town was fields that went on and on, farms, green, "go" green in all directions. Glints of sun in the trees were shining, distant lakes. The two of us went out in front of her house and she showed me a water garden her mother had made. Sparkling plastic gems still lined its bottom, and it was hopping now with tiny frogs.

We turned to face the house together. Now that I had been inside its mostly empty rooms, I sensed more deeply what had drawn Siri and me together: not just the loss of our parents, but the family stories never finished, like that mural in sun-faded pencil beside the stairs.

She took my arm, and we set out for a walk through her town, the all-night sun with us, a friend.

She pointed out her old elementary school, and the little red house of an old favorite teacher, and a stream where she'd once sailed hand-folded cardboard boats in the winter, when the water moved slowly and tiny floes of ice helped buoy them upright. The Swedish summer was peculiar and lovely. It felt like winter in its stillness, but with hot sun on my shoulders. I felt both young and melancholy-old. It was a mix of everything.

As we were walking back up to the road, a car came roaring toward us full of girls, honking the horn. They pulled over, and the three of them leapt out and tackled Siri, covering her with kisses.

Siri laughed and hugged them all. "These are my best girls!" she said to me.

From the mix of limbs and hugs, a skinny blonde extended her hand to me. "I'm Karin!" she said. "We've been waiting to meet you! We've come to show you a bit of our town. You ready?"

"Sure," I said.

"Where?" Siri said brusquely. "I want to show her the lake first."

"*Ja,* we're going to the lake," the girls said.

"Well, you said the town," Siri said.

"No. We meant the lake. See?" One of the girls pulled down the neck of her sweatshirt to show her bathing suit underneath. It was clear they wanted to please her.

"Okay, Lauren, well, you met Karin." She turned impatiently to the other two. "Can't you at least be polite and tell her your names?"

"Margareta," a heavyset brunette offered. She paused a moment and then kissed both my cheeks.

"Nice to meet you," I said, but I was looking at Siri. I had never heard her talk to anyone so tersely.

The other girl, white haired, tall, her face jutting with angles, simply nodded at me. Her lips were painted black, and her ears were pierced up and down the edges in a metallic C.

"This is Frida," Siri said, hanging on the girl's shoulders.

The girl looked away, squinting like she was trying to make something out in the distance.

"She's so shy today," Siri whispered in a taunting tone. When Frida didn't respond, I noticed Siri pinch her arm and chastise her in low Swedish until Frida shook her off and greeted me.

"It is good to meet you finally," she said.

Siri was smiling again. She was clearly the leader here, and I couldn't help but be taken aback that even Frida—imposing, two heads taller than Siri—had responded with such deference to her. It struck me too that this was the first time Siri was seeing these girls in months. She had so easily slipped back into this role with them. I wasn't used to Siri like this. She grabbed my hand and I could feel the other girls notice. Frida stiffened a bit. I tried to tell myself that Siri was feeling protective of me, that she just wanted them to be kind to me.

Frida's accent was thick, and her words felt practiced. "Do you swim?" she said to me, still looking at Siri's hand in mine.

"I love to swim," I said.

"We want to take you to the lake!" Karin said.

"Karin, you can swim?" Siri said.

"Oh, yeah, it's okay," Karin said.

"She just had a baby," Siri explained to me.

"Oh my goodness, congratulations," I said to the girl, who was fumbling with a locket in the scoop of her neck. She showed me the pictures inside, the baby's face in both sides of the oval.

We went back to the house for our swimsuits. When we'd left for our walk, I'd thought the house belonged to the ghosts who'd lived there once, but having seen her with her friends, everything now seemed to belong to Siri.

I heard loud music coming from behind the closed door of her brother's room. I know Siri heard it, too, but she didn't even pause. She raced past me, down the stairs. Did he not exist unless she wanted him to? My eyes caught on his shut door, and I followed her out to Frida's car. Frida handed her keys to Siri, and it was Siri who drove us to the lake.

WE WERE THE only ones there that afternoon. The lake gave off a screen of mist, but a tiny island was visible a short distance from where we stood, barefoot, on the planks of a narrow pier. My black one-piece had a skirt to cover my thighs. Siri and her friends wore bikinis under zip-up sweatshirts. Frida turned away and disappeared into her hoodie. Margareta yawned a lot, and I could see she had two extra teeth in the gumline above her canines. And

Karin smiled at me a lot, but it seemed that Frida's stony gaze out at the island was keeping us all from talking. For some reason, I could sense that girl did not want me there.

Karin knelt to untie a wide, wood-plank raft from a piling, and we stepped out onto it, lay down side by side. Frida had a six-pack of beer in one hand and a snorkeling mask in the other. Siri was on the edge and used a long branch to push us away from the dock. We floated out into a pool of stinging sunshine, round, yellow, certain summer. She let the branch fall to the bottom of the lake, and we drifted in the breeze.

"Frida is planning on going to Stella Maris in the fall," Margareta said.

Siri sat up. "Frida. Did you really send in your application?"

"*Ja, jag skickade det.*"

"You're not kidding me?"

"*Men jag är rädd,*" she said.

"Frida, English," Siri said sharply.

"I am afraid," Frida translated, embarrassed, but Siri didn't hear her. Siri was pointing up at the sky, wanting to show me a group of birds circling us. Frida slid on her black sunglasses, withdrew again.

"We're all so quiet," Margareta shouted. "The birds think we're dead!" She swooped up, rolled Siri with her into the lake with a splash, and we all laughed. Everyone but Frida.

"Don't you live in Washington, D.C.?" Karin asked me as we righted the float and balanced our beer cans between the slats.

"Just outside."

Margareta hoisted herself back up. Her black hair was slicked back now. "I thought you were from New York."

"I am."

"Why would you move from the center of the world to *Washington, D.C.*?"

"Oh, I don't know. I never really belonged in New York."

"It's true—you can't be shy and live in New York City," Margareta said.

I bristled at this, and Siri could tell.

"That's not the right English word, Margareta," Siri snapped. "Lauren is not shy. Besides, who would say something like that?"

"Everyone knows that," Margareta said. "So, have you ever seen your president walking around? Just like a normal guy? Going to the gas station, going to the market?"

"No."

"Nobody likes him, you know. We don't like him, no one in Europe, no one in Thailand—"

"Thailand? How would you even know?" Siri said. "Shut up, Margareta."

"You should have studied in New York City, Siri. It's all about who you know, and in New York you could have known everyone."

"Margareta, *var tyst!*" Siri said.

"What? I can't talk? I should be able to say what I feel."

"She's just asking you to be polite," Karin said.

"No, it's okay," I said. "It's fine. We're all friends here."

"Who are?" Frida said huskily. She lay on her back, her can of beer balanced on her belly. "You? And us?"

Siri glared at Frida. "Swimming! We'll swim," she announced, and she started pushing everyone off the raft. She swam ahead and gestured for us to make our way to the small island of tall, whiskery trees. Frida put on her snorkeling mask, and we all started in that direction like a school of fish.

Buzzed and jet-lagged, it was hard to swim. I was dizzy in the cold water, my legs heavy. Siri was already at the island. Frida and I swam as fast as we could to be next. Frida beat me, plopped herself down on the shore, and started cleaning out the mask with huffs of breath. She shot me a fake smile.

"Do you enjoy living in Washington, D.C.?" Karin asked kindly when we were all settled and our conversation lulled. "What are the people like?"

"I guess they're like city people anywhere. The people I work with tend to be ambitious. They're smart, but it can be hard to connect sometimes. How about you all? What do you like most about living here?"

Margareta laughed. When she saw Siri look at her disapprovingly, she threw up her hands.

"I'm sorry! The way we're talking, it's like some Oprah shit."

Water lapped at the shore, ruffling the skirt of my old-fashioned bathing suit. I replayed the conversations I'd been having with them over in my mind, realizing how forced everything must have sounded, how much older I must have sounded than them. I caught Frida staring at me. She narrowed her eyes and started carving shapes in the gravel with her mask.

"What do you do for fun?" Margareta asked. She took off her bikini top to splash away specks of seaweed under her breasts. I averted my eyes.

"There's a stable, and we sometimes go to watch the kids who take lessons there," Siri said.

Frida snapped her head toward us.

"Oh, Frida loves horses, too, Lauren. We all grew up riding at her family's farm. They have so many. We should all go riding here before you leave."

Frida lowered the mask back over her face and turned to the expanse of the lake.

"Frida, what's wrong?" Karin asked.

"*Inget,*" she said. Her mask was fogging.

"Why are you wearing your mask?" Siri asked.

Frida responded in Swedish, a long low string of sentences directed at no one.

"I told you we need to speak in English, so Lauren can understand," Siri said.

Frida sighed and stood. "I *said* because I don't want to see Margareta's flappy tits the whole of tonight!"

Margareta snapped her suit top at the back of Frida's head, and Frida caught hold of it and threw it in the lake. Siri jumped up and grabbed Frida by the arm and walked with her around the side of the island, where maybe she thought I couldn't hear her yelling. It was so strange to me, the way she was treating these friends. And it was bizarre to not hear Frida responding at all.

I turned to Karin, who was digging her toes into the sand.

"I've never heard Siri yell before," I said.

"Huh?"

"Is she often like this?" I nodded in the direction of Siri's voice.

"Oh. Well. You know. Old friends. You can just be yourself around one another. It doesn't mean anything."

I couldn't help but feel I was the reason for the way Siri was treating these girls. I'd disturbed their equilibrium. I lay back on the gravelly beach and looked up at the black birds circling us again.

When it had just been Siri and me, I didn't stand out. These birds could see something was off about me, that I didn't belong there. Siri nudged me with her toe, trying to get me to snap out of it. She and Karin lay down on either side of me and taught me dirty words in Swedish for a while, then how to count to ten, and then, giggling, the marble-mouthed word for "strawberry ice cream," *jordgubbsglass,* until Frida stood and removed her suit top.

"Okay then." She stepped out of her bottoms. "What is the phrase in English? *Last one in.*"

She dove into the water and the other girls jumped up to follow her in. Frida had seemed to hate listening to Siri talk and laugh with me. *She was just jealous,* I thought. It would eventually pass. I peeled off my suit and slid into the water, thinking how silly it was that someone like Frida could feel threatened by me.

That was the night Siri taught me the word *glöda:* "to glow." We picnicked as the sun held on—bread and beer. We all ate chocolate bars and swam in between bites. We left what remained in wrappers on the dock, and when we got out and finished them, drenched and huddled in blankets, they tasted also of lake water.

Later, Siri and I were sitting together with our feet dangling in the water, watching the other girls do cannonballs off the far end of the dock.

"They're like my sisters," Siri said. "We've known one another since we were babies. Frida—she comes across tough, but she's actually a really fragile person."

I nodded and waited. I thought Siri was about to explain more about her relationship with these friends, this rough side of *her* that I'd never seen. Instead she laid a finger upon my bare back and I jumped.

"I'm sorry," she whispered.

I hugged the blanket to me to cover myself. I knew she had seen the four equidistant circle scars that went down my lower back.

"What are those from, Lauren?"

I collected all the candy wrappers from the dock and pressed them into a wet ball.

"I'm sorry. I didn't mean to make you upset."

I remembered that night, crying alone in my bathroom, twisting to look at my back in the mirror, wondering if my vertebrae were exposed.

"I couldn't tell if they were real or a shadow," Siri said.

"They're both," I said.

We stared out over the lake. I didn't want to mar the night with the story of how I got those scars. And despite how she'd been with her friends, I still trusted her. I just thought we still had all the time in the world to tell each other such things.

After a while, Siri taught me *mångata*. *Måne* for "moon," *gata* for "road." It was a word that meant the roadlike reflection of the moon on the water. It was a word that felt like the night. A word that felt like the start of our journey.

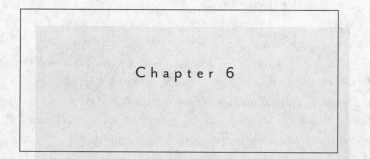

Chapter 6

AFTER THE LAKE, Siri and I walked back to her house in our swimsuits, carrying our shoes on the country road. It felt good with it just being the two of us again.

There was the hum of sleepy insects in the grass. The road narrowed into the trees and then dipped, so that a hill grew tall beside us. I soon had a feeling that we were being followed by something moving along the top of that hill. I looked up and saw a calf. She kept backing away from the edge but returning with curiosity.

There was a rock ladder built into the side of the hill, and we climbed it to see her up close. When I reached the top, I saw a wide expanse of field and about a hundred cows, lying in the grass in pairs. The one I'd seen from the road wore a bell around her neck that jingled as she moved. She went running toward the others, her young legs stiff and angular, full of happiness and announcement. The heads of all the herd turned toward us, appraised us.

I loved their scent and the lake air, the mint smell of the coming night. I looked over at Siri, and it was the old, sweet version of her. The way she had been rude earlier that day with her friends— maybe that was something left over from her childhood, an old hierarchy I just didn't understand. It felt utterly false now, and I wondered if she was embarrassed that I'd seen that version of her.

It was what Siri called the blue hour. Everything glowed as if through a sapphire filter. When we turned the corner and her house came into view, it took my breath away—the solitariness of it shining white against the sky.

We ran to the house. "I want to stay out all night!" I yelled. I had never run so fast, never felt so much inside my body. When we collapsed on the grass among the immense pink and purple flowers pushing up out of the earth, we both started laughing at their wonderful name: *blomsterlupiner*. Siri said we'd build our own house, the sky for our ceiling, the giant flowers our end tables, the rising moon our window, the still-out sun our door.

We were lying wet-headed in the grass, renaming everything in the field, when we heard a car pull up and its engine stop.

At once I felt the tension in Siri draw together beside me. By the time I turned my head, the screen door to the house was clapping shut.

"Who was that?" I asked.

She closed her eyes again. "Maybe he didn't see us."

"Was that your brother?" I asked.

"Yes."

I propped myself up on my arms and looked at her, and then at the old red car parked at an angle on the grass beside their house.

"Siri, is there something I should know about him?"

She didn't answer me.

"Siri?"

"It's better we just stay away from him," she said.

"Why?"

Birgit came to the door. "Siri? Are you out there?" She couldn't see us lying in the grass.

Siri sat up. "I love my brother. I do. But you know the story of how the frog is put in a pot when the water is cold, and when the stove is turned on, the frog doesn't realize it's getting hotter until it's too late?"

"Yes."

"Magnus is like that. He boils people up."

Birgit was holding open the screen door for us to come inside. She had changed into pajamas and was wearing a pair of eyeglasses with a taped hinge. When she saw our wet bathing suits, she rushed for towels. "You swam? It's still too cold! What were you think-ing?" While we changed, she stood outside our bedroom doors to collect our wet clothes, tsking.

"Come on," she said.

We went to wash our clothes. I noticed that Birgit and Siri stepped lightly past the closed doors, and I imagined Magnus was behind every one, a dog that might come charging out at us. His presence in the house now made them quieter. On the stairs, Birgit was careful to skip the step that creaked.

The sisters washed the clothes in the bathtub and brought them in a basin to a closet off the foyer. Inside, they lit a heat lamp and draped the garments on crisscrossing clotheslines and drying racks. I stood in the closet with them as they hung the clothes, sweat com-ing off of me in streams. Soon the walls were a heavy patchwork of damp fabric. The smell of detergent filled the room. The glow-ing disc of the red heat lamp made it look like a photographer's darkroom. I remember thinking that as they worked, their beauty rose more and more to the surface, like developing pictures.

We were in there when we heard a slamming sound in the front hall. They looked at each other, Siri burning up but Birgit's ex-pression still insisting that all was fine.

Birgit flung a shirt onto a clothesline above her. "We're in here," she called.

Nothing. They both watched the door of the drying closet.

"*Vi är här inne!*" she called again.

"Hush, Birgit. He knows," Siri said. "I don't want to see him either." Siri looked down at the now-empty washbasin, from which the last of the water had evaporated.

———

I WOKE IN the middle of the night with jet lag that felt like a hang-over, my skin smelling of the detergent they'd used for the laun-dry. I felt sticky with perspiration, as though I were wearing wet clothes. There was the sound of a creaky gate. The digital clock beside my bed read three a.m. There was half a chocolate bar left over from the lake on my night table. I reached over and touched it, surprised to feel that the heat of the room had not melted it.

I kept thinking about Siri at the lake and how she'd been so hard on those girls. At the time I had kept telling myself that she just wanted them to be kind to me, but Karin had remarked that it was the stuff of old friends.

I went to the window to try to open it and get some air. I thought of the way Siri had snapped at Margareta. How she'd pinched Frida's arm. How when Siri had pulled Frida down the beach to yell at her, Frida hadn't yelled back. These girls were used to this treatment from Siri, but I had never seen this side of her at all.

In the moonlight, I could see the window had been painted shut.

As I was pushing at it, I noticed a man standing in the field be-hind the house and stopped.

I knew at once it was Magnus. He was tall. Hair fell into his face over his brow, darker instead of Siri-fair. He held a metal shovel, and he was kicking at its glinting head, trying to push it into the ground.

His white shirt was streaked with dirt near his throat, and his mouth was a tight line, as though trying to keep his body from turning inside out. Everything about him was force and hunch, anxiety, sweat. He had broken the ground now, and I could see the lines where his muscles moved in his arms. He was the one hard thing in the soft field. Now he became the reason my room was hot. He was the reason the window was painted shut, the reason for walls and doors.

Siri had told me to stay away from him. I tried to remember that I had disliked him before this moment, when I could see him standing on the head of the shovel, falling forward with it, and then to his knees. He was at once at work and at the mercy of whatever was driving him. The dusk field was his soul, and he was lost in it.

I saw the hole he'd dug in front of him, and I saw he held the shovel, but it seemed that the hole wanted to suck him in.

I thought of my nights back home, staring through my blinds at the other apartment windows, inventing stories about my neighbors and how we might be alike. But with Magnus, there was something about his energy I immediately knew for sure, something that felt—like me.

The sudden sound of someone in the hallway made me jump. I went to the wall and snapped on the light to reorient myself, take a sip of water. After a few minutes, I shut off the light and tried to go back to sleep. I ate the chocolate bar in the dark. But then I was up and at the window again. Magnus was gone, but there was a mound of pulled-up plants on the ground where he'd dug. I wondered what it was. I wondered if he'd seen the light in my room go on.

Then I saw him.

He was standing off to the side, but closer to the house now, staring up at my window, right at me. It was definitely Magnus, though he wasn't smiling the way Siri would smile at me. His mouth was still a tight line, but I couldn't help smiling back at him. He dropped the shovel, and I dropped to my knees and crawled back to my bed, my heart thudding in my chest.

Shh, I told it when I heard the front door open and close with such force I thought the house might collapse to that side. *Shh,* I tried to soothe myself. I heard the door to the room beside me open and close. And a feeling of relief, of acquiescence to sleep or to possession, cooled me.

Chapter 7

THE NEXT MORNING at breakfast, Magnus was there. Like a fool, I stood when he came to the table and extended my hand to him, nearly knocking over a carton of milk.

Siri reached out at the right second and steadied it.

"Magnus, this is Lauren," she said.

He shook my hand, but he wouldn't meet my eyes. It gave me extra time to take him in. He had reddish hair and skin that had already tanned. He wore a dark blue uniform with *Bergström* embroidered on his shirt pocket.

Siri and Birgit were talking about budgeting, and a birthday present for their little cousin Fredrik in a northern city, and Siri's tuition for fall, which was not inexpensive. Magnus's gaze volleyed between them.

"What do you think, Magnus?" Birgit said.

"*Jag kommer att jobba mer,*" he said, shoveling a forkful of food into his mouth.

"That will help," Birgit said. She turned to me. "He's talking about more hours for his job."

"What do you do?" I asked him.

Silence. He piled all the dirty napkins from the table upon his plate.

"He's an electrician," Birgit said.

Magnus pushed back from the table and sighed. "*Elektriker?*"

"You make it sound like we're calling you a name," Siri said. "It is your job, Magnus."

"Then I'd best be off to it."

His eyes met mine, and suddenly I remembered the other details from his face the night before. Not just the fixed line of his mouth, but his eyes and the way they locked, the way his brows came together to make up his mind about me, the way my skin pricked at having him stare.

"Nice to meet you, Lauren," he said.

He left the room. I reached for the milk carton and sent it flying.

MAGNUS AND BIRGIT each did their part. Their house was neat. The dishes always done, the fridge stocked. They had a metal box in the kitchen for bills when they arrived. Birgit paid them in the evening at a little schoolhouse desk, drinking tea. I felt thankful to rarely see Magnus; he worked late like a dutiful father but went straight to his room when he came home.

It was different for Siri and Birgit, though. It was easy for them to discuss money and then run out into the field beside the house and see who could do the longest string of back walkovers. Birgit would come home from work and go straight out to the field to set up the badminton net so we could play late into the evening. Sometimes the sisters would argue, small old grievances coming out between swats of the rackets, tickle fights that ended in shouts and tears, then too-long silences at the times when it would have been natural for a mother to peek in to see if everyone was okay. In those moments, I felt we were all waiting for the same woman to come in and hush us.

Birgit wanted to know more about my parents. The day I told her how they'd died, I found the beats of the story more easily, and she held her cheek and stared at me, her taped glasses a little lopsided on her face. She marveled that I lived alone, that I'd moved away from my childhood home and sold my parents' furniture.

"I don't know what I would do without Magnus and Siri to care for," she said.

"You're amazing," I said. "I can't even take care of myself."

"But you're a college professor. It's a great accomplishment," she said.

She got up to pour us some juice, and the ghosts in the house nodded, affable. I wanted to say I was just an adjunct. That I appeared accomplished but wasn't, really. I appeared like I had things together, but I didn't.

"Lauren is going to interview for a full-time position at Stella Maris," Siri said.

"Do you think you'll get it?" Birgit asked.

"I don't know. I think they'll want someone who can also teach Asian American literature, and I don't have that background. And even if I could convince them that I knew enough, I don't have the degree they want. I'm sure they want someone with a PhD."

"She's reading all these books by Chinese writers. You wouldn't believe how much she reads," Siri said.

"Well, it's clear the students love you," Birgit said, throwing her arm over Siri's shoulder.

"I love you so much I brought you to Sweden," Siri said, raising her juice glass to clink hers with mine. She had her notepad and pen in front of her, a list of all the places she wanted to take me while I was there. I tried to read it upside down.

"Oh, if they knew I was here I'm sure any chance I have at that job would be shot."

"But why?" Birgit asked.

"They would see this as something . . . inappropriate," I said.

"They'd say there should be boundaries between students and professors."

"Well, I think it's great," Birgit said. "I think Siri needs someone responsible following her around on this"—she picked up Siri's carefully drafted itinerary—"this *agenda*. It's like my sister now has a chaperone so I don't have to worry so much."

I thought of how odd that sounded. Siri was the one who made the way safe for *me*. It seemed Birgit didn't know her own sister.

"Well, I plan to get Lauren into lots of trouble," Siri said. "After everything she's been through, I think she deserves a little fun."

I laughed at this, but Birgit caught my gaze.

"Siri can find trouble anywhere. She will have you out late every night if you let her. I don't want anything happening to you two while you're here."

It seemed Birgit was trying to warn me about something specific.

"For me, look out for both of you, okay?"

She reached across the table for my hand and squeezed hold of it. All the giggling stopped, and it sent a chill through me to feel the seriousness of her gaze on me.

"Please, Lauren. Watch out for her," she whispered.

"Stop it, Birgit." Siri snapped the juice bottle closed and slid it from her.

"You can't be so selfish, Siri." She patted my hand and then crossed her arms against her chest. "I don't want Lauren getting in trouble with the school. I mean, is that really true, Lauren? It could affect you getting that job?"

"Yes, I think so."

"Goodness. Why would you even *want* a job where they are so judgmental?" Birgit asked.

"The other professors can be difficult, but—it's the closest thing I have to a family. Teaching there has come to mean a lot to me. Birgit, you were saying that having Magnus and Siri to look after . . . it keeps you going. Teaching does the same for me. A full-time position someday would just—well, it would make it all feel a bit more permanent."

Birgit nodded. The look on her face made me worried I'd embarrassed her.

"I get it. But it does make me sad," Birgit said. "You two have so much in common. With the losses you've had, it's natural to be friends. You've lived the same story."

"No," Siri said quickly. "My story is nothing like Lauren's. She really suffered."

I turned to look at her. Was that what she really thought? She'd said that before, on the day in the adjunct office when I first told her about my parents' deaths. But certainly, she must have realized that our stories were similar. It was what drew us together, wasn't it? If not that, what? It felt good that Siri acknowledged my story as rare, a tragedy. But didn't she see we were algebra? A-B-A-B-A-B. That while A and B seemed different, they were really very similar. We were an essay in the comparison-and-contrast form.

Siri was wiping at some stain upon her sleeve.

Sitting in the kitchen, I somehow felt that if their dinette was a boardroom table, then I was the trustee too long absent and finally arrived, sitting in the place that had always been reserved for me. They awaited now my grief-shareholder's speech about how my story was worse. But I wanted to believe Birgit, that someone could look at me and Siri and easily see that we should be friends.

That's when it happened: an explosion.

We hurried to the pantry, where some of the cabinet doors had been flung open. Orange jelly oozed from the white shelves, spread across the countertop, and fell in fat drops upon the floor.

"Mamma's *hjortronsylt,*" Birgit marveled. Tentative, she opened one of the cabinets, and another glass jar burst with a little pop. It was cloudberry jelly. There must have been twenty jars in various states of ruin.

We heard Magnus's heavy boots coming up the stairs. I hadn't known he was in the house. He came into the kitchen and stared at the scene. He was wearing his work uniform, and the neat creases in his work shirt and down the front of his blue pants made it seem he was trying very hard to hold himself together.

"*Det blev för varmt därinne,*" he said slowly.

He motioned to the wall the cabinets shared with the drying closet. The girls had left the heat lamp on all night. The jars had gotten too hot.

"I tell you all the time to shut off that lamp. And the lights we are not using. And to turn off the water. And to stop letting the hose run in the grass—"

"*Äh, sluta,* Magnus!" Siri shouted.

I could see him trying to remain calm.

"I know you have not been here, Siri, for a while. But we have rules in the house," he said. "And practices we have enacted to save money. For your school, among other things."

"I'm glad they burst!" Siri yelled at him.

Birgit tried to put a hand on Siri's shoulder, but before I even saw her pick up a jar, she was turning from her and hurling one at Magnus.

When it landed at the tip of his boot, it popped rather than shattered. It looked like a glass balloon, still held together by some kind of thread skeleton, or by the jelly.

Magnus stared at the broken jar, as though contemplating what it would take to glue it back together. We were all quiet.

"You come back and bad things happen," he said to Siri. I realized he was saying this in English so I could hear it, too. "You can clean it."

"They had been in there too long, and that is *your* fault!" she shouted.

I'd never witnessed Siri so full of rage. She was pointing her finger in his face, and he backed away, stony eyed. He was used to this from her. I wasn't. I had no idea this had been underneath her skin all this time. I could feel the way she was yelling at him in my chest, the way a parade goes by and a bass drum thumps at your heart and throat. Birgit was starting to clean up, moving in a wide circle around her. I could tell that she too was used to seeing this kind of emotion from her sister. She got the trash bin. She filled a basin with soapy water. It was her way of dealing. Magnus left, his boots scraping shards of glass against the wood planks of the floor.

I felt angry that Siri was letting her sister clean. Angry that she had just let her brother leave. And I suddenly felt resentful of Siri, that she would take for granted this brother and sister. I felt resentful that she had family at all.

Birgit started pulling off long sheets of paper towels. "They'd just been in there too long. For years," she said to me, trying to pretend that all was normal.

Siri stood staring at the arched doorway through which Magnus had gone.

"The summer before our mamma died, we were visiting our cousins in the north, and they had cloudberries growing wild near their house. Mamma did the canning herself, and we brought these home. After she died, Magnus never let us touch it."

"I'm glad they burst," Siri said again.

Birgit went for a broom. "Yes, well. Let's just get it cleaned."

They let me help them but talked softly in Swedish between themselves. It was easy to tell they weren't talking about Magnus or the jars or Siri's rage. I caught words I knew. *Sommar. Mamma. Bär,* for "berries." They were trading memories of that last summer with their mother. Together we scrubbed the cabinets with soap and water. The deep orange jelly smelled sweet and delicious and got all over us no matter what we did.

Siri pulled a cardboard box from under a cabinet to collect the broken glass. It caught light from the kitchen window, and I recalled the sparkling geode paintings she'd shown me that first morning in our classroom, the mistake at the bottom of her canvas repaired with gold.

"Are you thinking of using it in your artwork?" I asked.

She smiled a little. "I wasn't. But maybe." She seemed to have come back into herself. I wondered if she was embarrassed by the way she'd behaved.

Birgit looked between us. "Siri, you should show her your

scrapbook," she said. "Our mother was the kind who kept everything. Do you want to see?"

Soon we were all sitting cross-legged on the bed in Birgit's room. Siri brought over a red album full of her childhood artwork. On the cover was a child's rendition of Pippi Longstocking.

"Have you read those stories?" Birgit asked. "We're planning to take you to Vimmerby this trip. There's a park based on the tales. We used to go there when we were little." She opened the book so I could see the playful pictures inside. Crayons and pastels. A self-portrait, where Siri was all teeth. Drawings of Magnus, redheaded, and Birgit, as tall as the book. There were empty pages at the back.

"I was eleven when our mamma left us," Birgit said.

"I was five when my mother died," Siri said. "She used to tell me I could draw and be an artist."

"Magnus and Siri got all the artistic talent," Birgit said.

"It's the only way he and I are alike," Siri said.

Birgit laughed. "She doesn't like to admit it, but she and Magnus are *a lot* alike."

"Don't say that, Birgit. I have a temper, but I'm not crazy."

"I hate that word," I said.

The sisters stopped and looked at me. Birgit seemed embarrassed. Siri just shook her head.

"You don't understand, Lauren. What I mean is he does crazy things."

"He works hard. He misses you terribly," Birgit said.

"*Syster,* you know what I'm talking about." Siri turned to me. "After our mamma died, I told Magnus that I was starting to forget what she looked like."

"Oh, I tell her even now—just look in the mirror," Birgit said.

"Magnus said he would help me remember. He started describing her to me at night before sleep. I would look forward to it. He'd sit on the edge of my bed. Tuck me in. Then I realized that he was always describing her in different ways, to mess with my head."

She looked up at a portrait of a woman on the wall above the bed. "That was one of many."

"It's accurate, Siri," Birgit said.

"But he painted ten others that were all different women. Some looked like demons. He just kept making them."

"We all handled her death in different ways," Birgit said to me.

"I couldn't sleep with them in the house. Even when I look at that one, I—I know it looks the way she did. But it brings back a lot of painful feelings."

"He wouldn't throw them away. He insisted on burying them out behind the house," Birgit said.

I looked at her.

"He'd go out at night and dig up the field and bury them. It was very strange."

Above her shoulder, the doorway. Magnus stepping into it silently. The girls' backs were to the door. They didn't know he was standing there.

I tried not to look at him.

"We have a complicated relationship," Siri said.

I could feel Magnus's eyes on me. He was waiting.

He wanted to see if I'd tell them that I'd seen him last night. I couldn't bear his gaze on me. I wiped at my face and got jam in my eyes.

"When Mamma died, Magnus was just a kid himself," Birgit said.

"I hate when you say that," Siri said. "Look at you. Don't act like you haven't had to step up and act like the oldest because of his issues."

"But he's a different person now."

"I don't believe you when you say that."

"It's the truth."

"You would say anything to defend him."

I found the desire to defend him rising in me, too. I fought back the urge to speak. Siri noticed my expression and breathed out, a smile. "Oh, your face, Lauren. You're making me feel like a bad sister."

"Good," Birgit said. "You don't understand how much you hurt him."

"Did your mother keep a book of Magnus's artwork, too?" I asked.

"No," Birgit said. "He was already at the age when he was private about things."

I looked up at where Magnus had been standing. He was gone.

"Do you have sisters or brothers, Lauren?" Birgit asked.

"No," I said. "It's just me."

She reached over and patted my knee. "And now all of us. Our difficult family."

We turned back to the scrapbook. The drawings gave a sense of how different their household had been when their mother was alive. The pictures were neatly arranged, dates beneath each one. You could almost see, making your way through the pages, when Siri's hand steadied, when her use of color became more purposeful, when she first tried shadow.

We passed the book back and forth, the room still smelling of cloudberry jam, the scent of the explosion. Siri reached out for my hand, like her contractions of pain and love and happiness and sadness were labor pains. I know Siri had felt release when the jars burst. Perhaps at a time when I least expected it, things would burst open for me, and I'd be relieved. But I couldn't help but think, holding Siri's hand, that this was the hand that had thrown the jar. And I couldn't help but think of the man now in his childhood bedroom with the music cranked up, for whom the pieces we'd swept up and trashed were more than just bits of glass. And sometimes I misremember, and it's Siri's startling fury that shattered all of the jars.

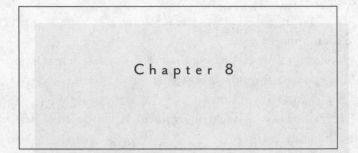

Chapter 8

SIRI KEPT ME busy the next few days. We went by ferry to Denmark and drank beer in Nyhavn, beside rainbow-colored port houses overlooking the canal. She showed me the one Hans Christian Andersen lived in when he wrote "The Princess and the Pea," and we shared with each other fairy tales of our own to pass the day.

Later in the week, we went to visit their family in Hamburgsund, a harbor town, to celebrate her cousin Fredrik's tenth birthday and watch him in his sailing race. We cheered for him from the rocks as he navigated his tiny yellow boat just out of the harbor and back. Afterward we all climbed a path that led to a rocky overlook to see a view of the whole harbor. Fredrik sweetly whispered to me that he'd named his boat *Ost*, the word for *cheese*, because his was the only yellow boat in his whole sailing club.

I loved that little boy and that harbor, and its rock cliffs and rain clouds that gathered around them—they made it look, for once, like it was getting dark when it should. With the sun out so early and so late, and the wind continually trying to push back summer, it felt like it could be any time and any season. We went back to their house for hot dogs and birthday cake, and after he opened his presents, we all fell asleep, exhausted, on the L-shaped couch in their living room. And I loved the long drive back to Olofstorp with Siri. She talked about all the other places we'd see, and she was so happy and gentle, it didn't seem possible she could ever break a jar.

SIRI ARRANGED FOR US to go to the Pippi Longstocking park that next weekend. I sat in the backseat with Siri. Items for our picnic were stacked on the front seat beside Birgit. With her closer to my age and so responsible, I felt I was stealing something by laughing in the backseat with Siri while she studied the map in the front alone.

I looked out the window at the flower beds Birgit kept. She was the sister who made beauty from order. Though Magnus was the oldest, Birgit embraced her role of mother to her siblings, caretaker of this house. She had Siri's same earnestness but not her carefree ways.

Birgit liked hearing our stories of our time in the United States, but it was clear she didn't want Siri to return to school in the fall. It was costly, and she mentioned that to Siri a lot. Mostly, she wanted the three of them under the same roof, as though they all needed to be present for anything good to happen for them. I stared at her neat rows of vegetables just starting to wind their way through the squares of a white lattice.

Magnus rapped on the door beside me and I jumped.

He was looking off to the side, waiting for me to open the door. I sat upright and rolled down the window.

"I'm coming with you. Open up," he said.

I opened the door, and he pressed in beside me.

Siri leaned across me. "You're coming to Vimmerby?"

"I think there's at least one thing we should do here as a family, don't you?"

Everyone was silent. I moved closer to Siri to give him room.

"Well, okay then," Birgit said, glancing at us in the rearview.

We drove. On the radio: soft, sentimental music from another generation. It wasn't long before Siri and Birgit were humming along. I gazed out the window at the blurring green. It was a beautiful, gray-skied day, the green fields glowing as if lit from the inside. Light came through the trees like honey dripping.

I read from my guidebook, a section on Swedish folklore and the story of a beautiful sylvan nymph called the Skogsrå, who guarded woodlands and lured wandering men to marriage or their deaths. After she slept with them, she'd reveal herself in her true form, the skin of her back made of bark, her torso a hollow trunk full of leaves. I felt Magnus reading over my shoulder. When I turned to him, he looked away.

I noticed Magnus's hands, resting on his thighs. They were still, but light flickered over them. I found myself listening for his breath, noticing the curve of my body that was against his. The undersides of his fingernails were all black.

Then we passed a lake and suddenly everything was water and silver-shining, bright-blue-sky openness—and I felt Magnus's chest rise. I looked at his face, and he was looking at me, too, as if we were sharing a secret. I imagined in that moment he was seeing all the different sides of me at once, and I thought of those portraits buried in the field. The girls were still humming, and he and I were just breathing. His scent of pine—I could imagine that sparkling lake was the place he disappeared to for the whole of every day, and now that I knew of it, maybe I could go with him there.

"Lauren."

Siri's voice.

"We all call that lake Bi Sjön—the bees' lake," she said. "When we were kids we swam there. There is a thick tree root that grows out over the water, and one day we discovered that the inside was hollow but full of dead bees. Magnus, do you remember when Mamma showed us?"

When I looked back at Magnus, there was tree cover again, like we were going through a dark green tunnel. His eyes were shining, and he didn't respond.

"Magnus, do you remember?"

At Vimmerby, we ate lunch sitting on long plank benches in the sunshine. Siri and Birgit argued a little. Actors dressed as characters skipped by. Teenage girls with yarn wigs were everywhere, sometimes two Pippis at once. In Swedish, she is known as Pippi Långstrump, and I loved the sound of that. We sat in the shadow of her multicolored house, Villa Villekulla, and watched as children ran up to men dressed as Pippi's horse, holding balloons in the shape of Pippi's monkey. Some of the pretty, yarn-headed teenagers stole furtive glances at Magnus as he sat wide-legged with his back against the picnic table smiling at them. Siri shot him a look and whispered, "*Nej,* Magnus."

I couldn't stop looking at him, either. He wore a white tank top, and my eyes kept going to the dark constellations of freckles clustered on his shoulder blades. The muscles in his back tensed as he scratched hard at the side of his neck, leaving a red mark where his fingers dug in.

His notebook and pencil were in front of me on the table. I'd seen him sketching throughout the day. I wanted him to turn to me. I wanted to feel that openness in him again. I picked up his pencil. I reached across the table and touched his shoulder with the rubber eraser.

He turned. I was still stretched across the table, smiling at him goofily, the pencil extended toward him. He took it from me and snatched his sketchbook up. His bottom lip was cracked in the center, and he had a dried bead of blood there.

"I have been wondering what you do," I said.

"My sisters told you. I'm an electrician."

"I saw those easels in your room. Were you an artist? Is that what you studied in school?"

He opened his sketchbook and pushed it toward me, flipping

through a few pencil drawings of animals we had seen in Vimmerby's petting zoo earlier that afternoon.

"I am an artist now," he said with gravelly confidence.

I told him they were good and slowly turned the sketchbook's
pages.

"I'm not good at drawing animals," he said.

"He's good at drawing people," Birgit said, her mouth full of
sandwich.

I noticed that in the backgrounds of all the drawings were shad-
owy ball-and-line figures, as though the people in the park were
made of wooden beads.

Siri came over and whispered in my ear. "He never shows anyone his drawings." She tried to see the animal sketches, but Magnus took the book back.

"Fine, Magnus—whatever. You know I think you're good."

"I think it's wonderful that you're both artists," I said.

"Yes, but we do very different stuff," Siri said.

"We're not that different," Magnus said.

Siri was quiet.

"Well? Say it, Siri. Say we're not that different."

"You don't even know what I've been working on," she said.
"I'm working in new mediums, and just being away from here has
provided a lot of inspiration. I mean, Lauren has seen my work.
What would you say, Lauren?"

He turned away from us, and Siri scoffed, gesturing to Birgit as
if to say, *See, he hasn't changed at all.* But I saw how it had hurt him.
The way he cocked his neck, the way he rubbed at his temple.
Some nearby children stopped their play to stare at him, and he
made an expression to make them laugh. It touched me, that he
was trying to put them at ease. Birgit went to him and spoke in
low Swedish in his ear. He nodded and took out a piece of paper.

"*Ja,* do it, Magnus," Siri said.

"What?" I asked.

Magnus turned to a fresh piece of paper. "I am going to draw
you."

Siri twisted around in her chair so that her back was to me, and she made a gun shape with her fingers like she was one of Charlie's Angels. "You do it, too," she said, elbowing me in the ribs.

Magnus stared at the blank sheet of paper.

"No, no," I said, lowering Siri's hands. "Be serious."

She leaned back into me. "I can't take him seriously."

She said it softly. I studied his face as he started to draw us, wondering if he'd heard her. He was the only person I'd ever heard Siri disparage, and it made me feel protective of him—and angry with Siri. There was the feeling of my hair and Siri's hair mixed together on our necks. His hand swirled on the page, the motion of a gravestone rubbing. I saw now why his fingernails were black—they were scraping up graphite from the paper.

Siri sighed against my back.

"Are you smiling?" I asked her, wanting to know if I should smile too.

"No," she said. "I have a *serious* expression."

She'd spoken louder this time, wanting to provoke him. It made me angry. Things had seemed better between them since the day the jars had exploded. Now I remembered how she'd called him crazy.

He erased something on his page.

He was drawing her, and she was sighing. He was drawing her now, like this, taking care to get her just right. I looked at him, wanting him to respond somehow, to defend himself or at least say something that would help me understand this breach between them.

Magnus kept his eyes on the circular motions he was making on the paper, and I kept my eyes on the aqua-colored shutters of Villa Villekulla. The two men in the horse costume negotiated their way up the bright house's porch steps. Magnus kept scrawling, slowing down, slower and slower. He removed his sunglasses from the top of his head and put them over his eyes.

"Hey," I said, trying to soothe him.

Suddenly, in the distance, Siri and Birgit were calling out my name. Somehow I could still feel her back against mine. When had they left the table? They'd crossed the field and were climbing wooden steps up the side of a red barn.

"Don't move," Magnus said.

I could still feel the pressure, the weight of Siri's body pressed up against my back, but now it spread around me like an embrace, at once keeping me seated so that he could draw me and pulling me in, pulling me in closer to him. I remembered his digging in the field, how he had seemed drawn into the ground, fighting not to be drawn into the hole. That was how I felt now. I was being pulled into the paper, I was made of graphite, I could smear on his fingertips.

I was always the kind of person who hated to have her photograph taken, dreading that instant when the camera might catch me looking stupid or at a bad angle, reduced to one version of myself, someone thinking that's all I am. Something like death in a photo. A stranger might pick it up, and to them that's all you'll ever be, this moment you had no control over, that had no before and no afterward.

But his drawing was alive. I could tell that he was contemplating my hair, my brow, my lashes. How would he do my neck? My shirt? My mouth?

My mouth was open, my lips parted. How would he render the things of my lips—my words, my breath? He was slowing down, but I wanted his hands to keep going, I wanted his eyes to keep me.

I saw in the drawing that Siri was as light as a feather, insinuations of a shape, just straight lines where her collarbone and shoulder met. But even from upside down, I could see all my lines were bold and dark and sure, clear curves, tiny details, eyes made bright by his hand. All of that came from his hands, upside down, everything, upside down.

He wanted to show me the drawing. He tore it from his sketchbook like he would give it to me.

"I have to go," I said.

I ran across the field to the barn. I climbed the stairs to the high loft, where Siri and Birgit were waiting for me. I could see them each turning—even now I see it in slow motion—one at a time the sisters launched themselves from the second-story loft into the hay below. Openmouthed and eyes closed, air gone, exhausted, laughing, motes of dust and pieces of straw drifting down, hanging in the rays of sun, magnets to the bars of light falling across them.

I breathed. I jumped. I remember feeling suspended, feeling my breath and heartbeat hanging in the air above me, even as I collapsed into the soft, sweet straw. I landed with my arms spread open to make room for my heart to fall back into my chest.

When I opened my eyes, I saw Magnus looking down at me with a pained expression from the high loft.

ON THE DRIVE home, the sisters recognized a road, a field they'd known as kids. I saw the name of the place in my guidebook. You enter beneath an archway of three stones—the remains of a passage grave. The massive stones had once been built into a hill, but the hill had worn away over hundreds of years, leaving only the two standing stones and roof stone behind. We parked on the side of the road and got out to explore it.

Before the stones, the ground was different. You could see pale stripes where snails were feeding on the lichens that matted the rocks. On the other side, there began a dense forest, where stones were flecked with copper or covered in moss. The forest part was an open room where everything was pied, shimmering with color and depth. I read as I walked, checking off the names of plants I saw there, spinning around to yell, "There's a tree here that is nine hundred years old!"

Magnus looked annoyed at me and my guidebook. He went off on his own while the girls and I went to find the old tree. It was a beautiful monster. Low down on its trunk, it split in two like horns, and the girls posed in front of it while I took pictures. The three of us played hide-and-seek, peeping from behind enormous red-leaved cabbages and climbing the massive, octopus-rooted trees. I wondered if everything there had grown up so giant from the dust of people once buried there, when all of this ground was yet inside a grave. I thought of my parents. How I would have loved the idea of a passage grave, a vault in the woods for safekeeping, where they would not be constantly shifting with the currents of memory, with the distant, mysterious currents of a lake bed.

I was hiding from the sisters when Magnus jumped out from behind the two-horned tree to scare me.

I felt like we became quickly enshrouded by massive ferns and trees that grew up to conceal us.

"Are you the beautiful Skogsrå?" he asked. "Let me check."

He pulled me to him and slowly slid his hands down my back. I wondered if he would feel the scars left there, the four hard dots over my vertebrae like bark. I stood in the tent of his gaze, the house of it, and I remembered Siri just as she came around the bend. I pulled away from him just in time but couldn't catch my breath.

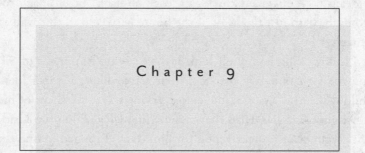

Chapter 9

IN THE DAYS that followed our trip to Vimmerby, Magnus occupied my thoughts. On the hall windowsill, in the dusty track for the storm window, I found three stubby pencils, their erasers gone. I wondered if Magnus had used them to make the sketches near the stairs, and I thought about how those drawings must have scratched the itches of the old house. One day, when Siri was napping and Magnus was at work, I found myself wandering the rooms, looking for more items of his left around. His jacket was where he always hung it, on the hook behind the kitchen door. His toothbrush was on the bathroom windowsill in a yellow plastic cup, beside Birgit's. I passed his room twice before deciding to turn the knob, which had been painted over many times. The old colors of the house were still showing where the paint had chipped. The door opened.

I went in. On his bedside table was a sketch pad and a half-drunk glass of water, a lens case, dust, coins. His easels were bare, the clips and dry brushes spotted with color. I breathed in the paint smell, touched the dried paint on the metal clips, catching a little underneath my fingernails. I had the sudden urge to run my fingers down his blanket, too.

I found myself breathing faster, trying to take in his scent from the sheets on the bed, which was positioned against our shared wall. I noticed that there were pencil lines all over that wall, just like the faint mural beside the stairs. Up close I could see eraser shavings stuck to the paint as he'd changed the flower shapes again and again. I imagined our lying back-to-back, or stomach-to-stomach, with just this wall of the house between us, this wall of flowers.

I hadn't really let myself look at the drawing he'd made of Siri and me at Vimmerby. Siri had been acting like an impertinent child while he'd scrawled and erased, trying to get the shape of her just right. And me. He'd drawn me while I was filling up inside with feelings of protectiveness for him. Now I longed to find the picture.

There was a mound of papers near his stereo, bills and paperwork from his job. I found myself touching them, wondering about his work, looking for evidence of his handwriting, all the while listening for any small sound in the hallway that could indicate Siri was awakening from her nap. I moved some of the papers, hoping to find that crinkly picture buried underneath, but found something else, made of fabric.

It appeared to be an embroidered kitchen calendar divided into twelve parts. Each square bore the image of a different macabre creature. A goat-priest with its heart exposed; a sow with sharp spines; a skeleton girl, her skull swimming with dots of frayed, bluish floss. The old embroidery threads appeared to be held together with rubber cement.

I touched an image of a black bird. It had a hole in one of its outstretched wings.

"That is Nattravnen," a voice said.

I turned to find Magnus standing behind me. I jumped back.

"The Night Raven. It's said that if you look through the hole in its wing, you'll see the thing you fear the most. Very bad luck to look at it. Better not look at the goat one either."

"I'm sorry," I said, closing my eyes to the bad-luck images, the sight of him standing there in his dark blue work uniform.

"What are you doing in here, Lauren?" he asked.

My eyes were still closed. I didn't know what to say.

"I could help you, if you told me."

He didn't sound angry, but I rushed from his room and into Siri's, where she lay sleeping on her bed. I locked her door behind me and stared at it, wondering if he would knock and demand I come out and explain myself. He didn't.

I turned to Siri's room. On the walls were framed compositions she had made, which felt very much like her. Paint infused with glitter, mosaics made with metal pieces and paper tissue, all scrunched up.

She had a little rolltop desk and papers there in neat stacks. I went to them. I saw that the papers were her old essays from my class, and that my writing laced the sides.

Tell me more, I'd written in one place. *This reminds me of a favorite story. It's called "All Summer in a Day."*

I knelt next to her bed. This girl had changed my life. She had clicked open my locked door.

In that moment, I promised myself I'd put as much distance between Magnus and me as I could. I had been two people ever since what happened in the forest. I wondered about these changes in her, if she was the one in the wrong, and I liked the way being around him made me feel. But I wanted to be one person—one good friend to Siri. I wanted to believe everything about Siri, even when she said there was something wrong with Magnus. She had asked me to stay away from him, and I wanted to promise that I could.

TENSIONS BETWEEN MAGNUS and Siri grew hotter the next day. I was in the shower when I heard them yelling in the hall. I put my head under the stream of water to drown out Magnus's voice whenever he responded to her, trying to focus only on Siri's side of the argument, saying that she must return to school, that there was no way for her to be the artist she wanted to be in Sweden. It was over by the time I shut off the shower. I heard him storming from the house as I was putting on my clothes, and he didn't come back that night.

I was grateful when Siri's itinerary involved our traveling by train to Stockholm for a few days alone, and it could just be the two of us again. I remember the long ride through the country-side, the gleaming lakes, trading music back and forth on her head-phones, playing hangman, trying fitfully to sleep, but the dreamscape being beyond the window, all that green, the gleam-ing lakes, the rolling fields.

I remember coming into Stockholm. There was a long, dark tunnel that went on forever until we seemed to blast out of it. Then we were gliding across the water—water on all sides of the train, a bright, flashing expanse. We couldn't see the track for all the water. The train might as well have been a speedboat. Or a rocket. My heart was racing so hard. I felt I was shooting through space. Siri slept, her face pressed against the window.

Once we arrived, the first place Siri wanted to show me was Gamla Stan, the old part of the city, and we walked the cobble-stoned length of Västerlånggatan, a bustling street full of tourists and outdoor cafés. Siri went down every tunnel-like alley. I poked my head through the doors of every church. She went into a store to buy candy, and I waited outside, taking photos.

There was a shop adjacent to an old church, and in its window, I saw painted woodcuts of saints, long faces with head coverings and gold halos. One immediately caught my attention. She was standing in sackcloth, had brown flames for hair, and was holding her own blue eyes in a dish. The shopkeeper came and pulled up the gate while I was standing there. "Excuse me," I asked. "Which saint is that?"

"Oh, her," she said. "Don't let her scare you. That is Saint Lucia." She invited me inside her shop and handed me a book.

"She went with her ill mother to pray at the tomb of Saint Agatha, and her mother was healed. Lucy was so overcome with joy that she pledged her virginity to God and refused to wed the pagan man to whom she was betrothed. He shocked her with his lust, telling her that he could see in her eyes the sexual creature she really was. So she plucked them out.'"

The book said that when Lucia gave away her pledged dowry to the poor, her enraged fiancé had her arrested. The guards came and found Lucia so filled with the Holy Spirit she was as stiff and as heavy as a mountain. They could not move her even when they hitched her to a team of oxen. She continued to pray even as a soldier thrust a dagger through her throat. They tried to burn her at a stake, but the flames did not touch her. It was only after she was given communion that she fell softly and peacefully into death.

"Is that the story you imagined looking at her?" the shopkeeper asked.

"No."

She moved behind the counter and smiled. "You are very sweet." She started to wrap the woodcut in brown paper. "You must take this. She is just like you."

"What do you mean?"

"You might as well be holding your own pretty eyes in your hand."

She handed me the package and wouldn't accept my money.

"She is the patron saint for the blind," she said.

I took it, but it made me feel exposed. What wasn't I allowing myself to see? I don't remember ever showing the woodcut to Siri. When I stepped back onto the street, she and I simply continued our walk along Västerlånggatan, she with a bag of licorice in her pocket, and I with the Santa Lucia. It felt so heavy, and so did I, heavy with shame that even a stranger could see that I was still borne down by my grief.

———

"STAY THERE! I'LL take your picture!" Siri and I were in a big out-door arcade known as Sergels Torg. There had been a picture of it in my guidebook, and gift shops sold postcards of its cityscape sunsets and large, black and white triangular tiles. She took the stairs two at a time, and I followed the dot of her in the crowd.

"Do something!" I heard her yell. People looked to see what I'd do. I waved. She kept opening her arms indicating *bigger,* some-thing *bigger.* I was being captured against a black and white screen. Wherever I stood, I felt I was a game piece and that something was about to happen to me.

What happened was rain. Out of nowhere. My blue jacket was immediately drenched, my bangs clung to my forehead, my makeup ran, and I couldn't stop laughing. I was a sky-blue top on that wet game board, my arms wide open, my side teeth showing. I spun, and my jacket floated out around my hips. When she ran back down the stairs, I hugged her.

She said, "*Finally free.* That's how we should caption that photo."

If Sergels Torg was a game board, the Tunnelbana continued the game underground. We avoided the rain by descending into the city's subway system and riding the trains to see the artwork that exploded against the cavernous ceilings, floors, and walls of the subterranean stations. We were inside the colors, the art spread out and around us like great wombs of pattern and noise.

"Magnus used to bring me to the different stations back when he was a teenager," she said, slowing down. "This is one he espe-cially liked."

We were in a vast vaulted chamber just before descending the escalator to the platform area of the Järva line, where an artist had painted silhouettes to depict workers constructing the station and the scaffolding they'd used.

"Magnus told me our stations were a marvel, that no other city loves art the way we love art. Because all of this is hidden from the street, you have to get down inside the station to know it. He'd get candy and let me eat the whole bag just to buy himself more gaz-ing time."

I had managed to put him mostly out of my mind that day. It had been the rain, the running around in the city, just being with her, so light and free of spirit like we used to be. Why did I now find myself wanting her to talk more about Magnus? I wanted to ask her questions. I wanted her to explain him to me—or explain him away.

I was determined to focus on us. Approaching each new station, I scrambled to read the guidebook passages. Departing, we made our own notes in the margins. In Alby, beneath the cavernous green ceiling: a teenage couple with mohawks, dressed in matching outfits, their hands in the back pockets of each other's pants. Siri drew them like a cartoon while I nodded. In Solna, the man with a violin. In Rådhuset, the ten enormous billboards advertising herring. We made a game of it. Our eyes had been sponges and we wrung them out into my guidebook until I was left wondering, *How can I record my breathing?* How to note how it felt to be beside her, to jump from the train platform and not be afraid, to give the last of my kronor to an oompah band in T-Centralen?

The guidebook began to feel similar to my dream journal, beloved and utilitarian. I was grateful that I'd have it, this record of our time together, despite the speed of the silver train and our hourglass running out, despite how, no matter how many words I taught her in English, she'd return to her first language when I left for home.

Two days later, on the nonstop train back to Gothenburg, there was a digital sign over the door that flashed through the names of towns we were passing and told us how fast the train was traveling. I'd wondered how fast two hundred kilometers per hour would feel.

I had the guidebook out. Now it was *our* book. I read aloud some of the funny things we'd written, but she was melancholy, smiling where I expected her to laugh, staring at the blur beyond our window like she was reading the paint of its long green lines. A table separated us. She listened to music on her headphones.

I thumbed ahead to a section about Öland, the island we were planning to visit the last day of our trip. It was long and thin with a lighthouse at each end, four hundred windmills in between. The guidebook spoke of ruined castles and windsurfing, the Iron Age, crowded beaches. The center of the island was a heathland known as Stora Alvaret, famous for being unlike any other terrain in Sweden. There were no pictures in this section, but they made the alvar sound like a windy desert swirling with tumbleweed.

The digital sign above her head marked the speed like a blood pressure cuff. "Look. Two hundred kilometers per hour," I said.

Siri took off her headphones and fumbled with the player.

"Lauren, do you agree with Birgit? Do you think I'm a bad sister?"

She'd caught me off guard.

"What? No. Birgit doesn't think that," I said.

"The way I treat Magnus. Do you think I'm wrong?"

I paused, and I hated that she saw it. "You feel what you feel," I said.

"What do you think of him, Lauren?"

"Me?"

"If you didn't know all the stuff between him and me? What would you think?"

"*Do* I know all the stuff between the two of you?"

She ignored my question, but I think we could both feel it, that there was something each of us was trying to hide.

"He told me I was avoiding him by bringing you home this summer."

"Were you?"

"I don't think I would have come back if you hadn't come, too."

"Why?"

I wanted her to say it was because she loved spending time with me, but she didn't. If that was the reason, she didn't know it. I could see her thinking, and in her silence, other ideas gripped me. That she'd brought me to bolster and surround her. I was a wall for her, a mask, a way to prove herself through my devotion. I wanted her to say it was because of love, if only to quell what I was feeling now—that I'd been used.

She laid her head against the velvet of the seatback. I was angry that she was allowing herself to rest without offering even a made-up answer. Maybe that's why my words came out sharply.

"Siri, what is it between the two of you?"

"The pictures he made of my mother," she said, staring out the window at the whizzing green.

"Yes, you've told me about them," I said.

"Yeah, I know," she said.

I was impatient. Magnus hadn't made her forget her mother's face. She was blaming him for the things that time does.

"If there *was* something else . . . would you tell me?"

"Don't you think that's enough?" she said. "I used to look up to him. I was a child. I told him I was forgetting my mother's face. I told him I was scared of spiders, and he painted her like a spider."

The light through the window made her freckles blink through the powder of her makeup.

"He believes her death was my fault," she said.

We looked at each other. This felt closer to the truth.

"That's why he paints her like that. To punish me. It's in the sketches on the walls. It's buried in a hundred holes in the field around the house. I imagined the paintings rising up again and coming to life. It's part of the reason I needed to get away from there."

I thought of the way she treated her friends and family. I thought of the wide berths people gave her, how much they forgave, how they didn't yell back.

"What happened with your mother, Siri? How did she die?"

Siri gazed solemnly out the window at the blur.

"She went for a walk and didn't come back," she said.

I felt a chill rush through me. I'd asked her about this before when she was a student in my class. *Nobody knows for sure,* she'd said. I'd assumed then that meant something too long undiag-

nosed. Something regular and sad. After all our talks, all our sharing, Siri had never told me more.

"Sometimes, lying in bed in that house, I find myself listening
in the middle of the night for the front door to open, the sound of
her returning," Siri said. "I feel it when I'm home. All of us in our
beds, listening for the front door. But it's always the gate. The
gate."

Her makeup had dried out, and there were lines around her
light eyes I'd never noticed. She got up and came to my side of the
table to sit beside me. Maybe so I'd stop looking at her. Maybe so
she could stop looking at me.

She laid her head against my shoulder, then turned her mouth
onto my skin. I could feel her lips move as she whispered. "I'll tell
you everything someday, Lauren. I promise. Until then, stay away
from him. For me. Please."

I know we both felt how fast the train was moving. I wanted it
to stop moving in his direction, but all I could feel was the high
speed at which we were traveling, the inability to stop it, the disas-
ter of not stopping it.

Chapter 10

Back in Olofstorp, everyone wanted to host Siri before she returned to the States. Everyone wanted to toast her. Frida had a party where people drank akvavit out of a long, hollowed-out horn. She'd gone around sulking most of the night with her arms crossed against her chest, shooting dark glances at me with Siri.

Siri's packed itinerary kept us out late, and both of us were starting to get a little sick, coughing ourselves to sleep each night. I worried that I would keep Magnus awake on the other side of our shared wall. Sometimes I would imagine him coming in with a wet cloth for my head or a cup of tea to soothe me. But Magnus was still gone. Birgit said that he hadn't come back since the fight with Siri, and he hadn't reported to work the whole time we were in Stockholm.

I know Birgit heard the coughing coming from both our rooms at night. She had pleaded with me to help slow Siri down, but I'd delivered both of us home from Stockholm sick. Often I saw her sitting alone on the window seat and worried she was angry with me.

We were headed out to see Siri's friends again one evening when Birgit jumped up and showed Siri that the freezer was packed with ice cream. "I went shopping for us. You could just stay in and we could watch movies the way we used to," she offered.

"I don't want to stay in. Come with us if you want to be with me," Siri said.

Siri went to get her bag, and Birgit went back to the window seat. I walked up beside her. I noticed that the window overlooked the road that led to the house.

"You're worried about Magnus," I said quickly. His name in my mouth felt like a jawbreaker.

Birgit turned to me.

"You're watching for him. You want to be here when he comes back, right?"

She nodded. "I need to try to fix things between them," she said. "You know, I see how you look at him, Lauren."

I sat down at the dinette table and stared at the blue and yellow pattern of the tablecloth.

"No. It's okay. What I mean is that you see he's not a bad person. Siri is too hard on him. He's been gone now for *days*. I so wanted them to fix this thing between them, but how can that happen now? And with the school vacation so close to being done."

Siri walked back into the kitchen. Her hair looked wet. She'd slicked it back.

Birgit brightened.

"But at least we'll have the weekend. Right, Siri?"

"*Syster,* I told you."

"You're not still thinking of going camping!"

"You can come with us!"

"I'm too old for that bullshit, Siri. Lauren is too old for it, too. She doesn't want to go there."

Siri tried to show Birgit a map of where we were headed that weekend, but her sister went out to smoke alone on the balcony.

"If I do not go out tonight, she will want me to stay home tomorrow, too, and the next day, and I *am* going back to school. That's what she wants, Lauren. You hear her. She wants me to not go back."

I wondered if Birgit could hear her through the glass. As we went down the circular staircase and out of the house, Siri told me we were heading to her favorite bar. Though she insisted it was the place everyone in town went to feel sentimental, I couldn't help but look back at their house, and at the second-story patio, where Birgit sat rocking among the yellow flowers and the orange stripes in the sky.

FRIDA AND MARGARETA met us at the bar, but soon many more people squeezed together at the corner table where we were sitting, all people Siri knew. Each conversation with a town friend sounded like she was picking up in the middle of a story. There was a local rock band in the corner of the room, the bass drum stuck with electrical tape, the lead singer droning on a high stool.

I caught Margareta looking at me.

"All this time, guys, and I don't think Lauren knows how to toast like a Swede!" Margareta put her arm around me and poured me a drink as the others raised their glasses. "I'm going to teach you. You look at all of us before you drink that drink. And then when you sip it you keep eye contact with the person in front of you. Okay? I will make the toast."

Siri seemed angry and yanked on her arm. Maybe she was afraid of what Margareta would say. Margareta was insistent.

"No, I will do it! And I'll do it in *English*," she said sweetly. "For once, let *me* make the toast. It's about you, too, our dear one."

Everyone laughed.

"If Siri is going to be away from here, and from us, we think it's a good thing that she has Lauren to watch out for her and be her friend."

She raised her glass.

"To Lauren."

"*Skål!*"

When I made eye contact with the people at the table, I felt I was drinking in a tiny bit of each of them to keep with me forever. I raised my glass to the person across from me—it was Frida. The only person with no smile in her eyes. I tried to keep eye contact with her while she drank, but she was taking forever, her gaze a strange glare I didn't understand.

"You see," Siri said, grabbing my hand, "you make everything better."

"Magnus is here," Frida said stonily. She hadn't been looking at me at all, but over my shoulder.

Margareta tried to head it off. "So? We don't have to talk to him."

He was on the other side of the bar, two pretty girls leaning over the partition of another booth to talk to him. Had he gone home first? Did Birgit know he was here?

"We'll go someplace else," Frida said, reaching for her sweatshirt.

But Siri was waving him over. *What is she doing?* I thought. Magnus picked up his jacket and carried it over to our booth. I could feel a wall going up between him and the others, but I found myself inching over, inching over, to make room for him. *What am I doing?* I thought.

"Hello," he said to the table.

There was a bandage taped across his hand. Frida and Margareta pulled out a compact and started applying sparkly makeup in the mirror together. Magnus sat down beside me. Had Siri told him to?

"Hello, Lauren," he said.

"Hi."

After so many days of not seeing him, we were body-to-body, me needing to press in even closer as more chairs were brought to the table. All I could think of was how he'd run his hands down my back and called me Skogsrå. I was sure he could sense my anxiety and hear the beat of my heart in the hollow tree of my body.

But Siri seemed relaxed. She asked him questions and answered him with more than just one or two words when he spoke to her. In him I saw a gratitude building. Certainly it couldn't go any larger, he couldn't go on expecting this volley of laughter to last much longer.

As the tension between Magnus and Siri eased, it was easier for me to be around him. "What was that?" he asked when I spoke and no one else heard me over the noise. "Your jacket slipped," he said, picking it up from the floor and draping it gently over the back of my chair. He was talking with me, and she seemed okay with it. Maybe something was changing between them.

From the beginning, I not only felt the space between them, I felt I *was* the space between them. When they were at odds, every muscle in my body was tense. But now that they were drinking together and toasting each other, actually looking at each other when they spoke, I was loosened, becoming unwound.

I was drinking too much. Suddenly everything was hilarious. The band grew louder, all synthesizers, disco, bass. Over and over Magnus slid his water bottle toward me and told me to drink. I sipped from it when Siri turned her back.

She kept turning her back.

I told him I was going to use the restroom. No, don't go, he said. Don't go, don't go. This song. *This* song. I remember it so well. It was a slower song. People were coupling up on the dance floor. He reached out his hand to me. Siri's back was still turned, but Frida and Margareta were slow-dancing, their eyes fixed on us.

I tried to walk past him, but Magnus caught me in his arms. When he felt the tension in my body he tried to make me laugh, dancing with me straight-armed and fast, like in an old-timey movie. I wanted to smile but couldn't. I stared at Siri's back. His hand touched my neck. Finally, she turned. I felt the floor sway beneath me. He took me by the waist and drew me to him. Over his shoulder, Siri and I locked eyes. In that moment I realized she hadn't brought him to our table to make things better with him.

She had done so to test me.

I waited for her eyes to turn to fire. Instead, she gave me an unreadable smile, lifted her bottle, and drank, an eerie toast. A toast to what? He spun me, and Siri turned back to watch the band.

She clearly wanted to see where my loyalties lay. For just a moment, I let myself feel him holding me. I imagined myself with him, not going home to America, but living on both sides of our shared bedroom wall, part for Siri, part for him.

"What were you looking for in my room?" he sang into my ear.

His question caught me off guard, and I pulled back to look him in his eyes.

"I was looking for the picture you drew of us at Vimmerby," I said.

He laughed. His face was kind. "You didn't even look at it that day. You ran away."

Because that's what Siri had asked of me, in myriad ways. That I always follow her, be there for her. That was why she had brought me to Sweden, wasn't it? To be in her corner, to reflect her light. I stopped swaying with him, looking again at the back of Siri's head. I thought of the picture he'd made of us, the swirl of our hair on our shoulders, back-to-back. I wanted that picture in my hands now, something to possess, maybe because I could feel her attention draining out of me. She had just toasted me, but I was stupid to think it could ever be permission. She wanted me to herself.

I went back to the table and reached across its slick surface to touch the back of her arm.

"Siri?" She didn't turn.

Magnus slid his water bottle toward me. I refused it. He asked me what artists I loved. He put it just that way: "What artists do you love?"

Siri was ignoring me. She was testing me. I was supposed to be proving something to her right now, but I would never be able to do enough to satisfy her. I wanted to drink. It took me a second to identify my beer from among the many bottles on our table.

"Or maybe you're an artist? I never asked," he said.

I drank. "I like Monet and his water lilies—the colors."

He stayed serious. "What kinds of colors do you love, then? Blue and green?"

I was in a bar with a loud Swedish grunge band, lifting my hand to the waitress to ask for a harder drink, and Magnus was asking me my favorite colors.

"I love all colors," I said.

"All colors?"

"Mostly colors."

"Most colors?"

"No, I mean, over subject matter." I knew he could hardly hear me over the music. "Mark Rothko," I yelled.

Siri made a face at us across the table. But at least she had turned.

"Who do you like, Magnus?" I asked.

But he'd been snared by Siri's expression. "What?" he asked her.

"Nothing."

"You have a better way to pose the question?"

She ignored him.

"You know, you're not just being rude to me. You're being rude to Lauren."

"You don't know anything about Lauren," she said possessively.

And just like that, everything was shrinking again, the trees growing up.

He turned to me. "She and I used to be close. She used to go to see the art in the Tunnelbana with me when she was a little girl. She liked the rainbows at Stadion station. When she was little, she was a *feeling* person, now she is only selfish."

His cheeks were two flushed rectangles.

"Now your question, Lauren. About art—you really do need to ask the question as, 'Who do you love?' It's the only really interesting way to ask that question. Not 'My favorite is,' or 'I like pretty good this one or that one.'"

"Magnus, you are being a bore," Siri snapped. "Who cares how she put the question?"

"No, it's okay, Siri," I said, looking between them. "He's just trying to make the distinction."

She held my gaze a second, then stormed off to dance. It was too loud in there; I don't think she'd heard what I said, but I know she sensed that I was defending Magnus, and it angered her. But I couldn't help it. Her hardness made me feel protective of him.

Magnus leaned in and tapped the back of my chair. "Let's go outside," he said, his breath hot on my neck. I shook my head.

I watched Siri dance, her back to us. I reluctantly went out onto the dance floor to join her, and she smiled a sort of thank-you smile, an everything-is-okay-again smile.

And I saw Magnus throw his body weight against the back door and go out. A ray of light streamed in and narrowed along the floor until the door fell closed.

I danced mechanically through two songs. When Siri went to get water, I slipped out the way Magnus had gone. The sun was too bright. I squinted. I saw him leaning on the side of the building playing with a lighter.

"She brought me to Stadion station," I said.

He looked up at the sound of my voice.

"The winding rainbows," I said.

"You're talking about the artwork in the T?"

"Yes. The flowers above that one bench that all look like rainbows. She took me to all of the stations in one day. She showed me . . . the one with the silhouettes. The men on the scaffold. She said it was your favorite."

I went to him.

I said, "She still *loves* it. Really loves it."

"What are you doing, Lauren?"

"What do you mean?"

"You want to make things better between me and my sister?"

"Yes."

"Why?"

"Because I see you both in pain," I said. But that wasn't it. As long as they were in pain, I was in pain. I was the breach between them and the reason she'd brought me home. If I could salve that, if I could make it better, she and I could be friends again.

He reached out his hand to me, the one with the bandage and tape. I took it. *Maybe this is all it is, all it's been,* I thought. *I am just trying to help.* I had to help this gulf between them, to narrow this gulf in me. I could smell the pine, sunshine, and sweat in his clothes. I noticed a dimple on his cheek for the first time. He wiped my hair back. *Oh no,* I thought. *Oh no.* He leaned in and his gaze swept me up. He was smiling, his mouth so close. There was wetness in his lashes.

I thought I heard the door to the bar open, and I pushed away from him. But the door hadn't opened. Only something in him, in me.

I walked around the other side of the building, through the parking lot, all the way to the road. Only then did I look back. The bar seemed then a temporary structure—a ramshackle cabin with a metal roof and a metal door looped with graffiti. There was litter on the ground, and cars peeling out of the dirt lot, and all was early morning sun-on-metal mist and dust.

WHEN WE GOT home, Siri apologized to me. She said that the way I defended Magnus made her feel like a bad sister. She said that I had an amazing sense of patience.

"I'm sorry," she said.

I didn't know if I believed her.

She reached across the table and pinched my arm, the way she'd done with Frida that first day.

I cried out and tried to draw back, but she grabbed ahold of my arm and rubbed it to soothe me. I couldn't help but feel she was trying to manipulate me, pat things down, smooth them out so I would accept her apology. She kept rubbing my arm and saying *sorry.* I think she could see in my eyes that I didn't believe her.

She was working hard on forgiving him for things but wasn't there yet, she said, louder this time. Would I forgive her?

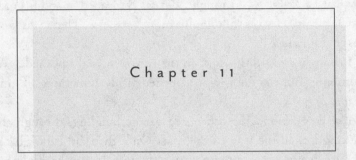

Chapter 11

WE HAD BEEN planning to go into the city of Gothenburg the next day, but at breakfast, Siri read over our itinerary with her head in her hands and ate lozenges one after the other. Her cough was sounding deeper and deeper. When I suggested we just go another day, she shook her head. "We're going to Öland this weekend. This is the only day we can do it."

"If you don't rest you'll get sicker and you won't even be able to go to Öland," Birgit said. "Which might be for the best, because that place—"

"Oh, *syster,* you must take her then," Siri said, bleary-eyed. "Take her to see the Poseidon statue. Take her to see the water. Bring her to the ice-cream place we always go."

"Are you kidding me, Siri?"

"I want her to see the city."

"I don't have time to entertain Lauren. You have your itinerary, and I have mine, okay? I have to wash these dishes, because neither of you have washed a dish since you came here. Then I have to go to work. Because I have *ett jobb.*"

It seemed her voice descended into Swedish to spare me, but I couldn't help but feel I'd let her down. Siri was back to her old habits, and now she was sick. I wasn't supposed to let this happen. She brought out a kettle and muttered to herself as she looked in the upper cabinets for tea. "You want some, too, Lauren?" she asked, but I could hear anger in her voice.

I loved Birgit. I immediately went to the sink and filled the basin with water. "I'm sorry," I said, and she watched me with her arms crossed as I started soaping the dishes.

Birgit helped Siri into her bedroom to lie down, then came back and dried dishes beside me with a white towel.

"It's just that I *asked* you," she said. "She pushes everything to the limit. God. I hate her being away. When she was at school, the fear never went away. That she'd do something so impulsive, so selfish, that I'd never see her again. But then she told me about you. We can make this work. You and I can be like sisters, okay? You can be her big sister in the U.S. You can call me. You can tell me if she's out of control. Can you do that?"

I nodded. She reached into the sink and removed the drain stopper. "Siri made me promise that I'd take you to Gothenburg. We'll go in an hour, okay?"

I agreed, then went back to check on Siri. I found her asleep in Birgit's room, curled up like a cat on the down comforter. The portrait Magnus had made of their mother hung above Birgit's bed. She had been dark haired like Birgit, but everything else about her face was Siri. The shape of her eyes, the delicate features, a sprinkling of freckles across her nose. Behind her ear she wore a purple rose touched with silver, and her eyes were partly closed in a shy, happy way. The portrait reminded me of a headstone, and Siri, lying there, like a girl asleep atop a grave.

I heard a snapping sound and noticed a piece of plastic had been taped across Birgit's bedroom window, where a section of the glass had been broken out. The old house had lots of places taped and bracketed and pinned together.

I went to the window and looked out. Birgit had a view similar to mine—the field behind the house, where Magnus had been the first night, digging, burying something. Had she been watching

Magnus out there, too? Had she known then that it was another portrait of their mother? Did she hope that this time, when he tried to bury her, it would stick?

I looked around her room. Into the edges of her dresser mirror, Birgit had stuck old photographs of herself with childhood friends, but there was nothing more recent. They reminded me of the pictures of teenage friends I had on my refrigerator at home. In the kitchen, Birgit was arguing with someone on the phone. I walked out into the hallway with my backpack on my shoulder and my jacket over my arm. When Birgit saw me, she went out onto the balcony and closed the door so I couldn't hear her.

Two ironing boards with bright daisy patterns were set up in the foyer. The sisters did their ironing there in the mornings, talking between puffs of steam. There was a narrow window beside the stairwell inlaid with stained glass, and I looked through the clear diamond shapes out onto the fields below the house. I felt then I was a girl between worlds. There was so much beauty here, but also so much that weighed me down. I waited, expecting that at any moment Birgit's phone call would end, and she would take me to Gothenburg.

Instead, Magnus came in.

"She's going to be a while," he said.

His red hair looked almost blond in the light of the foyer. He had been keeping his distance from me since the bar. Whenever I entered a room, he was always just leaving it.

He played with the button on the iron, and when a puff of steam shot out, we both jumped.

"I'm going into the city anyway," he said.

"You mean you'll drop me off?"

"No. I don't have work today."

I looked down the hall, at where Birgit was pacing now on the balcony.

"You want to ask her permission?" he said.

Birgit saw us talking and opened the glass door.

"I'm not going to be able to go for a while, Lauren. I'm sorry," she said.

"I said I'd take her," Magnus said.

"You did?" she asked.

"I better not go. Without Siri, I mean," I said.

Birgit covered the phone with her hand. "No. He has a nice idea, Lauren. You should go. I can explain it to Siri."

Her expression was insistent. She wanted me to go with him. I knew she didn't want him disappearing again for days. She wanted someone to make sure he would come home for these last nights before Siri left for school. She waved me on and shut the glass door.

"Magnus, I—"

"You won't come because of Siri?"

"No. I mean—with her, she just doesn't see—"

"But you do."

He took my hand. He went down the circular stairway backward, holding my hand all the way to the bottom. There was a crooked-smile proposal in each step, all the penciled faces whipping toward us as we passed.

Outside, heat rose from the gravel drive. We got into his car and he started the engine, which roared loud, an announcement.

"Now I've got you," he said.

His words sent a rush through my body. As he pulled onto the road, I imagined Siri sitting up straight on the bed, yelling our names.

"She will be furious, you know," he said. "No matter how Birgit explains it to her."

Part of me wanted to say *So what?* And *It was your fault, Siri*. I didn't make the seating arrangements for our car ride to Vimmerby. I needn't have been squashed up against him in the backseat all the way there, smelling how he smelled: pine, charcoal.

"But why?" I asked. "*Why* will she be angry? What is this thing between the two of you?"

"I heard you talking with Siri and Birgit that day with the scrapbook. Siri rarely talks about our mother's death without blaming me for it."

"Blaming *you*?"

"Hasn't she told you?"

"She hasn't told me enough for me to understand."

"No? Well, I'll leave that to her then, in her time. I imagine she gets the right to tell the story how she remembers it. She's *your* friend. You should hear it from her first. We can talk about something else. Ask me anything."

"Should I be afraid of you?"

He laughed and looked over at me incredulously. "Are you serious?"

"Yes."

"No. You should be afraid of Siri and her temper."

He drove fast down the winding roads, the roads all like tunnels with the treetops knitting together above us, shadows closing off everything behind. He revved the engine around a curve, and I felt intoxicated by the speed.

"Surely you have seen how she is with her friends here," he said, looking over at me. "You think you'll be spared much longer?"

Of course I had seen how she treated the other girls. And Magnus. And Birgit.

"I feel like I get her. And she gets me," I said, a little defensive. I found myself rubbing the place where she'd pinched my arm the night before.

"Have you asked yourself what will happen when she starts treating you like that?"

"I'm a little older than her other friends," I explained. "She wouldn't treat me that way."

"Yeah, you are older," he said with a flirtatious smile.

"Shut up."

"I'm just saying that I can see you're a sensitive, good person. I heard her telling Birgit about what happened with your family.

I'm sorry about that. I just think you need to take care of yourself, you know?"

All Siri had done so far was pinch my arm. But I'd felt her in charge of me here. In the forest playing hide-and-seek, when he ran his fingers down my back, all I could think of was her. The day Magnus had found me in his room and I rushed back to her. Her strange toast to me in the bar when I'd danced with him. Outside the bar, when I'd run off before he could kiss me.

"For example, you have feelings for me," he said.

"What?"

"You like me. But she won't even let you feel that I am a normal person."

I stared at the trees flying past, the side roads, the telephone poles. I could feel his eyes on me, and it scared me.

"If you're going to drive this fast you need to watch the road!" I said. I slid my guidebook out of my backpack, intent on making the day about the places we were headed and not him.

"That book again," he said.

I opened it. The first things I saw were Siri's marks, her purple drawings, her cartoons.

"What do you want to see today?" he asked.

"There is a famous statue. Of Poseidon?"

He nodded. "Yes. Fine."

"Do you like the city?" I asked him.

"I don't like most people, and there are fewer in Olofstorp," he said.

"What do you want to see in the city?" I asked him.

"Me? I have seen everything."

"Is there something you would prefer to see, I mean? Other than the statue?"

"I guess we could go to Fiskekyrkan."

"What's that?"

"It's a fish church."

"Fish church?"

"A fish market that looks like a church." He shrugged.

"You're not much of a tour guide. Maybe I should have waited for Birgit."

I didn't know if he would like my teasing him, but to my relief, he smiled. "No, you shouldn't have." He looked at me out of the corner of his eye. He gunned the engine, and my heart sped.

In Gothenburg he parked the car in a public lot near the harbor, where small vessels were docked and men with extreme sunburns sat on wooden pilings drinking beer. I heard some of them talking in English and turned my head toward what sounded like a New England accent, but Magnus took my hand and pulled me along.

I followed him like we were both late to something. We walked past the city's opera house, and through its immense glass windows I could see its interior was curved like a hull and the wooden floor resembled the deck of a ship. Everything in the city felt maritime, from the shapes of the buildings to the hidden canals.

We soon found ourselves in a busy central area with cobblestone streets and mobs of people crisscrossing our path. The energy of the square seemed to charge him, and he walked faster, talked faster. Above us, colorful banners ruffled in the hot sun. The sounds of glass and silverware being laid out in cafés tinkled around us. We passed the city's central food market, Saluhallen. When I tried to pull out my guidebook and read its entry, he snapped it shut and pulled me down an alley where every door was painted a different raucous color.

The quiet alley was narrow, high, full of shadows. I was suddenly nervous that the scarlet, violet, and yellow doors led to single rooms with mattresses on the floors.

"Where are we?" I said.

"Shh."

With his eyes fixed on mine, he opened one of the doors. I heard a bell jingle above our heads. We were met with the smells of wood and paint.

It was a small gallery full of canvases. A white-haired man sat at the rear of the store, sawing wood for new easels. "*Hallå,* Magnus," the man said amicably.

"This is a friend of my sister," Magnus said.

Magnus positioned his hands on either side of my lower back and moved me in front of the paintings he thought I should see. Each time we passed him, the old man smiled to himself. When we left, Magnus took my hand and led me to the shop next door, where all the narrow-faced portraits looked the same, and all their eyes watched us back.

The alleyway was full of tiny galleries, and all the owners knew Magnus but didn't talk with him much. I asked him if these people were his friends.

"They are people I know," he said. "That first man—Jens—he used to be a great artist. All the others, they get one successful painting and then open a shop where they sit inside and celebrate themselves. No one ever comes here but other artists. But everyone is nice to one another."

"Are you going to open a shop someday?" I asked.

"When?"

"When you have your famous paintings."

"No. I won't need this mutual-affirmation society."

He was determined to show me as many paintings as possible. Portraits of black-eyed women. Geometric patterns like melted-down Calders. I found myself searching his eyes for an indication of what was interesting to him, but we were going too fast. His attention fluttered from piece to piece. I let him tow me along, from one bright door to the next.

"I have another idea. We'll have to take the trolley," he said.

My feet hurt from walking on the cobblestones.

"Wait," I said. "I didn't get to see the statue."

"Which statue?"

"Poseidon."

We turned the corner, and there it was, as though he had conjured it. It was massive, bronze green. Around its perimeter, sea creatures—mermen and strange fish with human faces and scales like coins—lurched away from the figure of Poseidon. Bright nickel arcs of water shot from their mouths up around the god's body, as though he were a man caught in sprinklers.

I pulled my guidebook from my backpack.

"You are such a tourist!" he joked, trying to grab it from me. "Tell me all it says. Who made this thing? Why the spitting fishes?"

"Stop, Magnus," I laughed, pulling away from him.

Magnus looked so happy. He climbed up to sit upon the edge of the fountain and spread his arms wide. "This magnificent example of Swedish sculpture of a god and his several fish was installed in—" He reached down for the guidebook to check the date, but he started to lose his balance. When he reached behind to steady himself, the book slipped from his hands into the fountain.

"No!"

I climbed over the side. I saw it in the water and waded in to retrieve it. The fountain sprayed over my head, and then I couldn't see. I knelt down, feeling for it.

When I found the book, it came up thick and heavy.

I tried to pull the pages apart, but it was soaked through.

It had been our illuminated manuscript of this trip, with memories like condensed diary entries in its margins. A cherished record, for when I was alone again, of a time when I hadn't been.

One page: art in the Tunnelbana, Siri's cartoon drawing of the mohawked teenage lovers, now pulpy. Another: a map of Öland, the margins impossible to write in now, when there would surely have been so much to say about our last day in Sweden.

The water around my legs was cloudy. Siri's purple ink, words, pictures, our shared memories, rippled away from me.

I looked up and saw Magnus before me, water shooting against the back of his head in an explosion of white rain. He was already drenched, letting the water hit him, his mouth open, waiting for a cue from me that it was all right for him to smile, to laugh. I shook him off my shoulder, but he kept trying to grab me, to make it a game.

"Lauren, it's only a book," he said.

I shouldn't have left Siri. Why did I do that? I thought about all the notes we'd made in that guidebook, praying I would be able to remember them on my own.

Magnus was running through the water, around and around, with big, dancing strides. He was trying to reach me, to make me laugh. The sounds of traffic intensified. I was all at once aware of the everydayness of the avenue—the people sitting on the steps of the nearby museum, all the people just walking by us.

But Magnus was gone. He was a satellite. He might as well have been that far away, that distant. I climbed out of the fountain and sat down on a bench. I closed my eyes and listened to the rush of the water bursting up and coming down, thinking about calling the house, envisioning Siri answering, how impossible that would feel.

"Are you mad at me?"

He was beside me again. I tried to put some distance between our bodies, but I could still hear him breathing. The rise and fall of his chest, the rise and fall of the water.

"I'm sorry," he said. "There is a bookstore nearby. I'll buy you two of those guides."

His hair was tousled and wet, his eyes pleading.

"It's okay," I said. "Let's just get out of here."

I'd let him back in. He knew it. He sidled closer to me and asked if my legs were cold, though he was the one wet from head to toe. "Come here," he said, coming closer. He turned me so that I was facing him. "Come here."

"I'm right here."

"What about your arms? Did your arms get wet?"

We stood up, and he rubbed my arms while I tried to glare at him. I loved that book. But I was growing intoxicated with his now-cataloging of my body, what parts were wet, whether I was cold, was I still mad, did I have a fever. I found myself leaning into him at the street corner when we were waiting for the cars to stop. I stuffed the wet guidebook down into my bag.

The light changed. We crossed. I felt we were running through the streets. This was how Magnus and Siri were alike, I thought, the speed of beginnings, how fast things could change. When we returned to the house that night, it would have to be over, but right now we were just starting.

He paused on another corner. He sensed my keeping up with him, keeping up with his thoughts. His hands closed around my cheeks and drew my face toward his.

"How old are you?" he asked.

I pulled away.

"I just want to know," he said.

"Twenty-eight," I whispered.

"You have such a soft voice."

"Twenty-eight," I said a little louder.

"I heard you," he laughed. "Why are you embarrassed?"

"How old are you?"

He shook his head like a dog, drizzling me with water from his hair. "I am gray. All this is red paint!"

I reached up and touched his hair, and he caught my hand as it grazed his neck.

"One more place to show you," he said, leading me down the street and through another door.

It was a shop filled with postcards, Swedish souvenirs, and candy. There were convenience-store smells, the ink of magazines, the salty oil of fried food. He brought me to a line of small paintings in the back of the store.

The colors were distinctly Swedish—the blue and honey-drop yellow of the Swedish flag. They made good souvenirs for tourists, here in this shop so close to Central Station, everyone leaving and wanting to grab one last memento of the harbor city.

I picked one up and turned it over to see the price. It was only about six U.S. dollars. In the center of the canvas was one small, yellow, daffodil-like flower. Its tiny, translucent petals had been worried over, in contrast to the swipe of sea-blue and white, spackled-on crest. It was floating, lost, out of place.

"What do you think of this?" he asked.

"I like the colors."

"With you, always colors," he said. "What about the flower in the middle? How can you stand it? So detailed, so out of place from the rest of it."

I tilted the canvas in my hands; its white lines sparkled like the fizz of sea foam. "My father brought me to a Salvador Dalí museum in Florida when I was a little girl," I said. "There was one painting as big as a wall. But if you got up close to it, right at my little-girl eye level, he'd painted a tiny silver fish. You could see its pink gills and all the parts of its eye, like he'd done it with a razor blade. This reminds me of that."

Magnus looked at me like he was waiting for me to say something else, but the memory of that silver fish, of standing beside my father, was so close all I could think of was that St. Petersburg museum full of air-conditioning, the streets outside full of steam. In the gift shop, my father had bought me a perfume because I'd loved that its gold bottle was shaped like an ocelot.

"Why did you want to show me these paintings?" I said.

"I didn't." He took the painting from me and fit it back into its place among the others. "I wanted to show you the ocean."

I looked again at the wall of paintings. In my mind, the silver fish darted away.

They were all similar, the tiny yellow flowers now disappearing against a blue background. The white swathes now approached as one long breaking wave. The creamy lines set side by side made for a beautiful effect, and above the crests, an indigo horizon slowly settled along the back wall of the store.

His eyes flashed to see it moved me.

Perhaps because the paintings' coming-at-you energy was so like him, because he was a wave that was always building, I knew then why he'd wanted me to see them.

"These are yours," I said.

He smiled. That sunlike smile from the car ride to Vimmerby. So pure, because he felt seen.

We went outside and stood beneath the shop's awning. I had this feeling that the wave would come through the revolving door at any moment and knock us over. Those were his paintings, a solid wall of them lining the back of a convenience store. It'd taken him the whole day to trust me enough to show me: that this is where they were sold; that they did not cost much; that they weren't selling; that together, like him, they were a wall and they were a wave.

"Are you hungry?" he asked me. "I could take you to dinner."

"It's getting late," I said. "Maybe we should go home."

He smiled a little, shook his head. He grabbed for my hand again. He wanted me to know that he enjoyed being with me this way. Seeing that I liked his work had calmed him down. I could feel it in his body. He turned to face me, put a hand on my shoulder. With his other hand, he tucked my hair behind my ear. *Where to now, then?* I wanted to say. He put his arms around me and drew me close to him. He lightly touched my back, where the scars were. He went right to them, beneath my shirt, like he knew exactly where they were. His eyes, so light. Like water. I could hear him breathing, each exhalation rolling against the sand of me.

He kissed me, so light. A friend's kiss, maybe. Just a thank-you kiss. Then another because we knew it was coming. Then harder, because *you* knew this was coming, Lauren, this wave, this wave crashing over you now, this thing you must have, more, please, a scramble of hands to each other's faces, this kiss rather than breathing.

INSTEAD OF TAKING me home, or to dinner, Magnus took me by trolley to Liseberg, an amusement park in the center of Gothenburg. All evening we braved roller coasters and free-fall rides. Now we were sitting, pressed against each other on a bench, his fingers in my hair.

He looked at me intensely, and behind him, the lights from a fountain danced and changed from white to red on his face.

"Why—" I started.

I had so many questions.

He kissed me. I couldn't be close to him anymore without wanting to be in his lap. I kissed him back. I kissed his hands, and I could taste the sugar from the long ropes of licorice we had eaten instead of dinner.

All those days of his walking out of a room just as I was entering—my not following him always felt like flipping a hidden coin in my pocket. Magnus was one side of me, Siri the other. I'd wanted to be like her, but I felt that I was him. The love she showed me felt beautiful but demanded more of me. Thoughts of Magnus were dark, familiar, and easy.

And being with him felt like a respite from the house, as though I'd been seen and claimed by him, taken out and fed the meal I deserved, all sugar, shown the places I was supposed to see, my body kissed and tossed.

I fingered the collar of his shirt, still damp from the fountain that afternoon.

"I can't help feeling that you and I are similar," I said softly.

"What are you talking about? Your shirt isn't even wet."

He meant that he'd been the one who'd ruined the book.

"I've been thinking about the first night I was here," I said.

"Yeah?"

"When I saw you. Out in the back of the house."

"And I saw you. By the light of the moon," he said, singsongy, a twist of my hair, a nod to the water behind us. "All white now," he remarked of the fountain lights.

"What were you doing that night?"

"You heard my sisters."

"I know. I want to hear it from you."

"I'd done a portrait of my mother. I was putting it in the ground."

"Why?" I asked.

"It wasn't right."

"Why not just throw it away?"

"Because there was something in it that was of her."

"You could have put it in a closet. But you—"

He cut me off.

"The portraits bother my sisters. They think they're bizarre. They are. The whole thing is bizarre."

I thought of how I had tried to protect my parents' things. Part of my mother in this copper pan she cooked with; part of my father in the matchbook cover he used as a bookmark.

"Siri had come back home. My paintings upset her. I didn't want her to see."

"I saw the one you did with the purple rose—"

"Yeah, yeah. They liked that one."

"But the ones you bury?"

"No roses."

"Okay."

"Maybe a crown of thorns. Bees where her eyes should be. Her face blue with frost. Smiling and clutching a bloody heart. Maybe her, but ripped in two like that old tree you liked near Vimmerby."

I suddenly remembered the creatures from the old embroidered calendar I found in his room that day. When I didn't speak, he just laughed and looked back at the fountain.

"Why do you paint her that way?" I asked.

He shrugged and nuzzled my neck where my shirt wasn't wet. Then his hands were up underneath my blouse in the back, tracing the four dark circles that had once been scabs and had each come off in one piece, like bark.

"Was she troubled?" I asked.

"Yes. She was in a deep depression after my father died. It was a hard year. Sometimes I think I'm the only one who saw it." He tried to harden his face. "All that's in the Öland cemetery of my mother is a name marker."

"Öland? She's buried on that island?"

"We had a summer house there. Our happiest times. But no, not buried. They never found her body."

"Siri said . . . she'd gone out walking?"

"Is that what she said?"

"Yes."

He shook his head. "No one knows what happened to her that night. But lots of people had ideas. And I was young, trying to make sense of it all. The images come from that time, from a younger me."

"But you're not that boy anymore."

"Aren't I? Won't you always be the age of the girl whose parents died?"

A chill went through me. Yes. Every part of my body was ringing *yes*.

"I was trying to capture something of my mother in those paintings, and I was failing, over and over. I understand Siri was young. She wants to remember our mother one way only. But our mother was grieving the death of our dad that whole year. Going around in his shaggy brown sweaters. Writing us notes and signing them from him. She was depressed. Some days she didn't get out of bed. She was a beautiful spirit. But she was also all of these other things that scared and angered me. I was trying to remember her then, even when she was in our house. I felt her slipping away. I didn't want any part of her to slip away. Siri only wanted to remember her smiling, with a purple rose in her hair. . . ."

His voice trailed off, and I realized that was the Siri I knew, too. She wanted things simple. Me on her side. Us having fun. Everything just better, all the time. She wanted everyone to focus on her, so she wouldn't have to focus on her grief. Magnus buried portraits in the ground. She buried all the complicated versions of things inside.

"Siri said your burying the paintings in the field around the house makes it feel like a cemetery."

"It helps me to think part of her is in the ground and she's not just . . . out there walking."

"Maybe you could show me those paintings someday," I said. "Maybe it would help to talk about them."

He drew back. Maybe I'd crossed a line.

"What is it?" I asked.

"I tried to tell Siri before you went to Stockholm. We fought about it."

"Fought about what?"

"I entered some into a competition. They won. The judges saw them. They *liked* them. Siri said absolutely no. And Birgit says to put them on display would torture Siri. She's trying to convince me not to do it. But they don't see that these are of me. To have someone look at them and see I'm not a bad person—it means something to me, Lauren."

"Did you tell Birgit that?"

"She said some things should be off-limits. We screamed at each other. I punched out a window, and we don't have the money to fix it. She told me I scared her. The usual-usual."

I looked down at his bandaged hand. I thought of the plastic stretched across the window in Birgit's room.

"You still think you and I are *similar*?" he whispered in my ear.

"Why? Because you punched a window?"

"Because I'm selfish about my art. I might make a decision that hurts my sisters."

"I don't think you're the selfish one," I said.

That made him quiet. We were so close I could feel the blood rushing in him, his heart pounding, the sweat on his hands.

"I'm sorry," I said. "Was that wrong to say?"

Magnus put some distance between us on the bench. "I think all this time I wanted to convince you that I wasn't a bad person. I wanted you to see what she does, the way she is with her friends, how she pushes people away. But it was hard for me to hear you call her selfish."

"It's hard for me to see the way she treats you."

I put my hands on either side of his face and tried to get him to look at me, but his eyes were fixated on the colored fountain, the whites going red and blue.

"I just feel like I'm seeing everything more clearly," I said. "And that's not a bad thing."

"As much as I hate it, she is going to go back to that school," he said loudly. "I need her to have a friend there. I don't want to drive a wedge between you. She needs you. When she was over there, I couldn't sleep. I couldn't work. She didn't return my calls. I felt crazy all the time."

"Birgit said the same thing to me. Of course I'll look out for her." I gently touched his bandaged hand. "But who will look out for you?"

"Birgit says I'm crazy."

"No."

"She wants me to see a psychiatrist. Wants me to go on medication."

"Would it help?"

He stiffened.

"What I'm saying is that people have also told me that I should," I tried to explain.

"Why not, then? Aren't we *similar*? Aren't we just open wounds all the time? How long has it been for you? Ten years, right? There's something wrong with the world if the world thinks that ten years is long enough."

He stood up from the bench. He was so loud now, people turned to listen to him.

"I've watched you since you've been here . . . with Siri, and her friends. You even let them dye your fucking hair. You want to be accepted, you want to be close to other people, but we're different. Siri is little Miss Fun All the Time. Not me. Not you. Whatever makes us different, it keeps us *separate,* and there's no medication for that."

The fountain suddenly went dark. People started walking out of the park.

"We should go back," he said, his words clipped. He carried my sweater. When we got to the park gate, he handed it to me. We rode the trolley back to Central Station and sat straight and forward, hardly talking to each other, but I wanted to talk. I wanted to tell him I understood him. I stared at his hands, wanting to hold them. I noticed the tar beneath his nails. I swore at that moment he smelled of charcoal—of dirt, things red-hot and compressed.

We walked to the car, where it was parked by the opera house. Water lapped at the bellies of the rocking boats. His faith in me was receding. He didn't want to look at me. I didn't understand what was happening. By the time he was fumbling for his keys, all the dark tree cover had grown back between our bodies.

At the house, Birgit was awake. She told us Siri was still sleeping but feeling better. Magnus and I went to our separate rooms. It felt like an ending. In my bed, I thought about pressing up against Magnus while waiting on line for the roller coaster, when I had reached up under the light material of his button-down shirt and touched his chest. About the things he whispered to me in Liseberg's sculpture garden—how beautiful I was, how long he'd wanted to touch me. That we were two lost and grieving people trying to find relief in each other. His fingernails had grazed the small of my back when we kissed. I imagined him pulling the bark off my back one sliver at a time.

In the guest room, I held my breath and listened for him to talk to himself, to play the songs I knew he liked before sleep. But the sounds on the other side of the wall were just rustling, a drawer opening and closing—all calmness. I felt so foolish.

In the middle of the night, I thought I heard Magnus in the front room, and I rose to go out and apologize to him. I wanted to tell him I *did* understand the way he grieved. That I did still feel like that eighteen-year-old inside—my own kind of eighteen, the alone eighteen, the floating eighteen.

I opened my door and padded softly across the wide-plank floors to the foyer, where I'd met Magnus that morning between the ironing boards. There was a glow underneath the door of the drying closet, and I saw the door was ajar. I opened it and peered inside.

Siri sat in the red light of the heat lamp, her hair combed back and wet from a shower, cross-legged on the floor. Her cheeks were red. She was peeling apart pages of a book.

My guidebook. She was trying to dry it out.

She looked up at me, and with her hair combed back that way—what had her father said to her as a child? That he brushed it back because he wanted to see her beautiful face? I saw it. I saw all the complexities of her, the vulnerability, the fear that she was losing me, too.

There were still so many days left to go.

Chapter 12

SIRI HAD ONCE written about how a deer with antlers jumped into the family car one Midsommar and wouldn't budge until her sister coaxed it out with a plate of strawberries and cream. In her essay's margin, I'd written *Charming* (happy face), then *Verisimilitude?* But on our five-hour drive from Olofstorp to Öland, I found myself checking for a deer sitting inside each time I opened the door to her small car. It had become so easy to believe in magic by then. I'd seen it and felt it in the places we'd been; in words, in light, and then that morning, in the inky flowers that bloomed in the water at Neptuni Åkrar, where Siri, Karin, and Frida's blond hair all took on just the slightest tinge of blue from swimming.

It had been five days since I went to Gothenburg with Magnus. Five days of Siri growing more critical of me, doing things on her own, calling friends from her bedroom phone and shutting the door. *Hej* for hello, cheerful *hej hej* for goodbye, always loud enough for me to hear, over and over, an unending number of friends. I often found myself sitting with Birgit on the balcony amid the yellow flowers, rocking in those two chairs, staring off into space.

The guidebook had dried out. It was bloated now, all the pages crisp, the binding ruined and gluey. It sat on my night table, and I thought about going through it page by page to write over the faded words and reclaim the memories we'd recorded there. But the trust between us was torn. Siri had found the book that night— after going through my backpack, looking for something. There had once been a time I didn't mind her going through my things. I remembered, back home, her going into my bedroom that morning after the red-backed man had left. I realized then that I'd *liked* her going through my possessions, being so at home in my apartment, my things her things, and then this book—our book.

But it didn't feel like that anymore. She'd gone through my backpack while I slept. Just what was she trying to find? Things felt bloated, faded, changed.

I had been looking forward to the camping trip because I thought, somehow, we'd have more time to be together than we did in the house. We'd have to work together to pitch a tent. I imagined we'd gather berries and tell stories near a campfire. We'd make up.

It was only going to be us. But the day before we left, she invited her friends.

We were driving to the campsite from the beach. I would be leaving Sweden the following evening. The plan was to camp, then leave for Olofstorp at sunrise so I could make my flight home. Time was slipping away.

I fiddled with the dial on the radio, though we had not been able to pick up any stations for a long time. Beyond the window, I could see a windmill with blades like bat wings; pretty, abandoned pottery on the roadside; a long, dreamy path that led all the way to the other side of the island. A bicyclist with a white wicker basket full of ferns waved at us. Frida waved back like a little girl. He rang his bell, and I watched him in the side mirror until he was a silver dot far behind us, and the ringing just an imagined note. When Frida saw me smiling at her in the mirror, she crossed her arms again and closed her eyes.

"When Frida comes to the U.S., we will all three be friends there," Siri said.

Frida shrugged, her eyes still shut. "I still have not heard anything from the school. I think I would have heard by now."

"You and I will be roommates." Siri kept turning around to look at her until Frida opened her eyes and laughed.

We turned onto the campsite road, gravel popping against the underside of Siri's car. An old man in what appeared to be lederhosen came toward us, and when Siri rolled down her window to pay the entrance fee, Margareta leaned over the seat and peppered him loudly with questions, patting my shoulder as she talked. The smell of cigarette smoke hung in her hair. After he answered her, Margareta sent out a long, shrill list of complaints in Swedish until Siri reminded her to speak in English so I could understand.

Margareta spat out her translation. "We cannot come back onto the campground after ten o'clock if we leave with the car. I think this is stupid." Margareta added, "Also, that old man thinks you will not have fun here."

"He did *not* say that," Siri said.

Margareta laughed. "Well, I will. I will say it. You won't have fun, Lauren."

Siri said something to Margareta in Swedish, and I looked out the window. Sometimes my inability to communicate in Swedish made me feel free. Then there were times when my red, downcast face said too much. It's easy for people to see through you when the only thing they can do is see you.

"In English, Siri! English!" Margareta laughed, her top teeth bared. She enunciated each word for my benefit. "Siri just whispered that I am not supposed to tease you. Are you really that sensitive? Give me a break." She slumped back between the slim blond girls on either side of her, the collar of her jacket rising up over her mouth.

I want to remember that Siri hissed at Margareta then, but it was probably the heat rising into my face and ears. Earlier in the trip, Siri would have snapped, "*Sluta!*" or, in English, for my benefit, so I could hear her defending me: "*Shut up.*" But since that night I had seen her in the drying closet with the wet guidebook, she'd stopped defending me to the other girls.

Siri parked the car, and we dragged our camping equipment from the trunk. The air smelled of kerosene. Karin and Margareta thrust their backpacks at Frida and gave each other piggyback rides, all of us following Siri down the path, toward our numbered plot. Siri: the leader, the queen bee. I felt a sense of foreboding, that she'd be buzzing like this the whole night, this version of herself that made me feel so utterly alone.

Beyond the squat seagrass and the small hairy dunes that buffeted the dirt road, the campground's trailers and domed tents came into view. No one tended a blaze that rose from wood stacked in a teepee shape in the distance. The girls cooed, as though the fire were a baby. And then I noticed all the people.

It looked like a vast, partially clothed tailgate party.

The lots had trailer hookups, and RVs were parked everywhere. The campground reminded me of an old drive-in theater. I thought I could hear the crisp white noise of those speakers you would hang on your car window. But it was the sea, somewhere in the background, beyond the straggly wood that surrounded the campsite.

Different kinds of music competed from each direction. Close by, two women sunbathed topless on sleeping bags outside their tent.

A clutch of teenage boys sat in a circle of lawn chairs in the lot across from us. They all wore colored wigs and their camper was missing its wheels. A clothesline stretched from their window to a tree, hung with gray clothes and beach towels. They were drinking beer and had a boom box in the middle of their circle. When they saw us, one of them reached forward and turned the volume way up, trying to get our attention.

I suddenly felt much older.

"Ignore them. They are *raggares,*" Margareta said, pulling a cigarette out of a pack with her mouth. "How do you say? *Lowlifes.*

Don't tell them you're from America. They'll never leave you alone." The cigarette dangled from her lip as she barked orders at the girls, who wrestled with the camping equipment and goofed around. "It is my family's tent," Margareta complained. "They should be more careful."

Margareta's English didn't last. When I placed the metal stakes too close together, she breathed out a string of Swedish condemnations, grabbed them from me, and hammered them in herself. Karin and Frida unfolded the noxious brown tarp that would form the tent's walls, and Margareta yelled at them when they complained how bad it smelled. There was a small piece of flowered fabric and we attached it with buttons to the inside of the tent— a curtain for the tent's one window. They took pictures of one another peeking out from behind it.

The boys across the lot turned up their techno music again. I could feel its beat in my stomach. One of them, tall, wearing a bright purple wig, came over and started speaking to me in Swedish, pointing at my camera. He was offering to take our picture. He said something about the tent that made the girls laugh. I handed him the camera and the girls posed for him. I went to our pile of equipment and rooted out our night's provisions. Aside from my case of beer, there was a box of sandwiches and a clinking pillowcase full of heavy bottles—scarlet, amber, absinthe green— taken from Frida's parents' liquor cabinet at home.

Frida spread out a furry blanket on the ground beside the tent. Though it smelled lightly of wet dog, it looked soft and inviting. I lay down on my back upon it, and she caught my gaze.

"*Älg,*" she said.

"I'm sorry?"

"The blanket. It is moose," she said, opening a bottle of vodka.

The other boys made their way over to talk. I could feel the tip of Siri's toe poking me in my ribs. I squinted up at her.

"What are you doing?" she asked.

"Other people are lying down." I gestured toward the topless girls across the way.

"Stand up and talk with us," she said.

"Where do I go if I have to use the bathroom?"

"Say again?" She couldn't hear me over the now-booming music.

"I need to use the bathroom."

"That way. See that building?" She pointed to a square white building in the distance. "That is the toilet block. Want me to come with you?"

"No, I'll be fine."

I excused myself and navigated between trailers, homey encampments and trees, beach blankets, little campfires, and sleeping bodies. The scene quickly grew more complex, so that soon I had to edge sideways to make my way through the crowd.

The building smelled of pine and mildew. There was a line for the toilets. Inside, a shallow flood coated the buckling, tectonic tiles, and the girl in front of me stood barefoot in it. She wore ropes of jingly anklets and had long, straight blond hair. I noticed her bitten-down nails when she clutched the door frame. She turned to me.

"Are you American?"

"Yes."

"I love Americans." Her light blue eyes drifted back into her head. She lurched. The girls at the front of the line caught her just before she fell facedown on the wet floor.

After using the toilet, I stood at the sink and took stock of my image in the mirror. I looked tired and pale. The blonde staggered up and stared at me in the mirror. "*Hej* again," she said. "I'm Sunny."

"Lauren."

"Is that your real hair color?" Her fingers floated near my head like she was trying to trace the shape of it. The bottled blond had lost its luster, and the two inches of black dye on the ends made me look strange. I pulled my hair into a tight ponytail and wiped at the makeup that had settled under my eyes.

"No, it's not real."

"I'm not feeling well," she said. She splashed her face with water and got some on me. "Would you walk me back to my blanket?"

The campground had an eerie, greenhouse light. When we got to her blanket, Sunny released her viselike grip on my arm and collapsed onto the bunchy fabric, staring up through the trees into the sunshine.

"Stay with me. Eat candy," she said, tossing a plastic bag up to me. They were the white and pink car-shaped marshmallow candies called Bilar. "Tell me about America."

Pools of gold light dappled the hoods of nearby vehicles, patches of grass, the centers of sleeping bags. The clear solstice light had been my reason to teach Siri the word *gloaming*. I loved that light.

"I've been trying not to think about America. I've been here for three weeks. I return tomorrow night."

"You don't celebrate Midsommar in the USA."

"No. One of my friends told me that I should come see it for myself."

"Did your friend tell you about our ghosts?" Sunny asked. "They get confused because there is no darkness, and then they get caught up in the trees, the flowers, even our dreams. Do you have ghosts in America?"

"Some," I answered.

"Did any of your American ghosts follow you here to Sweden?"

Her eyes were red around the rims. She stretched her arms over her head, closed her eyes, and stuffed her mouth with Bilar.

I walked away without answering her. She was drunk. She was a teenager who didn't know anything about my past. Her questions shouldn't have upset me.

I had a hard time finding my way back. Hundreds more people seemed to have arrived, and things were getting louder and out of control. I was sure it was evening, but the sun just stayed out, hanging there with its one orange eye.

When I got back, the girls and boys were flush with rumors they'd heard while I was gone. Siri translated them. There was a skinny dog running loose down on the beach, and they didn't know who it belonged to. She looked like she was dripping milk—wasn't that sad? And there was a man selling salted licorice, but no one had seen him yet. Desperate for conversation, I tried to ask the girls if they were going to try to find the dog, or if they wanted licorice when the man came by, but they didn't seem to hear me.

Were my own ghosts floating around me? Were they hanging on the cuffs of my sleeves? I felt I'd dragged them across the camp-ground as they clutched my ankles. Their hands were on my throat, now, muffling my voice, making it softer and softer. Vaguely I heard my name, and I saw Siri reaching out to hug me. She kissed my cheek. Her hair smelled of salt water and was still tinged blue from the swim at Neptuni Åkrar.

"We're going to do a dance now!" she said. "You can follow us. It's not hard."

Karin and Frida screwed their big cans of beer down into the dirt. The girls all clasped hands and danced in a circle, singing a traditional song called "Små Grodorna." For a moment it was easy to imagine them as children in costumes and braids, and not as the netherworldly teens with whom I had crossed the bridge that morning. The refrain resounded across the campground, and peo-ple came out of their tents to cheer them on, swinging their arms over one another's shoulders and swaying. When the girls finally fell to the ground in a tumble of giddy missteps and exhaustion, a roar went up around us.

The adrenaline of the dance slowly drained away. I stood in various clusters of people as they talked in Swedish. I smiled when they smiled, and I laughed sometimes when they laughed. I had thought before that being without language was like being a child, but maybe it was more like being a dog, watching for clues and picking up on pack rhythms. After a while, I crawled into the tent for refuge.

A few minutes later, two immense RVs pulled up and parked side by side on the adjacent lot. I could feel the bass of their sound systems thumping in my chest. I looked out. People were standing around staring at the vehicles, which both had the Playboy bunny spray-painted on their sides.

Siri came into the tent and zipped us in. "They are going to be loud and annoying, right?" She came to my side and peered out of the window with me. "But we will be louder and more annoying, yes?"

"Do you have gangs in Sweden?" I asked.

"Hmm. Yes. I guess we do. But those guys are not gangs. There are no Playboy gangs." She reached across me and buttoned the curtain into place, as though that would keep them out.

I fumbled in my pocket for my lipstick and applied it, feeling for the outer edges of my mouth. Siri stared at me until I looked at her.

"Are you going to just stay inside the tent?" she asked.

I was exhausted from smiling and from the crowd, the pit in my stomach that told me something was wrong between us. I stared at her, willing myself to see her the way I used to, so simply, so clearly, only good. With a chill, I imagined her with a purple rose behind her ear. Was that what I'd been doing? Only allowing myself to see her one way?

Margareta tapped on the side of the tent, and the fabric fluttered near my head. "Siri! *Karin såg Magnus vid bilarna.* He came."

I looked up.

"I don't want to see him," Siri said. "If he comes over here, tell him I'm gone." She pulled a pair of aviator sunglasses out of the front of her shirt. "Look at these. Some guy gave me these." She slid them on.

"Did she just say that Magnus is here?"

She held out her palm for my lipstick, and I handed it to her, trying not to meet her eyes.

"I don't even know why he would come here. This isn't his kind of thing." She quickly traced her mouth and handed the lipstick back to me. "I'm sorry," she said. "It's not your kind of thing either."

I smoothed the flannel of my sleeping bag and felt her staring at me.

"Come out of the tent, Lauren. Please? It is your last night here. We can still make it fun."

I didn't want to make it fun. I wanted to find a way to talk to her. I wanted us to be alone again, where we could find our way back to what had pulled us together at the start.

Siri unzipped the tent and scuttled out, calling my name like a song. Did she want me here anymore? Were we pretending? I crawled out behind her. A tall boy in a purple wig named Viktor was opening bottles of beer and handing them around. Everyone was dancing. It felt like pretend.

I looked up for the sun and saw it glimmering in the wet green leaves above me. I pulled out my camera to take pictures. I looked through the viewfinder and moved it around the scene: Margareta and Viktor, now kissing each other on the neck. I adjusted the lens up above their heads, to the tops of the vehicles, to the trees, to a Mylar balloon caught in some branches, a clothes hanger stuck on another. I pulled the camera away from my face and looked with my own eyes.

The trees were blooming. Siri came up beside me. She noticed me looking at the flowering boughs. Her friends were dancing spasmodically now behind her, all waving limbs and stripping themselves bare.

"Why don't we walk into town?" she said softly. "It is a beautiful old town, and I bet we could find a Midsommar's pole."

A flash. Viktor had Siri's camera, and he'd captured me, probably looking so relieved, so eager to have her to myself again for a while.

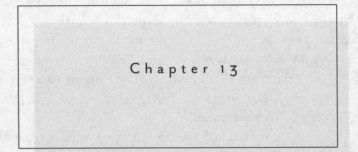

Chapter 13

Siri and I left the campsite, and we made it to the village square in Loftsvik by late afternoon. We flip-flopped along the town's stone streets and poked into different storefronts, my head clearing as we went. We walked into a surf shop, its doorway strung with beads. There was a boy behind the counter with shaggy blond hair and a necklace made from shell pieces. Siri asked him where we could find a *midsommarstång* in town, and they talked in Swedish while I strolled around the shop. The walls were covered with rock music posters and advertisements for Mr. Zog's Sex Wax. Candy-colored bodyboards were propped in the corners, and racks were stuffed with everything from bikinis to winter coats. All the seasons, all pressed together.

Siri was soon by my side, rifling through the bathing suits. "He hasn't seen a Midsommar pole in town. I don't get it. Usually they are easy to find." She found a suit she liked and held it up. "I'm going to try this."

She went into the dressing room and its saloon-door partition clapped shut behind her. "We're not going back to the campsite until we find a *midsommarstång*." I could see that she was barefoot and standing on tiptoes, like the floor was cold.

I knew she wanted me to experience the traditions that made her love Midsommar so much. I was supposed to be feeling carefree, but she must have known that something was off between us now. I needed to find a way to talk to her about Magnus. I started picking through some sweatshirts folded on a table. One had a Swedish word in jagged lightning-bolt script.

Siri hummed to herself, one of the poppy techno songs we'd listened to over and over during the trip. In a mirror, I pressed the sweatshirt against my body. I noticed some young men watching me. I tried not to meet their eyes, but they came over, swift and slick. They were surfers. I could see the wetsuits underneath their plaid flannel shirts, and their faces seemed permanently windburned.

"You shouldn't buy that one. That's not for you," one of them said.

Another pointed at the jagged-lettered word. "Don't you know what that says?"

"No."

"*Fäbodjäntan.* The farmer's daughter."

They talked in Swedish. I could see the mean edge of their grins and knew what they were saying wasn't kind. I looked to the partition of Siri's little dressing room and saw her still shadow. She was watching through the slats.

I placed the sweatshirt back on the table.

One of them said something else to me, and suddenly Siri threw open the dressing room door to yell at them. She was wearing the bikini she'd gone in there to try on. It was pink, dotted with green robots. I'd been intimidated by the men, but she only had to give them the annoyed look I'd seen her give Margareta, and they skulked away. She went back in to change into her clothes. I stared at the shadow of her body against the door until she came out. She hung the bathing suit back on the rack and hooked her arm in mine.

"What did they say?" I asked.

"Don't make me translate everything all the time," she said, glancing behind us and squeezing my hand.

WE LEANED OVER a lot of fences in our search for a *midsommarstång*, even wandering behind an old stone house to check a family's backyard, where we saw a long stone table set with bowls of heaped red and white strawberries, silver herring, sour cream. I felt suddenly nauseous and turned to lean against the fence.

"Lauren, you're so pale. Maybe I should take you back?"

"No. I've just been drinking too much."

"You haven't been eating."

I hadn't had a real meal for days, my appetite held at bay by Bilar and my stomach torn up with guilt over Magnus and over Siri's distance. She said he'd come to the campsite. With whom? And who did he follow here? Siri or me? Back in the square, Siri bought me a Coke and some roasted nuts from a street vendor. We sat down on a bench with our backs against the wind and shared the nuts from a wax paper bag, soon shiny with our fingerprints.

"I bet we could find a Midsommar pole in the countryside. Or some beautiful *väderkvarnar,*" she said. She coughed. "The windmills here are hundreds of years old."

"Siri, your cough is so bad. Should we go back?"

"No, no." She smiled and cleared her voice. "It's Margareta and her cigarettes. She doesn't stop." She looked down at my sandals, where a piece of straw was caught in the straps. "Hey. Do you know there are Vikings buried *right under your feet?*"

I smiled.

"Are you all right to walk?" she asked.

"Yes. But I don't want to go back to the campsite yet, okay?"

"We'll go into the countryside," she said.

There was real silence away from the town, away from the campsite, and I basked in it on the walk with Siri. We climbed a path that went from asphalt, to gravel, to trodden grass. There were purple flowers everywhere. Few homes, no cars. The defunct windmills she'd promised peppered the landscape, but despite the strong wind, they didn't stir. If there was any noise at all, the wind pushed it past our ears before we had a chance to catch it. There was no responsibility to hear, to do anything except be.

This is what it had always felt like to be alone with Siri. When it was just us, I could be confident in the quiet. I could be my slow-healing, mourning self. My sometimes-frightened, sentimental, youngest self. From the top of the hill, I saw the flashing seas that surrounded the island. Rain clouds were gathering, making it look, for once, like it was getting dark when it should. I felt I was standing at the top of a playground slide and gravity was pulling me down, down.

"We're up closest to the sun now," Siri said. "We can ask it not to set. Then the day will last. You won't go home."

We got down on the ground and lay on our backs. I didn't know where we were, only that we were close to the sky and the sun might listen to us.

She reached out for my hand and held it in front of her face. "Look at this. When I first knew you, you were self-conscious of your nails being bitten down—remember when you would point to the sentences on my essays with your knuckle so you could hide your chewed fingernails from me?"

Overhead, the sudden sound of raucous birds. They were swans, flying overhead and low, their wings beating like sailcloth.

"Tell me what you will do when you go home," she said.

"I'll prepare for my class. I'll get the new roster and go over my students' names so I know how to pronounce them the first day. I'll read the new book of essays they want me to teach from this year. At night I'll write poems about this trip. I'll make a scrap-book with our pictures."

"And Mrs. Vallapil will bring you plates of biryani with raisins—your favorite."

"Yes."

"And Annie. You will have Annie back with you."

My beautiful Annie. The Vallapils had been taking care of her all those weeks. I imagined Khushi following my dog around with the little silver whistle her parents made her wear around her neck, hurting Annie's ears. Annie was arthritic and slow, and the Vallapil apartment was Technicolor, with pungent altars in all its corners.

"Yes. I'll take Annie down to the soccer field and walk her along the edge of the woods," I said.

"You should walk her by the stables to see the horses we love."

"Rockabye and Irish Cloud," I said.

Siri closed her eyes and breathed deep. I could feel it through the ground. I felt a rush of all the things we knew together, all the ways we'd been good for each other coming back to us now that we were alone. It was like the Siri I had once known was waking up from sleep.

"When I was a child, my father told me that if I blinked, I could miss nighttime. Each Midsommar's Eve, we would play a game to count the seconds between dusk and dawn. I could never stay up for it. I would awaken to him counting, and the sun would be rising." She rolled over on her stomach and laid her head upon her hands. "You must come back here when you have your own children, Lauren. Tell them stories like that."

She said it like Sweden belonged to me, too. I wanted to believe that. I stole a look at her peaceful face, the one I loved.

"How long will it stay dark tonight?" I asked.

"For a little while. The sun will set about ten and come up again around four. In the north, the sun does not set at all this time of year, but we are pretty far south. The day will still be really long." She sat up. "East of us now is the campsite. And that way to the bridge"—she pointed—"that way to the cemetery. That way to my old summer house."

"I'd like to see it."

"No, it's probably torn down now," she said quickly. "Lauren, this island . . . it used to feel more . . . wholesome."

"That campsite's not wholesome," I said with a laugh.

"No." She picked at a snag of flowers growing beside her. "You know, the graveyard is not too far from here. My father. My grandfather. My mother's headstone. I was thinking—would you want to go with me there tomorrow morning?"

Her mother's headstone.

"That would mean a lot to me," I said. I'd been hoping she would tell me about what happened with her mom. Maybe there she would finally confide in me. There was still so much I didn't understand about her. We'd traded words, and we'd traded stories, but it had all been weighed and measured. We needed more. All of it. If she could really confide in me about what happened with her mother and Magnus, our friendship might be real. I imagined her as a child on this island, her family at the top of a hill, her running down it to get away.

"When we're back in the U.S., we can take the bus to New York. They have those buses that go up and back for twenty dollars. You could show me the places that were important to you when you were small."

"I guess we could," I said. "I haven't been there in years. We'd have to take the train or rent a car to get to Long Island, though."

"I could see your old house. And meet your old friends," Siri said.

It struck me that she should know this; that I had told her; that our whole friendship was built on this—that there was no one left for me there.

"I haven't spoken to many of them in a long time."

"When were you last back there?"

"I haven't gone back there."

"What? Not at all?"

"No."

"But it would be good to go back, right?"

No. No, it wouldn't. She knew this. Hadn't I told her everything? I looked around me at the long blades of waving grass.

"I figure either I'd be talked about all over town—or people would not remember me. And I'm not sure what would be harder."

We were quiet for a moment.

"Then fuck them. We don't have to see any of your old friends," she said defiantly. "I want to see what made you happy. What would make you happy?"

"I don't know anymore."

"That's the problem with staying away from a beloved place too long. You start to forget. We'll go. You'll remember the parts that were wonderful."

That might be possible, I thought. With her by my side. If she could vouch for me. If she could make the way safe. I nodded and looked out again upon our vista. It had been so easy to lose track of time on the island. I didn't know where any of the paths led or how to get back to the campsite, but the island was already in me, the way a memory is in you, affects you, even though you might remember all the details wrong.

She looked at me seriously. "What are you thinking?"

"I'm thinking about us. How important your friendship has been to me. And how I want to be there for you, too," I said.

"You are." She smiled.

I gripped her arm, somehow feeling she was sliding away from me with that smile.

"No, I really want to talk about it. Things have felt off between us, and I hate it."

"Oh, things could never really be wrong with us, Lauren."

"What do you mean?"

"I know you did not grow up with other girls like I did. Frida, Margareta, Karin—they are like my sisters, and I am lucky to have them. They are witnesses to my whole life, I think. But, Lauren, they see but they don't see. You and I . . . we've always understood each other, you know?"

She hugged me. Right out there in the field, my heart against hers and the whole field beating with us. I wanted to believe her. I held on to her.

"We'll go to New York," I said.

"It's decided. We'll go." She nodded. A promise.

"I mean, it's suburbs. Strip malls and pizza places. Lots of traffic. But you're never far from a beach. We could drive all the way to the end of the island."

"I bet it's beautiful there."

"Not like this, Siri." Öland was the most beautiful place I'd ever been—wildflowers everywhere, the all-night sun blurring the edges of everything.

She got up and brushed off her pants. "*Allemansrätten*. Remember I taught you that word?"

I did remember. It meant "Every Man's Right." It was a beautiful word, a beautiful law. People here were free to venture outdoors anywhere they pleased, as long as they didn't disturb the landowner, steal, or make a fire.

Siri suddenly started running down the hill toward a windmill. I leaned up on my elbows and saw her waiting for me at the bottom. When she called my name, I got up and ran to her, my heart a stone flying from a slingshot.

But really, my heart was flying backward in time—that's how it felt, to be running, to be free and unafraid. Free, before loss tangles and addles you. To be young again. To have ever been young.

We approached the windmill together and discovered a small door in its back constructed of wooden planks. Slowly Siri opened it and we peered inside. The old stone and wood works of the windmill were awash with the sunlight coming in through the top. And graffiti. Names scrawled into the wood. Names + Other Names: lovers. Hardened bubblegum spots making a mosaic of the grinding stone. Siri and I climbed up inside. I thought of the night on the playground when I'd been stuck inside a structure not unlike this one. I wondered, if I called out for my father here, would he hear me? I closed my eyes and heard the sound of him in the bathroom, shaving before his night job. I heard the click of his razor against the sink, the crumple of my mother setting his brown-bag lunch on the table beside the door, the tinkle of his spoon from his empty teacup being left on the counter. He'd wash it when he returned at daybreak. I opened my eyes and saw Siri looking out across the field. "There's a house," she said. "Not too far!"

We climbed down and walked in the direction of the farmhouse she'd seen. Siri pointed at blooms and told each one its name. She showed me a dandelion-like flower and called it *backklöver,* mountain clover, *backklöver* . . . she went hazily between Swedish and English, as if the eyes of the black-centered flowers she was sniffing were poppies. She talked to herself as she walked on ahead of me, and I could only make out every other word. That wind again, scrubbing hard enough that it might erase things. I let it break against my face, my chest. Then I thought I heard her say *Magnus.*

I caught up with her and tried to listen. She was talking to the giant pyramidal *blomsterlupiner.* They stood grand and imposing, their petals a knit of riotous fuchsia.

"He told me not to come here, I did anyway, and now he is here to make sure I don't get in trouble. He is so fucking controlling. Birgit likes to think being with you keeps me safe. But that's not enough for Magnus."

She looked at me like she was wondering if I believed her. Another test. The field felt like a place of confessions. All she would have to do was ask me how I felt, and I'd have to say it.

"We should make a *midsommarkrans* from wildflowers. A crown. Do you want to do that? That's a special tradition in Sweden. We would need to gather many different kinds of flowers."

I could hear tension in her voice all of a sudden. She brushed her hand over the heads of some indigo blooms. Their color was so rich, I almost expected her palm to come away dripping ink. She was upset, thinking about Magnus, but she kept talking about the crowns. We needed a bendy reed that would be strong enough to braid, she explained, and then we could tuck whatever flowers we liked into that. *Sandklint* were bright pink poms. *Rödklint* had fragile sun-ray petals that turned to dust between your fingers. She showed me the natural depressions in the field. "This is where two roads would have come together a long time ago," she said. "You always pick flowers at a crossroads."

But she had brought up his name. She wanted to talk about him.

Siri pulled up bunches of lilac chicory and added them to her bundle.

"And there's another tradition with flowers," she said. "For when you are lovesick. Maybe I should teach you that one?"

She knew.

It would be easy to say that my feelings for Magnus came because he was off-limits. But I don't think that was the reason. The only thing more intoxicating than being with someone you long to be is to be with someone who feels like the misunderstood parts of you. In so many ways that perhaps only I could see, Magnus and I were alike, and it scared me, the idea that Siri might see that and reject me, too. He wasn't a vial marked "drink me." He was a looking glass.

"What did you guys do in Gothenburg that day?" she asked.

I took a breath. I told myself I'd tell her the truth.

"We went to see some of the places you and I had talked about going."

"How did the guidebook get so wet?"

"It rained," I lied.

"You were with him the whole day," she said. "How was he?"

"He was fine," I said.

"I saw the guidebook. I thought maybe he did something to our book."

"No," I said.

"He is always complaining about the way I live my life. He complains that he has to work to support me, that he's not able to spend more time on his art. But I say . . . so what? You know? He's not that good an artist."

"I think he's good, Siri."

She waved off my comment. I wasn't going far enough. I needed to tell all of it. Not just how I'd held his hand, kissed him, imagined us as lovers, but that I really did believe he was, as a person, good.

"He's not," she said loudly. "He's a fool."

She watched for my reaction, to see if I'd grow protective. I squinted at her, where she stood in the sunlight, trying to get her into focus, trying to understand this side of her.

"I think he wants to impress you," I said. "He wants you to approve of him."

"That's ridiculous."

I'd wanted to impress her. I'd wanted her approval.

"He's so controlling," Siri said. "Don't you see it?"

An opening. Why couldn't I just tell her everything? I needed to fix this. I was going home to America the next day. I needed her to be my friend again when we were there together. I couldn't imagine my life back in America without her.

"You saw it," she whispered. "I bet you that day he did something bad and you're hiding it from me. Tell me the truth."

I was quiet.

"You have feelings for him," she said, walking deeper into the field, the grass and plants up to her shoulders. "Something happened that day between the two of you."

Yes. Yes.

"*Hallå, hallå!*" came a voice in the distance.

We looked up and saw an old man in front of the large farmhouse, its Swedish flag flapping. Smoke curled from an outdoor stove built from wide, stacked stones, and the smoke smelled of an inside winter night, not the bright evening. The man was standing on his porch wearing a T-shirt, suspenders, and shorts.

Siri ran toward him. "*Hallå, hallå!*" she yelled.

I was angry that she hadn't given me the time to find the words to speak. She would fly toward anyone ready to give her attention. Even this old man, this stranger.

I followed her to where she stood conversing with the old man in Swedish. She looked suddenly happy again, as though a flock of birds had flown from her, taking all of her resentment with it. When she told him we were collecting flowers for Midsommar crowns, he said something that made her laugh.

"He thought we came to steal his flowers," she translated. "He

wants to show us something inside his house." Siri dropped her
bundle beside his fence.

The man opened his white gate and waved us in. He saw me
hesitating. "Really, really," he said, like it was the only word he
knew in English. Siri walked through the gate and turned to me.

"Lauren, it's okay. He is a nice man."

What was she doing? Why was I following her in?

Inside the house, newspapers and books were stacked almost to
the ceiling. I felt it: the way his things must have talked to him, the
way he walked by them like the piles were people. The windows at
the back of the house were painted over. We followed him up the
stairs, and with each step, I resented Siri's avoiding our talk this
way. The man waved us into a room at the end of the hall. I wanted
to turn and run out.

In the bedroom, two yellow dogs lay sprawled on the floor, but
they were lying at strange inclines—the center of the floor was
sunk in from age. Some of the furniture had shifted away from the
walls toward the dip in the center of the room. There were signs
that this had once been a well-tended home. A cupboard displayed
pretty crockery and a collection of small wooden Dala horses,
most of them glazed bright red. Lace doilies draped the bedside
tables.

I felt that at any moment the room could collapse from our ad-
ditional weight. The man hurried to a dresser and grabbed a bunch
of pink silk roses from a vase. They were dusty and stained. He
gave one of them to Siri and one to me.

That was all.

Outside, we picked up our flower bundles and left him sitting
on his porch petting the dogs, which had followed him out. Siri
explained that the silk roses had been his wife's, and she was dead
now, buried somewhere in that field we had explored, but she
would have wanted us to have them for our Midsommar crowns.

She pointed now to where the grass was sprung with daisylike
flowers. "Oh, those are very important for the crown. It is a traditional flower. They call it *prästkrage*," she said. "This is similar—it

is called *baldersbra*. You have to pick it yourself to make it lucky."
She watched as I gathered a few, then she moved on. "And these
here are called Jacks! Sometimes we call them Jack-go-to-bed-at-
noon."

We were on our way back. I walked slowly, and she had to wait
for me to catch up. She placed her bundle on the ground and rolled
up the cuffs of her pink pants.

"You're mad at me," she said. "I'm sorry. I should have asked if
you wanted to go in his house. But he was nice, right? He was like
my grandfather. With that big belly! He was sad. He missed his
wife."

"No, that's not it, Siri. We were talking about something important."

"You said all you needed to say. Okay? I am fine. Enough of
this."

Siri looped her arm in mine and we climbed the dirt path back
over the hill. No, there was so much more to say. We had just been
getting to it. I didn't want to avoid this anymore, but soon the path
became asphalt, and we were descending back into the village
square, and heading back to the campsite.

Chapter 14

THE CAMPSITE CAME into view. I wished we were back at the start of our adventure, or even back in that old man's plain, collapsing room, with time to talk between ourselves. At the mouth of the campground, Siri pointed at a wooden sign. "It's nearly ten o'clock," she said. "We are in for the night. After ten there is no readmission, even by way of the pedestrian gate."

That felt like an announcement of nighttime, of an ending, though the sky was still as light as it had been when we left. She didn't want me to tell her about my feelings for Magnus. She knew, and she wanted me to know she knew and feel guilty, and that was the end. There would be this long, all-night party with strangers, the time in the car with the girls back to Olofstorp, breakfast at her house—but our time together, alone, our story-telling, word-sharing, whispering time, was done.

We walked toward our plot with our bouquets draped over our arms, the long reeds fanning the ground as we strode along. The place appeared, now, like a military encampment. We passed tiny campfires and rows of overflowing garbage cans. People saw our bundles and called out to us, "Are you going to make crowns?" "Make me a crown!" Beer cans littered the ground.

Siri's friends seemed jealous that she'd taken me to gather flowers. Siri sat down on the moose-skin blanket and spread the flowers before her. She plaited some stems to form the shape of the crown and wove in flowers until it grew large. The other girls tried to pick up some unused pieces to start their own, but Siri slapped their hands away, saying, "No, these are just for me and Lauren."

Margareta slinked toward me. "Do you even know what a *midsommarkrans is*? Or why it is *for*?"

"*Sluta,* Margareta!" Siri said.

The girl pursed her lips and fell silent.

"I'm serious. I'm tired of you all being rude to Lauren. Back up!"

They did as they were told and glowered at us from the perimeter of the blanket, scolded into silence. She was back to defending me, and the girls hated that. I hated it. I knew there was something false about it now.

Siri went back to trying to show me how to make the flower crown. I tried to follow her example, but I was conscious of the girls' silence, and my flowers were falling to pieces. I had collected flowers primarily for their beauty, but Siri had known to choose hardier types. Some people came around to watch Siri finish hers. When she was done, she popped the old man's pink rose in the center, placed the crown on her blond head, and smiled. It was perfect.

Strangers asked to take pictures with Siri, and she posed with them. Her crown was a hit. I told her she looked like a movie star, and she snapped out her sunglasses and slid them on for effect.

As I pulled my array of broken flowers into a pile in front of me, Viktor came over to us holding clear plastic cups with purple drinks. They looked like decomposing Jell-O shots. He told us that they glowed in the dark, but it was still too light out to see. He gave Siri a cup, and she lifted it in the air to toast me. When I looked into my drink, I could see the gelatin separating into chunks, a film of dirt on top, a blade of grass.

Siri held up her empty cup. "Look at me. I toasted you," she said. "Did you even notice? Now you toast me, Lauren."

I was tired of her pushiness, but I lifted the cup.

"To you, Siri," I said. I held my breath and drank it down.

Frida came back from the Playboy RVs. She said the boys wanted to talk to the pretty girl with the crown.

"*Bygga broar?*" Siri laughed. "I will be right back."

I looked over at one of the RVs. Two boys were sitting on the roof with their legs hanging over the side. They saw me look up at them and they waved. The Mylar balloon from earlier in the day winked among the trees.

"Siri, no—stay here," I whispered. "Make me a crown."

"I will be a second. I just want to see what they want."

She was so at ease with her beauty. The extra beats of a man's gaze against her chest. The way men's voices grew louder in her presence, as if each meant to stake his claim to her by outshouting the others. The shyer ones, furtive, their longings that read like anger. None of it gave her pause.

"I'll make you a crown," Frida said. She came over and undid my hair elastic, combed my hair through with her fingers. "I can braid your hair the traditional way."

Frida was never this nice to me. She was drunk. I could smell her body odor as she worked with her arms raised.

"You could come with me, Lauren," Siri said. "It might be fun."

I didn't answer her. She shooed Frida away.

"Lauren."

My eyes stung because I knew they were just teenage boys, but in the dark, now, they looked like men. And the invitation was the invitation of certain men: They wanted to talk to the pretty girl; they would wait for her to come to them.

And she wouldn't listen to me. Because I held no authority here. In her eyes, I had taken all my insecurity, deep troubled nonsense that I'd confided in her—I'd given her up and thrust myself at the one person she didn't want me to be with.

She picked up the braid Frida had started. She dropped some of her unused flowers into my open palms. "Hold these. I'll put them in your hair."

Siri braided my hair tight. My head hurt but I let her continue to do it. I looked down at the weary daisies in my cupped hands.

"Are you going to just sit here all night on this stupid blanket?"

"No."

"*Bygga broar.*"

"What does that even mean?"

She pulled my hair back. "It means 'building bridges.' Getting to know people."

"You know I'm not feeling well. I almost got sick before. Remember?"

"I know you are full of shit right now."

"They look like assholes, Siri. And what if there are drugs over there? I promised Birgit I'd watch out for you."

"I don't think there will be *droger* there," she said. "But you know I'm young. I want to do things."

"I know," I said.

She was at the age when she was supposed to be reckless. I was at an age when I was supposed to be responsible. I could hear Birgit in my mind, entreating me to keep her safe.

"You worry about me so much," she said quietly. "And I thank you for that. You hear me? I do thank you. But I need you to stop being so controlling."

I turned to look at her. That was the word she so often used to describe Magnus.

"You've got to stop now, okay?" she said.

She went off in the direction of the Playboy RVs, her crown streaming petals as she ran. It was the first time I hadn't followed her.

I sat in the center of the moose-skin blanket surrounded by smoke, and garbage, and drunken revelers, and trees, and somewhere, beyond the dune, the sea. I tried not to look back at Siri. It was unfair that she'd called me controlling. Surely she knew that I hated worrying about her like the mother of a teenage daughter, half feeling that I must do everything in my power to protect her, half that I must be her fun best friend and look the other way, lest she hate me, storm from my house one night, and never come back.

I crawled inside the tent and into my sleeping bag, listening to the mix of beats, ecstatic singing, and drumming music. The Playboys turned on their headlights and a globe of yellow light made a perfect circle on my tent's wall.

Then the headlight was a spotlight, and my heart was lit up with pain from back home. I didn't know how I would manage when I returned home, alone. I had no technical-writing work lined up yet. There would be two months of empty time before school started again. The simple schedule I'd imagined with Siri on the hill—spending my days reading, writing, and eating biryani— would have been manageable were it not for the apartment I lived in, which could be so loud with pain. I stared up at the white circle of light as if to ask it what it had to show me.

Someone was making a shadow animal against the light—a dog. It was a man; I heard him clear his throat. He made the dog bark, then run about in the circle. It made me smile. I would be happy to see Annie. My poor old Annie. The dog became a rabbit. I closed my hands and slid them under my head. After the bunny came a bird, flapping its wings. I thought dreamily of the ocean beyond the dune. I closed my eyes and let the bird sing to me of its wings beating down ocean-thick air. When I opened my eyes again, there was an animal I could not quite recognize, and I said this aloud in English. I waited for him to reposition his fingers, but he went away.

"Don't leave," I said.

The light went out.

Then darkness.

I wanted to believe it was Magnus. His light, his wings. Siri thought Magnus was controlling, but he had only been trying to love her. Every time I saw him, he was loving her and she was pushing him away. Calling him controlling. Turning her back and running toward something or someone else. All we wanted to do was protect her, and she couldn't handle it.

I crawled on my belly to the front of the tent and zipped it open.

The darkness outside had depth and edge, but I couldn't make anything out. People slid continuously across my line of vision. They were gathering, walking, clapping, but they might as well have been dancers, counting out beats in the dark.

How long did Siri say it would be nighttime? Minutes? Hours? I thought of the game young Siri had played with her father, where she'd fall asleep counting and wake up to his counting. My heart beat fast; it was up in my ears, counting.

I was overcome with the idea that he was out there. I wanted to believe it had been Magnus soothing me through the tarpaulin. I wanted to believe that at any moment his face would float toward me through the night like a sun, looking at me the way he had on the car ride to Vimmerby.

It started to rain. Someone ran by me, kicking up dirt and getting it in my eyes, forcing me back inside the tent, forcing me to listen to the drumming that echoed from the vein in my own neck.

That tent was like a one-chambered heart.

The drumming became louder and quicker. I felt it moving in my stomach, then against my temples.

I thought the sound was coming from inside me. The pulsing of growing sick. But it was the rain. Rain like fingertips tapping on the tent's top.

I AWAKENED LATER to a glinting gold oval, a pendulum swinging—Karin's locket as she leaned over me. Then voices as Siri, Margareta, and Frida crawled into the tent. They were whispering. *Sover hon? Är hon sjuk?* Frida and Margareta pulled the dirty moose-skin blanket inside and draped it over me. It was strewn with spent cigarettes and smelled sour, dirty from the afternoon of people dancing, smoking, and eating upon it. Wet, too, from the rain. But the weight of it, and the girls leaning over me, and their Swedish, comforted me.

Siri touched my forehead and brushed the hair away from my eyes. I could sense the concern in their voices. *Är hon okej? Är hon okej?* Margareta's coarse black hair hung loose near my face, and Karin fiddled with the locket at her neck, breathing hard, like she'd been running. Siri leaned down to whisper in my ear. "Lauren, you're okay, right?"

"Are you having fun?" I asked her.

"Ah, so you are awake. Are you feeling any better?"

"I don't know."

"Rest. I will find something for you to eat and bring it back here."

The girls smiled at me and backed out of the tent. Siri's denim jacket smelled smoky. My long braid lay upon my shoulder. Softly, she combed it out with her fingers and removed the flowers from my hair. "We picked these at different crossroads, remember? There was that cloud of *baldersbra,* white and fresh. You picked these yourself."

She arranged the flowers gently by the edge of my sleeping bag.

"Where is your pink rose? The one the man gave you?" she asked.

I pointed to where it lay by my bag and she placed it with the others.

"I'm going to teach you that other tradition, the one with the flowers. But you have to make me a promise, okay?"

"Okay," I said.

"On Midsommar's Eve, if you sleep with seven different kinds of flowers underneath your pillow, you will dream of the man you are supposed to marry. It's even more powerful when you pick them from a crossroads. It's magical that way. We didn't do a lot of the magical things I had planned for us. We couldn't find a *midsommarstång* in town. We didn't really swim here. I was hoping to, but you were right. It's too cold. But this—this is big magic. This is a good thing to do on our last night here."

I lifted myself up on my arm, and Siri slid the flowers under my pillow. "What do I have to promise?"

"This is serious."

"Okay. I promise. Tell me."

"You have to promise me you won't dream of Magnus."

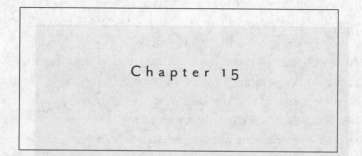

Chapter 15

WHEN I WOKE, there were sounds like whirring motors close to me, grinding sounds, mechanical sounds. The sound of a shovel. When the sounds were human, they were screams. Real or imagined, my own, I don't know. I tried to get away from the sounds, but I was underground. I was in Magnus's field, buried alive, and the rain had made quicksand of the ground and sucked me under.

It was the tent. The tent had collapsed from the weight of the rain. The thin vinyl was stuck against my body and face like plastic wrap. I couldn't breathe. Scraping at the tent with my fingernails, I peeled it off and choked for air. Water poured onto the ground into the grass, in streams.

There was a light burning in the square window of one of the Playboy RVs, and I could hear voices laughing inside. I rushed toward it and tripped on a metal stake. I couldn't recover my footing. The mud was gripping my shoes. I crawled to the RV and opened the door. Pillows were propped in a circle on the floor and a bucket was catching water coming through the roof, but now there was no light, and no one inside. There were food wrappers all over the floor, and the air smelled sour. In the corner of a wide glass aquarium, a large white snake, jawing something, coiled slowly. I backed out, and the door clapped shut.

Siri had gone to get me something to eat. How long ago did she leave me? The campsite had changed while I slept. Now it was imbued with a mean magic, and I couldn't tell what was real and what was not. It must have been Viktor's drink. I could feel the pieces of gelatin in my throat, the dirt, the grass. I told myself I was hallucinating, but it didn't help me.

In the distance, I could see tents, and bright dots like fireflies that could have been the glow of cigarettes. Drenched and cold, I moved from tree to tree trying to find shelter from the rain. The water in the grass was rising, and everywhere I stepped I was tripping on a soggy body or stepping into a dead campfire. The strings that tied tents to their stakes coiled and struck out at my bare legs.

I would not be able to find my way back to our drenched tent in the dark. It lay on the ground someplace, inside-out upon itself. I cut my foot on a broken glass bottle, and blood trickled into the grass. The campsite drank it up.

In the morning, when it was light, I might be able to make my way back along the grass through the woods to our deflated tent. But now, I was compelled to go farther into the darkness, farther from the center of myself. Around me, shadows danced black-on-black. They were the Nix rising from the wet ground, a swarming, thriving, waterlogged assembly. They reclined near the trees. Some snaked toward me over the tents with long, pale limbs. Some were legless, flailing their arms; some were Mylar-skinned satyrs with silver tails.

Some, I knew, were Näcken. The ties of the tents were his fiddle strings, and anywhere I stepped could be a sinkhole that could suck me out to bob adrift on the sea. The girl in Siri's story made the decision to stab herself in the heart rather than go to live with Näcken, and the pale water lilies of his pool turned red with her blood. All around me, flowers sprouted like hungry leeches in the moonlight, mouths gaping, anticipating I would make a similar decision.

I felt crazed, thirsty. My skin was soaking up the rain, and because of the water, the insanity of the campsite, I suddenly knew—I just *knew*—that Näcken had first drowned in a car.

I would never find my way back. I saw people standing by the toilet block. I launched myself toward them; I'm not sure what I thought I would do—how would I greet them? I was so afraid, so wet and shivering and sick. When I came to them, they looked at me with disdain and disappeared. Maybe they were ghosts. If so, they weren't my ghosts. My ghosts liked to rub their hands in my hair. They talked with voices like syrup.

I stumbled inside. It was empty. The wall was piled high with clear trash bags. I washed my face, and my skin felt so chafed and loose, like it could be rubbed right off. But there was something about the buzzing fluorescent light that was calming me down. I knew I was seeing things and couldn't trust myself. I dried my face, neck, and legs with brown paper towels. Beneath the radiator, I found an abandoned comb and parted my hair so neatly. Calm, calm. I could breathe again.

The front of my long, wet sweatshirt was emblazoned with lightning-bolt lettering: *Fäbodjäntan*. So I had bought it. The surfers had said it wasn't for me, but it was. *The farmer's daughter.* When did I buy this? Before or after I drank another cup that Viktor had made especially for me? Hadn't he poured it for me in their broken-down RV, under a blacklight, a drink that glowed like he'd squeezed all the jelly from a neon sign? I took off the sweatshirt, wrung it out in the sink, and draped it over the radiator. I stood beside it in my bra impatiently, as though I were waiting for a train.

I hurried into a stall, suddenly sick. When people came in, I watched them through the thin crack between the door and stall until they left. My skin burned. Looking down, I could see that name again, its lightning-bolt script tattooed upon my chest, red edged, infected. I couldn't tell if it was misspelled. I thought, *What a shame if it is misspelled, this tattoo that covers my whole body*.

I heard someone call my name. I resolved not to respond un-

less it was the sun itself calling me. I stared through the thin
crack between the door and stall and saw one blue eye looming
back.

"Lauren, are you in there?"

The person jostled the stall door, then reached underneath to
grab at my feet. I tried to stomp the person's hands.

"Stop it!" the person yelled. "Lauren, it's Karin."

She busted open the stall door and pulled me into the light.

"Oh my God, you were in the rain!" She took off her jacket and
handed it to me. She had an umbrella with her and propped it
against the radiator.

"I cut my foot on a bottle," I told her. I looked down at my feet.
There was the cut, but it was closing. I reached for the sweatshirt
I'd left on the radiator, but it was gone. I was still dressed, and in
the same clothes I'd worn all day.

"It was that stupid Viktor's drink," she said. "Can you walk?" I
was terrified that the hallucinations would begin again if I went
back out into the dark. I cried into her shoulder, and she stroked
my back. After a while, I let her lead me outside.

She narrated our journey in careful English. *Now we are near the
big trees, now we are across from the swing sets.* The rain was easing, and
people were coming out again. They were at home in the blackness. I wasn't used to it. I didn't want it. I had come to Sweden to
see the night erased.

"Where have you all been?" I asked.

"There was a party," Karin said.

A group of girls came toward us. Siri was among them in her
cropped pink pants and giant, unruly crown. They made her laugh
and she coughed hard. She wore her aviator sunglasses and was
being held up by a girl I didn't recognize.

When she saw me, she shouted out: "Professor!"

Professor, teacher, Ms. Cress. I hated when she called me by these
names. How long had I lain slumped in the bathroom stall? I imagined all my bottled blond was grown out to gray roots. She tried

to embrace me. Her body was cold. Her hands were freezing. Leaves from her crown scraped my face around my eyes.

"Are you having a good time?" she asked.

"I'm not feeling well," I said. "I hurt myself. I hurt my foot."

She turned from me and sang a few lines of a Swedish song with a girl I didn't know. They were holding hands, clasping their hands together in one thick fist and shaking it in time to their melody. All of her was in that fist, none of her left for me.

A few feet away, I saw three older men standing beneath a tree, staring—they were watching Siri. When it started to rain again, Siri grabbed Karin's umbrella and twirled it. The men laughed. I tried to see Siri the way they saw her. There was something jittery and staccato about her movements. Siri spun the umbrella over our heads, and when I went to steady her from falling, I could feel her shaking all over.

"Siri," I whispered, "what was in Viktor's drink?"

"Karin, what was in Viktor's drink?" she asked dreamily. Karin didn't say anything; I could see she too had noticed the nearby men. The tall man in the center had a bright yellow stripe across his jacket.

"The tent collapsed," I said, bargaining with Siri's drunkenness. "I've been seeing things." I wanted her to snap out of it. "I'd like to sleep in your car. Give me your keys."

"I don't know where it is," she said. "It's all the way back in the parking lot. And it's dark now. You won't be able to find it."

The men stepped forward. They asked Siri something in Swedish.

"I don't know," she said. She turned to Karin. "Just how young am I?"

"Let's go," Karin said.

Siri took off her sunglasses and I could see that her pretty eyes were nearly black, her pupils so wide. The man with the striped jacket smiled at her.

"Siri, let's go," I whispered, reaching out for her.

"Leave me alone! Oh, my God! You are such a bore!" She fell down and the man with the striped jacket reached forward to help her.

"She's okay," I said. I pushed past him to lift Siri's head from the dirt. He looked from me to her.

"English?" he said.

"American!" Siri yelled out, laughing. Her shirt was up around her stomach. Karin knelt down and together we lifted her up.

"American. Which? Who is American?" the man asked.

"You like Americans, huh? You want to fuck an American?"

"Siri, stop," I whispered.

"She is such a bore, but yes, she is American," Siri said. "She's a fucking bore, but she likes to do it. She'll do it with anybody," she said. "Even the worst person. Even the *one* person . . ."

Her words sloughed off my drunk-sick fog.

"Don't any of you want to fuck an American tonight?"

She was laughing as she said it.

"Siri, please stop." I heard my voice crack.

The man in the striped jacket turned to Siri. "*Nej.* But you might be fun."

Siri yelled something in Swedish and took Karin and me by our hands. We pushed past the men and ran toward the parking lot. Siri held my hand loosely. For the first time, I got the feeling that if I slipped away she would not have stopped.

Karin and Siri rapped on the side door of a red van I hadn't seen before. It slid open. Many people were inside, avoiding the rain. Arms reached out, grabbed Siri, pulled her inside. Karin and I climbed up after her. I sat opposite Siri. They slid the door closed.

It was warm. We were all sitting on a mattress that took up the area behind the front seats. The inside walls of the van were bare red metal. Above us a tiny disco ball caught the light and shot it out in squares around us. There were bodies bundled up inside down comforters on the floor. Others sat around the perimeter of the van.

I could still feel that sensation in my palm, the way her hand had been slipping from mine. What was I doing here? I needed time alone with her, to talk this out, to hear the lilt of her regular speech, to feel her eyes rest on me instead of darting away.

I didn't recognize any of these faces. I wondered if Margareta and Frida were buried somewhere in the blankets. People passed around a box of chicken-flavored crackers. Siri stared at me from the other side of the van, until Karin saw it and slid the aviator glasses over Siri's eyes to spare me.

Even the worst person, she'd said. *Even the* one *person.*

I had confided things to Siri I rarely admitted to myself. I'd traded myself away too easily. I'd told her of my old house on Long Island in the days after my parents' death. Beautiful, repaired, blooms of impatiens, the neat porch, the watered lawn. How I'd made our house look pretty again on the outside, but with all the men coming and going, and the darkness and crudeness they brought with them, my parents' home became, on the inside, a dark Villa Villekulla. All was awry inside. A horse may as well have been standing in my living room. A shrieking monkey made my bed and made it again. My parents are buccaneer captains lost at sea, that's all, they're coming back, you must leave now, please go before they return. That man smoked in their bed while I twisted in the mirror, trying to see my own back.

I'd told her about the night when two men came calling at the door of my apartment at once. They fought outside my apartment until Mr. Vallapil came out and chased them off with his broom. Ravi and Khushi were protective of me after that. I was so ashamed. I thought I'd left that behind me in New York. But my vulnerability was a feral scent. And no matter where I moved, it came with me.

My eyes adjusted to the light. A teenage boy sat at the back of the van. He wore what appeared to be a crown with a large star in the center. His eyes were flat and dark, but he smiled easily. When he asked for the cracker box, it was immediately passed to him. He told me his name was Björn and that this was his van. He asked me if I had everything I needed, and I said yes, looking away.

The rain started hard again. The cadence of the soft conversation, the closeness of new men, Siri's little foot poking out of the blankets by me—I was somehow lulled to sleep by these sad instruments.

Chapter 16

I WATCHED SIRI sleep across from me. I could just see the top of her flowered crown. Sweden. It had been impulsive and stupid to come here. Drunk or drugged and sick, surrounded by teenagers. The van was warm and red and glowing, a capsule, shuttling me toward something. I wiped at the sweat on my cheeks, pushed the blankets off with my feet. Sweden no longer felt like a place of magic. It felt like a mistake.

Siri reminded me of who I was once, of the person I might have been at eighteen, who I could pretend to be on this other side of the world. But that night, lying in the mud and with bloodshot eyes, she'd told those men I was a bore and a slut. There are reasons students and teachers shouldn't be friends. Sometimes the rules only seem silly because you aren't able to see far enough ahead.

I tried to push it out of my mind. She was just drunk, I told myself. People say things they don't mean sometimes. But she was the one who knew all the parts of me. The Siri I knew had X-ray vision. She could see through me. Not everyone could.

Sometimes after classes ended, as my performance adrenaline waned, I would gaze back at my neat, chalk-written notes upon the blackboard like they'd appeared out of nowhere. Grammar examples bearing my father's name so I could read it over and over during my grading. The final paragraph of a sample essay—arguing, in conclusion, something about my hometown, far away, a place the students didn't know to be real. The names of the two ferries that docked in Port Llewelyn at night after making their hour-long passages between the north shore of Long Island and Connecticut. Mapped sentences with words from my own life. Perspiration between me and my clothes.

A boyfriend once told me, "Other people have lost their parents. You're not the only one."

But Siri.

I thought of our horses at the stables, stuck in that ring together, no place to go but around and around. That is why I thought they were us. If they could jump the rail and run, would they go in different directions? Round and round, stuck in grief. I didn't think of it that way then. I was stuck because I kept myself at a distance. Siri was stuck because she kept the people who wanted to help her away. She'd throw them from her back and run.

No. When Siri woke, I'd tell her that I'd forgiven her while she slept. We needn't mention it again. Go back to sleep, I'd say. I'll be right here counting the moments left until the sun comes up in the van windows. The way your father used to, like we're family. It won't be long. Seconds left of darkness, and then all will be right.

I thought of that man, Jason, at the stables that day, who had been so entranced by Siri, her high voice, her beauty. That was the day I told her I was scared to be alone. That I had a way of convincing men we shared a connection. Had I tricked Siri the same way? Or had she tricked me?

But we had traded stories from our pasts.

Not the stories that mattered. You never told her about your scars. She never told you about her mother.

But we had traded the words we felt were beautiful in each other's languages.

Languid. Gloaming. Verdant. Do you even remember any of the words she shared with you? Or was this just another version of your game?

I couldn't shake it. Things felt different now, and all those memories that I played over for myself didn't feel comforting, but like grief.

I imagined them like that instant photograph Jason had taken—a blur, soon fading, something Siri would throw away.

EVERYONE WAS ASLEEP but me and Björn. Two other boys had passed out upright, with their backs against each other. One girl lolled in the center of the van. Karin and Siri slept, subsumed by the covers.

Björn looked either college-age or just out of school and in his first job. He reclined with his legs stretched toward me. He was chewing gum, or maybe tobacco.

"Where are you from?" he asked.

"The United States."

"Your friend is so much younger than you."

"She's not that much younger."

"Well, you're older. Older than all of us, right?"

There was a flash of lightning in a faraway cloud. I smelled the after-rain air. Things were peaceful, damp, and cool. I found myself thinking about "All Summer in a Day." Sitting there in the van with the door open, feeling the breeze, looking into the expanse of sky, it was like I was sitting with my legs dangling from Margot's open closet door. Now the lock is picked open. Now what? *Someone come and take me home,* I thought back to myself.

"Hey. Have you ever seen fjords?" Björn asked.

"No."

"Have you ever been to Norway?"

"No."

"How about we go there tonight? We cash in your ticket home and make our way to Oslo. Then Hardangerfjord, Sognefjord. How much did your ticket cost? I bet it would be enough money for everyone here to travel for a month."

I didn't say anything. Björn was watching me. Then we heard a sound in the distance.

"Is someone coming?" Björn asked.

"I don't see anyone," I said.

"I thought it was maybe your friend's brother again."

I looked at him. "Her brother was here?"

"Yeah. She threw a fit when she saw him. She ran off, and he went after her."

I felt suddenly uneasy. I looked out into the dark.

Could it be Magnus coming back? I could see the line of the big dune in the distance. The ocean panted beyond it. I wanted it to be him. I didn't feel like myself. A teenager's drug was wearing off. The blankets were oily with teenage sweat, gritty with dirt from a teenage campsite, and damp with rain from this eighteen-year-old part of the earth. Siri was the unlocked closet door. Magnus was the rocket ship. I thought I'd wanted to be young again, but now I wanted him to be looking for me, coming to pull me out of there, somewhere into space.

There was the crunch of gravel, and then the ruffle of underbrush. A man drifted forward from the woods, and I sat up straight.

It wasn't Magnus.

I saw the yellow stripe across his jacket.

"Hello!" the man called out in English.

I turned to Björn. "Can we close this door?"

"What? Why?"

The man pressed forward. "I know you!" he shouted cheerily. "Right? We met earlier tonight. I met you and your friends."

The man had a flashlight and swept it over the others' sleepy faces just before I pulled the door shut.

"How do you lock this?" I asked. Björn reached forward to snap the latch, and I looked at Siri, awake, rubbing her eyes. "It's one of those guys from before," I told her.

The man pounded on the van door, awakening the others.

"What does he want?" Björn asked.

The man started calling out in Swedish. I couldn't understand it, but it was the same line, over and over, a rhyme, like he was singing. Siri suddenly reached into the strata of blankets for her shoes.

"What are you doing?" I asked.

She didn't answer me. I grabbed her wrist to keep her from touching the door handle. She shook me off. The man continued to call out.

"What is he saying?" I asked.

"He wants the girl in the pink pants to come outside," Björn said.

Siri found her shoes and was pulling them on.

"Siri, no," I said.

"What did she do?" Björn said. "I don't want everyone here to get in trouble for something she did. She should get out."

Siri looked around for her aviator sunglasses. "He wants to take me swimming."

"Swimming? But there's lightning. And you've been sick this trip."

"She should get out," Björn said.

"Stop it!" I said. "Siri, stop. It's too cold. Don't you remember how cold the water was at the beach?" I tried to grab Siri's shoulder, but she slid open the door.

The man leaned against the van, his legs crossed at the ankle. He had a handsome face, but his hair was gray in places, and his lips were dark and chapped. Looped over his arm was Siri's yellow inner tube—the one we'd used at Neptuni Åkrar. He turned on his flashlight and shined it in her face.

Siri scrunched her eyes.

"Well, come on, then." The man peered into the van. "Anyone else want to come? Everyone is welcome."

I suspected he was speaking in English because of me. Maybe he thought Siri wanted me to give her permission to go.

"Hey, American girl. Tell your friend I'm okay. I just want to party," he said.

Karin crumpled against me. "Tell Siri not to go," she whispered.

He looked odd. But it was also his age. His face was half-subsumed by shadow, but I could see now that he was older—like me—too old to be hanging around the campsite with these kids.

"Tell her, Lauren!" Karin pleaded.

"Don't go, Siri," I said.

"*There* she is," the man laughed, swooping the flashlight into the van. "I knew you were in there."

Siri turned and found my eyes, even though that man couldn't, even though I was sitting way back in the dark. Could she see in my eyes all the other things I was feeling in that moment? That this man with the stripe across his jacket, with his way of coming just for her, that he was—or might as well have been—Näcken. He'd take her down to the bottom of the sea.

"I've always wanted to swim in the ocean at night," Siri said.

"Siri, you can't. Please, stay with me."

"You sound just like Birgit! The two of you always want me in your sights!"

The man with the striped jacket started laughing.

"I don't think it's safe," I said.

"Why do you *care*?" she said. "You care *so much* it's making you crazy. You know who you're like?"

"Don't say it."

"You're like my brother," she said. "You're exactly like my brother."

This had been the true violation. Not that I'd desired him. Not that I'd had *feelings*. She didn't want me to be like him. And now I could see that she was ready to write me off like she'd done with Magnus. She was pushing me away, like she had done so many times before with Magnus and Birgit. I could be Magnus, crunching out of the room in anger after the jars broke. I could be Birgit, sadly rocking in her balcony chair. But Siri was going to go with this man.

I grabbed at her, but she dodged out of my way.

"Fine. Go then," I said. It was a dare. I didn't want her to take it. I thought another argument could buy us some time. But she took the man's arm. I remember her pink capri pants with the strings dangling about her calves. I remember her backless sneakers.

Then the van door was closed again, a drawn curtain.

People in the van were talking casually.

"Your friend is a lot younger."

Björn.

I nodded.

"So where did you live in America? I only know New York."

"Yes, I lived in New York."

"No, you didn't. You didn't live in New York."

I was supposed to go after Siri. I was supposed to protect her.

Björn again: "You don't look like you lived in New York."

I tried to shut out his voice.

"You look like a teacher," he said.

Yes. That is what I was. What was I doing here? How did I get here?

There was the sudden sound of a horn being leaned on, and everyone reacted in tandem, as though it were a siren. Björn pulled his gaze from me and crawled into the driver's seat.

"Let's get out of here!" he yelled.

A girl scrambled up beside him to help him navigate his way through the tight maze of parked cars to the gate.

I kept thinking that if we left, there could be no readmission to the campsite until morning. I didn't know then that there was never going to be a way back. This was the end.

Karin did not hesitate. I saw her leap through the van's open back doors and scramble teeteringly to her feet. She turned, waiting for me to follow her. She grew small as Björn drove us quickly off the campsite. And I—I did not jump out.

Fall

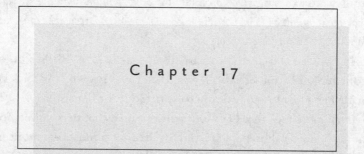

Chapter 17

WHEN I CAME home, I hesitated to look at any photos from the trip. I thought of each of our cameras, full of the summer past. Skinny-dipping pictures: still places along the shore where you could see ice, thin as cellophane—and there's me with my nipples out and sharp. There was a picture of me from the last night—the worst night—on the campground in Öland. I was giving a fake smile, but I was still the only person smiling in the whole group. I have trouble thinking about that night. I don't look at the pictures.

What if Siri showed the photos to friends in her fall classes? What if my colleagues at school saw them?

I never knew you owned so many tube tops, Professor Cress.

I didn't buy them until I got to Sweden. Everyone was wearing them. Even women my age. I've dyed my hair back to all brown. I'm still the same smart girl-woman I was last spring.

I remembered the first morning after Siri bleached and crimped my hair, after we'd shopped at the only clothing store in her town, which carried mostly cutoffs, studded T-shirts, and off-the-shoulder tops. I came into the foyer to catch a glimpse of myself in the skinny window that overlooked the field behind their house and felt so confident, so tended to. Then I'd turned and seen Birgit sitting at the dinette, looking at me, seeing that Siri had so taken me over, marked me as hers. I think Birgit wanted me to be on her side, to be another adult. She started asking me questions right then about my life back in America, as though trying to remind me of who I'd been here. I didn't want to remember. Her questions were exacting. *Do you know the other families who live in your apartment building? How far from the school to your apartment? How often do you see Siri outside of school?*

In Sweden, I'd been a tourist, temporarily free. Birgit's questions reminded me of who I was, that I was grown, and that I'd made her a grown-up promise to watch out for her sister.

That closeness, that I could have ever been that person, seemed far away now. I'd been back from Sweden for almost two months, and I hadn't heard from Siri. I didn't have her phone number in Sweden, but I'd called her U.S. cellphone number periodically since coming home, and she'd never picked up. I made excuses for her in my mind, mostly that she was angry with me and Magnus, that it would take time for her to get over it, but that she would. Certainly, she would.

I went to campus for an adjunct orientation in late August and saw some students moving into their dorms. I thought Siri *must* be back. I called her number again, and this time it went straight to voicemail. I left messages, more and more. At first with a mother's pain that her teenage daughter had lied and not come home. Then with a child's anger, that her mother had lied about there being magic.

She was being selfish. A lot had happened that last night on Öland, and memories of our last day together now left me feeling betrayed. I wanted to tell her that seeing how she treated Magnus made me want to care for him. I couldn't help it. I wanted to tell her that in Sweden, I had seen how she treated her friends, and I wanted no part of it. That I'd seen what she truly was. But each time I called her number, her sweet voice on the recording melted me, and I felt an urge to apologize. I told her that I was sorry for what happened with Magnus. I told her I'd give her space if she needed it until she was ready to talk with me.

But she didn't call back.

I was being shut out.

I had seen her scream at those Swedish friends she called her "best girls." I felt tormented as more days passed, angry and jealous that I didn't deserve even that much.

Those early days, I answered the phone for any unfamiliar number, so eager to hear Siri's voice again. Always they were calls for short technical-writing assignments, and I'd solemnly look for a pencil to scrawl the details. I accepted every contract I could, desperate for the distraction.

When I was in Sweden, I felt the country belonged to me, that it just always had and I'd never known it. It was so far removed from my regular life, it sometimes felt I'd never been born to parents at all, but born of Sweden's glades and overlooks, my mother the clear water you could dive into, and my father a dinner spread on raw wood tables, heels of bread with liverwurst.

Back home, the things in my apartment berated me. Their part-forgottenness stung me afresh, all of them wanting to make me listen, again, to their stories of the past. They were disgusted with the souvenirs I'd brought home. The eerie woodcut of Santa Lucia, which I hid on a back shelf in my closet. I don't remember if I had ever even shown it to Siri. A Swedish travel magazine, taken from a train. A woman on the cover had her head thrown back, eyes closed, arms wide to take in summer. The magazine was still dog-eared to mark the places I'd once thought I'd return to someday. But it was Siri who'd let Sweden be a part of me. If she was shutting me out, Sweden did not belong to me anymore.

I tried to tell myself that I just wanted things to go back the way they were before Siri. But things had not been good before her.

My birthday came, and I spent the day alone. I tried to make it through the day without calling her old number, but by evening, I was dialing it. I found myself leaving a voicemail about a dream

I'd had that my parents were alive again. I was sitting on a patio reading a book, and they were talking softly together inside a house, in a dim summer room. And when I finished the book and I walked into the room, it was empty. The dream had left me so shaken, I told her. I laughed a little, embarrassed, but I could almost see her compassionate eyes in my mind. When I went to hang up, I realized that my story had gone on too long—the voicemail had cut me off, and I'd been talking to no one. I waited for her to call me back. She didn't.

And then, I knew she wouldn't.

My pain from that was so great. She knew the depths of the grief I'd shared with her. She knew she was the only one to whom I could tell something like that dream.

I resolved that we were done, and when, later, long international numbers appeared in my voicemails between the tech writing calls, I made myself delete them without listening. It felt like I was setting a healthy boundary. It felt like self-care.

STELLA MARIS WAS built upon a hill, with its four main academic buildings huddled around a square, three stories deep, a labyrinthine series of stairs-to-gardens in triplicate. It bottomed out at an amphitheater informally referred to as "the pit." Some said the three-level square was inspired by the architectural designs of Frank Lloyd Wright. Siri used to say it was reminiscent of Escher's famous drawing of piled-up, interlocking stairs.

There were benches on each level of the pit, and lion-faced fountains that bled rust. They didn't run in the winter, but they gargled through the last of the hot autumn days. Students sometimes stood around the top of the pit and called to each other. On my first day back, I kept hearing Siri's voice in the mix. I scanned around for her blond head. But then I'd hear the girls' voices in my mind from that last morning in Sweden—*She is nowhere*—and I moved on, angry at myself for caring.

It was the opening day of the fall semester. Members of a student committee were passing out white and purple balloons, and the sky was dotted with them. Ahead of me, two girls swung glossy white bags stretched by the weight of new textbooks. I passed each cluster of students with my head down.

I didn't know what I'd say to Siri when we ran into each other again. I cataloged the places I was sure to see her and tried to imagine a map of the campus without them. But Stella Maris was small, and our memories together formed a chain of interlocked places I couldn't avoid, no matter my path.

I found myself walking toward the tiny campus chapel. From outside, it looked like a plain white box. Its two old priests often walked in and out of the confessionals like they were phone booths, but I never saw any confessors. There was a peacock-blue rug that ran down the aisle. On one side of the altar there stood a carved wooden statue of Mary with her hand over her plump wooden heart. On the other side, there was a statue of Jesus with his hand extended.

Like the Rose Walk and the late-night library, I early on claimed the campus chapel for my own. It was a place I could breathe deeply.

That first day back, I went in and sat down in a rear pew. I'd brought Siri to the chapel once. There she'd told me she sometimes went to the Lutheran church in town because they had a Wednesday night service in Swedish and it helped her feel less homesick. I wound up telling her about my meeting with a pastor once, not there, but after my parents died, back in New York. That pastor had a circular office with candy-colored stained-glass windows. There had been a tinkling sound the whole time, and I'd tried to identify it, thinking there must be wind chimes. In my memory, his window rained pieces of rainbow glass upon his office floor.

I told her that I'd gone to that pastor because, after my first visit to his church, someone from the congregation had come to my house with a loaf of bread and told me they'd like to see me the next Sunday. It had made me want to go back. I had been going to a Catholic Mass before that, but when I held my hands the wrong way during communion, the priest told me he couldn't serve me if I wasn't Catholic, and people stared at me as I walked to the back of the church and out.

I had told Siri that I was doing all the things then that I thought one did to grieve healthily, but I wasn't grieving healthily. I remember that in the days after their deaths, I was going through my father's toolbox and found a razor blade, rusted, popped from his old box cutter. There was a box of long nails. There was a small handsaw. I used to take these things out one at a time and lay each object upon my coffee table. A voice in my head narrated the things I did: *"She just wants attention." "She would love someone to see this." "If she really wanted to kill herself, she would have done it by now,"* and *"She just wants someone to knock this razor out of her hand."* But I was alone in that place. No one *was* there to knock it out of my hand.

Why couldn't the pastor have sent me a loaf of bread after our meeting in his round office? Why couldn't he have asked me if I had a box of nails, or a razor blade, or a plan? Instead he gave me a book he'd self-published on the Ten Commandments with a clip-art cover and told me he couldn't meet regularly.

"Are you even a Christian?" he asked as I was walking out. "That's the question you need to be asking yourself."

I hadn't even said that I wanted to kill myself. Only that I'd wanted to be with my parents again. If I could have only admitted to myself that those were the depths of my feelings, the seriousness of it all, maybe I would have sought more help.

Alone in the campus chapel without Siri, I found myself feeling that same sense of desperation. I watched the altar candles, which burned without movement—there were no doors opening, no one passing through this place to make a breeze. It was just me, sitting still. Before leaving, I went up to look at the candles, to make sure they were real.

ON OPENING DAY, I decided to go to the Mass held on the bottom level of the pit that all the students and faculty were encouraged to attend. I looked over the top-level railing and saw Dorothy Wisch down below, directing volunteers as they set out white folding chairs. A girl was passing out free hot dogs under a rainbow-striped umbrella. I took one for Dorothy and went down the stairs to see her. She was wearing a Miss America–style ribbon across her body with the word *English* on it and rolled her eyes when she saw me smile.

"We all look like a bunch of suckers." She nodded toward her colleagues, who were standing in a group, all wearing similar sashes with their department names printed on them. She tugged at the sash and tried to smooth a wrinkle from it with red, arthritic fingers. "What happened to your arm?"

My wrist had been in a purple cast since my last day in Sweden. "Oh, I fell. It's just a fracture. Nothing serious."

"Did you hear about the lit job?" She took a bite of her hot dog. "I hope you're going to interview?"

The names of the writers I'd studied flooded back. *Sui Sin Far.* *Onoto Watanna.* They were tick marks on a timeline wadded up in a pocket of my brain.

"I don't think I know enough about Asian American literature," I said softly.

"Listen. You're a good teacher, Lauren. Remember—I write your evaluations. Don't take any shit."

"The kids are so great. They never give me problems."

"You really enjoy teaching in the international program?"

"Dorothy, you're talking like you gave me the worst possible assignment. I love it. I probably wouldn't have been happy in the lit job anyway."

"You enjoy giving grammar lessons all day?"

"The students are always interesting," I said. "They make it interesting."

I felt a pang of missing Siri.

Her colleagues were beginning to congregate on the stage. She reached into her bag and drew out her gold-edged day planner. It was stuck with tasseled bookmarks and Post-its. She flipped it open to check something. "Hey—I never saw your syllabus for this semester."

"It's the same as last semester's."

"Don't *say* shit like that to me. You have to at least pretend like you prepared." She laughed and straightened her jacket. "What did you do this summer? Anything?"

"No, not really. I visited my parents in Michigan. They were doing some work on their house, so I supervised their antics."

I had lied about my parents being alive many times before, but not since Siri. I bit my tongue. I could feel more lies in my mouth.

There was the traditional striking of the big brass gong that had been wheeled from the music room, and everyone stood up. "That's my cue," she said. "Take it easy."

She walked away to join the line of academics and march affably to the stage. "Take it easy," I said, though she was out of earshot. I could feel my smile fade. The president stood at the podium and instructed us to take our seats.

Paper programs were passed down the line. The school's symbol, a lighted oil lamp, was embossed upon the cover, and I traced it with my fingertip. Some music was played. A trumpeter. A house in Michigan. I had never been to Michigan. I knew it was in the shape of a mitten—little else.

Tentatively, I looked around for Siri in the crowd.

Her hair could have been Kool-Aid red, brown, blond, blue. She dyed it a lot. It could have been longer now; it had been two months. I scanned the assembly for a girl with her mannerisms, her speed of movement. Part of me thought that if I did see her, I'd see myself beside her, the two of us talking softly amid the commotion.

If there were a house in Michigan, she'd have been there, too.

Her friendship was like that. All my old memories were woven through with her. When I think back on the day my parents' bodies sat in the morgue while I feverishly sold what I could from our

Long Island house to afford a funeral, Siri is inside that memory, too.

The idea of my parents' possessions going all at once had terrified me. Someone told me to advertise an estate sale, where people could leave after bidding on the larger items and I'd have some time to think about their offers before deciding whether to sell at all.

After the ad went out in the *Pennysaver,* a man called, saying he and his brother would be at my house at six a.m. sharp with a van, and they planned to load it up. When the two men arrived, they were twins in matching clothes, impatient. I tried to explain to them how the bidding would work, but they didn't want anything they saw. They picked over things, saying *this is cheap; this is fake sterling,* all but daring me to keep bringing things out to impress them.

There was a beautiful, middle-aged woman who came in a minivan covered with bumper stickers. She asked me what my parents had looked like, trying to remember them from anywhere in town. As people milled around touching things, I showed her their pictures. She said she was interested in our dark wood dining table, the one my mother had loved and bought the year prior. I told her to write down how much she'd be willing to pay for it, and I'd get back to her.

We sat on the couch together while she scribbled onto a yellow card and I looked into space with a fixed smile. I almost didn't care what she wanted to pay for it; I just wanted her to take it before those men decided it was worth something and loaded it into their van. I wanted it to go to someone who might love it the way my mother had.

A sudden shout from my parents' bedroom. "What size are these?"

The woman and I looked at each other. I ran upstairs and found the men crouched on the floor of my mother's closet before her prettily-lined-up shoes. One wore a pair on his hands. "You should at least mark what size these are!" he said.

I asked him and his brother to leave. I walked out into the front room and told everyone to go. When people dawdled, I stood in the middle of the room and yelled. I was thankful that the kind woman had already left before seeing me that way. I closed and locked the doors and turned around to the picked-over house, returned to my parents' bedroom, and started straightening my mother's small shoes.

After I got myself together, I went out to the living room and saw the kind woman had left her yellow card on the dining table. It was almost like having a friend in that moment. I turned the card over. She hadn't left me her first name. Just: *MORRIS*. Her phone number. Her bid: fifteen dollars.

And then Siri, sitting at the dark wood table, shaking her head at the idea that the woman could have been so hurtful, Annie's white face peering up from her lap, the brown spots at the inner corners of her eyes like the stain of tears.

The professors were asked to stand and everyone in the pit applauded. I turned forward quickly and clapped along, unsure if I was supposed to stand up. Onstage, Dorothy chatted with someone beside her. She seemed like a teenager at her high school graduation. The air was crisp, and the hill's big trees were dropping red leaves down into the pit, upon the crowd.

At the end of the service, the college president delivered his message with his hand over his heart. The school's two old priests stood and blessed the student body. There was the swinging out of incense, then a hymn, for which we all stood up to sing. Then there was the dismissal of the students, the announcement of an ice-cream social later that evening, and the gong again. When we rose to leave, everyone sang the doxology, which floated all the way up out of the pit.

As the professors and priests left the stage, I filed back up the stairs of the pit with the students. Someone brushed past me, and I had to grip the railing to keep from falling. I looked down at the purple cast on my left arm. It was supposed to have been cut off at the beginning of August, but I kept missing the appointment. I

think I wanted to be able to show it to Siri. Just one time—as
though it could serve as proof of something about that last night.
I looked over my shoulder at the sea of people filing back up the
stairs. Surely she was in this crowd. I could feel her. People pushed
past me. I was holding up the line. I turned around and tried to
keep myself from searching for her.

Rock music blared from the stage speakers just as I reached the
top of the stairs. I turned to see a performance artist arranging
paint cans in front of him like drums. I stood beside the railing to
watch. Beneath me I could see the other levels of the pit and the
artist on the stage. He was painting with his fists, splashing buckets
of color onto the immense canvases in time with the blaring music.

I could see now there was a girl standing on one of the giant
speakers. I felt a pang of longing. The girl's hair was blond. She
had Siri's same way of moving, and she was dancing to the music
despite the chaos around her. I could feel the sheer number of
bodies and the pit like an arena.

There was now something electric and watery about the crowd,
and a feeling that the tall speakers near the stage were about to be
pushed into the human current rippling in the pit, and the girl
would fall. I couldn't help myself. I brandished my cast, waved my
arms, tried to push my way back down the stairs.

"Come on, now!" I yelled. "Stop it, all of you!"

The crowd packed the stairs. I couldn't get down.

I thrust my backpack onto the concrete and started to climb
over the metal railing that separated me from the three-story drop.
I could feel the height. I felt my legs saying no, their muscles freezing, the muscles in my one good arm saying *Yes, do it,* pulling me
up and over. Now I was sitting on the railing. I could see the girl
better. It wasn't Siri. I hated myself for thinking it was her—
I hated myself. Now I felt off balance. It would be so easy to let
myself drop. I heard a siren; it was the sound of people below
howling up at me, all their mouths long O's.

At the last second, an arm caught me around the waist and I
tumbled backward.

I pulled away from the man who'd stopped me. He had silver hair and short sleeves. He seemed nervous about having touched me, and angry, and compassionate.

"Were you going to jump?" he said.

I looked around for my backpack. "No. No."

Over his shoulder, I saw the girl again. She was laughing and practically charging up the stairs. She was taller than Siri, and older in the face, and dressed all in brown, which would never be her.

"Are you okay?" the man asked, handing me my backpack.

I slid my hand along the metal railing, gazed down at the people below, remembering their expressions when it looked like I might jump. "I wasn't trying to hurt myself. I have to go. I have class."

"Which way are you heading? Let me walk you."

I walked away before he had a chance to ask me anything else. I lifted the strap of my backpack higher on my shoulder and made my way through the crowd.

I tried to think through my first-day notes. I would touch on the importance of twelve-point font, Times New Roman, and all the due dates stretching deep into the wintertime. I would go over their names on the roster and write the phonetic spellings in the margins of my grade book. I would show a video of a man talking about Arthur Rimbaud's fondness for pissing on critics who disliked his poetry, which would make them laugh, and then break them into small groups to practice describing pictures using rich language. I would tell a story about how I stole my first thesaurus and dismiss them early to get on their good side. As I walked, I stretched the muscles in my legs, trying to lose the sensation that I was still standing on a high railing about to jump.

I taught my class in Dominican. The building had a gleaming blue and white patterned floor that reminded me of a Delft porcelain plate. I could see the janitor, an old man named John Sled, pushing a mop at the far end of the hallway, sliding the pattern of the tiles toward me, all its Netherlandish blue ribbons, its diamonds and swirls, its shine.

I sometimes dreamed about walking across that floor, the click of my boots, my silhouette reflected in the glass of the display cases I passed. When I was just working in the library, I wore my same black-pants outfit every day. I'd go the whole day without noticing the tiny knots of hair and lint on my clothes. A boyfriend once picked one off and asked me why I couldn't take better care of myself. Now having to get up in front of people, to be prepared, to be on time, helped—but I only looked more put together on the outside.

I passed John Sled, and he looked up at me. "You," he said as though he'd been waiting for me to return all summer. "You have a great class today. God bless you."

His skin was covered with tags, his beard patchy, scabs showing through his white whiskers. His cart was overhung with bags and bore his name on the back like a license plate. Markered Styrofoam cups along the top were filled with things he found, and a small white stuffed bear with a red bow tie rode near the bottom, by the Lysol canisters. I knew that people avoided making eye contact with him because of his intensity at even the slightest opening. I had once heard a professor warn her students to stay away from him while he was still in earshot.

"God bless you," I said back to him, and he tipped an imaginary hat at me. I sometimes felt relief that he could see through my outer appearance, recognize that I was just as lonesome and on the outside of this world as he was.

I passed the other first-day doorways and looked into the rooms where professors sat with their backs to their whiteboards, blond wooden crucifixes hanging above their heads. Straight lines of desks. Everything quiet, quiet.

Around the bend, Gwendolyn Shoales stood in her doorway. She was an esteemed professor who liked to pick fights with other professors on behalf of the school. She always laughed as you approached her, like you were doing something foolish just by walking. She had been a well-known poet, and she often bragged about being on a panel once with Toni Cade Bambara. She wore a dress with two pockets in the front, each with a pack of cigarettes inside. It was as though she sewed pockets on the front of all her dresses for just that purpose.

"Lauren," she said in her low, gravelly voice. "You look exhausted. Aren't you sleeping." She didn't say it like a question. The ends of her sentences always went down.

"I just have a headache," I lied.

Some students passed her to enter her classroom and she laughed at them, too. "Mr. Andrews, I get to have you again, I see. Adonis, Adonis, stop, what are you doing entering my room." She addressed them all by name, her voice a spill of rocks. She had a cadre of repeats, all young men.

I walked to my classroom, the same one I'd taught in the previous spring. I felt a rush to be inside of it again. I kicked away the rubber stopper to shut the door.

My room was the only one with an old-fashioned chalkboard. I loved to write in chalk. I pulled my chair around to the side of the desk and sat down, tugged my roster out of my bag. I looked at the front seat in the first row. It was the desk with the uneven legs that Siri had occupied last semester. A young, skinny Korean man sat there now, looking afraid of me. I smiled at him. He glanced down at his book quickly.

Few of these students would continue on at Stella Maris after one year. The program had become something of a stopover for kids looking to live in the United States. They came because they said they wanted to study the visual arts, but they were eighteen-year-olds on their own in a new country, and soon they all wanted to be fashion designers and go to FIT in New York, or they realized how quickly people could get well-paying jobs with a certificate in graphic design and left to pursue that. But now they were shy. When kids ran in late, I made a point of smiling at each one of them.

I went into my first-day speech and felt my teaching joy start to come back into my chest. I played the Rimbaud video and everyone laughed, even the young man who was so hesitant before. I went around and asked people to tell me something about themselves. They all seemed to be opening up.

I liked them all so much already. I went to the wall and shut off the overhead lights. I asked them to move their desks into a circle, and they shuffled around the darkened room, the desks groaning.

"One last thing before you go. I need a writing sample from each of you. We'll talk something through first. I want you to watch the others' faces as you talk. Notice how the words you choose matter. I thought we could make it fun and tell scary stories."

I wasn't sure how it would go over, but they loved it. I, on the other hand, regretted it immediately. I expected standard spookiness, the kind that would make us jump and laugh, but they enthusiastically derailed into horror. A woman named Cecile talked about her father's losing his arm to marauders in the Congo. She told the tale with a storyteller's wide-smiling glee, but I was so shaken I wanted to snap on the lights again.

A middle-aged woman named Linda, from Scotland—why was she in my class?—told us how her dog had predicted her miscarriage. A girl named Ana who spoke with a fierce, deep voice told a story of her village's plague and how the beautiful white lace veils its women made for the dead contributed to its spread. They were all enthralled with one another's tales and rushed to raise their hands and offer new ones.

A boy named Nikhil wanted to tell us of his life in the jungles of Nepal. He wore a long soccer jersey and sandals, and his thick black hair fell to his shoulders. "I raised a tiger from birth," he said. "When it was small, it would drop gifts of headless birds and rodents on our doorstep. When it got big, my father became afraid and brought it to a distant place in the jungle and abandoned it there. But one night, it came back to see me. It missed me. It hitched a ride on a bamboo raft and rode all the way down the river until it got back to my village. It snuck into my hut at night, where I was lying in my loincloth outfit, then rose up on its back feet to put its front paws on my shoulders and hug me. My father thought it was trying to attack, and so—*whizz!*—he blew a blow dart at its face and killed it. I loved that tiger very much."

Everyone was quiet. Cecile and Ana had covered their eyes, as though the tiger had fallen dead right in front of them. Nikhil was looking around expectantly for other reactions. I could see the faintest glimmer of a smile at the corner of his mouth.

"I'm joking, people."

"That's not fair. We all told real stories," Ana complained. But she was the only one who was upset. The others applauded. Ana, tall, with the broad shoulders of a basketball player, watched my face for a reaction. She didn't like it when I smiled.

I passed out blank sheets of paper and continued the lesson, telling them, "Don't worry about grammar. Just freewrite for about ten minutes. When you're done, you can pass them up to me."

Emotionally exhausted, I slumped into my chair while they wrote out their scary tales. They were all writing happily. Nikhil kept searching out my face. When I finally allowed myself to meet his eyes, I tried to shake my head at him, but a laugh burst out of me like a burp, and this made the others laugh again. Suddenly the door creaked open. A girl walked in.

Her blond hair was longer than before and pushed back with a thick headband in a preppy American way. Her collar was sticking up out of her sweater. She looked at me with wide eyes.

It was Frida.

"Are you my teacher?"

"Are you in this class?"

She handed me the white slip with her late registration information, and I stared at it unseeingly, my heart pounding. Frida *had* said she might come to study at Stella Maris. It had not occurred to me that she could wind up in my class.

"There's a seat in the back," I said.

She maneuvered between the chairs and dropped her bookbag on the floor. It was covered with colorful round buttons, and she wore black boots that laced up the front to her knees. Ana turned to Frida and told her the assignment. Frida looked at me and scowled.

"It can be any story," I told her. "I just need it as a writing sample."

She didn't hold her pen right. She wrote with a bunched fist and didn't blink.

This girl had seen me drunk, vulnerable, topless. She'd seen me try to connect and to be like her friends. When I'd tried to make jokes, she had not laughed. She'd seen me giddy. Happy. Her best friend had loved me, and because of that, she'd tried to like me but could not. For all those reasons, I told myself it was natural for me to be uncomfortable with her sitting in my classroom now.

But there was another reason. Frida would never have come to the United States on her own. If Frida was here, Siri was back in the United States, too. And she had really not sought me out.

Frida was done with her paper before many of the others and sat back to appraise me. The papers drifted to the front of the class-room, and I collected them.

When I dismissed the students, Frida lingered. She stayed at her desk with a peach-colored paper map of the campus spread open before her.

I walked to her with my arms crossed in front of my chest. Her fingers were covered with rings, and I could see tattoos poking out near her wrists like the sleeves of an undershirt. I didn't remember her having tattoos. I leaned against the back wall and cleared my voice.

"Well, how are you?"

She was silent. I didn't know how to take it. I felt anger rising in me, but I didn't want it to show.

I sat down in the desk beside her and pointed at a square on her map. "That's Goering's Bookstore," I said. "It's the best bookstore in the city. There's a shuttle you can take there. It leaves from out-side the administration building a few times each afternoon. You can get the schedule from the secretary."

"This is weird," she said.

"I know. I . . . I can't believe you're at Stella Maris."

She folded up the map and put it in her bag.

I wanted to ask about Siri. Was she well? Were they roommates after all? Which classes did Siri have? I readied myself to ask, but Frida was impatient.

"This place is not what I expected. I thought I'd be getting some kind of American experience, but they have us living with internationals, taking all our classes with internationals—I feel separated out."

"I've heard that from other students. Siri used to say that a lot last year."

She looked at me hard. "Have you been talking to people about her?"

"What? No."

"But you two were such great friends."

"People here—they'd have opinions about how she and I were friends. They wouldn't approve."

"No one here knows you were friends with her?"

The finality in how she said that. I tried to steel myself.

"I tried not to make it public. It was just easier."

She looked down at my purple cast.

"How is your arm, Lauren?"

Immediately I felt the break inside the cast, the sweat and water trapped within it, the blue tinge from the swim at Neptuni Åkrar.

"It hardly ever hurts anymore," I lied.

Her cat-eyed gaze was a transcript. She gathered up her things and left. I imagined her carrying my words back to her dorm in her black bookbag, emptying them upon Siri's bed like small, headless creatures.

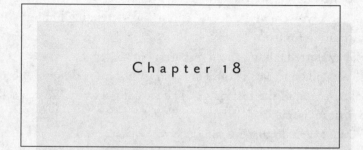

Chapter 18

THERE WERE MANY obstacles on the way out of the campsite. Double-parked cars. Sheep blocking the highway. It was as though the island wanted us—me—to stop and go back. One of the girls, a blonde named Mia, hung on Björn's shoulders and urged him on. She wore a sleeveless concert tee and a black velvet ribbon tied in a bow like a choker, so tight its knot dug into her neck. The others were looking through the rear windows and shouting. They were afraid. I knew then that they must have done something wrong to be so afraid.

For all their urgent narration, there were no sirens, no police cars following us. Mia directed Björn toward the head of the gigantic bridge that stretched over the Kalmar Sound and back to the mainland.

"Let me out," I said.

We passed beneath highway lights. They made a slow strobe upon Björn's face. "We need to keep going," he said.

The others quieted down, and with the ease of adrenaline came a sudden recall that there was no readmission to the campground after ten o'clock.

"There's no one following us. I need to go back," I said.

Björn glanced into his side mirror as though he still anticipated a chase. Mia turned to stare me down. "Look. He wanted this van ever since he saw it *Wednesday*."

Another girl was shaking. "We've gone too far," she said. "This is like we stole it. This is different."

So the van was not theirs.

"The keys were in the door," Björn said, defending himself. "It was waiting for us."

They started talking about going to Norway.

"We will go to Mia's house first and gather some things." Björn looked at me in the rearview. "Then we'll go west. We can sell your ticket home."

"No, I can't do that," I said.

"But Midsommar is just the start of everything!" Mia said.

I should have gotten out with Karin. My legs were still tensed for the jump I didn't make. I crawled to the back of the van. Through the back windows, the threat of my real life was coming up. Nothing tailed us—no sirens, no recourse. No bright-headed Siri, poking her head out into the highway, waving me back. Just a new day and my trip home. I didn't want to go home like this. Not back to my friendless grief, all-the-way dark all the time.

"First Oslo. We'll plan a great escape into the world from there," Björn said. He was still wearing his felt crown. He seemed to expect me to follow his reassuring, monotone directions all the way to Oslo, help them navigate the stolen van through the crevasses of fjords or as deep into Lapland as he wished to take me.

"I don't have any money. I don't have anything to sell. Please take me back."

Mia reached into Björn's pocket and drew out his pack of cigarettes. I watched her light one. Pursed lips, slow exhale, a flick of her tongue when she noticed my staring. "She doesn't want to come. Forget it," she said.

Björn laughed. "No, she wants to go back and wait for that asshole."

"What?"

"That asshole who was in the van before. The girl's brother. I saw your tits light up when I told you he'd been there."

"No."

I went for the door. The others saw me try to open it and yanked me back, afraid I'd jump out. They yelled at Björn to pull over and he did, finally, but I could still hear the sound of wheels, or rushing, or panting—

Mia slid open the door. "It's the water!"

A wave came toward us, white crested. When it hit the jagged rocks of the shoreline, a mist sprayed into the van. The road had been running adjacent to the shore all along, but I couldn't tell because of the dark.

The others jumped out. Björn and I followed them. Above us, the stars were so large they might all have been planets. When my eyes adjusted, I saw that we were nearly at the place where the long silver bridge met the land. I could see one spot of light, far in the distance, floating across my line of vision—one little car crossing to the island. Björn stared hard at me.

"If we sold your ticket, we could all travel for a long time," he said.

"You keep saying that. I don't even have my ticket with me."

I wondered if he was able to follow my English as quickly as I was talking. No rail separated the road's shoulder from the slant of rocks. I stepped toward the water, to get some space, to breathe, but Björn grabbed me around the waist. His hands on my body felt too familiar. They were small-of-my-back hands, the kind I fell into when I felt lost. How young are boys when they first learn to spot weakness? Does someone teach them?

"You said yourself that the van was just left there. No one's looking for it."

"There was a siren."

"It was a car horn."

"I could get arrested. Or I could drive and take my friends to see fjords. And we're all friends now, aren't we?"

"I'll walk back," I said.

"All the way back? It is five miles."

"I can walk five miles."

"Did you see the first windmill when we passed it? No, you weren't looking. You were crying, with your face in your hands. You won't recognize it for a landmark. There are hundreds of windmills on this island. You'll turn at the wrong one. Or one will reach down with its arms and fling you into the sea."

Had I been crying? On my knees with my face in my hands? Of course I had.

"Drive me back. Please."

One of his arms was still around my waist. He pulled me closer and grabbed ahold of my ponytail.

"They used to tie women by their hair to the arms of the windmills. People think the windmills are picturesque. They don't know the dark history of this island."

I tried to wrestle away from him.

"I'm giving you a story. Don't you like history? You are a teacher, right? I'm giving you a story to use in your classroom."

I elbowed him in the stomach, and he grabbed my left hand and bent my wrist back. I heard it crack. Björn heard it, too, but it didn't slow him. Pain rushed up my arm. He pushed me against the side of the van and reached into the back pocket of my jeans for my wallet. Then he pushed me into the gravel, climbed back into the van, and honked the horn to call the others back.

I clutched my wrist to my chest. The kids ran up the road and hurried into the van, like they knew this had been the plan all along. The van's wheels crunched out of the gravel shoulder, left me in the dark.

I was stupid, so stupid.

I mentally went through the contents of my wallet: about forty dollars in Swedish crowns, a torn piece of paper I'd been using to pen details from the trip since losing the guidebook, the phone number for Siri's house in Olofstorp. My passport, my plane ticket, and a wad of American cash were still back at that house.

Here: There was wind. Darkness. The bridge like a long arm,

like a needle, like a false thing that had been erected just for me, and I didn't take the chance. Now it could fall into the water.

The sounds: only wind. At times like a chime, a whistle, a groan, but only wind. It carried scents from the interior of the island. I could smell wood smoke. Chimneys. There were houses nearby.

I turned, a blind dog each time the wind shifted. The smell of a hearth. Someone who might take me in and keep me.

My wrist was surely broken. It felt heavier than any other part of my body. But the hurt made room in the center of my chest for an old, familiar feeling: that I'd be all right. I would be all right if I wanted to be all right. I could hide, adapt, get by on my wits. I was on my own again, but I knew how this worked.

A cloud shifted, and out came the moon. I saw a windmill in the distance and thought about what Björn had said. I knew there were ghosts on this island—since we'd arrived here, I could feel the press of them from all sides—but they weren't my ghosts. Mine swelled up in my injured wrist, pressed up against the underside of my hand. They said, *We will be your witness that you need to be treated with kid gloves. That you are the sensitive type. That you are world-wounded and allowed a certain extra number of mistakes.* They stroked my hair and called me *so lonely.*

Why hadn't I jumped with Karin? Because I was afraid. Because that man, swollen and pockmarked, seemed a leftover piece of my hallucination. Because if he was Näcken, then Siri was the girl from the story standing at the edge of the water, delighted with his attention, willing to go with him though she should have known better.

Is that why I was angry? Had I sought to punish her for being that girl?

Taking a chance, I turned at the first windmill, and the campsite was visible down the straight shot of road. Heat seemed to rise from it. I knew it had taken me a long time to convince them to pull over, and it would be a long time before I was back there. I could walk five miles, but I didn't know how long I could be alone with myself.

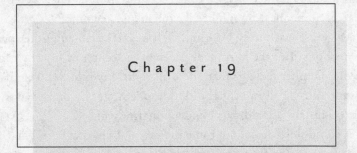

Chapter 19

In Siri's essay for the compare-and-contrast assignment last spring, she'd written of the Norse god Odin and his two pet ravens, Huginn and Muninn. Huginn represented thought. Muninn, memory. Each morning Odin would set them loose. They would fly around the world and bring back news to him so he could know everything.

Odin had wolves, too—everyone remembers the wolves. But it was the ravens that Odin feared. They didn't have wolves' teeth or ravenous appetites, nor were they killers. What made the birds frightening was that after he set them loose, they might not return.

It had been weeks since I'd written in the journal I kept by my bedside. More and more my dreams were about the time I'd spent in Sweden. A pause at the end of a line—this is where she would laugh or smile; now no one to listen. No need to pause. It became sheer rambling, no punctuation, no landings. When they came back to me, my ravens were illogical, hazy: I heard the sound of Siri coughing. The metal clack of the bill box on the wall of their house. I used to dream of my parents floating; now I dreamed of them contained, prisoners, in a metal box with a lid, and I dreamed of them coughing, coughing.

EVERY DAY I was anxious about seeing Frida in my classroom. I imagined that after class she went right to Siri to report what I'd talked about, how I'd looked, whether I still wore the purple cast on my arm.

Sometimes I thought I'd said something in class that made me seem like the good person I used to be, and that for sure, *for sure,* she would go back to her dormitory and tell Siri I should be given another chance. But each class Frida was darker in mood, gaunter in the face, faster out the door. She alternately sulked when people asked me questions, punctuated my responses with non sequiturs, vied for my attention like a despondent child.

In an early assignment, I asked my students to write a short poem and read it aloud to music. Frida refused to do it, but the others put forth beautiful efforts. Nikhil misunderstood the assignment and sang a cappella about his grandfather, who was dying in Kathmandu. He sang about the clouds in his grandfather's eyes and how the old man hadn't remembered him the last time he was there, and it was all so heartbreakingly beautiful that when he finished, we all were breathless with appreciation that he hadn't made it another joke.

The last one to go that day was a man named Adnan. With a full beard and sun-hardened skin, he looked much older than the others. Usually he wore his long blond hair tied on top of his head in a knot, but that day he shook his hair loose and played speed metal at high volume. He shouted the lines of his poem and no one could understand him. A few minutes in, Tenny came to my classroom door to complain about the noise, but I just held up my hand to her and asked him to continue. My students all leaned forward toward Adnan like the line they would understand was coming if only they were ready for it. Toward the end of the song he was banging his head, his hair flailing.

The music ended.

"Lauren!"

Gwendolyn Shoales had pushed past Tenny and come into my room. She was much shorter than us both. She wore a cream-colored polyester suit with a deep V. I could see the bones of her chest, her skin shiny from her body lotion.

Gwendolyn stared at me. She wanted me to apologize for the noise, and she wanted me to say it in front of my students.

Everyone was quiet. Adnan collected his papers and went back to his seat, looking from me to the two other women with trepidation, tying his hair back up into a knot.

Tenny widened her eyes at me, imploring me to apologize. She always aligned herself with power. But I couldn't bear it. I felt protective of Adnan—of Nikhil, of all of them who'd been willing to be vulnerable that day.

"This young man had something to say," I said finally. I turned to the class. "Give Adnan a round of applause, everyone."

The students clapped their hands. Gwendolyn tried to put her mouth into a straight line, but she couldn't help but bare her teeth. Turning to leave my room, she walked into the janitor, John Sled, and yelled at him to get out of her way. Tenny watched Gwendolyn leave. I could tell she was trying to figure out if I'd just won a challenge or gotten myself in deeper trouble.

Class was over. There was the screech of chairs as the students got up from their desks. Frida started to approach me, but when students swamped my desk, she gave me a sad smile and walked out.

That smile. It was an opening. What would she have said to me?

And what did she say to Siri, back at their room, about the way I defended Adnan? I wanted Frida to tell Siri that I had stood up for him, that I still had it in me to do something like that. I wanted Siri to be proud of me, to say I was that kind of person. I stared after Frida, as though I might hear their conversation if I listened hard enough.

Slowly, one of my students, Hae-Won, came into focus. She was standing right before me. She'd been saying my name.

"I'm sorry," I said. "What is it?"

With two hands, the girl slid a clear glass jar of kimchi across my desk. She said she'd made it herself back home in Korea by burying it in the ground for a year to make it the traditional way. "The heat of summer," she said. "The cold of winter. You need to have both or it does not taste the same."

I thanked her and set the jar upon my desk while I talked to other students. They wanted to know if I'd read their papers. Yes, of course, I said over and over, I remember what you wrote. But it wasn't true. This thing with Siri was making it impossible for me to focus. My hands dove to the gritty bottom of my bag, shaking. Writing back to my students on their essays had always been my favorite part of teaching. I thumbed through the pages, realized too many of the paper clips were at the bottom of my backpack, the papers were out of order, some graded, most not. All the while, Hae-Won's jar sat upon my desk, a lava lamp of summer and winter, red and black.

I was still shaking when they all departed. I looked at the large jar and the viscous scarlet leaves floating inside. I thought I'd slide it into my bag, but there was no room with all the unmarked papers. I carried it in my hands and, turning the first corner, ran right into John Sled's cart. The jar slipped and crashed onto the sparkling hallway tiles, the red and black cabbage flowers like organs caught up in the patterns of the vines.

I hurried to the bathroom to grab paper towels. I could smell the kimchi. My eyes stung, and then I was crying, hanging on to the sink and staring into its tiny drain. I chastised myself. *So stupid. So thoughtless.*

Outside the bathroom I could hear the students' voices. "What happened?" someone said.

I prayed that Hae-Won was not among the students in the hall, that she hadn't seen me so spectacularly destroy her gift.

"Where did she go?" I heard someone say.

My shoes were stained from the kimchi. I felt something stinging me between my toes. It was a shard of glass.

A voice, full of calm, full of concern: "Was it Miss Cress?"

I turned my head toward the door. Siri.

In the mirror, I could see I was disheveled. My purple cast dark-splotched from the sink, the front of my blouse wet from leaning against it. But I didn't care. I didn't care anymore that I didn't know what to say or who was there to hear. Or about the unreturned voicemails or the space I was supposed to be giving her. I burst from the bathroom, afraid she'd already left, just wanting to see her again.

John Sled was mopping up the mess. Some students stood in a circle near him. I rushed to them, looked into all of their faces. Siri wasn't there.

"Are you okay, Miss Cress?" one of them asked.

I nodded, but I noticed John was staring with concern. I wiped at my eyes, and he looked away, squeezing out the ropes of his mop head.

The students dispersed before noticing that I was barefoot and bleeding between my toes, that I wasn't breathing. After that day, each time I walked down that hallway, which had always been my favorite, I could still almost smell the pungent wreck of that jar and see the stain of red mixed up in the vines and flowers, and I imagined it came from an open cut on my own foot.

THAT NIGHT, THE Vallapil children, Ravi and Khushi, were playing with a tricycle in front of the apartment building when I got home.

"Where's your friend?" Ravi asked. "We never see her anymore. I still remember all the words she taught me," he said. "*Jordgubbsglass* means 'strawberry ice cream.'"

"You pronounced that perfectly," I said.

"Do you know any new ones?" he asked. Their mother came out onto the patio to listen.

"She once taught me the word *mångata,* which means 'the reflection of moonlight on water.' *Måne* is how it sounds, 'the moon.' *Gata* means 'road.' The reflection in the water makes a road of light. Isn't that pretty?"

Khushi stood for a moment looking up at the sky, her mouth open. I followed her eyes.

"That's a satellite," I told her softly, and the kids walked me to my door.

An envelope sat under my door knocker.

"Someone left something for you," Ravi said.

"Who was it?" I asked. "Did you see?"

"I don't know. We were playing," Ravi said, mounting the tricycle and hoisting Khushi on the handlebars.

I smiled and opened the door to find Annie sitting on the arm of the sofa, looking at the fishbowl, nose-to-nose with the small red betta that lived within.

"Hi, my girl."

She came ambling toward me as fast as she could, like she had been waiting all day to tell me something.

I ruffled her white head and opened the envelope. Inside lay a ticket to a Santa Lucia holiday service at the Lutheran church in town.

I sat down quickly. Was this from Siri? I stared at it. Had she come to my apartment again, raised my door knocker? I felt hope rushing in, but I didn't trust it. I looked up at the opposite velveteen chairs we used to sit in, and I remembered when things with her were good, and I felt a rush of sadness.

In the breezeway, Ravi was singing. Annie knew his voice. She tilted her head, shuffled her feet like she was dancing.

"You want to go out with your friends?" I whispered to her. "You feeling strong?" She wanted to play. I looked around for something I could use to play with her and realized it had been a long time since she'd had any toys. "Maybe we could find you a ball," I said to her. She followed me from room to room while I searched.

In the laundry room, I came upon a box that held my mother's old knitting. I opened it on the floor, so Annie could smell the old yarn. I found a ball of string and wound it tighter. It still smelled lightly of my mother's Chanel No. 5, her spearmint gum, so many years on. Annie pressed her body against the box and leaned her head inside. It seemed she was remembering the time after my parents' accident, when she didn't eat for days and lay near my mother's open closet door, staring at her lined-up shoes.

I looked again at the chairs, the ottoman Siri and I used to share. I hadn't used them since I came back from Sweden. That was where our ghosts sat.

When I knelt to give Annie the ball, she leapt upon my lap like a young dog and then into the box, where she circled round and round three times, snuggled down, and pressed her nose into the knitting. And I put the ticket atop my dresser, where it slowly collected dust.

THE NEXT CLASS, Frida approached my desk with a huge piece of oak tag flapping.

"I wanted to show you my artwork," she said. "These are some things I have been working on."

She spread the messy collage onto my desk. It ruffled with Swedish magazine clippings, pictures of small-windowed yellow buildings, some of her own drawings.

"That last assignment. The story you had us read," she said. "It inspired me."

I suddenly remembered Siri's art, the sheer weight of it. Anything she wanted to show me would take two arms to lift. She took stuff from life, the heaviest stuff—metal to weigh her ghosts down, glitter to baptize them, spackled-on layers of paint to suffocate them. When looking at her work, I'd always thought about depth. But it was height, a pile, a burial mound. Magnus had his in the field; Siri's were on her canvases.

Frida lifted up the edges of some magazine clippings so I could see clearly a drawing she'd done of a girl with long, light hair.

"You didn't know her when she had her hair long," she said.

"You're studying art here, too?" I asked.

"Yes."

Other students had come in. I looked up and saw Ana watching us.

"Let's get this out of here now," I whispered, anxiety rising in me.

"I wanted you to see. . . ."

I turned away, but she slid it across my desk so the part with the drawing of Siri would be in my line of vision.

"What do you *think*, Lauren?"

"Not now, okay?"

She was hurt. She turned to see the other students looking at her and took the collage back, embarrassed. Some of the magazine clippings fell off as she walked to her desk at the rear of the room, and the skinny boy in the front row collected them from the floor and passed them down the aisle to her one at a time.

In the previous class, I'd had them read Alice Munro's short story "Meneseteung." In it, a narrator imagines a time in the life of a small town's poetess by piecing together newspaper clippings from the town library. I asked my students who their favorite artists were, and we did some in-class writing. They were to imagine a day in that artist's life strictly from the works they remembered. What did that artist love? I said. Can you guess from what they painted? *Not like, but love,* I said. *It's the only interesting way to think of it.*

I was writing instructions on the board when I remembered who first said that to me. Magnus, that night at the bar.

I turned back to the class. "Have fun with it," I said, my voice high and wrong. "There is no need for any of it to be true."

Frida laughed out loud, and the other students turned their heads toward her.

"Why are you laughing?" Cecile asked.

"Who would even read this?" she said, gesturing toward the freewriting instructions upon the board. "I don't understand the purpose of what we're doing."

The students ignored her and turned back to their work.

"I'm just saying there is not one person in my life who would read this and care," she said.

"Miss Cress cares!" Nikhil called out.

"I don't think she does," Frida shouted back.

It seemed impossible to me that Frida and Siri were such close friends, that they'd shared an adolescence, that they were people of the same town. Siri drew people to her. Frida was pushing everyone away. I hated having her in my classroom. Why was she the one who still got to be in Siri's life?

I thought of that night at the bar again, when I learned how to toast the traditional way. That night Frida had been sitting in front of me. Her eyes had seemed to bore into me, just as they did now. Mine had gone to her throat to see if she was done drinking, if I could look away.

I looked at her throat now, at the way she appeared to be swallowing hard.

"Some people won't care about what we write, Frida. Some people won't hear the depths of our stories the way they are meant to be heard," I said. "But there are those who will."

She pulled up her hood and slid down in her chair. I watched her, and soon she took up her pen and was writing.

I thought maybe I'd broken through to her. But when she turned in the assignment, I saw that Frida had only written a few paragraphs—about Siri. I scanned her sheet: Why Siri had wanted to study in the United States. How Siri had applied for the scholarship herself, announced to her brother and sister her decision to go, but never asked their permission.

I hadn't known that. I found my eyes dragging on Siri's name. I wanted to read it all, but it was painful to see her name written there.

"This wasn't the assignment," I said to Frida. I handed the paper right back, holding it at the end of my extended arm to keep her at a distance. Other students pressed forward, asking me my opinions on their papers cheerfully. I felt Frida watching me as I gave them feedback. She returned to her desk, looking at her paper.

"This isn't fair," she erupted from the back of the room. The others went silent.

"Frida, give me five minutes."

"I did what you asked! Maybe I didn't understand what you wanted. You said someone who listened to you!"

She waited until everyone else left.

"Why are you treating me this way?" she asked. "Why are you shutting me out?"

I stared at her. She was keeping Siri from me. This was never about me and her. Why was she *writing* about her? Just to torment me?

"This wasn't supposed to be an essay about Siri," I said.

She bristled to hear me say her name, as though she were tasked with protecting it and she was the only one who got to use it.

"You said our favorite artist!"

"You can't yell at me in class."

"Maybe I just didn't understand your stupid instructions!" she screamed. She pushed the sleeves of her sweatshirt up like she was gearing up for a fight. On her forearm, I saw she had tattooed the outline of a girl's face.

I couldn't breathe.

"My plan was to avoid you," she said. "That was probably the right idea."

"Avoid me?"

She stuffed her collage back into her bag. "I want a different teacher."

I said okay, and my voice cracked with distress.

"Don't worry," she said. "I won't tell them the real reason why."

Frida gathered up her bag and sweater and clopped out of the room, her high-heeled boots sounding her way down the long, long china-plate hall.

Chapter 20

THE ÖLAND HIGHWAY back to the campground was so clean, with fresh blacktop and no cars. In the distance it seemed the whole of humanity was on that site and the rest of the island was floating free.

It was jarring when I came upon a small concrete building lit up with fluorescent lights. *Polisen.* A shield with three crowns.

It took me a moment to realize what it was.

My thoughts flew. I could ask an officer to drive me back to the campsite. Surely I'd be let back onto the campground if I arrived with the police.

I rushed in. A white-haired man in uniform stood at a counter, typing with his index fingers. Several young men sat in colored plastic chairs along a cinder-block wall. The long cord of a green telephone stretched across the room and looped around the officer's chair leg. The officer put its receiver down when I walked in and slid a form toward me across the counter for me to complete.

I imagined reporting my complaint: *My friend abandoned me, and then a stranger broke my arm and stole my wallet.*

I was taking too long to write. The officer was staring at me. It felt strange to be under the fluorescent lights after walking so long in the dark.

The form's headers: *Brottsplats. Brottstid. Brott.*

"*Vad betyder . . . brott?*" I asked the officer, who had already gone back to his slow typing.

"It means 'crime,' " a familiar voice behind me said.

I turned toward the voice, toward the row of men sitting on plastic chairs.

And then I saw him. His blond-red hair. I had to tell myself it had been so long since we were in the fountain together—how could his hair still be wet? He wore a white tank top and had a red flannel shirt tied around his waist. What were the chances of his being at that police station?

Only one hundred percent.

"Did you come for me?" he asked, standing up.

He had a bruise under his eye and lines of dried blood coming down either side of his mouth. His bottom lip was busted open, and his shirt was streaked with mud.

"What happened to you?" I asked.

"I was camping," he said. The blood from his mouth had stained the area beneath his bottom lip pink.

"You got into a fight?"

"Of course," he said. "And you?"

He saw how I was cradling my wrist against my body. "Yes, I guess I did, too."

Magnus asked a question of the officer in Swedish, and the man pointed toward the door.

"You can leave?" I asked.

"He just wanted to make sure I had a ride. I have my papers. He wanted to make sure I had someone to take care of me." He nodded toward the form. "Did you have something you needed to report?"

I imagined Siri swimming, phosphorescent, full of Viktor's neon jelly, a firefly moving along the surface of the sea.

"No," I said.

"Then let's go back," he said quickly. One of the other boys sitting against the wall yelled out something in Swedish at Magnus. "That kid says he wants to kick my ass more before I leave, but I think we'd better go." He took me by my good hand and led me out into the parking lot. He was looking at the cars, looking for Siri's.

I looked down at our entwined fingers.

"Whose car are you driving?" he asked.

"I don't have a car."

"What do you mean?"

"I walked here from the bridge."

I realized then that he must have thought Siri was out in the parking lot waiting, or that she had sent me to pick him up. Had she seen him get arrested?

"She didn't send you to get me?"

"No," I said.

He wiped at the cut on his lip with his flannel shirt. "I shouldn't even be walking," he said. "I probably have a concussion."

"Should we call a taxi?" I asked.

"There are no taxis out here. Come on."

He seemed upset that Siri hadn't come for him. He glared at the still-distant campsite, where light was rising like steam.

"What was your fight about?" I asked.

"Oh—everyone fights here. I didn't know those guys."

He walked with long strides and it was hard to keep up. "When did you get to Öland?" I asked.

"This afternoon."

"Did you come alone?"

"Yes."

He wasn't looking at me when he spoke; he clearly wanted to get back to Siri. But there was also something in his manner that seemed like he was exhausted—tired of him caring and her not. It had been the same way with her and me. I was new to that feeling, but he had lived with it for years.

We walked for a while without talking. It seemed he was angry that he cared so much, but he was still walking quickly to get to her. With each step, I felt the anger growing in me, too, that we were now both walking in her same direction, at that same speed.

A blank expanse grew to the east of us, a level, void blackness of ground-sea-sky. If we stepped off of the road we'd be sucked into space.

"They call this part of the island the alvar," he said. "It looks barren but there are relic flowers out there that don't grow anywhere else in the world.

"Not too far from this spot, there are standing stones. It's too dark to see them now, but they are large. They used to bring people out to those stones to execute them. One is carved with the story of how a father and son were executed out there. This was in the very olden days. They would make the doomed people run back and forth between the stones. When they were exhausted, they would say, 'We will let you go free if you can jump over one of these stones.' But even the lowest of the stones is to your waist. A tired man cannot jump in the air. But the people always tried. That was the scariest part."

There was something different about his voice. I wanted him to turn so I could see his face in the moonlight. I wanted to ground myself in his black eye, his split lip.

"Our summer house was not too far from here. My aunts sold it after what happened with our mother. Whenever I come back to the island I go to visit it and look it in its face. I went this afternoon."

I remembered Siri telling me that their summer house had already likely been torn down. Surely she knew otherwise. I was suddenly angry that she hadn't wanted to show it to me when I'd asked her.

He stopped walking and pointed out at the alvar.

"When we stayed here, there were times my father would punish me by leaving me out there to find my way home. It was hard for me to get my bearings. There is the sky and the highway. Those stones. But if you get spun around, it's hard to figure out which way to go. I would just stand out there thinking about killing him."

He looked at my face to see if that had shocked me.

"And no trees. No way to take cover from anything," I said in his same rhythm. I wanted him to hear it in my voice, that I understood him, to make up for what had happened that night at Liseberg. "All you can do is be afraid."

"People say there are no trees, but Siri and I once found a whole stunted pygmy forest," he said.

"I heard you came looking for her at the van," I said.

"She's always getting herself into trouble."

"And out of it."

"Yes," he said. "Nothing sticks to her, as they say. Maybe I shouldn't worry about her so much. It drives her away."

Worry did push her away. And anything that smacked of disloyalty or disinterest. A pile of blue, broken pottery lay on the roadside where I stood. I recognized it from the morning, when we first drove onto the island. Magnus knelt and tossed the chipped cups and vases into the darkness like he was skipping rocks on a black lake.

"I wish I could show you this place in the light. It is usually on and on of nothingness. But after a rain, like tonight's, it is an old map. Lines come up on the ground, and you can see all the ancient roads. Lines that went to ancient towns. There were people who lived out here. Can you imagine it? This high-screeching sound of the wind in your ears all the time? I wonder how they did not go mad."

He put his hands over his ears, though the wind was low.

"When the water dries up, the roads dry up again," he said. "But for a while you can imagine the people walking by from the past. And you don't feel so alone. Sometimes when I walk here I wonder if I might meet my mother on the road. Did Siri ever tell you anything about that?"

"No."

No. She never told me what it was like to lose them, despite all I shared with her. I had asked, hadn't I? Despite everything, there was a wall between us that she'd put there.

"Do you remember the calendar you were looking at in my room that day? With the Nattravnen?"

I immediately thought of the eerie embroidery I'd found. When I looked out at the alvar and tried to make out what Magnus was seeing, it was those macabre creatures I imagined, embossed over the blackness.

"When I was a kid, after our mother died, there was this rumor that our mother never wanted to come back that night. Some people said that she wanted to be rid of us. Some said she'd found a lover. It was mean stuff. But one day, someone told me there was a way that you could see a loved one again after they'd died."

I wondered what this had to do with those creatures. We were walking, our eyes on our own feet.

"You go a day without food or water. At midnight you go out into the woods alone. You might meet some of those creatures along the way, if you're lucky. They help you know you're on the right path. If I could make it past them all, maybe my mother would meet me in the dawn."

"Did you do that?"

"I was distraught. I was depressed. I would have done anything anyone told me to do," he said.

I remembered doing all the old funeral director instructed me to do: I was to press two browning chrysanthemums in a Bible; I was to stand at the door to greet the visitors; I was to fill my car with flowers to its roof.

"What happened the night our mother died was my fault," Magnus said.

"What?"

"There is a winter holiday—a saint's day. The idea is that this woman comes in the night, bearing light, casting away the darkness on the darkest night of the year. Every year girls compete to be chosen in a kind of a beauty contest, and the winner gets to lead a procession at church and sing.

"Siri wanted so much to be chosen but she was still small. She decided to go out in the night and knock on doors, sing the procession's songs to our neighbors, like a little campaign so they'd vote for her. Our house was asleep. I'd heard Siri moving around downstairs. She'd taken a candle and lit it on the stove light. I heard her go out. From my window I saw the light from her candle moving from the house and to the gate. I rushed to our mother's room and told on her, and our mother went out after her. Our first neighbor on the road brought Siri back right away, but our mother—she never came back."

My heart was in my throat.

"I could have gone out after her myself," he said.

"You can't blame yourself for that. You were a child, too."

"After all this time, Siri is still going out into the world knocking on doors trying to convince people to choose her, that she is a bringer of light. It's like she has been set into some kind of perpetual motion, to escape this house, to have her candles blown out, to have someone bring her home again. And it's like, now I am always at the window, wondering what to do."

I remembered Siri on the train saying that at night she often found herself lying in bed, all the siblings quiet, everyone listening for their mother to open the front door. *But it's always the gate. The gate,* she'd said. The creaky gate. I'd heard it the first night I was in Sweden. It was the same sound I came to associate with Magnus as he dug into the earth. The same gate she'd opened to go down the path with her white candle in the snow.

I could see her in motion. I could hear her steps. They were inside of me, a beat I'd learned to respond to—for every action, a reliable reaction from me. He was sitting at his window. I was the neighbor at the door. *How beautiful,* the neighbor must have said upon seeing Siri standing in the snow. Did she ask, *Where is your mother?* or did she just bring Siri home?

"Did Siri even tell you anything about our house here?"

"A little."

"Ah, of course she said *nothing*. Nothing here matters to her anymore."

Magnus looked at the way I was cradling my wrist.

"What did you do to yourself, anyway?"

"I think it's broken." I didn't want him to touch it.

"I know you didn't get in a fight. You're too good."

He untied his flannel shirt from around his waist and tore off the sleeves with quick motions. He fashioned a little sling and tied it carefully around my neck. He brushed the loose strands of my hair away before tightening the knot.

"I liked your hair better when it was brown," he said.

"You don't like it now?"

"I don't like that you thought you had to change it."

The sky was turning golden-green in the distance. "Can you ever see the Northern Lights from here?" I asked.

"On Öland? No. We're too far south. That's dawn coming up."

The fields stretched out on both sides of us now, like desert. On the very edge of the roadside: *blomsterlupiner, baldersbra*. I said them to myself in Siri's voice. I remembered her walking in the high fields earlier the same day. The wide, padded straps of her lilac backpack sliding down her arms. How she touched the faces of flowers. In my mind, she turned to face me, and all the flowers closed.

"Why did Siri leave you alone?" he asked. "You don't know your way around here. I'm mad at her for doing that to you."

"No, it wasn't like that."

But it was kind of like that, wasn't it? She had embarrassed me on the campground in front of those men. She never apologized, and then she pushed me away. While the rain clobbered the roof and I sat there thinking over ways to forgive her, she *slept* in the van. She must have known that she'd hurt me. She knew that, didn't she?

I felt Magnus's hand picking out a leftover, wilted daisy from my ponytail. "You are so *svensk* to have flowers in your hair on Midsommar," he said, putting it behind his own ear.

"You should have seen Siri tonight. She made a flower crown."

"Sounds like her."

"She loves you, you know."

"She avoids me." He spread his arms wide like he had a paintbrush in each hand, and birds rose out of the field, squawking, like black tar pencil across the morning's now-pasteling canvas.

I let my hand fall onto his shoulder. I wanted to comfort him. I wanted Siri to have to answer for his feelings. I was convinced that she'd gotten him wrong.

"I'll never give up on Siri," he said.

He was beautiful and open. Wounded. That statement, a beating drum. I felt everything in me rushing toward him.

"Did you know," he said, "out there on the alvar—there are flowers that bloomed during the glacier age. There's a whole palette of flowers that can only bloom here."

"That's what you said."

He reached out his hand, and I looked into his palm again, like he had taken something from the sky and was presenting it to me as a gift. He laughed and grabbed my good hand, pulled me into the alvar.

It was a gunshot, marking the start of a race. My heart banged like a pinball. Would my guilt soon set in, the metal ball sucked down into the machine again? I knew what was about to happen, but in that moment, I let it. She didn't want me. But he needed me. He ran backward into the dark field, laughing. I chased him into the blackness.

"I'm going to jump the stones!" he yelled.

We were so far off of the road I thought we'd never wind our way back, and I didn't care. We were in space, where I'd always longed to go. Everything black, deep, and vast, a place to float. My wrist didn't even hurt, the way he'd tied it against my chest. He turned to charge deeper into the alvar. I followed him by the brightness of his white shirt and stumbled on a rock. He came to nurse my skinned knee with kisses. He unfastened my sling, then he unfastened my buttons and pulled me beneath him.

It was selfish of me, I knew, but I could sense both of us pushing her out of our thoughts. It felt so good. There was nothing between us at all. His mouth gentle on my neck, his breath like he was about to say something just for me, over and over. He reached under my shirt and slid his hands over my breasts. He squeezed my nipples with his fingers; his palms felt for my heartbeat. Every time he touched me, I felt the thousand instances he'd wanted to. I could feel him letting go, letting himself do the things he'd wanted, and I loved it. There were flowers beneath my neck, crushed into scent. There was the rub of grit behind my knees. The way he was pushing into me, it felt like he was trying to push me underground, to put some version of me in the ground. When he looked at me, his pupils widened and widened until his eyes were black as night and I was completely taken in. It felt real, and the earlier events of the night seemed like a dream drying up.

Chapter 21

PREPARING FOR A conversation with Siri on campus wouldn't serve me. When our paths did eventually cross, it would be in some unexpected place. She'd be silent. I'd be forced to start. What if my colleagues were around? I'd speak too softly. *What?* she'd say, and I'd be caught off guard, and I'd have to start again. In my mind, I started that conversation over and over.

But not on campus, I'd think. In Stockholm. Let's meet again on that rainy day in Sergels Torg, when everything was just joy. Me in my sky-blue trench, she with her hair spiky and dusted with glitter, when we'd floated across the large black and white triangular tiles in the marketplace that had reminded me of a game board. Siri kept stepping from black triangle to white, taking pictures of me. With each step, I thought, *What now?*

I remembered our ride through the stations of the Tunnelbana, looking at all of that artwork and writing about it in the guidebook together. In one station there were gears along the walls like a hundred plain shortbread cookies. And in Näckrosen, it was silver all around with palm-sized rocks like barnacles spackled into the posts. Green lilies painted on the ceiling put you underwater. It had been a beautiful day. It was a time I would never get back.

Siri's own artwork was mostly pieces of concrete and metal, brass, like armor, on a canvas. But the underworld stations she loved most were playful and ethereal. I loved that about her, the way her eyes lit up at Stadion's rainbows. How Järva's line of black figures on red clay made us both feel as if we were wrapped around a Grecian urn. How Tensta's white walls made the station a shining pearl with sculpted penguins on rock-face shelves. We'd been on an adventure—two friends on a subway, talking about art and family. Alby was a heavenly, kelly-green woodland. And Solna Centrum was blood red, making the long escalator down feel like a descent into hell.

I SAW TENNY in the basement office the week after Frida transferred out of my class. She didn't say more than hello when I walked in. At my desk, papers were starting to pile up, rustling in the breeze from the open window. I reached for something to place upon them to keep them from blowing away. I opened the drawer of my gray desk and saw the gift Siri had given me, the bud vase in the shape of a lemon, its finish that of a lemon rind. It was the only personal item I kept in the office.

"Did you apologize to Gwendolyn Shoales yet?" Tenny asked.

"For what?" I asked.

"The way you embarrassed her in front of your class." She came over to my desk and lit a cigarette beside the open window.

"No. I haven't," I said.

"I bring it up only because she's been appointed to the hiring committee for the position that's coming open. Professor Trela's. Are you going to apply?"

"I've been thinking about it."

"You should, you should," she said, smoking, blowing out a long breath of air. "You're the right kind of person for it. And you're so young. You could have a long career here."

She watched me set the lemon vase back on my desk in a way that would catch the light. She eyed it with a little jealousy, I could tell. I know what Tenny saw. I was still the teacher who got little gifts. Sparkly cards from students. *We hope you are having a good day!* written on the board before I came in.

"Here, I got your mail for you," Tenny said. She retrieved a pile of papers and envelopes from her desk and handed them to me. "I also got your student. Frida Dahlström. What a sullen little bitch she is."

I looked at her as she blew her nose.

"I know," she said. "I shouldn't say that about a student. I just hate them all this semester. But I'm good at not letting it show."

From the way she was changing the topic, it didn't seem that Frida had told Tenny her reasons for transferring out of my class. Tenny was the type who couldn't resist a piece of gossip. If she knew the slightest bit of the story, she'd want it all.

From her bag, she held up her illuminated volume of Dickinson.

"When things got too hard for Emily, she shut herself up in her house. She would listen to the children playing down in the street, get to know their personalities. She would fill a little basket with candy, tie it to a bedsheet, and lower it down to them. They only saw her slender white arm through the window, but they came to love her. Sometimes I think if I could only conduct my classes through an upstairs window, I would be a good teacher."

"You're too hard on yourself," I said.

"Maybe. You don't seem to have those problems, though."

"No. I mean . . . sometimes I do," I said. "We all do."

She looked at me appraisingly. "What kinds of problems do you have, Lauren?"

I'd been trying to convince myself that since Frida had left my class, things were going better. I'd attributed my tension to her, and when she left, I thought I'd be relieved, but I wasn't. More and more I had to ask students to repeat themselves. Sometimes I would be talking in front of the class and realize I'd said the same thing twice. They'd stare anticipatorily, as though waiting on me to become that teacher from the first day again, the one who asked them for scary stories and could bear things like that.

When I pulled out construction paper and asked them to make paper snowflakes, they humored me. I asked them to write their favorite line from a personal essay on their snowflakes, and they did, though I still hadn't returned most of their papers. I planned to say something about their voices being like snowflakes, but suddenly a blond girl breezed past my open doorway, and my throat clenched as I thought for a moment she was Siri. I was suddenly sapped of the confidence to broach sentimentality. I went to the door and looked down the gleaming, empty hallway.

"Miss Cress?"

Back in the room, I didn't put the snowflakes in any context. I just taped them to the windows and dismissed the class.

I TOLD MYSELF that before Sweden I had been getting better. I had found a friend. I was going to apply for that full-time job. I was going to make up for lost time. Afterward, here I was, *that* person again. The one who couldn't sleep at night, the one who walked the aisles of a twenty-four-hour store to pass the time. Up and down the rows, just looking at things. I had to be out of my apartment, among people. I felt that if I withdrew any more inside myself, I risked disappearing entirely.

I met a man there late one night, when I was feeling particularly bad. He was an employee there. He had black hair that he slicked back, and he was very thin and tall. He asked for my number. *Since Siri,* I thought, *I'm not playing that word game anymore.* But I started it up again, with him. He called too much. I stopped answering my phone.

And on a day toward the end of September, I showed my students a scene from a gangster movie. A man shot another man in the head after calling another man a racial slur. I asked them to compare and contrast the two cruelties. On the board, I went through my algebra, making a key to indicate the A's, B's, and 1-2-3s. I talked through it—the blood and gore, the racism, the ignorance, the pain. When I had filled the board with chalk, I turned around. They were all silent. Slowly, Adnan raised his hand.

"How can you talk so coolly about death?" he asked.

I brushed at my pants, covered with dust from the chalkboard. The old TV was on its dusty rolling stand in the corner, shut off, but they were all looking at it so as not to meet my gaze.

"You think I talk coolly about death?"

As had become my habit, I dismissed class before the end of the hour.

I found myself staring at Siri's old desk. The desk's legs were uneven, and whenever she was writing, she'd gently tip the desk back (click) and forth (clop) as she wrote, a soft, slow pendulum that no one else seemed to notice. She would sit so straight in her chair I could see the pattern of her breathing.

I reached into my bookbag for my grading. So many ungraded papers, all of them the beginnings of conversations. Looking at their opening paragraphs, I could see that my students were trying to do what I told them. Writing is a way of connecting, I'd told them. Here's your topic—what is the first thing you think of when I say (*blank*)? I wrote in their margins less and less. Click, clop—a beat of memory with no outside dissonance. A little quiet. A little focus, and slowly, memories: The number of people we had to ask before finding a bottle opener at that outdoor bar in Nyhavn—sixteen. The name of the tiny sailboat Siri's young cousin captained in Hamburgsund: *Ost,* because in that sea of children steering white boats, his little yellow one looked like a wedge of cheese. Siri, in her lavender jacket, turning to face me, her hair blown by the wind.

I looked toward my open classroom door. The memory of Siri was so present then. It seemed she would reappear immediately. I felt an unreasonable hurt when she did not. Condensation dripped on the big windows. I heard footsteps out in the hall and listened hard, trying to figure out if they were coming closer or moving away.

It was Tenny. She filled the doorway space.

"Did you release your class early again?" she asked.

"Yes."

She held a book in her hands like an open hymnal.

"I want to ask you something," she said. "Did something happen between you and that student?"

"I'm sorry?"

I was caught off guard. I tried to think of a fair response, but none came. I did all I could think to do—indicate the empty chair opposite me, where she might sit and talk about what had happened. But she didn't come farther into the room. She wanted me to answer for something, but I couldn't speak. She shook her head and walked away.

My hand was still extended toward the chair. The first seat in the first row—Siri's chair. I pulled my hand back as though I might be burned.

On the other side of the water-patterned windows, students talked. Their mouths moved mechanically. I went over and pulled on a string to lower the blinds. The entire contraption came down with a dusty crash, and I jumped back.

I stood blinking in the powdery air as the desk that had been Frida's came into focus, its top covered with black stars, drawn in pencil. They were similar to the ones that jutted at Frida's wrists.

What did she tell Tenny?

Lit up with grief and adrenaline, I went to Tenny's classroom. She was sitting at her desk with neat piles of papers before her, writing with her hand bunched like a fist.

"You walked away without explaining. Which student did you mean? The girl named Frida Dahlström?"

She gave me an inquiring look.

"No, not her. I thought you knew who I was talking about."

"Who did you mean?"

"That blond girl from last year. I would see you with her quite a lot. You were friends with her."

I tried to stay composed.

"I know who you mean," I said. "She was very sweet."

"What was her name?"

I paused. "Siri Bergström."

"Yes. People were talking about her today."

"What people?" I asked.

She laid her book open flat on the desk and folded her hands upon it, as though her long fingers aimed to cover a secret.

"You never talk to me anymore, Lauren. We used to be good friends here. Why don't you just tell me the truth?"

I looked at the door, then at the window. I wanted to run from that room, but I felt frozen there.

"What was your relationship with that girl?" she asked. "Your student."

"Yes, she was my student."

"I don't want to get into an argument with you. That's not what I meant to do at all," she said. "It's just that people saw you together all the time."

"You keep saying 'people.' What people? Faculty here? She was my student. She didn't have very good self-esteem and had a hard time adjusting here. I offered her a listening ear."

She nodded. She tilted her head to one side and blinked.

"Tenny, I hardly knew her. In any case, you needn't be concerned about it."

"I'll mind my own business," she said.

"Yes," I said. I was accustomed to Tenny's being deferential to me. To everyone. I hung in her doorway, my nails digging into my palms while she returned to her grading.

"Tenny."

"Yes?"

"What did she say?"

"Who?"

"Siri Bergström. Did she say something about me?"

Something changed in her expression. Like she was doing mental math or buying time.

"When was the last time you saw her?" she asked.

"In the spring."

"The spring."

"Yes," I lied.

"Lauren, that girl didn't return to school."

"What?"

She took up a letter opener. She was still staring at me as she plucked an envelope from among the papers.

Slowly she slit it.

There had been that opening-day Mass in the pit. That day with the splattered kimchi and the feeling of Siri passing by my open classroom door. I would be someplace on campus and suddenly feel the memory of being there with her, and I'd flee. Or I'd be standing with colleagues and laugh a little louder because I felt, I just *felt* her presence nearby, and I wanted to show her that I was okay.

The ticket. The ticket to the Santa Lucia service at the Lutheran church. Hadn't she left it for me? Whenever I passed it on my dresser, I told myself I'd see her at that church, if not before. I'd see her there. That was the church she went to when she felt homesick. She had invited me home again.

I spun from Tenny and hurriedly walked back to my classroom, where my students' paper snowflakes quivered in the air from the radiator. I grabbed my things, put on my coat, and left the building.

I thought I'd been giving her space. I had thought there was a chance, however small, that we would fix things and go back to the way we were before.

In Gamla Stan's narrow caramel alleys, in Stockholm's silver subways, in the streets, with her purple backpack bouncing ahead of me—I'd felt lighter.

When she walked ahead of me down the cobblestone tubes of the Old Town, she made the passage safe. Her presence vouched for me.

I was the one who needed protecting. She was supposed to protect *me*.

I'd replayed the last night on Öland over and over in my mind.
If what I had done to Siri that night was not a betrayal, denying
our friendship to Tenny had been. To whom could I apologize for
that? She hadn't come back.

Lying had become second nature in my adult life. It was a way
to spare strangers difficult conversations. The lies only ever per-
tained to my own information, and nothing I said was ever that
important; the lies only served to keep me smiling, to keep the
conversations from going off the cliff of sympathy, to keep me
from breaking down.

But my lie to Tenny that Siri hadn't been my friend—it was not
white.

It was a lie that aimed to black out everything.

Chapter 22

When we got to the campsite, things were awakening like a morning house. We trod over the fanlike seagrass that grew near the now-open pedestrian entrance, walking one behind the other through the maze of cars that dripped with condensation in the new light. I led Magnus past the glimmery splutter of campfires to the place where I'd helped pound in the stakes of our decrepit tent the day before.

There, beside the moose-skin blanket, the girls sat in a circle of plastic chairs, bundled up in sweatshirts. Over the embers of a dying campfire, they were making coffee in a silver pot. They ate cookies. It seemed so strange to be seeing people doing ordinary things here in the daylight—picking up debris from the ground, frying sausages, packing up. The Playboy vans that flanked us gleamed, freshly rinsed from the rain.

When Magnus and I approached, one of the girls turned, slowly, to look over her shoulder. Frida. She saw me cradling my wrist and blew out her cigarette smoke.

"It's broken," I said.

"Where is Siri?" she demanded.

Karin was with them. She was slouched in a lawn chair, a bag of ice on her ankle. Both her knees were scraped and bloody.

"You never caught up with them?" I asked her.

"No, I never caught up with them," Karin said angrily. "Where did you go?"

"Isn't it clear where she went?" Margareta said, staring at Magnus.

The girls glared at me. Frida poured what was left of the coffee onto the grass.

"Who did she go off with?" Magnus asked.

"Some man," Margareta said.

"We have been all over the campground. She is nowhere, Lauren," Karin said.

I'd never seen such disgust in Karin's face. Of the girls, she had always been the kindest to me.

"You were stuck to Siri all this time, Lauren," Margareta said. "Why didn't you stay with her?"

Frida started shaking, her eyes suddenly full of tears. The girls tried to comfort her. I undid the straps of my sandals. There, on my right foot, was a long red line from where I had stepped on the shard of glass the night before, as if to assure me the dream had been real.

Magnus looked at me with his eyes wide. "Why didn't you tell me that something happened to Siri?"

"She just went off. I told you that."

"What did this man look like?" he asked the others.

"Well, Lauren? You saw him! What did he look like?" Margareta said.

"Tall," Karin said. "Broad. There was something wrong with his skin."

In my mind I saw the too-tight skin, the too-tight smile, the way his skin was pocked like a sponge.

"He was older than us. He had a deep, strange voice," Karin said.

The sound of the waves, then, was the sound of breathing, rasping for air, the first breaths after being underwater for a long time.

That man had wanted to take Siri swimming.

"Did you check the beach?" I asked.

I could barely speak. Would my English conjure her? Would she come toward us again through the woods, dripping from head to toe, from the bottom of the sound, take me someplace where it could just be us again?

"Of course," Frida said.

The girls started talking to one another in Swedish, purposefully shutting me out.

"Did you check the water?" I asked.

"What?"

Magnus heard me say it. "What are you talking about?" he hissed, as though I were wishing something evil upon his sister.

With each passing second, the feeling inside me grew. If there was ever a connection between Siri and me, I felt it then. I felt her. I left them, walking in the direction of the water. A moment later, Magnus was beside me, and then we were running together toward the high dune.

We had to climb it to see the water. Pieces of fencing poked up from the sand, shards of glass, a doll's head. My steps sank in, exposing things—chunks of concrete, a shoebox. I was losing my footing, and my fingers curled into the sand looking for something to hold on to, but the whole thing was as delicate as sugar, the dune about to collapse beneath me. Magnus had made it to the top. He was reaching back for my hand to help me over. I clambered up to where he was.

When I saw the Kalmar Sound from the top of the dune, it was lit up with sun. A silver balloon was riding a current of air straight out over it. Even in my panic, I thought I'd never seen anything so beautiful.

We caught our breath and walked along the top of the dune, one behind the other. He squinted out at the water. "Siri's a good swimmer," he kept saying. "Don't worry."

But then the Kalmar Sound folded in on itself and there emerged from its crease a yellow dot. The inner tube. My mind raced with fear. Was that it? The one I'd sat upon, that we'd packed in the hatchback of her car?

It dipped beneath our line of vision for just a second and then Magnus was racing down the side of the dune, kicking up stinging sand. When I was able to focus, I saw him bounding into the water. And when he turned, he was carrying Siri in his arms. She was not moving.

I hurried down the dune toward the water and splashed in. The water was up to my waist. Siri's eyes were open. Her yellow inner tube was looped on Magnus's arm.

He placed her on the sand and bent over her, his cheeks already red from the cold. She kept saying that her legs hurt, and I saw how thin she was, with a bruise on her knee. When she saw me, she grabbed my arm with so much strength that I stopped crying and yelled out.

"How long were you out there?" Magnus leaned down and rubbed her arms to warm them.

"I swam out far," Siri said.

"Where was he?"

"We were partying on the beach, and he wanted to go for a swim. Then when I tried to swim back in, I was too cold. I couldn't move. He just left me."

Except for the light waves and Siri's breaths, all was quiet then. The man hadn't been a premonition, a nightmare come to life. He wasn't Näcken—is that what I'd thought? The idea of it felt so foolish now. He was just another selfish, careless person. It was morning now, Midsommar's Day, and we were just three people gathered on an empty beach.

"Siri, I think we should take you to a hospital," I said.

"He didn't touch me."

"But you're freezing. And you've been sick this trip."

Siri looked at me intently. "No. It was Viktor's drink. I can still feel it. I don't want to get in trouble."

"In trouble with who?" I asked.

"You think someone put something in your drink?" Magnus asked.

Siri nodded.

"I should have stayed with you," I whispered to her.

"I didn't want you to stay with me," she said.

Her words hurt. I looked at her, her hair wet and pressed against the side of her face, her lips dark. I wanted to help her. Why was she still pushing me away?

Magnus put his hand on the small of my back and talked over my shoulder so she wouldn't hear him. "*She needs to go to a hospital. Her skin is ice, she—*"

Siri's gaze was retracting. Pulling back, back, far enough to really see me and her brother beside me, the hour hand upon my back and the seconds beating in his fingers. She got us into focus. It was an alarm going off. She pointed at me, at him.

"Did you dream of him, then?" she asked. "And he came true?"

Magnus scooped Siri up from the sand, whispering words to calm her. He carried her across the beach and over the dune, leaving me there with the yellow tube, slack jawed and staring at the writing on its side, all dots and vowels.

The island was no longer a place of magic. I was no longer a girl between worlds. I sat looking at the water for too long after they'd gone off. I picked open the clear plug on the tube and pounded and pushed until all the air was out.

When I got back to the campsite, her friends were combing her hair and dressing her in warm clothes. She looked so small, so different. I don't think Siri ever told anyone everything that happened that night, though it was clear every one of them had a story in her mind that held me accountable.

The girls looked at me with disdain. Siri, however—she looked at me with what could only be described as sympathy, as though she could foresee the many long, questioning days that lay ahead of me in my life.

Everyone was encouraging her to go to the hospital, but she did not want to go. They were still arguing with her when I left the campground. Without any discussion, Siri arranged for me to travel back to Olofstorp with Margareta.

On the drive back, Margareta did not speak in English again and smoked a lot. In Olofstorp, Birgit drove me to a clinic, where a doctor properly cast my wrist. The doctor also refused to speak to me in English, but Birgit translated that it was only a tiny fracture. And then to the airport. And then I was in the air. And then I was home.

Chapter 23

THE NIGHT AFTER Tenny told me that Siri had not returned to school, I ransacked my apartment, looking for Siri's contact information in Sweden, but I could find nothing. I dialed her D.C. cellphone again. This time, instead of the robotic greeting, I got a message saying that the number was no longer in service. I dialed it again. It was as if the tones were trying to tell me that the number had never existed. I thought of voicemails from the strange numbers I'd deleted those days my feelings had been bruised, telling myself it was self-care. Self-care! Had it been Siri calling then, to tell me why she wasn't returning?

It must have been Frida who left the ticket for the church service, I decided. She had somehow found my address, come to my apartment, lifted my door knocker to leave me something that she knew would hurt me. She was here in Siri's stead. She was studying art like Siri, walking the same paths we used to take together, taking up my time like Siri. She was a trespasser.

I had to teach the next day, and it went poorly. When Gwendolyn Shoales strode up to me at the end, I thought she was there because she'd seen it all—how I'd lost my breath while reading a poem aloud; yelped after leaving my hand too long on the hot glass of the overhead projector; opened the wrong side of the chalk case and dropped the pieces on the floor, where they broke into bits too small to use.

"Lauren, how are you," Gwendolyn asked huskily, shaking my hand. I motioned toward the seat at the teacher's desk, but she shook her head.

"What's with snowflakes in September?" She went to the window and touched one. She noticed they bore handwriting. "Are these things the students wrote?"

"Yes. Lines they liked."

She read one of them under her breath. "Not very clever, this one. But I get the idea. All this construction paper . . . from outside, this looks like the window of a preschool."

"Do you think I should take them down?"

"No. I mean, who cares?" I realized one of her hips was jutting out. "I want to talk to you for a minute."

"Yeah, of course," I said.

I sat down in the chair I'd offered her. She went on.

"You think of yourself as a 'fun' teacher, right? You give easy A's. Maybe you're too much of a pushover—would you agree?"

"To which part?"

"What are you talking about?"

"Well, you just said three very different things."

"Let me just say that you should stop being stupid. I'm here as your friend today, okay? There have been complaints about you."

"What?" I felt a sense of dread. "From who?"

"Whom," she said, correcting me.

She looked me over.

"Lauren. I know you're young. You're not much older than the kids here. But you need to draw a line between yourself and them. Some things are off-limits. If you are ever wondering if you are getting too close, then you are—yes, you are. Draw back. That girl who transferred from your class? She told Professor Ryan the way you conducted class made her uncomfortable."

"Uncomfortable? You're making all sorts of statements. What exactly was the complaint?"

"People are calling it 'inappropriate behavior.' I think it's all unfounded. I do. Everyone here has a weakness for gossip. I don't think you are a bad person—I just think you're a poor teacher. I'm coming to you today as a friend, okay? I'm your friendly colleague, here to tell you to wise up."

"What exactly did Frida say?"

But she was already out the door. I grabbed my things and rushed to Dorothy's office. I had always been enamored with the campus, the mossy conversation of its trees, the edged paths, the marble steps. Now the scenery felt oppressive. The light of evening—I remembered the golden word I taught Siri my first night in Sweden: *gloaming. There you are again, gloaming. Like I need a spotlight illuminating this race to Dorothy's office. Go away, gloaming. No one needs to see this.*

I approached her open door. She was on the telephone. She turned around in her chair when she saw me standing in her doorway. I was breathing hard from running up the steps to her office, and I'd caught her off guard. She pointed to the phone she was holding and came toward me. Why did I think she was going to hug me with her other arm? She didn't. She closed the door in my face. I was sure she'd come talk to me as soon as her call was over. I waited out there like an idiot, thinking any moment she'd open the door and apologize to me. She didn't.

THAT NIGHT, I drove across the campus in the dark. A one-lane road separated the boys' and girls' dormitories, and above the road there was a narrow walking bridge, from which the campus bell hung and rang out each hour. I circled the building a few times, looking up at the bell, looking up at the dormitory windows, where some of the curtains were pulled back. I could see figures moving inside like dolls.

There were spaces in the front, but I parked behind the building and turned off my headlights. I would find Frida's room. Maybe Siri would be there. Maybe Tenny had gotten it wrong.

For so long, I didn't know what I'd say if I saw Siri again. Now I wrapped my scarf around my neck, around my mouth, to keep the words from spilling out before I got to her. My fingers curled through the holes of its knit. *Why did you leave me? Why didn't you return my calls? You know me! You know what I've been through, what's made me the way I am. Why didn't you come back?*

She hadn't come back. She wasn't in that dormitory.

I hated her for not coming back. And I hated Frida for being here instead. How dare she be here, taking Siri's classes, making collages, showering on her hall, sleeping in her bed?

Inappropriate behavior. Did Frida tell people I'd harassed *Siri*? How could I even mention Siri's name now, ask anyone about her, without bringing more suspicion upon myself?

I screamed into my bunched scarf.

How could I even say Siri's name now without shrieking?

I clapped my palm against my mouth and felt tears between my fingers.

I turned on the overhead light to look at myself in the rearview mirror. My cheap jacket. My hair—too long again. No lipstick, no blood in my face. I was scared of the anger I saw in my eyes. I thought of the ticket she'd left me at my home. I didn't trust myself to go into Frida's dorm. I felt I could kill her.

A gaggle of girls came out of the entrance to the dorm, hanging on one another's arms and laughing. I turned to roll up the window and shut out the sound of them. I looked over into the car beside me.

Tenny.

Was she watching me? The amber glow of her visor light made two long shadows of her eyes. A red dot near her cheek—the burn of her cigarette. She brought it to her mouth and turned her face upward, and the way the light shifted, her eyes elongated down, down, like two black slashes.

I put the car in reverse and backed out as fast as I could, nearly hitting a student. I motioned for the girl to go ahead. She wouldn't move—she just stared at me with her mouth open. Frantic, I waved her on and pulled back onto the one-lane road that ran beneath the bridge.

A class must have just let out. A river of kids separated and curled around my car. There were so many students I had to stop. More and more kept coming. Clutching books, bundled in coats, bookbags, purple and gold college sweatshirts, contorted faces blanched out by my headlights—hands on my car, they pounded on the hood and one started yelling at me, others started yelling, one unified, fierce, riotous mob drumming upon all my windows.

Then it was just forty to fifty individuals, dis-coagulating, laughing at the joke and becoming people again in my rearview, lit up red by my brakes.

Chapter 24

My next teaching day, I was in my classroom when Frida came in. I worried she'd heard I was outside her dormitory. I was full of anxiety at the sight of her, but she seemed entirely placid.

I cleared my throat, a sudden rushing sound in my ears, a furnace switching on inside me.

Frida slid into the chair beside my desk. She flicked her hair. It smelled of incense.

"I have something to give you," she said.

She reached into the pocket of her denim coat and pulled out a folded piece of paper dotted with lint. She wiped it on her jeans before handing it to me. It was a printed image of a painting—a very good painting—of two girls, back-to-back, smiling.

It was a rendition of Magnus's sketch of us at Vimmerby.

It was like she'd handed me a picture of ghosts. My hands were shaking as I took it from her. Hers were, too.

He'd captured Siri perfectly. Her openmouthed, laughing smile, the way her eyes sparkled. I was overcome with tears upon seeing Siri's face. I was overcome by the fact that we could still exist anyplace together, though it was only a picture of a painting.

"You look beautiful in it," Frida said.

I let myself look at my image. Magnus had painted my eyes blue-green. There was copper in my hair. Leaning against Siri's back, our hair mixed together on our necks. I could still *feel* that. I looked self-conscious, but the way I was smiling—I didn't know at the time I was being seen that way. I remembered that happiness right on the surface of my skin again.

Frida made a motion to grab my hand, but I drew back.

I put my hands under my desk, so she wouldn't make that mistake again.

She seemed a little embarrassed, but she continued speaking. "It's pretty famous now in Sweden. The painting was on the cover of a magazine. Magnus was on television. Apparently, he won a prize," Frida said.

"What kind of prize?"

"It's a famous painting now. He thought you would want to know about it. I said I would give this to you."

"When did you talk to Magnus?" I asked.

"I didn't. *I* don't. This picture came by way of my mother. She mailed it to me."

"And Siri?"

Her name had spilled out.

"Everything Magnus does is for Siri now," she said as though scrambling to take Siri's name back from the air. We were still jealous of each other; Frida, perhaps, of this painting, I of her ability to say my friend's name out loud.

"I still can't imagine you purposefully putting an ocean between the two of you," I said.

The radiator at the back of the room grumbled on.

"An ocean?" she said.

Emotions flashed on Frida's face with strange speed. Some students started to come in. She turned to see who was there, then faced me, full of heat.

"I spoke to Birgit. She asked about you," she said.

I was sweating. The radiator was on high.

No, it was a furnace. It was inside me: a broiling thing that filled in all of the space of that room. A hot-air balloon inflating my chest. A heat that made me shake, that gave me a blacking-out feeling. A circle of blackness that aimed to grow and grow until it squeezed out any memory of Öland.

I wanted the long, steely bridge to the summer gone. I wanted to explode whatever was at the end of the bridge.

"Birgit thinks you and I should be friends here," Frida said. "Do you think there's ever a chance of that?"

I remembered how Birgit had entreated me to keep Siri safe. How it hadn't proven possible. How I'd failed her. Was Birgit asking me now to protect Frida? I couldn't do it. I couldn't keep my own head above water.

"We can talk another time."

I slid the picture into my backpack.

"Why not now?" she said. "Lauren, why not just say that's what we are? That you and I are friends?"

"How?" I whispered. "With all that you have been saying about me?"

"I have not said anything! This is your own guilty mind—"

"No."

"I heard you that day, you know. I heard you say that you hardly even knew Siri."

She pointed to my backpack.

"The name of that painting is *Två Flickor: Two Girls*. That is *your* face. It proves you were there."

Some of my students were standing outside, hesitating to come in. Frida wiped at her eyes like she wanted to rub them out.

"I could make copies. I could post them everywhere in the school so everyone knows it!" she said. "That's your biggest fear, isn't it?"

"It's okay!" I waved my students in. "Class is going to start in one minute."

Frida turned like a ringmaster to them.

"Everyone, yes, please come in! Miss Cress is getting ready to tell you about the best way to express yourself. To connect with the world through writing!"

She pointed at them with her fingers splayed, her lower jaw jutting out, her bottom teeth bared.

"Miss Cress wants you to be authentic! So you better tell the truth!"

SIRI: LAUGHING. HER mouth is open in a daring, crooked smile. Mischievousness. Her fingers in the shape of a gun, like one of Charlie's Angels. Her blond hair tucked behind her ears, all her freckles out, her green eyes challenging but twinkling. Like she is ready for a fight. Or flight. Something in her look: fleeting. She is not going to stick around very long. She didn't, of course.

Me: my back to Siri. The swirl of our hair made us look like we were of one body, connected at our shoulders. Our hair mixed on our necks. Though Siri and her friends had dyed my hair blond, Magnus had painted my hair bronze-brown, the way I looked when I first arrived in Olofstorp. I am looking down to where our hair is swirling together. On my shoulder, the three tiny freckles my father once called my trinity. Magnus painted them blue, pink, and green. The colors of Monet's water lilies.

Now: nighttime in my apartment. By the gray cast of the television, the picture thumped in my hand like it had a heartbeat.

In the actual photographs I took at Vimmerby, Siri and I both look young, like there is little difference between our ages. But our friendship bridged that span of time when women try to figure out who they want to be and what parts of themselves they want to leave behind. I should have known who I was by then.

All of the pictures were out of order. I didn't have any of Magnus. But he was in *Två Flickor*. I could feel Magnus staring at me when I looked at it, just as I'd grown breathless when he'd done the sketch at Vimmerby.

I was attracted to Magnus long before I promised Siri not to dream of him. And Siri knew it. I wanted to be like her, but I felt that I *was* him. Siri was going to rescue me by pushing me over the hill. Magnus was the cold-wind top of the mountain just before you go over, the standing there, being able to see forever.

He smelled of snow-topped pine, of charcoal. Siri smelled of strawberries—those were youth. Wild strawberries in milk, delicious and rare.

Två Flickor. Two Girls. I went to my computer and typed the title in English. Then I typed in his name:

Magnus Bergström.

And there he was.

Result after result . . . had enough time passed for him to have accomplished so much? A professional shot of him in Malmö, near blue water. In another photo, his arms were crossed before him on a table in a café. One was snapped of him looking pained, and the angle of the shot made it appear he was falling out of the frame.

I went to my desk and took out a sheet of paper. I decided—for all the things I'd left unsaid—I would write to him.

Magnus, congratulations on your success with Två Flickor.

Magnus, who would have ever thought that your simple sketch at Vimmerby would amount to something so acclaimed? No, that suggested I hadn't believed in him then. No, better to just say that I was glad it had come to this. That people had recognized his talent. Because sometimes, people's talents go unnoticed. Things go unnoticed. *I just want to say that you really have an eye for things, and that I feel, beyond the skill of your painting, that you saw me. People don't often see me. I thought your sister saw me. I was so sad that she didn't come back to school. Am. So sad. Please tell her that. Please tell her: Siri, I have been lost this fall without you. I miss your cheerfulness, the coffees in the cold classroom before the bell rang. I remember your hejs, which always sounded like you were about to tell me something more, something important. Let's try again. For all the things we've yet not said, for all the ways in which we are similar.*

Annie was standing in the middle of my living room, barking as though I were a stranger. I looked across the room at the orange light, the opposite velveteen chairs. Annie was beneath the otto-man Siri and I would share when she'd come to read and drink tea with me. I caught my image in the mirror over the fireplace. My hair, brown again, hung in my eyes. My face was wet from crying. The white sheet of paper shimmered in the light from the televi-sion, vacant.

Siri was done with me. I'd trusted her, opened up, given her part of me, and she'd rejected me. Why couldn't I let her go?

IT WAS LATE enough that I thought I might avoid the other profes-sors. I descended the stairs of Wells, heard voices inside—and turned to leave just as a young adjunct was walking up. He rushed to hold open the office door for me but saw me hesitate to go in.

"You doing okay?" he asked.

Inside, several professors sat talking with Tenny. They all saw me. I had no choice but to go in.

There was an immediate hush.

"I didn't know you were still here," Tenny said.

"Did you think I'd been fired?"

"Because it's *evening*. You don't teach in the evening," she said, looking at the others, sucking in breath, half-laughing.

This was new. This semicircle of professors around her, like she was holding court. The dismissiveness in her laughter. She had never been like that with me. I saw her lean back and slide her hands into two pockets on the front of her dress.

At my desk, my things had been moved again. My tattered blot-ter was propped against the wastepaper basket on a piece of broken tile.

"I just want to get my papers and get out of here," I said.

Tenny appraised me. "Yes, your students have been leaving *lots* of notes for you. And I'm always getting your mail for you—if I didn't, your cubby would overflow!" She swept the notes on the desk toward her. "These are both from early September," she said.

"Do you even hold office hours anymore? What should we tell your students when they come looking for you and you're not here?"

I stood waiting until Tenny wheeled back so I could get into the top drawer. I couldn't bear her oppressive perfume—musk and citrus, like furniture oil.

I noticed her illuminated copy of Dickinson on the corner of my desk, where my lemon vase used to sit. I pushed past her, and she rolled away from the desk to give me more room. I opened every drawer.

"Where is it?" I said.

"Where is what?"

"The little vase. The one like a lemon. I used to keep it on my desk here."

"It's stupid to keep something important in a shared space," Tenny said. "This is a shared space."

"This desk is my space!" I yelled.

"Lauren, you are the *last* person who is allowed to take that tone with me." She turned to the others. "Can you believe her."

The end of her sentence didn't go up. It was a question, but she said it like a statement, like she was spitting. She said it like Gwendolyn.

The others in the circle were sitting back, looking away. Not one of them would meet my eyes.

"Lauren, let me ask you something. Can you believe that girl Frida came here? After everything she has been through?"

She knew something. She wanted me to know that she knew.

I rushed from the office. I didn't go back.

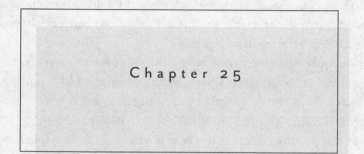

Chapter 25

WHEN I FINALLY had my cast removed, and the nurse cracked open
its husk, tossing away the short strips of Swedish tape, and the
Swedish gauze, stiff with the sweat I'd sweated then, I was shocked
at how shriveled my arm looked and how it bore a blue sheen. The
doctor reassured me that it would puff up again in no time and
that the color of my arm was normal, but to me it was the hue of
the flowers at Neptuni Åkrar. Walking to my mail cubby that afternoon, I tugged my sleeve down all the way for fear that people
would ask about it.

As I pulled out the books and papers, a plain manila envelope
dropped to the floor. No address. If I were being fired, is this how
I'd receive the word? I pressed my fingertips against the sharp
metal wings of its closures, lifted the flap, and slowly tipped out its
contents.

Inside were thin, glossy pages torn from a copy of *Kupé,* a free
magazine given out to passengers on the SJ railway in Sweden. I
glanced at the pages and slid them back in. I left the office, my boot
heels clopping on the floor as I hurried to the ladies' room and shut
myself into a stall.

I sat down and pulled the pages out again. Two girls, bare

chested and reclining on their elbows. They looked out from the painting at the viewer unabashedly. No self-consciousness. Just wide-eyed—could it be called that?—innocence. And then, the incrimination of their nudity.

It was a magazine article about Magnus. There was a photograph of him, a small black and white shot. I didn't know enough Swedish to read the article, but I could tell he was being celebrated for another painting of two girls.

We looked like mermaids, up on the shore for the first time in our lives. The painting was at turns damning and exquisite. Though the images were more impressionistic, less precisely rendered, the girls were definitely supposed to be me and Siri.

In this painting, our skin was blue in patches. This was Öland—Neptuni Åkrar. The beautiful day, the silent day. It had only been Karin, with her tender cesarean scar; Margareta, with her black hair whipping in the salt air; Frida, looking grumpy even while skinny-dipping; and Siri and me.

The painting suggested Magnus had been right there with us, with an easel balanced on the wide, flat rocks of the beach, telling us a story that had us rapt and interested.

I didn't want this moment in a picture. This was my last good day with Siri. I wanted it to be just for us. We were innocents there, but no one would look at this painting and see that. I was angry that she had let this be our last day. My heart ached for her.

Neptuni Åkrar—Neptune's Fields. Blue algae had slicked the horizontal shingles of limestone where the water came in. I had imagined azure flowers were swimming with us. Siri had gotten out of the water right away because of the cold.

Magnus had painted my hair copper and dark again, and it was streaming down my shoulders. From where we lay on the rocks sunning ourselves, we had been able to see all the way up and down the empty beach. There was no one else there. Was he working from a photograph? I didn't remember taking pictures there—and this, this looked like someone working from feelings. My feelings—of childhood—unencumbered, uninhibited.

I tucked the envelope under my coat and made my way to my classroom at the end of the hall, where all the windows converged into a point of glass.

Frida waited for me there.

She shuffled her boots against the floor.

"Aren't you late for your class?" I said sternly, nodding toward Tenny's room.

"I left you something in your box."

I stopped, blinked, and pointed toward the back door of the classroom with such force that she had no choice but to follow me.

We went out the metal door. There was an elevated stoop with a few steps that led down to the school's soccer field. She leaned against the railing.

"Siri looks pretty in it, right?"

I still clutched the envelope beneath my coat, against my chest. I didn't want her to comment on it. I didn't want her to have even touched this picture.

"It's called *Sjöjungfruar*. That means 'mermaids.' It's a little private, I guess, with you both being naked." She frowned and boosted herself up onto the railing. "I don't think people would recognize you in it. You looked a lot . . . different then. I guess it is the same for me. I don't recognize myself in the mirror anymore. I have pimples from stress and dark circles under my eyes from bad dreams. Do you have bad dreams?"

How could I tell her I had nightmares? How every day was a walking nightmare, that this moment was a nightmare?

She laughed when I did not answer. She made me feel like a third wheel, though it was just the two of us standing there.

"Magnus keeps painting you with her. All set in different places from the summer. It's a big deal back home. He wants you to see them."

I envisioned my office mailbox stuffed with more incriminating pages, paintings of my breasts and my smile. I thought, too, of the embroidered calendar in Magnus's room—the goat, the sow, the skeleton girl—and my face overlaid all its figures. I felt a twinge of fear. He was blaming me for something. Behind the glass, I sensed my students watching us.

"Why does he want me to see them?"

"Why *wouldn't* you want to see them, Lauren?"

Because the painting was an accusation.

"Frida, you can't leave things like this in my mailbox. I need you to understand . . . this job . . . it's all I have. If people found out about the time I spent with you this summer—"

"This is not about your *job*. You're afraid to face what happened."

A student breezed past, and I crumpled the pages of the magazine against my chest. I hated Frida being this intermediary between us.

"I don't get why Siri was so keen on you. You act like you don't even care about her."

"Of course I care."

"You shouldn't be able to *function*."

"Is that what you wish for me?"

"I wish you would talk to me!"

"You told people I did something . . . inappropriate. Didn't you tell people I make you *uncomfortable*?"

"I haven't said anything to anyone about you."

"You're lying."

"I haven't. I *wish* I had someone to talk to here. I wish *you* would talk to me."

"That's not going to happen. I don't trust you."

"I've helped you keep this secret, you know. Yes, people are asking what is wrong with me. It's not like I haven't had opportunities to tell many people what happened over the summer. You should be more grateful."

"Grateful?"

"I thought we could confide in each other."

"I don't want to confide in you," I said quickly. "And I don't want you coming near my home again."

"I don't go by your home," she said slowly.

"Didn't you leave me that ticket on my apartment door?"

She was quiet.

"I feel hounded by you. And Magnus. It's too much."

"You didn't deserve her as your friend."

"Probably not," I said. "But it's over now." I tried to say it with force, to make it true.

"No." She flipped up her hoodie and tightened the strings. "It's not over."

"Are you threatening me?"

She walked off.

"Frida!"

I looked across the soccer field. Frida was already on the other side. I pushed open the metal door to the classroom, letting it shut behind me with a clang. My students were all there waiting for me, staring back quietly. I knew they'd been watching the argument through the window.

I gave the class a new assignment, a speech on a topic of their choosing. I thought it would help. In my bag, my pile of ungraded papers was getting out of control—this would be one fewer written assignment for me to grade. I tried to explain the project, but I couldn't focus. I made notes for them on a transparency, but the plastic sheet grew damp from the heel of my hand and I smeared it all. I kept having to stop and consciously breathe. One by one their hands went up, but I couldn't bear to call on them. I snapped off the projector and told them to freewrite.

I could see Frida was still walking the perimeter of the soccer field, a white marble against the green pitch. I watched her for too long. I went to the blinds and snapped them shut.

"Professor Cress, this is bullshit."

"Excuse me?" I turned back to the class. Ana was staring at me with an indignant look.

"This wasn't on the syllabus, and we haven't even gotten all our papers back yet."

"You'll get them back next class," I said. I tried to use the voice that sounded like the previous semester's version of me. "You all have given me a lot to work with. Lots of good ideas. They've been taking me longer to grade. The comments I give you on these papers . . . I really want you to take them to heart, okay?"

"And you still want us to do a speech?"

"It can be about anything you choose."

"You're not even giving us topics?"

"If anyone wants a topic, come to my desk, and we'll discuss possible topics."

The students all got up at the same time.

I put my hands up. "Okay, okay. I'll assign one general topic. Just give me a minute to think."

The envelope containing the pages from *Kupé* sat on my desk. Frida was still visible beyond the glass. *Sjöjungfruar.* I stared down at my hands, bunched into fists. I remembered the slice on Magnus's hand from where he'd punched out Birgit's bedroom window. They'd been fighting about his paintings. She'd told them some things should be off-limits because they could be torture. I went to the blackboard, picked up my chalk, and wrote in letters that took up the whole wall.

Should anything be off-limits in art?

"For those of you who need a topic," I said.

The students wrote it down and looked back up at me for further explanation. I wanted to go further, to say the answer was yes, because some things are torture, some things *should* be buried.

"What if we have a problem speaking in public?" Ana asked.

"You obviously don't," I snapped.

She slid down in her seat and crossed her arms. Someone leaned over and tried to reassure her. She shouted out, "Bullshit," one more time before I assigned them pages for reading and turned to stare at the closed blinds.

Chapter 26

THE WEEK'S DEPARTMENTAL meeting was a den of women professors. They all stopped talking when I walked in. Lately I would see
Tenny whispering in the hallway with Gwendolyn. People were
saying she was a shoo-in for the new full-time position. I hadn't
even applied. I was losing my footing. She was coming into herself.

The hands of those women moved across their students' papers
in unison. Marking splices, missing apostrophes, V's for where the
student should add an article, but never more information. Instead
they drew long lines through sentences, whole paragraphs, X's
through pages to indicate *this is tangential; this is not interesting; this is
not even your original thought*. But what student would offer up any
part of themselves in their straight-rowed rooms?

When the meeting ended, there was the chair-scrape of all the
professors getting up at once, filing out. They walked down the
hallway ahead of me. There were no footsteps, just a swishing
sound, maybe all their floor-length skirts dragging. Then they all
slowed down together, turning to look at me. Their mass parted,
and I could see Frida at the end of the hall, sitting in a too-small
orange chair, her thin legs splayed, her arms at weird angles. Her

blond hair was pulled back from her face in a tight bun, her eyebrows so light, it just looked like bone there.

I could see it. Plainly. I recognized Frida's desperation as my own. I could see from her face she had the same hot, black cloud inside of her that was always full and ready to burst inside of me.

"There's that girl," one of the professors whispered.

Frida approached me.

"*Du måste ringa Birgit,*" she said.

The other professors grew quiet, wondering if it was possible I spoke her language.

Frida pulled off her long sweater, revealing a sleeve of tattoos on her arm. A web of them. A spider on her bicep. Mostly black lines, the outlines of tattoos waiting for color. But there was one long red line, an unraveling ribbon, that went from her bony shoulder to her elbow. And the outline of a girl on her forearm, moving as Frida moved.

The women, now on either side of me, stiffened. They snaked around us and went down into the stairwell, leaving us alone in the corridor.

I took in Frida's gaunt face. Siri had once described her as fragile, and I felt I was seeing it for the first time. Her normally steely demeanor was now a clay urn, fissured with grief and ready to burst. I pushed down that part of me that wanted to embrace her.

"Birgit has been trying to reach you. She says you're not picking up, so she has been calling the school." She handed me a slip of paper with a long stretch of numbers. It was the phone number for the house in Olofstorp.

I thought of Tenny pushing all those notes toward me on my office desk. I thought of the unheard voicemails I had deleted. Now the guilt was setting in. It was Birgit trying to reach me, to call me home, home to the terrible person I was, the selfish, bleach-haired tourist in her foyer, the person who had let her down by not watching out for her sister.

"Birgit wants you to know that Magnus gained a lot of attention from his paintings since the summer. He is having an exhibition in Stockholm. Birgit thinks you should come and see them when it's up."

Birgit thinks.

She started running her black fingernails up and down her forearm, scratching at the tattoos as if to knot and tangle the lines.

"Fine. Forget I said anything," she said. "But I don't want to be their messenger anymore. *Ring henne,*" Frida said, and she went down the stairwell the way the women had.

Ring henne: call her. Why did she say it to me in Swedish? Did she think I knew more than I let on, even a whole language?

I couldn't sleep that night. Around my apartment, nixes bloomed like fungi, playing violins. There was a scratching sound coming through my wall, and I let myself imagine it was Magnus's pencil, scrawling flowers that turned into the face of a sow, of a goat-priest, of two mermaids on a beach, of a large, black bird.

The slip with Birgit's phone number sat on the desk beside my computer. I was afraid to call her. Siri had been sick before that trip to Öland, and she'd begged me to look out for Siri. But Birgit couldn't control her, Magnus couldn't—I couldn't. We were either at the window with worry or bringing her back home like the neighbor woman. I remembered Magnus carrying her off the beach. I remembered the girls holding a cup of warm milk to Siri's lips.

The day of my students' speeches came. I had not expected Ana to participate. But that morning she was there early, in the corner, fiddling with my shoddy overhead projector and its lamp.

"Hi, Professor." She sighed in a cheerful but exhausted way.

Once we got the overhead projector working, I left it on, and it hummed through all the presentations. Two of the students read banned poems from their languages, and I found myself paying attention to the lilt of their speech and remarking on the passion with which they explained the words in English. A girl played a song for us, and though it sounded like a pop song—she said it was an alternative national anthem of her country—it somehow sparked the kind of discussion I used to lead all the time, the kind that changed the room to a place where everyone was safe. I felt almost like my old self.

"Last but not least. You're on," I said to Ana, who went to the front of the room, positioned the overhead projector, and drew down the screen. The machine whirred loudly.

Ana's hand fidgeted before the projector's lamp and made shadows upon the screen. "I always thought of impressionist paintings as old-fashioned versions of those crazy Magic Eye pictures— where if you squinted really tight you could make out the scene, you know? What I am going to show you is an impressionist picture, and it reminds me of the ephemeral nature of time."

She slid her transparency upon the glass.

"Okay, that girl is naked," Adnan said, and the class laughed.

"You can see her breast, but you can't really see the woman's face," Ana continued. "Her mouth is just a slash mark. You can tell it is modern times from the hair, though. She is like a punk."

The painting was done in light colors like a disappearing Monet. There was a black blotch in the middle, meant to represent the woman's mouth. There was a cliff wall. A woman reclined on the sand, voluptuous, everything rounded, except the dimensions of her hair: sharp, blunt bangs, hair like a white triangle, black on the ends. Her face was amorphous and bleak, as though it had been smeared away like a mistake after hours of diligent work. Some aspects of the painting were sharp and accurate. Others were mysterious and upsetting. Perhaps it was the beach setting. Nudity again. I stared at the hair of the grotesque woman and drifted closer to the screen.

"I like the woman," Ana continued. "She is scary and sexy at the same time. I think back to the stories the women in my family told, and they were always about women like this, who ruin things. Can you see what is in the distance?"

There was a white wave beneath the cliff, and upon it, a yellow object strangely suspended in the white paint. I thought, at first, of Magnus's daffodils in the paintings he'd shown me that day in Gothenburg. Then I noted the shape.

"It's an inner tube," I said breathlessly.

"I think it's a boat," Ana said. "I think the woman has made it capsize. It is the woman's fault. I think about in my culture, how it is always seen that way."

"How did you find this picture?" I asked. I felt my anxiety rising. The students were only looking at me now.

"What?"

"Did Frida Dahlström give this to you?"

"Frida? No. What are you talking about?" She came forward to collect her transparency from the glass, but I blocked her way.

"Sit down, Ana."

I stared at the picture enlarged on the screen. I could not deny the strange hair and the terrible downward gash that was my mouth. There was something like tar gurgling from it, molasses full of larvae and hair, a representation of lies. I could feel the light of the overhead projector outlining my body.

"Who is Frida?" someone asked.

"That Swedish girl from the beginning of class. The one who was friends with Siri Bergström," someone said.

A wave rose as they started to murmur to one another.

Someone asked how the last name was spelled.

"B-e-r-g . . ."

"Shh!" I snapped off the projector.

"*Ström*," Ana finished, looking at me narrowly.

I couldn't bear the hiss of their whispering. They were all talking about her now, each their fragments—

"That girl who went to school here . . ."

". . . last semester . . ."

"Quiet, all of you!"

"The girl who died."

I stood, frozen.

"I heard she drowned," someone said.

"When she was found, she was blue," another said.

"Who said that?" I said.

I searched their silent faces, like the words could still be hanging in the air before them. But there were no words hanging in the air and no words inside of me for the feelings now, no words—

"Who said that she died?"

My eyes went to the transparency. The woman held in her hand a bag, a pink bag. I knew what was in the bag. It was candy—Bilar, my favorite. From the sea cliff floated a blotch of blue—the country's flag that floated from every red barn, every lavender-doored cottage, every place.

I remembered Frida's words: *Everything Magnus does is for Siri now.* It was a realization as big as a blue ocean wall, coming toward me with a crash.

But I *saw* Magnus charge into the water and drag in her inner tube. I saw her friends shake out the moose-skin blanket and wrap her wet body in it. They heated up milk in a pan and gave it to her to drink. They coddled and soothed her, and when they talked about bringing her to a hospital it was just as a precaution. She was okay. She had to be okay. I needed her to be, so she was.

I had last seen her lying in front of the tent. I had last seen her there, so she was there. The moose skin was tucked beneath her chin, a cup of milk being raised to her lips, and she was giggling because it had run down her chin on both sides. Somewhere on the other side of the world, the beautiful girl was still laughing. She never answered my calls because she was still camping. She didn't come back because she was still swimming.

Heart pounding, I grabbed the transparency off of the glass and rushed to Tenny's classroom, where Frida sat in the back row, doodling in her notebook.

"Professor Ryan, excuse me," I said. "May I see your student Frida Dahlström?"

All the students whipped their heads around to look at me. Frida's eyes were wide. She gathered her things while I waited in the doorway. Tenny said nothing—just stood there looking shocked.

Near my classroom door, I could see my students gathered in

the hall, watching me. Moment by moment, the focus on their lenses was growing sharper. They were beginning to see me for who I really was. I was losing all approval. I was losing hold.

Frida came out into the hall. I jabbed my finger at the transparency. "Is this supposed to be me?"

"I don't know what that is," she said.

"Don't lie to me! You know Ana. You were friends. You gave her this to shame me." I shook it at her.

"I don't know what you are talking about!"

"That flag. That yellow spot—it is the inner tube. Siri's. From that morning." Now my tears dripped onto it, making the image as hazy as my memories of the real time.

"You think *Magnus* made this?"

"Didn't he? To punish me? Someone in the classroom just said—"

"Now, why would Magnus want to punish you, Lauren? It's not like you've gone months without contacting them. Or like you've spent the semester telling people you and Siri weren't friends, or pushed me away—her one friend here, who could also have used a friend here."

Now the square of blue was actually a circle, now a pool—it wasn't a flag. It was sky. I tried to make sense of the image. I could only see the scrollwork design of the hallway's blue tiles through the plastic sheet.

"I—I'm just not remembering," I said.

This was the black cloud.

"What don't you remember?" Frida said, standing straighter. "You're not allowed to *not remember*."

This was the nighttime-dormitory-parking-lot desire to explode my long steel bridge to the summer. The feeling that Frida was the bridge. This was the desire to clap my hands over Frida's mouth, and this was the horror when I pulled my hand back and found my own dark lipstick in my palm.

"We have to accept it," she said.

I wasn't ready. I would never be ready. This was the moment

she would tell me how Siri had died. This was the moment I'd hear it, and the scenes would be sucked into my ears and into me, and I'd never be able to erase them. I pulled Frida toward me until I had her by the shoulders and she was trying to push me off of her. She opened her mouth, and I felt the vibration of her screaming beneath my hand, the wideness of her mouth stretched out. She yanked her face away.

I watched her wipe her mouth. I watched her tighten her ponytail.

"I will make you remember," she said. "I will make you feel what I feel."

We both turned at the same time. Tenny was coming toward us. Frida gave me a final look over her shoulder and raced off.

"You can't put your hands on a student!" Tenny said.

"Leave me alone."

"Did you see her face? You're terrorizing her."

"You don't know what you're talking about," I said.

"The hell I don't."

"You know nothing about that!"

"About the morning the girl was found? Oh, I know."

It was like all the blinds in the school crashed down at once.

"I know it all. Frida confided in me. You didn't think it was possible, did you? You think you're the only person the students open up to? I must report this."

"Whatever you say, I'll deny it," I whispered. I looked at the lipstick marks on my palm. "And they'll believe me," I said. "Because I am a great fucking liar."

Chapter 27

IT SEEMED EVERYONE knew about the day I'd lost it in front of my students, and that the painting Ana had shown was just an early Joaquín Claussell. I'd never heard of the artist before, but now his name was on everyone's lips. I'd given the Mexican impressionist a modern-day revival, with everyone talking about his work, and about my breakdown.

What they didn't know was that my mind had the capacity to work with a technique like Claussell's, filling and embellishing, mixing and overpainting to nine layers. I'd told Tenny that I was a great liar, and I was. I had the capacity to black things out if I wanted.

I had spent months pretending nothing had happened in Sweden and that Siri had meant nothing to me. *What kind of woman befriends a teenager?* everyone would have said. *What does that say about that teacher, that person, that she can find no friends her own age?*

I'd been afraid that I'd be found out, but I'd done it so well. No one at the school had sought me out. My secret had been safe. As far as the school knew, I had been nothing to her, peripheral, as forgettable to her as she was to me. But once I heard it with my own ears that day in class, I was sawed open by my grief. And I wanted them to see it in me: All the different versions of me are right here, like the rings of a tree. Siri's was the ring of a sunny season after one of too much rain, but after that, a charred ring, evidence of scorching.

It was not a teaching day, but I came to the school early, before the academic buildings opened, and I wandered the campus for hours, trying to ground myself, to make sense of the last months. I walked past the pit and my body remembered the way it felt to balance on the railing, the way the wind had even wanted to give me a push over.

I felt desperate. I went into Dominican Hall, looking for Dorothy. I stood at the small auditorium door and watched the last minutes of her class. Her students were laughing. They loved her.

"Lauren, Lauren," came a gravelly voice.

Gwendolyn approached with an open bag of microwave popcorn in her hands.

"What are you doing just watching there like a stalker," she said. "Come in with us, have a snack."

I followed her dazedly into the faculty lounge to see some other women professors congregated, sitting deep in plush, nonmatching chairs around the long conference table. I didn't know their names, but they seemed to be waiting for me.

"Here's a chair," Gwendolyn said. "Sit down."

The vinyl arms of my chair had been picked at, and the crispy yellow stuffing inside was flaking out. Slowly I started to recognize the others at the table. They were the women from the regular English department who were serving on the hiring committee for Professor Trela's open position.

"What's the matter with you," Gwendolyn said. Again a statement, not a question.

She laughed a little when I didn't respond. I was digging into my backpack, looking for my blue notecards. I tried to remember the names of the writers I'd studied. *Sui Sin Far. Onoto Watanna.*

"You have another of your headaches? Let me try something."

She gripped my wrist and turned it over, applying pressure where my blue veins came together. The whole underside of my arm suddenly looked pale and fishlike.

"Close your eyes," she said.

For a moment I couldn't do it. I felt that if I shut my eyes I'd lose my place in time. I felt my pulse going beneath her fingers and wondered if she could feel that I did not have a headache.

"I do this for my nephew when he gets them." Her voice was different. Almost kind.

I tried to relax. The voices of the other professors floated into the background as I concentrated on not crying. I had a sensation that Gwendolyn had stoppered my blood and it was all up in my face, damming against the backs of my eyes.

"So much tension. It's these students," she drawled. "But you're learning, though, this semester, aren't you. Everyone has to go through a semester like this."

I tried to pull my wrist away from her, but Gwendolyn held on.

"A trial by fire," she said. "But tell us. What happened with that girl? Why didn't you tell us you were going through something like that?"

Because anything else would have been too much. Because my undercurrent was *All is not lost*. That was what I'd agreed to believe. That was my beating drum. And if my depression was a planet of crushing, continual rain, my faith was the forest that kept growing up despite it. To admit that Siri had died would be a burning down of that forest in my one hour of sun, all the way to the deepest root of me.

"What are you going to do now?" one of the women asked me. She had a big slushie drink and was drinking it with a spoon-straw.

"No, this was only a part-time job for her," Gwendolyn explained.

"But you were being considered for the new full-time position, weren't you? Gwen, wasn't it between her and Tenny?"

"No, I never applied," I said.

"Well, that's not what Tenny thought," the woman snickered.

Another professor asked, "Lauren, you teach somewhere else in addition to here?"

"I'm a technical writer."

"A *technical* writer. Oh."

Gwendolyn said, "Dorothy was mandated to bring on more adjuncts with, how do they say it—real-world experience."

Another said, "Because we don't live in the real world, right?"

"She doesn't *seem* particularly technical," the first woman said.

"But how can you say you didn't know?" Gwendolyn said, pressing me. "Tenny said the sister was calling here and leaving phone messages for you."

"The sister?" the woman with the slushie asked.

"Yes. Apparently the whole family was very close to Lauren," Gwendolyn said.

I picked yellow stuffing from the arm of my chair. My thighs felt pressed against the bottom of the table. I shuffled my stack of index cards. One read just *MORRIS, $15*. Another bore the list of tasks I needed to do before their bodies could be released from the morgue. All of the cards were soft with erasures.

"There were two," I said, a whisper.

"*Two* sisters?" Gwendolyn asked, leaning forward.

"They were Chinese American women authors. One did memoir. The other fiction."

The women stared at me in silence. They clearly thought I was crazy. Gwendolyn laughed, this time a dismissal, letting go of my wrist so abruptly, it fell to the table.

I rushed to the ladies' room. In the mirror, I noticed a dark spot on the shoulder of my jacket and picked it off.

On the waist of my jacket, another dark spot. I pinched it off and looked at it. Hair. Wound round, round, a tight little ball of hair and lint. On my lapel, another. I heard the voice of my old boyfriend: *Why can't you take better care of yourself?* I picked them off until the sink was dotted with them.

I stared hard in the mirror, trying to find my eyes, rubbing the spot on my wrist Gwendolyn had pressed, as if to reroute my blood again. I was losing my place in my body and in my mind. There were no tracks, no veins to me. My blood coursed in waves, sloshed in me when I bent at the waist. I was losing all my linearity.

In the days since that class, I had kept dreaming that Siri drowned in the Kalmar Sound, but I knew that hadn't happened. Siri was a strong swimmer. At the blue beach, she was the first one in, and she was able to hold her breath longer than any of the others. The beach at the campground had no real waves. It was tranquil, at times a mirror. Had she been confounded by the darkness? The dune separated her from the lights of the campground. The moon was in and out.

Mångata.

Had there been a road shining on the water for her to follow back? Maybe she couldn't even see the shore.

In my dream, Siri is on the harbor dock, her legs kicking back and forth over the sides. The rest of us stand behind a perimeter of police tape. Up comes my parents' car, pulled from the bottom of the harbor with cranes. I see the bumper stickers—that the car has climbed Mount Washington; that they have a daughter on the honor roll at Liberty High School. Water spills out the sides like two waterfalls until it doesn't. Then it just hangs, suspended there, while authorities on the dock try to decide where to move it.

In my mind, Siri arches like a dolphin and disappears into the water.

"Lauren, may I have a word?"

I turned, and it was Dorothy. The women from the conference room were clustered behind her, peering into the restroom, where I stood, my head soaked from the sink.

IN HER OFFICE, Dorothy told me she wanted all of my ungraded papers on Monday by noon. She had heard too many instances now of my erratic behavior. *Going forward,* she said, everything had to be from the textbook. She had to approve any topics I taught. I was not allowed to use the overhead projector. She didn't say why.

She said I could proctor the midterm and we would talk about the new semester after I turned in my grades. *No more,* she kept saying to my pleading. She was silent when I cried. Then: *I'll see you on Monday, Lauren.*

At home, I worked on the leftover papers through the night, just points and check marks now, knowing that Dorothy would see them and judge me for anything I wrote that was too personal. But it pained me to read them. As the stack grew thinner, the version of me who listened well to them grew thinner, too. Annie curled against the small of my back. There was no skin between her and my spine. Through the wall came the familiar sound of the Vallapils' dishwasher whooshing on.

I stared out into the courtyard of my apartment complex, watching for movement in the other windows, but there was none. I thought about that night months before when the liquid-green lights bounced against the buildings. That night I had been entranced. I'd thought I was witnessing something magical. The next morning I had rushed to tell Siri, but instead, all my history had poured out, and I'd thought the way she understood me was magical, too. Now I realized they were probably just searchlights, or a child playing with a flashlight and tinfoil, something ordinary and sad.

I fell asleep among my students' papers. In a dream I revisit the lavender-doored house. It is the morning after Liseberg. Magnus has practically been wooing Siri, pouring her juice, hanging up her sweater. He has cut her violets. He does his best to please Birgit, too, apologizing when he slams the door, making a list for the morning shopping without being asked, cold air breezing out around him as he stands before the open refrigerator with a pad and pen.

We all sit quietly at the dinette table. I keep stealing glances at Magnus, but he does not look at me. I am wrapped up in my thoughts of him, of kissing him in the sculpture garden, of the adventures we had in Gothenburg, of how he felt and tasted. When he gets up to go around the wall to the kitchen, I follow him in and ask for a glass. He hands it to me without looking my way, his arm extended fully, as if to keep me as far away as possible. I am hurt. He is willing to let me go so easily.

Birgit is on the patio. Siri goes into the bathroom to take a shower. As we stand in the kitchen together, I turn to see if Magnus is okay. All the light in the kitchen, the sunlight pouring through the windows and flooding the wide planks of the floors, the chrome of the chair legs, the porcelain arms of the water pitcher, the clear body of the juice carafe. Then he is beside me, shoulder to shoulder.

"This thing between us," he says.

I can't get air in fast enough. He motions like he is going to grab my shoulders and shake me, but when he makes contact, his hands grasp my hips, drawing them toward his, and I can feel how hard he is, and that he wants me to know it. There is a relenting between us, a falling into each other, an entanglement. His mouth is wet on my neck and shoulders. He lifts me onto the countertop and reaches under my skirt and pulls apart my knees and looks at me. I can feel myself opening to him, I can feel my body changing to let him in, can feel him moving inside me, but also things suddenly changing in the house—the room getting smaller, the roof lowering down just a bit, all the walls growing thinner, all our breaths stronger, ruffling the curtains, shaking out the gutters. I can feel the house coming against me. I can feel Siri stepping into the water, I can feel Birgit leaning over the balcony, her cheek brushing the faces of the soft yellow flowers. With every thrust I fall deeper and deeper into that version of myself. And then: an explosion. The counter creaking from our weight like the whole house could come down on us and on Siri and on Birgit. And then it does.

I awoke screaming, shaking. From outside, something hit the glass, something black. I crawled away from the window, Annie

barking. It seemed to drop: a black splotch on the grass, illuminated by the courtyard lamps.

I clipped on Annie's leash and we went outside to see what it
was. A small black bird, sitting queerly in the grass. Have you ever
seen a bird fluttering on the ground, its wings moving frantically,
a motorized fluff of pain, unable to lift off?

THAT MONDAY, I returned to Stella Maris to hand in all the papers
and proctor the midterm exam. In my classroom, where unfamiliar students sat waiting for the test to start, the old paper snowflakes fluttered in the window. My students were in another room.
Dorothy always switched up the teachers during midterms and
finals because she thought it helped ensure objectivity in grading,
but the prompt was still the same as last semester's: *In what ways
have you changed since you came to the United States?* I looked through
the crowd, down the center aisle between their too-small desks,
and I imagined the pile of essay grading to come.

I read them the prompt. I told them to begin and they hunched
over their work. I watched a young man scraping out an outline in
the corner of his paper. He realized I was looking at him. I dropped
my eyes to the floor and watched the bouncing shadow of my
boot. The students were all quiet. Before long, I called time, and
the students passed up their blue books and filed out.

I was alone in my classroom. I went to the back window and
started to pluck the snowflakes down, looking at the sun-faded
writing upon them. *Where I was lying in my loincloth outfit.* Nikhil.
Even after everything that had happened, the thought of him on
that first day could still make me smile.

Dorothy came into the classroom and took the pile of blue
books from the teacher's desk, switched them with another stack.
"These are from Professor Ryan's class," she said, as though to an
empty room. "Due Wednesday."

She left the room and the door closed behind her. I drifted
toward the desk and sat down, slowly separating out the blue

books across the desk like I was playing solitaire. Somehow, I knew what was coming. Part of me wished Frida hadn't sat for her midterm, that I could avoid reading her response to this question— but when I saw her name on the front of the essay booklet in red ink, I pushed all the rest aside. Frida would talk to me.

> Dahlström, Frida
> Comp 003
> A Time I Experienced Change
> What is change? A lot of people probably think I have a lot to write about in the way of change. I am nineteen years old, and I am away from home and in America for the first time, that's change. But the change that I will write about in this essay is the change that occurred in my way of thinking about coming to America. In this essay I will discuss my original dream, how I planned to obtain it, and how it came to be.
> I had many friends from school but my favorite and oldest friend had her own dream, which was to be living in the United States doing anything. Her name was Siri. She was one year ahead of me and the thought of her leaving hurt me, but I endured it for one year. She came back to see me in the summertime and brought with her a friend from the U.S. who had been her professor. My friend had already grown up and become so different since I knew her. I saw her having in common a lot with this teacher and it hurt me more than having lost her for the whole year. I tried to reclaim my friendship but it was so difficult I always felt at odds with them both. I decided to make my dream to move to the U.S. as well.
> My friend helped me figure out how to apply to this university for being able to stay in the U.S. with her too. She said I could join her in the fall and be her roommate. She talked to me about her dream of being independent coming true. Everything was going to be back to the same

or even better. Then, a nightmare in real life. My friend died during our holiday we call Midsommar.

We all blame Professor Cress. She let Siri go off with a strange man. She should be ashamed. I bet she is ashamed, and that is why she does not return the family's calls. Here at school she acts like it never happened. She denies being friends with Siri. She thinks we're all her friends. How sad! To pick out the pretty girls in the class to make her own club. She tried to recruit me, but I'm too sharp. I transferred out. Flirts with the male students. Her shirts are too low cut. Makes us listen to all her old stories, her ideas on things. She made us sit around her in a circle like she's our leader or something. She uses us to get her own needs met, just like she used Siri Bergström. She uses her class like her own personal therapy session. We don't care about your dead parents, Professor Cress! Get over yourself!

Do you know what it's like to be the one person who does not fall in the golden circle? She is cruel with favorites. She has never shown any compassion toward me. So I say she is a fraud.

Why did she pressure me to transfer from her class? Could it be because I know what really happened between her and Siri? That she invited herself to Sweden, where Siri sought a respite from her with her family and old good friends? How every minute had to be spent together to the point that Siri even told me she was afraid of her?

What is change? Looking in the mirror and not knowing who you are anymore. That is change. I still came, I thought it was a good decision, but I was stupid, and I'm failing all these classes. My opinion is changed. I knew that Siri would want me to have this experience or else I would not have come. I thought I would feel closer to her to be here, but I don't feel her spirit in this place, and she was too good for any of the people here. I thought I would come here and

live out our dreams for both of us. In conclusion, I believe
living for one person is hard enough.

The blue book had eight wide-ruled white pages. The writing
stopped after the third page, but I continued to turn them, white
page, slowly, white page, until I was finally shutting the little blue
book and staring at its back cover. I was supposed to give the essay
a grade, then pass it on to one of the others to read and assign a
grade. The final grade would be the average of the two.

I felt dizzy, like I was spinning. I didn't believe what Frida had
written, but I knew she was desperately trying to get to me and
hold me accountable for *something*. She would connect with me or
destroy me. I couldn't push her away anymore. I grabbed my blue
books and my coat and rushed outside.

If the bell that hung from the dormitory bridge could have
rung, it would have sounded then.

Chapter 28

I DROVE DOWN to the spot on campus where the two roads fed into one. The boys' dormitory on the left, the girls' on the right. I backed my car into a space and got out, all slow motion. I told the girl at the front desk I was looking for Frida Dahlström's room. Third floor—the international floor, she said.

I ascended the stairs. There were sounds of people above, below, all my steps amplified. Colorful ads for local bands and sorority rush lined the halls. On the second-floor landing, music was playing. Many of the doors on the hall were open and girls moved in and out of them, calling to their friends. The smell of shampoo. A girl brushed past me with her toiletries in a pink case. Her hair was wet and draped over her shoulders, darkly soaking her shirt.

The third-floor landing had a big picture window that framed the foggy campus. I noticed one dark rooftop way in the distance. A small triangle, the edge of a bandage. I imagined tugging it, peeling away the blankness and exposing the other buildings, the parking lot, the chapel, the dune, the beach, the Kalmar Sound, like a wound.

It didn't occur to me that Frida might not be in her room. She was surely in, waiting for me. I passed a Coke machine that buzzed like a bug zapper. On the cinder-block hallway walls, there were magazine cutouts of skinny models, girls with huge, doelike eyes, signs along a path. Perfume ads. Men hanging on girls; girls reclining in boats in bikinis; girls embracing each other.

I stopped before an open door. Inside, Frida stood on her tiptoes, peering over a hot plate, stirring ramen noodles. She wore striped socks to her knees and shorts in the heat of the dorm room. There was an open box of wheat crackers on her rumpled bed. She looked at me in an unsurprised way, her eyes ringed with black eyeliner, making them look as big as those staring out from the perfume ads in the hall.

"Am I in trouble?" she said.

On her bed was a pink plaid comforter. Above it, glossy pictures: Margareta's double-toothed smile. Karin with her baby daughter in her arms. Lots of Siri. The photos were arranged in a heart shape. On the opposite side of the room there was an empty desk and a bed with a bare, striped mattress.

She followed my eyes. "I don't have a roommate. They assigned me one, but the girl left early."

I went to the bare bed and let myself sit down upon it. A round candle was burning on a trunk in the middle of the room.

"Siri was supposed to be my roommate this year. Remember?" I pulled the blue book out of my coat and showed it to her, damp from my skin. "Why did you write these things?"

She sat on her bed and scuttled back against the wall.

"I have no one to talk to about how I'm feeling." She scratched at her head, her neck.

"Then tell me."

"She was found floating in the inner tube—"

"No. She didn't die at Midsommar. I was there."

"That man made her go swimming—that man *you* let her go with—and he just left her there. She couldn't find a way to swim back in. The water was too cold. She floated out in the cold water until Magnus found her."

"I was there. Frida, I was with Magnus when he found her. She talked to me when Magnus brought her out of the water. She looked up at me. She was angry with me. Don't you think I remember every second of that?"

"Karin told me you let her go with that man."

"Siri did what she wanted! She never listened to me!"

Frida closed her eyes. She couldn't see my hands bunched into fists.

"Karin went after her. *She* went looking for help."

She shook, though her legs were pink from the radiator heat. Her ramen started to steam. Something was changing in her.

"She didn't want to go to the hospital. She thought that guy Viktor had drugged her drink and that she'd get in trouble. She was afraid that if she got arrested, they wouldn't let her return to school. We wrapped her in the blanket. She stayed in the tent."

"What happened, Frida?"

Even though I knew I needed to, I didn't want to hear it.

"It was chaos. You left with Margareta. Magnus was yelling at everyone. Where were you? Back to the United States! You cannot miss your plane, yeah? You were done with us. She kept crying that Viktor's drink was in her chest. But it was water in her lungs."

Her voice seemed to be turning inside out. It was a strong tide suddenly reversing, and I could hear her hatred for me going inward. I felt the undertow of her.

"She begged me not to let Magnus take her. She said it was another instance of him being overprotective, and I listened to her. Oh God, I had missed her. I loved her. I loved being the one to zip the tent closed, to scream in his face, to tell her what he looked like when he stormed away."

Her eyes were so blue. It was like she was looking through me, into space. Her voice was a shell I crushed to my own ear.

"I couldn't ever say no to her," she said. "Saying yes kept us close."

And with that, everything stopped.

The wave of emotion, the pull of her, the anger in me—it stopped.

That day at the lake, that first day, when we were floating on the wooden raft—didn't *I* push them off one by one, hand Näcken each of their ankles, until together we formed a human chain to the bottom? I blamed myself for everything that had happened from that day forward. And I could see, now, that Frida did, too. That was why she had been trying to connect with me. That was why I had been trying to push her away.

Blaming myself was a pause. It bought time. Making it about me meant Siri's story hadn't yet ended.

Frida was a ball on her bed, rolled up on the pink covers, a snail with no shell.

"Frida," I whispered.

She wouldn't look at me. Her black-rimmed eyes were fixed on the striped mattress across the room.

"It wasn't your fault."

"I tried all semester to talk to you about what happened. You kept pushing me away," she said.

"I didn't know."

"How can you say that? You *knew*. You had to know."

I looked around for the blue book essay I'd brought with me. Like we could review it together, line by line.

"Right, Lauren? I wasn't alone here this whole time in this, was I?"

Had I known? Had I known it in my bones since the fall, even from those first unreturned calls? Is that why I deleted all those voicemails without listening, why I wanted to jump that day into the pit when I caught sight of similar blond hair? I'd wanted to jump then because I'd wanted to jump from the van, because the feeling in my legs had never been right again since then.

It was all too much. "I'm sorry," I managed to say. I backed out of her room. "I'm sorry," I said, rushing toward the stairs, past the posters of girls looking at me wide-eyed. In her room, Frida let out a scream, the loudest, loneliest of screams. The scream of a killer, of one being killed.

Somebody should see if she is okay, I thought.

But no one would, I thought.

If they did, they'd find her a twist of embarrassment and pain. She wanted her story and she wanted her blame. Easier to keep arguing inside about who should take the blame. Our kind of grief waited on revision.

I kept going. Past the Coke machine, past all the doors that were shutting, one at a time, falling dominos against her screaming. I went down the steps and out into the fog. I could hear the rain pummeling the roof of the red van. I remembered the way Siri looked so disdainfully at me on Midsommar's Eve, when we sat across from each other in the van, wrapped in blankets, surrounded by sleeping bodies, in silence.

Chapter 29

IT WAS AFTER five o'clock in the Humanities office, and people were leaving for the weekend, taking with them their clutter and noise so that Dominican felt empty. I went to the mail cubbies and slid my midterm grade list into Dorothy's box.

"Those are late," she said.

I turned and saw Dorothy standing there. She was wearing a flowing skirt that seemed to take up the width of her doorway. Her hair was pulled back, and the rings on her red fingers glittered. When I paused, she smiled and beckoned me into her office.

I let out a breath as though it were that day I'd run to her office, that day I'd stood outside her door, desperate to be let in.

"I don't want to believe these stories," Dorothy started. She pulled out a chair for me and I sat in it. "But is it true? You hit Frida Dahlström outside of your classroom? And that you went into the girls' dormitory and upset her?"

Her eyes searched mine. When she spoke next, her voice was low and resigned.

"You know what I'm going to tell you."

"You're firing me."

"We're just not *inviting you to return*. Let's say that. Adjuncts enjoy employment here on an at-will basis. You were never a full-time employee here. So nothing bad on your record. No record."

"No record," I repeated.

"That's right. We even . . . wish you the best." She managed a smile.

"You said I was a good teacher."

"We wish you the best," she repeated. "*I* do. You know I do. I wish you the best. Don't make this any harder than it has to be, Lauren."

I stared at the gold-edged planner on her desk and noticed, beneath it, the cover of a blue book.

I started going through the lines of Frida's essay in my head while Dorothy rolled her great copper rings around and around her fingers. Those rings were like the beads of an abacus as she moved them back and forth over her knuckles. The skin on her hands was shiny, as though rubbed to a polish.

"Frida Dahlström's essay," I said.

"What?"

"What she said on her midterm about me and Siri."

She stared back in confusion.

"Frida said I harassed her, but I didn't harass her. I went to Sweden last summer because she and I really were friends. A teacher and a student can be close—"

"Who?"

"Siri Bergström."

"Lauren, are you talking about that girl who died?"

I knew. So surely everyone knew. Surely *she* knew, and this was the reason—

"Did you just say that you were with her this summer when it happened?"

She moved her planner to scan the year on her desk calendar. She moved the blue piece of paper to her waste bin. It was not Frida's blue book. No, I'd left that crumpled on the desk in Frida's room.

I was being fired because I was losing control. And not grading

papers. And found that day soaked from the sink. And yelling at
Ana in the classroom. And at Frida, in front of Tenny.

"You were in Sweden with her? Over the summer? How do
you explain that, Lauren?"

"She was my friend."

"When, friend? You met her when she was a student in your
class?"

"I—"

"Lack. Of. Judgment," she said.

"She was there for me when I needed a friend."

"Oh, God!" She laughed. "It's a damn shame, Lauren. You really
are talented and smart. It's just a damn shame that you are so
needy."

The word hit me in my stomach.

Yes, of course that was what it was. She picked up her phone.
Was she going to ask security to escort me out? I drifted from her
office. It was over.

THAT NIGHT, I dreamed that I was the one who drove the van away,
with Siri in the back, fussing at me for having driven off the campsite. I floored it down the highway to the bridge, and when we got
there, I slammed on the brakes and our van skidded off the road,
over the shelf of rocks. The back of the van went in first. All the
kids were laughing as the van filled with water and we drifted
down to the bottom of the Kalmar Sound. I kept my face up near
the ceiling to breathe in one inch of space. Soon even my eyes were
covered over with brine, but I could see it through the window—
the Port Llewelyn ferry was coming in. We would soon crash into
its underbelly. Bodies loosened themselves from the blankets, and
the striped mattress floated, suspended. We were all in space. All of
them drowned dotted with bubbles, and Siri's body rose to the
top, petals from her crown floating around her.

No, I convinced myself upon waking. *That is not how it happened.*
But my memories were never the same twice. They were waves

building one upon another, changing, disappearing. I was going crazy, in a process of trying to label each wave.

THE VALLAPILS KEPT coming by, but I didn't answer. One day I woke to see Ravi standing over my bed with my fishbowl under his arm like a football. I sat up quickly, and he rushed to set the bowl back down on my nightstand.

"How did you get in here?" I said.

"I need to feed the fish."

I remembered I had given him the extra key to my apartment so he could take care of my pets while I was at work.

"We've been worried about you. My mom prays for you," he said.

I could hardly bear his large brown eyes, his earnest expression. I looked over at the little red fish negotiating the rocking water.

"You can keep the fish. Just tell your mommy I'm okay."

Ravi picked up the bowl again, the water sloshing. "I will take good care of him."

"I know you will."

He walked slowly from my bedroom, making sure the water stayed even.

Another day, I heard his mother talking outside, and I thought she was talking to a neighbor, but when I got closer I could hear she was talking softly through the door to me, telling me it was all going to be okay. Tears streamed from my eyes, but I couldn't open the door.

ON MY NIGHTSTAND, a ring in the wood where the fishbowl had sat. Bunched tissues. Half-drunk cans of cola, the Latin workbooks. I didn't know if it was morning or evening. Light was light. I screwed up my eyes against it.

When Magnus and I get to the campsite, things are awakening like a morning house. A house with all the curtains thrown back,

its furniture pulled out onto the patio, all the scuff marks showing, dust rising into the sun. There are police cars, red and blue
lights swinging, and an ambulance, and all the kids who were free
and dangerous the night before are serious now.

The girls sit in a circle of plastic chairs, bundled up in sweatshirts.

"Why didn't you stay with Siri?" Margareta asks.

"Me? Where were you? Where were any of you?"

Frida is shaking, her eyes full of tears. The girls try to comfort
her. Then the police say it is time. We all go single-file to the dune.
I see little bits of paper in the sand, and I pull them out and they
are whole portraits. One is of Siri with a lavender rose behind her
ear; another is of my mother, who looks also like me.

"Siri's a good swimmer," Magnus says. "Don't worry."

A giant crane is pulling Siri's body from the water, and water
rushes off of her like waterfalls on either side.

We are all standing behind cones and police tape, yellow police
tape with big, black-marker, hand-drawn letters that run the
whole length of the ocean.

"*Vem var mannen?*" a policeman asks me.

I look around.

"*Vem var mannen?*"

"Tall," Karin says. "Broad. There was something wrong with
his skin." She speaks in English, as if to spur me to join her in a
description of him. They are asking about the man Siri went off
with. The waves now are like breathing, rasping for air, the first
breaths after being underwater for a long time.

"He had red skin," I say. "He taught technical writing."

Out of the corner of my eye I can see the girls screaming, falling
to their knees on the sand, a collective organism. I never had
friends like these: witnesses to one's whole life. The crane is rotat-
ing her now and she is hanging above our heads, an arching circus
performer on a swing. It is lowering her down. It is laying her
gently before us on the beach.

"Who was the man?" the policeman says. He is on the phone.

The long cord wraps around our legs and around the metal workings of the crane, and he isn't going to let me go until I answer him. In the water, fiddle strings wag, beer cans clink, a wicker-waisted bottle with colored wax bobs. Then the colored wax melts into the water, and the horizon rises to stripe the morning sky.

They are perplexed about the blue tinge to her skin, those peculiar flowers from Neptuni Åkrar. They wonder if she floated from the other side of the island.

It is morning. All I want to do is cry, to have my anguish, to fall to my knees on the sand, but they want me to answer questions, work through probate, identify their bodies, take my mother's necklace home in a plastic bag, fill out the forms, the pen is not working, but here is a new pen, continue.

Her eyes are open. Magnus's face is wet, as though he has dived under to get her. Her hair is wet, and her face is pressed in on one side. I rush to touch her round belly. *We have the same belly shape,* I say. Her lips are a silvery purple. For a moment I think I can see the barest smile there, a loving erasure of all dark things.

I am yelling *I'm sorry.*

"Lauren, we need you to focus so you can help us."

I start to recite beautiful words Siri taught me during the trip. *Glöda:* "to glow." *Mångata:* "the roadlike reflection of the moon on the water." *Blunda:* "to cover one's eyes."

"It was the man who lives in the water," I say.

"What is that?"

"He sits on a rock, out there in the water."

"Like an island?"

"No. Not an island. Underneath."

The policeman pulls me away from the others. "Did you know the man?"

"He . . . he drags women underneath and makes them live with him forever."

"Who does?"

"Näcken," I whisper.

I can see his eyes changing as he goes from thinking it is a translation issue to thinking I'm out of my mind.

They think I am in shock. Birgit is called and drives all the way from Olofstorp. She is beside herself, but when I am taken to the country hospital, where they give me medicine and I sleep, she stays with me, and keeps saying, "Yes, I forgive you. Please don't think on it anymore." The doctor barely speaks to me in English, but Birgit translates that it is just the shock of it all, a tiny fracture, but all will heal again, when I am ready. She gives me an index card that lists all the things I must do to get better. And then to the airport. And then I am in the air. And then I am home, checking off the things I must do every day.

The card was just the back of my airline ticket, worn soft from handling, and from—when things were too hard—the erasures.

Chapter 30

THE WAY I was remembering things scared me. It was like my brain was trying to show me how fragmented I'd let things become. There was a loop, this potential for perpetual motion, jumping from the van or not, making love to Magnus or not. But I was slowly coming to terms with what had happened despite myself. I wrote in my journal and scrutinized every line to make sure it was absolutely true. I didn't want to lie to myself anymore. I felt there was something I needed to do to make it all stop.

The ticket to the Santa Lucia service had a different message for me every time I passed it on my dresser. That I had once thought it came from Siri. That I had once thought it came from Frida to taunt me. That it was a ticket back in time, and to go would be to confront something I had been fearing. When I picked it up, it bore an energy in my hand, as though if I were to let go, it would flutter like a sail.

I went into my closet, and there on a back shelf was the wood-cut the shopkeeper had gifted me in Gamla Stan. Santa Lucia, holding her own blue eyes in a golden dish. The shopkeeper had told me I was blind. I ran my fingertips over the grooves in the wood, the place where the saint's eyes stared back at me. In that moment, it struck me that Frida had left the ticket under my door-knocker the very day she had smiled at me in the classroom, the one day things had gone right. That day I'd imagined her going to Siri to report to her that maybe I wasn't so bad. Frida had been lonely, and she'd been blaming herself, like me. She'd left me the ticket to try to connect.

I decided to go. The evening of the service, I got myself to-gether and drove to the old chapel in town. For a long while, I sat in my car, staring at the places where melting ice pied the black-top. It took me some time, but I went in.

Inside, the church was bright and crowded, alive with voices that sounded like the summer past. There was a man in the vesti-bule tuning a long, narrow violin with buttons like an accordion. I asked him what his instrument was called, but he said it so fast, I didn't catch it. That, too, felt like the summer.

There was an old woman collecting tickets, her long skirt pat-terned with vines and flowers. "It is a *nyckelharpa,*" she said, nod-ding toward the man with the instrument. "Very traditional. He'll play later, when we dance."

I handed her my ticket.

"Do you have a daughter in the program tonight?" she asked.

I shook my head.

"A sister?"

"No. Why?"

"It's no problem. It's just that this ticket is a special one for fam-ily members of the girls and boys," she said.

I took a seat in the back row, right on the end, and the nave went black. From behind me came the sound of girls singing. It sounded so distant, as though it were coming from outside, from beneath the icy trees.

People turned to see the girls enter. I did not expect my tears. An extraordinarily beautiful girl with flowing, white-blond hair came down the center aisle. The girl's white robe was tied at the waist with a red satin sash. Upon her head she balanced a frightening crown adorned with lit candles. She moved slowly, her head perfectly still.

A luminescent procession followed—twenty girls filling the church like white smoke, their white robes swishing. Each girl held a single candle before her face, singing the slow, entrancing refrain, "Santa Lucia," their candlelight illuminating the stone walls.

I didn't let myself look at the girl with the crown. I had come here to face something, but now I was afraid. I feared she was holding my eyes in a dish. I feared I was made of wood. I feared I'd burn up.

The young women congregated upon risers at the front of the church, each of their clean, fresh faces prettier than the last. When they were all arranged, their angelic chorus died away. The one with the candle crown sang it through one time more, alone, in a dreamy mix of Swedish and English that reminded me of being with Siri's friends. Lines floated up to me:

> *Natten går tunga fjät,*
> The night walks with heavy steps.
> *Skuggorna ruva,*
> Shadows are brooding.
> *Stiger med tända ljus,*
> Bearing lighted candles.
> Santa Lucia, Santa Lucia.

I was suddenly tremulous with recognition.

The girl with the white-blond hair, the one who sang alone, in the center of them all—it was Frida. She looked so innocent. And, as impossible as it seemed that she could see me in the darkened nave, she was staring at me.

As their musical director led the girls through a series of cheerful Swedish holiday songs, I tried to avoid Frida's gaze, but her eyes were locked on mine.

The singing ended, and the girls proceeded back down the aisle two by two. Frida came last. One of the candles on her crown was slightly lopsided. It seemed the candle could fall at any moment and catch her bright hair on fire. But she walked with confidence, the long sleeves of her robe falling back from her thin white wrists, her star tattoos nowhere to be seen. When she passed me, she began the "Santa Lucia" chorus again, singing alone, even as the doors closed behind her and her volume diminished, as though she were singing inside of a box.

The lights came up and everyone applauded. I felt ill. I told myself it was just the seasickness of hearing all that Swedish again in the dark. But it was Frida. That she had wanted me here after all that had happened with Siri. I gathered my coat up from where I had been sitting upon it. From my coat pocket I grabbed my hat and gloves.

People waited their turn to file out of the church, some of the older people needing help to leave. I had no choice but to stand in line. All those puffy coats, people all around me. My anxiety grew, and I fixated on little yellow flowers an old woman in front of me had pinned into her hair.

By the time I made it to the door, Frida was waiting for me. She had changed into regular clothes, her crown gone, a long, wool-lined denim coat thrown over her shoulders like a cape. People pushed by us, moving into the church hall.

"I can't believe you came," she said. "I left you that ticket when I thought us friends."

With all the people around us, I was pressed up against Frida, our faces nearly touching. I could see wax in her hair, from where the candles had dripped. I waited until I could step back again before answering her.

"It was beautiful," I said. "You have a beautiful voice."

Some of the other girls from the procession laughed and pushed by us, tapping Frida on her arm as they passed. Frida didn't acknowledge them. Her eyes were on me.

"I hope you will stay with me awhile and have some food in the hall." She pointed to the ink stamp upon my hand. "I told some people you were my mother."

I pulled on my gloves.

"Just for a few minutes," she said. "Please."

She turned and went through the double wooden doors to the church hall, then looked back at me with a semblance of a smile. I followed her. In the hall, people in traditional Swedish dress stood behind tables of handicrafts and food. Red-glazed wooden horses, clay trolls, crocheted ornaments, pastries in the shape of curled-up cats with raisin eyes—I didn't belong among these things. I tried to push aside the eeriness it made me feel because I could sense there was a reason Frida still wanted me there, and I needed to know it. I kept her bright hair in my line of vision. I followed her until we were shoulder to shoulder at the refreshment stand, where a woman handed us Styrofoam cups brimming with deep-scarlet liquid.

Frida and I sat down on some folding chairs away from the crowd. "It's called *glögg*. Try it. It's strong."

I sipped. It burned my throat. I could feel it in my nose. At the refreshments table, I watched some boys reaching for cups of it and an old lady swatting at their hands.

"There was a time I thought Siri had left me the ticket for to-night," I said.

"Thinking of Santa Lucia makes me feel close to her. But Siri would never have come to something like this. I think you know that."

"What do you mean?"

"Didn't she tell you what happened to her mother?"

I shook my head, and I expected Frida to thrill at that—that she'd known more about Siri than I ever did. I think she expected it to thrill her, too, but it didn't.

"Siri only told me that she died. Magnus told me a little more." Frida scoffed. "Magnus."

Small children were starting to gather near a Christmas tree in the middle of the church hall. One of the little boys came to Frida and pushed himself into her lap, laughing and demanding attention. She set him back down on the floor, and he ran off, leaving behind his conical hat. Frida spun it in her hand, and its glittery star caught the light.

"You heard in the songs tonight how Saint Lucy comes with her candles to cast out the darkness? Magnus heard her go out. He woke their mother, and she got dressed and went out after Siri in the terrible cold."

Magnus had called it a saint's day. But of course. It was this day. Santa Lucia.

It had been the smell of candles—that was surely what had made me sick during the service, the candles, and how all the girls went out the back door into the night, into the memory of the story Magnus had relayed.

I remembered asking Siri how her mother had died. *Nobody knows for sure,* she'd said. Her mother had always worn a necklace that appeared to be made of silver coins. A beautiful detail—a check mark in her essay's margin.

Nobody knows for sure.

All Siri had told me was that her mother wore shift dresses all year, but in the summers, she was always in a too-small black bikini, the first to jump into the cold water, gathering her and Birgit and Magnus in the glade to tell them stories charged with magic.

That's what I knew of her mother—how she'd laughed and jumped and loved to swim. That was very Siri, always looking for the living parts.

My story is nothing like Lauren's. She really suffered, she had said.

I hadn't even pressed her. I felt aggrieved that I'd asked so little when I had the time. For so long I'd been angry that Siri had revealed herself to be selfish, but I'd been selfish, too.

Magnus had said that since that night, he and Siri had been fixed in a state of perpetual motion—she going down and unlocking the gate, he at the window, trying to decide what to do. Maybe, for Siri, it was the going after her that felt like love. She going out, the lover or the brother or the friend chasing after her. The girls at the campground that morning had despised me because they believed to love Siri was to go after her, and I hadn't done it.

The musical director came up then and hugged Frida. "We are so glad you were able to come here tonight and be present for Frida," the thin woman said. "It has been hard for her to be here in the U.S. alone. She's been missing Sweden so deeply."

The woman walked on before seeing that there were tears in Frida's eyes, then tears slowly moving down my own face. I realized that for Frida, I had been the closest person to Siri she had in America. Part of me now wanted to reach out and embrace her.

"Birgit told me she has still been trying to reach you."

Her knee bounced. She was holding a paper plate with a pastry on it, a shiny braided cake meant to look like a kitten with two raisins for eyes.

"At the school? I was fired. I'm not there anymore."

"I know. They told Birgit that. She was devastated. She knew how much the school mattered to you."

It meant a lot to me that Birgit had remembered that. "She told me once that taking care of Magnus and Siri helped her through her depression. I told her teaching had done the same for me."

"And then Siri, of course," Frida said. "She helped you."

"Yes," I said.

Frida had finished her drink and was scooping slivered almonds from the bottom, eating them with her fingers. "She was complicated, and she drove us all crazy, but she wasn't afraid of sadness in people. I think that's rare."

I had once thought that Siri was going to fix me, that this golden girl had been put into my life to thaw me out. And then I thought of how angry I had been at her because she'd deserted me, rejected me, after coming with a candle to my door.

I drank my *glögg*. I remembered the glue and gold glitter she'd used to patch her artwork, not to cover what went wrong, but to give it light. Being with her had sometimes felt like gold running through me.

Siri was imperfect. She could be rude and selfish. But she could also mend things with her lines of gold. For so long, I'd thought only of myself and what she hadn't ultimately been able to be for me. I could see now that her friends and family weren't chasing her down to fix themselves. They were trying to get her to see how much she was loved. Did she ever really know it? Did she ever know she could slow down, let herself rest in it?

"You've got to go back and see them, Lauren. Birgit and Magnus."

"No. There's no way, Frida."

"They want to see you. They want you at that exhibition of Magnus's work."

"I can't. I don't know what I'd even say to them."

She tossed her cup and plate in a nearby bin. "You wouldn't have to say *anything*. You don't always have to have the right words," Frida said.

I remembered standing as I had been told to do, by the front door as people came into the funeral home, and all those wrong, wrong words they said that didn't go away, and all those people who had nothing to say but rushed to stand nervously in their curious clusters around the room, and I shook my head at Frida.

"I'm going back," Frida said. "I thought I'd feel closer to Siri here, but it has been . . . a nightmare."

"I understand," I said.

I needed a break from talking. I felt out of breath.

"I'm not coming back to school after the holidays," she said.

"I wish you the best," I said, and I remembered that was exactly what Dorothy had said to me when I was being dismissed.

Frida got up from her chair.

"Is it the English teacher in you that thinks everything can be fixed with words? Sometimes it's just enough to be around people who loved the same person you loved."

She went off to pour herself another cup of *glögg*. I watched her drink it down. I thought she was coming back to me, but she didn't. She pulled on her denim coat and walked out of the church hall into the night.

Chapter 31

I WAS SUPPOSED to get up and go after Frida, take her hand, follow her all the way back to Sweden. But in the days after the Santa Lucia service, if I left home at all, I was careful to avoid the roads near the college, for fear that I might take a wrong turn and wind up in Magnus and Birgit's gravel driveway. I kept the curtains drawn for fear I'd see the spires and rooftops of Gothenburg, dive into the ocean from my apartment, swim to its shore.

But I did return to Stella Maris. One day, when the school was on its winter break, I drove past and saw that the student parking lot was empty and the guard's gate was raised, with the kiosk empty. I turned onto the campus road and parked beside my old building. As I entered, I saw the janitor, John Sled, salting the path near the main entrance of Wells. Down in the stone-walled basement, I could smell where he had the coffeepot on.

The door to the adjunct office was open, but no one was inside. I went in and locked it behind me. To my surprise, my old books and papers still lay on the desk. Some were marked with coffee rings where someone had set a mug upon them.

One by one, I opened my desk drawers. Empty. I went to Tenny's and opened hers. Nothing. I started opening all of the drawers to all of the desks, pulling them out, the metal innards whining and screeching, all of the drawers semester-break empty, nothing but pencil shavings and paper clips inside.

I heard the rattle of keys and the door to the office unlock.

John Sled opened the door, pulling his cart behind him. His blue jacket hung from a broomstick on the top. He saw me and stopped.

"Miss Cress."

"Hello, John," I said.

I held an empty metal drawer in one hand.

He came into the office, looking at his keys, shaking them. I noticed his cart blocked the doorway. I held the metal drawer against my body like a shield. He noticed.

"You've been gone."

"Yes."

The palms of my hands were pressing into the metal runners of the drawer.

"You were, uh, close with that girl," he said. "That pretty girl. The blonde. Sometimes I'd see you leaving campus together," he said.

I wondered if he could hear my heart beating against the metal. I couldn't read his expression. What had he heard, pushing his cart past my colleagues' doors? What had he read from the wastepaper baskets of this place?

"What's her name?"

"Siri."

"I've been looking for her to come around. Do you think she'll come back to school in the spring?"

"Yeah," I said. "Sure."

"She was kind to me," he said. "You can tell her that. But I bet she doesn't even remember me."

"Siri remembers everybody," I said.

"She seems like that kind of person. She used to talk to me sometimes."

I thought of how other people would dart their eyes, ignore

him, pretend not to see him coming. Of course Siri had slowed down and spoken to him. She'd probably made him visible to the whole school on those days.

"I'll tell her you asked about her," I said.

"You will?"

It was lying about my parents that contributed to my forgetting them. It was when I started lying about Siri that those memories grew tangled, too: First, that we hadn't been friends. Then, that I hadn't known something was wrong. That the good might not have existed because of the bad. That the friendship never meant anything because it didn't mean everything. The distance, this ocean between me and Sweden, was even letting me lie to myself, tell myself that Siri might still be there, that she would be the person I had to answer to if I went back.

"She died last summer," I told John.

"What?"

"I'm sorry. I didn't know how to say it. She got very sick after a camping trip."

"Oh my God."

I had told the truth. I had said it out loud. I felt a breaking-open in me, a place for the truth to live and take hold in a way that it hadn't been able to before.

But for John, all his energy drained away. He seemed younger suddenly, the way grief makes all of us younger. Like we have a separate timeline of wakefulness to this shock of the world, and all of those events are strung together, the line itself hidden, an ancient road that rises up after a rain and then drains away again into the past.

"Wait," he said. "Just wait."

Anxiously, he started going through the items on his cart. There were plastic baggies of twine and balled T-shirts. A Styrofoam clamshell container with tiny items sorted by color: plastic figurines, dice, a small Rubik's cube that was once a key chain. Suddenly he was presenting me with a damp clump of paper towels. He opened them like petals of a flower.

Inside lay the lemon vase.

"Someone put it in with the garbage. This was yours, wasn't it? I didn't think you would have thrown it away."

My heart was beating so fast. I took the vase and turned it over and over in my hands.

I noticed for the first time that there was glitter in its glaze. It looked like lemon sugar candy. It was so heavy, for a small thing. It was a sign and it was a memory—of Siri, and of *blomsterlupiner*, and of unexpected gifts. All good things. It was what I had come for, what I had been searching for in the drawers.

"I was afraid I'd lost it," I managed to say. "Thank you."

He didn't respond, but when I looked up, his back was rounded again, and he was tapping the items on his cart to count them.

After he unlocked the wheels of his cart and pushed on, I sat down in my chair with the vase in my lap. I ran my finger over its curve and felt a ridge I'd never noticed before.

I held it up to the light and saw that there was a spot of gold glue along a tiny crack in the base. Siri had repaired it the way she repaired so many of her artworks, in a way that illuminated the break. She had said that repairing it with gold could make the thing more precious. Like the wounds that leave different marks on each of us and change us.

The colorful flyers, the sunlit desks, the new ice trapped between the screen and the glass of my picture window. I had loved this desk at this school, my window. It would belong to someone else in the spring.

I had started to gather the papers scattered over my desk when I noticed an envelope tucked underneath my tattered blotter. It was a letter. The long envelope, addressed to me at the school, had Birgit's name in the return address. Its postmark was August.

I picked up Birgit's envelope from the table.

I opened it and read it through. She had known I was in trouble. She didn't want me to blame myself for anything.

It was an opening. It was a gap in space, and to open it, read it—

her words delivered me out of the warp of memory to the realness of that place and time again. It was my ticket back.

I'd been trying to find a way to make the loop stop, and I knew then that Frida was right. I needed to go back. Easier to go across the world one more time than to do it unceasingly in my mind for the rest of my life.

I put on my coat and ran to the car. I turned on the radio, thinking of Adnan in my classroom, his unintelligible grief poem, his head-thrashing, honest mess, delivered in front of all of us, given freely from his soul. I turned the music up as loud as it went. I screamed, and this was a hundred jam jars bursting, this was the clay urn splitting, and this was the hot balloon of my grief exploding. Finally. The latex splats of it, the shreds drifting down, the hot air going out.

Chapter 32

I GAVE THE taxi driver the address.

"This is Tunnelbana," the taxi driver said, pointing at a sign on the street. "You take the T right there."

I didn't understand. He sighed, and we fought traffic to get across the city. It was midafternoon but dark as night. We passed parks flooded by giant spotlights so that kids could play on the basketball courts as though it were still sunlit day.

I laid my temple against the coldness of the taxi window. Just hours before I had been coming out of my bedroom with a packed suitcase. Annie had kept walking ahead of me to block my path. I knew she didn't want me to leave her again. I'd crouched and run my hand from her soft, curly head to her white, wagging tail. She'd pressed herself against me, lengthwise, like she wanted to feel as much of me as she could.

"I love you," I told her. She licked my face, and when I smiled, she tried to lick my mouth, like she had never seen me smile before and it looked delicious.

I took her over to the Vallapils, who had agreed to watch her again. I'd never been inside their home before. The small pictures on the walls, all nailed a little too high up, bore the serious faces of gurus, and the smells of spices were lovely on their side of the door. Annie went straight to a corner, and Khushi rushed to her with a folded blanket.

"That's how she was the whole time you were away last summer!" Ravi said.

Annie lay on the blanket, and Khushi petted her back. The girl whispered to her in her high, rare voice, then laid a row of tiny plastic dolls before Annie's nose.

"No, *that* is how she was," Mrs. Vallapil said with a smile. "Inseparable all summer. Best of friends." She touched my shoulder. "You needn't worry about her. You just go and have a meaningful visit with your family."

I hesitated, and she looked at me with concern.

"It's not my family," I said.

"What do you mean?" she asked.

"I don't have any family. I had a friend who passed away recently, and I am going to go pay my respects."

Her hand went to her mouth, and she closed her eyes. "Was it the young woman with the colored hair?"

"Yes," I said.

She threw her arms around me and hugged me hard. The father and the children stopped what they were doing to watch us. The next thing I knew, Ravi was hugging one of my legs and Khushi the other.

I felt loved by them. I thought of the familiar whoosh of their dishwasher, the kids' voices in the stairwell, the mother coming to me with plates of food—there was a long list of ways they'd loved me, though I'd been blind to it.

Annie barked at me when I handed Ravi her leash, and it made me feel good to know that she wanted me to come back for her. When I left, Mr. Vallapil lifted Khushi up so she could kiss me on the cheek, and he leaned in to whisper to me.

"You better come back. I don't mind the fish, but I'm not keeping the dog."

I nodded.

"You better come back," he said. Gently, he reached out and touched my hand.

"This is it," the taxi driver said now. He stopped the cab short and pointed at the glowing sign for the T. "I told you. That address you gave me is for a station."

I paid and stepped out. Lining the curbs were stalls, all painted the same color red, their clapboard awnings held open with stick shutters. A thin layer of snow iced the ledges of the old buildings, and along the tops of the stalls, ovals of sausages hung like garland. It was a Christmas market. There was *glögg* for sale, and reindeer meat to sample, and knitted ornaments. A man dressed as Santa poured hot chocolate from metal thermoses, one in each hand, and the top of his hat brushed the ceiling of his kiosk. People carrying shopping bags pushed past me, disappearing through the entrance of the Tunnelbana.

I looked up at the station lights. I wondered whether Birgit had given me the wrong information. We'd talked on the phone before I left the United States. She'd been polite, said she'd heard everything from Frida, and pushed away any semblance of apology from me. I looked at my watch. I was a few minutes late. I wondered for a moment if she'd recognize me, my hair dark again, all these layers of winter clothes.

But then I saw her, coming toward me on high, wobbly heels. She'd cut her bangs blunt, and where her coat was open at the neck, I could see she was wearing a necklace that Siri used to wear all the time, a tiny cross. At once I felt ashamed that I'd forgotten about the cross.

She embraced me. Her small frame—it was like holding Siri. I could smell her hairspray. She was crying. The rock of her crying against my chest was my own rhythm of grief. But she was hugging me. I'd been so afraid of what to say, and here she was expecting nothing. Here she was holding my hand as she paid both our fares. Here we were, together going through the subway turnstiles.

I thought we were about to board a subway car. She'd told me to meet her at this address, and she'd take me to the exhibition of Magnus's work. The air was acrid. With so many people pressing against me, I felt I was being carried along by them, inside a vein. We descended the escalators to the train platforms, where the walls arched and spread around us with long blue and green arrows pointing deeper down, down. There was a smell, familiar and woody, growing stronger the deeper we went. Then I realized what I was smelling.

It was paint.

Paint that bled off paper that had been put in the ground. The images, buried, had dripped down through the ground and re-materialized.

"Lauren, what do you think?" Birgit asked.

On the rough bedrock of the station wall was Siri's face. And my face. Neon colors with tiny flashes of silver and bronze.

It was a two-story-high rendition of *Två Flickor*.

Was this a trick? It felt like an exposure. It was an explosion, like I'd burst open completely, and all my months of missing her were on the wall.

Someone bumped me from behind. I looked to the left and the right—there were more. There were some above the tracks, lit up by an oncoming train, animated by the flash of its approach.

In one, I walk ahead of the viewer through Gamla Stan's cara-mel alleys. I look over my shoulder with a beaming smile. I have excitement in my eyes. I am wearing a white tank top, and on my shoulder are the three freckles, pink, blue, and green. My skin is golden brown with a suntan, and my hair is the same color, tinged with copper. It was the early morning we had run down the main street of Old Town. The mouths of yellow alleys had reverberated back our laughter. How could I have forgotten that morning?

Another painting, on the side of the station stairs: me, lying in a mound of hay. Vimmerby. I am viewed from the side, and the hay around my face makes me look like a lion. My eyes are closed, and I am laughing with my nose scrunched. Bars of light fall upon me.

People milled past. They were all about to board a train or coming off of one. The shock that had first seized me fell away. We had been those people. We had been happy, looked at each other that way, lain that close to each other's bodies. In every painting where I could see her eyes, I saw her compassion, and it made me so happy because I knew Magnus had painted it and despite the way she treated him, he knew it had been there inside her, too.

There were gradations in the rock, and our faces were distorted in places, but Siri was just as beautiful as a giantess on these walls as she had been as a pixie in my classroom.

I heard Birgit laugh, and it made me turn to her quickly. I almost couldn't believe she was able to laugh like that while still grieving.

"Birgit, I'm so sorry," I said.

"I told you please not to apologize to me—"

"I *knew* something was wrong, but I didn't want to acknowledge it, so I let myself believe all semester that she was just angry with me. Better that than—" I stopped.

"I remembered you telling us that they would have looked down on you for being in Sweden with Siri. You told us how much teaching there meant to you, and you were going to apply for that job. I didn't want to ruin that for you. You said how much it meant. That you didn't have anything else. I know that feeling. And I knew Frida would be there. I thought you two could help each other."

"It didn't work out that way. I was terrible to Frida. Terrible to all of you."

Her blue eyes shot toward me, at the crack in my voice, at the tears streaming from my eyes.

"No, Lauren. Frida is doing the same thing and she is living in a hell. What happened this summer was no one's fault. There is nothing for you to worry about with us. Do you understand me?" She looked over my shoulder and gestured to the other side of the station. "We're all just glad you are here now."

I turned, and the train that was there was pulling off, and I could see, suddenly, clear to the opposite end of the track, where Magnus was.

He stood against one unpainted wall, the world moving in a blur around him. He was staring at me.

"You're the person who finally helped soften Siri's heart to him," Birgit said.

He drifted toward us. He was wearing a suit; Birgit and I were in black dresses. We were all clothed for a funeral. When he reached me, he started taking off his tie, fumbling like he'd never worn one before. I felt we were both trying to get in air.

"You were the one who told me she still loved the paintings in the T," he said.

"Yes," I said.

"Everyone in Stockholm knows your face now. You are famous," he laughed. "More famous than me."

He handed me a program with the Tunnelbana symbol on it. The booklet discussed the history of art in the Stockholm underground, which dated back to the 1950s. The title of Magnus's collection was printed at the top.

"*Guidebok*?" I asked.

"I promised her at the end I'd help you see." He pointed up at a portrait: Siri and me sitting with green beer bottles between our ankles beside a harbor. Black and white lines of ships jut up behind us like scaffolding. "That's Nyhavn," he said.

Yes, it was. But he hadn't gone with us there.

He slid his hand into his suit jacket and drew out a book, bloated and faded.

I gasped. It was my old *Per Vikander's Guide to Sweden,* the same one we'd illuminated with memories in the days before Magnus threw it in the fountain.

"You left this behind," he said.

"I thought it was ruined."

I'd thought the trip was ruined. The friendship.

I opened it and saw my old handwriting, bleached out from

having been in the water. But written over those ghostly entries, in purple pen: new writing. Siri's hand. In some places, she'd traced what I'd written to make it legible. In others, she'd drawn pictures. Places circled—the places we had traveled. In the blue sea beside the map of Öland, a list of the flower names she'd taught me. *Baldersbra; Jack-go-to-bed-at-noon; sandklint; rödklint.* Just as I'd listed them in my mind, sitting alone in the tent that rainy night.

I looked up at the giant paintings on the walls with new vision. Me in Gamla Stan. At Neptuni Åkrar. My eyes-screwed-shut profile in the hay—it was Siri who laughed beside me and with me from that angle. He'd taken our memories from the book and enlarged them here.

I clutched the guidebook against my chest. My fingers stretched and curled around it. I ached to reclaim every piece of her inside it, every bit of the wholeness that had evaded me since the summer.

On the inside front cover, there was a note that trailed down, getting smaller near the bottom, curving up to write sideways along the page's edge. Arrows telling me to turn the page. Parentheses where it left off, directing me somewhere else, where it would begin again. The letters growing smaller and squashier, not enough margin space in the world for everything she wanted to say.

Then: *Kram*—a hug, *och puss*—a kiss. Like the book was the end of a long, long letter.

The cover was soft from old water, but also from the way Magnus's hands must have opened and closed it a thousand times to see her handwriting.

I closed the book. I thought of the long comments I used to scrawl in the margins of her essays, the small spaces first allowed us.

The subway cars zoomed in, breathed, pushed on. I closed my eyes, let myself feel being beside him, this man who knew her and grieved her and loved her. I was afraid that the sound of a train taking off again was the sound of his moving on, but he remained beside me, perfectly still, another person who had loved Siri. I'd been attracted to Magnus because I'd thought him wounded, like me. I think it was because Magnus and I knew we had been loved once, and we were trying to get back to that. We were flying parallel for a while on the way back to that.

Birgit had come to stand with us. "He did a good job, yes?"

"It's incredible," I said.

"He wanted to record every detail. But it's hard to remember everything. Thank God we have others to help us remember. But you know, even if all of this washed away tomorrow, it would all still be okay. It would all still be written on the heart of God."

Someone came to Birgit and asked her a question in Swedish. Magnus stepped away to sign someone's program. I sat, those words repeating over and over in my mind against the music of their talking.

My whole life, I'd been working to remember every detail about my parents, feeling that all fell to me. But in coming here, making the decision to come back here, I knew this time I didn't have to go through this alone. It could be different this time.

Frida had said that it might be enough to simply be with other people who loved Siri. With the proximity of our bodies, I think we felt the same thing: that we each had a piece of Siri inside of us, parts that only we would ever know. It made me feel like we were connected.

Birgit came back to me and looked at me like she was reading my mind. "You have us," Birgit said. "Our difficult family."

It was something she'd said to me last summer. I remembered my heart racing when she first said it, lifting at the possibility that I might ever be seen as a part of their family. Now, standing with them in this place, after all that had happened, I knew it to be true.

On the wall before us there was a painting of a white horse. Five girls sat upon its long, long back. I recognized Karin, Margareta, Frida, Siri, and me.

"That is *Bäckahästen*," Birgit said. "It's from mythology. We call it the Brook Horse. The story goes that children would be mesmerized by its beauty and leap upon its back. No matter how many children, its back would grow longer and longer to accommodate them all. Then the horse would jump into the water and swim to the bottom, drowning them."

In the painting, Margareta is smiling with her extra teeth bared. Karin's golden locket is open in the scoop of her neck. We all look exuberant. But that horse did go on to drown us, didn't he?

A drowning. It felt truer than what I'd been told: That pneumonia had overtaken Siri's body after she was pulled from Kalmarsund. That she'd spent time in the hospital going through the guidebook, writing over the faint ink and talking to Birgit and Magnus about the things we'd done.

In the horse painting, white-haired Frida is holding on to Siri, her face buried into her shoulder so hard one might not know it's her, unless they know how hard she held on, always, to Siri.

"Did you notice?" Birgit said, reaching out to touch the mural. "The horse's feet do not touch the water. I think Magnus painted it that way for a reason."

This moment is the joy just before they go under, I thought.

Chapter 33

THE TREES CAME together over the road so that I was driving through a long, long tunnel, with only clicks of light. I'd find that beautiful hill we lay on, I told her. The one where we could see the water from all sides. I imagined that she was the sun, and I could be closer to her there, for as long as the sun stayed out that day. I drove looking for that town with the surf shop, the one with the path that led in all directions away, into the fields of windmills and sky. But it was winter, and the sun had come out late and was setting fast. It was almost down when I saw, on the side of the road, the entrance to the campground, now deserted.

There was the gate, rolled back. There was the empty kiosk, where the man in lederhosen had taken our money, and the registration building, its windows dark.

I rumbled over the familiar gravel drive. I parked and walked down the road where Margareta had once carried Karin upon her back toward the tall bonfire. Between the slender bodies of the trees, I could just make it out: the tall dune, dotted with snow.

Now, in the distance, a man's figure, making his way toward it. Another figure swept past—a woman. A cold wind spun round me. I could suddenly smell my father's smell, feel my mother's hands. My father was running with a white sail behind him. Or was it snow being moved by the wind? They ran past me, disappeared.

Were they all waiting for me on the other side of the dune? The touch of my mother's rose-petal hands, the smell of my father's black coat. I felt them calling me. The vibration of girlish laughter: Siri, saying, *Everything is fine, follow me, I will make the way safe.* She was waiting for me to swim with her, just as she'd made me promise to do at Midsommar. It was cold, and everyone said you must not swim, so of course we had to.

I used my hands to claw my way up the dune. When I got to the top, the sky flashed with a familiar, glowing green light—it was like the light I once saw outside my apartment window. And then the lavender of her front door, and lemon-drop yellow, all in bright lines that whipped back and forth, like long ropes of candy. Then there were flashes like waves being viewed from underneath, like the whole arc of heaven was the body of a fast whale, and the sky bore the iridescence of shells.

I would remember those lights as the Northern Lights, though Magnus had once said it was impossible to see them that far south. He told me that what I thought were the Northern Lights was actually the dawn. I would remember feeling seen there, as I was seeing them.

I went down to the beach, where a white line of foam had frozen on the sand, and I picked out some reeds that had been made pliable by the lapping of the water. I tried to braid them into a circle. I started to speak the names I remembered, and in my mind, they appeared. *Jack-go-to-bed-at-noon. Baldersbra. Chicory*—Siri's favorite. Up they came, blooming from the snow.

I put the frail crown of reeds in the water. As it drifted away, I wanted to remember all the flower names. I wanted to remember everything, and I felt that fear again, that forgetting such things about my parents, about Siri, would disconnect me from their love forever.

But what had Birgit said? *It would all still be written on the heart of God.*

When I was young, I used to think that if God was bearing witness to our lives, it was to record our names and the good and bad we'd done. But in that moment I had the feeling that if there was any book, it was a much bigger one, with all our stories, all the ones that I remembered and had forgotten, and not just what had transpired, but all the narratives there ever were, all the trajectories our lives could have taken, all our dreams come to fruition, all the bad decisions leading to good luck, all the sadness leading to a bursting open.

Maybe a true friendship is being able to hold, equally, all of those pieces. I was broken, but now there were people who held me, just as they held Siri. I had experienced a true friendship, a precious friendship, and there could be more. There could be other versions of family, of love.

I saw Siri first as someone who might save me, then as someone who had failed me. But love was holding all the pieces at the same time. And it's always true, whether we remember that or not. Perhaps because of that, though there are things we might forget, nothing is ever really lost.

Our book was a big book, and it would have names for not just the grave markers but everything we ever were, all our hopes and dreams, every broken piece of us, and tons of notes in the margins, winding their way all around. In our book, all our pictures were in order, and any torn pages were repaired with gold.

I headed back through the wood to my car. I saw a path. A pressed-down place in the snow I had not seen before, an ancient road that had risen up to meet me.

The woods ended in a glade. And there, standing crookedly behind an abandoned red house with white-framed windows, was a *midsommarstång*.

It was tall, covered with ivy, and draped with striped ribbons that snapped in the wind. This is what Siri and I had gone looking for in Loftsvik that day—what she had wanted to show me. A symbol from her childhood, of better times. The ivy was dried, and the ribbons were blanched. I realized the pole must have been there since last Midsommar.

We would have danced around the *midsommarstång*. We would have laughed like nothing bad had ever happened in our lives. A memory of it would have been recorded in the margins of our guidebook. A painting might have been rendered from that memory. At home, I would find myself remembering it with as much joy as if we had danced around it. I would come to realize that there are things that you don't see when you are lost in grief. But things were coming back to me now.

ACKNOWLEDGMENTS

To ALL WHO are struggling, who don't know if their voices matter; to the writers and artists who wonder if all they do will forever be invisible, I honor you.

To the tellers of stories for which there are no comp titles; the writers of "unlikable" female narrators; to the misfit writers; the parent-writers scribbling after their babies go to sleep; the writers writing in their heads; the writers writing in their cars; the writers living in their cars; retiree writers who feel too old to start; the young writers whose families tell them it's not practical to continue; the twenty-year "overnight successes"; the poor ones, the sick ones, the baffled, the lost, the marginalized, the slushed, the ones with no writers groups, the ones with destructive writers groups, the ones who want to clear a path for others—I see you and urge you to keep going. You are not alone. Please believe in yourself, even when you don't believe in yourself.

I send thanks and love to JW, my exceptional friend, who has always been able to see when someone is hurting. You came into my life when I needed a thawing out from grief, and you welcomed me home into a new world. This book is partly a list of the things I feared could go wrong. They didn't.

I send gratitude to my loving and dedicated agent, Katherine Fausset. Thank you for standing by me through everything, and for showing me so much compassion and friendship. This book would not have been possible without you.

I send love to my incredible, otherworldly editor, Clio Seraphim, visionary, motivator, friend, who believed in me and these characters when I feared no one else would. Thank you from the bottom of my heart.

Thank you to everyone at Curtis Brown and Random House. Thank you to Sarah Horgan, Diane Hobbing, Nicole Ramirez, Aja Pollock, Ayelet Gruenspecht, and Melissa Sanford.

Thank you to all who have ever been part of the Writer to Writer Mentorship Program, the most heart-driven phenomenon of literary service I have ever been a part of. I am forever grateful to the mentors who have freely given of their time and talents to the next generation of writers.

I am grateful to all the people who have nurtured and loved me and let me love them back.

I want to give thanks to Julia Phillips, who is such a model for me of the kind of writer I want to be in the world.

Thank you to my extraordinary writer friends: debut-author-sister and angel Natalie Jenner; Sandra Gail Lambert, who fought breast cancer at the same time I did; Lori Ostlund, Jerod Santek, Liz Paley, Terry House, Ananda Lima, and Martin Wilson. Thank you to Liz Stein. Thank you to Alice McDermott, Rebecca Makkai, and Tania James—the women workshop leaders I needed so much. And deep thanks to two of my early writing teachers, Nick LaGrega and Sam Ligon, both beloved.

Thank you to Sue Adams, Annie Werbitzky, and M3.

Thank you to the communities at Sewanee, Bread Loaf, the Tin House Writers' Conference; The Muse Writers Center in Norfolk, Virginia; the MFA Program at the University of Florida; Svenska Skolan in Washington, D.C.; and the American Scandinavian Association for their winter Santa Lucia services that marked each of the twelve years I took to write and edit this book.

Over those years, I had a baby, worked full time, and went through cancer treatments.

Thank you to my fellow 2020 Debuts who have had to have their dreams come true in a different way because of the pandemic.

I know your words will still find their way to the readers who need them.

This book would not be here were it not for my kind and beautiful husband, Blair, who sacrificed so much to give me the time necessary to create. All those years of "Can I go upstairs for ten minutes?" "Can I have a four-hour block?" of being the only person to take our daughter to birthday parties and to care for her while I was at conferences or writing in the car down the street—thank you for believing in me and being my partner. Thank you forever.

And finally, to my beloved Sarah, I pray that you can always look up into the sky, dark or light, and know that you are not alone.

The
ALL-NIGHT SUN

Diane Zinna

A BOOK CLUB GUIDE

IF MY BOOK

by Diane Zinna

Originally published in Monkeybicycle

IF *THE ALL-NIGHT SUN* were a wake, it is my father's, and I'm fifteen, there with teenage friends. We break away and go down into the funeral home's basement and sneak into the showroom where they sell the caskets lined with satin that my family couldn't afford. My friends put their feet up on the flower-print sofas, open the drawers to end tables, find straight pins, and make jokes "This is what they use to pin the eyes closed!"

If *The All-Night Sun* were a voice, it is the Long Island accent that my friends shed first because they could afford out-of-state schools.

If *The All-Night Sun* were a spray of coffin flowers, it's chrysanthemums because they are the least expensive. They turn brown around their edges the fastest, usually before the service is over.

If *The All-Night Sun* were a meal shared with family, it's a cold cuts platter handed to you during break time at the funeral home that you carry home on your lap in the passenger's seat, the Saran wrap sticking to your tights. You put it on your dining room table and your aunt and cousins gather around to criticize it and the fact that the coffin was closed. They say, "Why couldn't you even put his picture on top of the casket?" They take all the seats around the table and you and your mother eat ham rolls off of paper plates in the living room with the TV set turned off.

It's a question—what if you dove into the water and came out blue? What if you made love in the grass and turned green? Sat out in the all-night sun and turned orange, just stayed that way? I have stayed that way.

If *The All-Night Sun* were a taste, it's salt licorice in long ropes; chocolate bars mixing with the taste of lake water after a swim; sticky marshmallow candy, making you sticky all over.

If *The All-Night Sun* were a crematory, it's the kind that sends home ashes in a plastic bag inside a cardboard box, a box to be discarded in a hotel lobby trash can at a popular family resort. (I've stopped telling people which one. They are always shocked.)

If *The All-Night Sun* were the beach, it's that time you stopped for water pills at the supermarket before meeting friends.

If *The All-Night Sun* were a country, it's not this one. If it were a school, it's the kind that closes for plagues. If it were a bird, it's one that sits so long on the branch outside your kitchen window it makes you Google, "Bird Omens."

If *The All-Night Sun* were an urn, it's brass and it's sealed, like a metal football, dropped in a lake. You can't remember if it was inscribed with your last name or had those peely sticker letters that would have washed away by now, with all the tides and whatnot.

If *The All-Night Sun* was a cacophony, it would be the crowd of people shouting that something has rolled up on the sand that looks like a metal football.

If *The All-Night Sun* were a closet, it's a mouth.

If *The All-Night Sun* were a monster—it's that luminous horse that appears beside lakes. Children cannot resist jumping on its back, and it stretches its back longer and longer to accommodate more and more children, and then it jumps into the water and dives to the bottom.

If it were a crown of flowers, it's one long drifting on the sea, discovered on another shore, maybe by you.

If *The All-Night Sun* were a meal eaten alone, it's at Subway in black clothes, when the sandwich artist rolls their eyes at me, and I say that I just came from a funeral to make them feel sorry. I don't tell them the funeral was ten years ago.

If *The All-Night Sun* were a psychic's reading, it's one that shrugs, "They're there, but they are doing their own thing in separate rooms and not really wanting to talk right now."

If *The All-Night Sun* were a dress, it's black with white fabric roses around the neckline that you can twist when you are nervous. The flowers self-replicate and grow larger when your voice trembles. Soon you are only a décolletage of white fabric roses that grows up around your head and conceals your face.

If *The All-Night Sun* were a chair, it's broken. If it were a moon, it's a sliver, and you're looking for its other parts on the grass. If it's a pond, there is a whale inside it, singing its mournful song and never hearing any echo-y answer back.

If *The All-Night Sun* were a friendship, it's the kind that sits in a photo under a magnetic frame on your fridge and surprises them years later when they come to visit.

If *The All Night Sun* were a gift, it would be received with, "You don't just give someone a rabbit! You need to check first to ask if they want a rabbit!" Then it would be possibly rehomed/possibly adored, best pet forever.

If *The All-Night Sun* were a thread, it's a lifeline. If it's an article of clothing, it's a life vest. It's no day cruise out of Tampa, I can tell you that.

If *The All-Night Sun* were a piece of pottery, it's broken, repaired with gold. There are Japanese artists that mend broken pottery with gold as a way of showing that a thing—or a person—is made more precious by the ways it has been hurt. Here is a vial of very fine, gold glitter. I like to throw this shit on everything.

QUESTIONS
AND TOPICS FOR DISCUSSION

1. Lauren and Siri's relationship is the central tension in *The All-Night Sun*. Was their relationship inappropriate? If so, when in your opinion was the first line crossed? Did their relationship remain inappropriate after the school year ended and Lauren was no longer Siri's professor? Why or why not?

2. Both Lauren and Siri lost their parents at relatively young ages. How does each react to her fate differently? How do these reactions affect their lives?

3. When friends and strangers ask about her parents, Lauren often lies. "The idea of their drowning in a car—I feared that by sharing it, the image would continue to live in other people's minds," she says. "I came to believe the most polite thing to do was let the memory of it die inside me. And part of me started to die away with it." Do you agree that lying, in some instances, is the "polite" thing to do? How do these lies keep Lauren from processing her grief?

4. Lauren often talks about how much she loves her teaching job—she considers it one of the only things she has in life. And yet, she's quick to risk it all for the chance to travel to Sweden with Siri. Why do you think this is?

5. What did the Sweden trip represent for Lauren? What was she hoping to find? What kind of person did she hope to become?

6. Where else have you seen the Midsommar festival represented in popular culture? How do these representations differ? How are they alike?

7. In Sweden, Lauren begins to see a different side of Siri—cold, cruel, full of anger. Do you think this side emerged when Siri went home, or was it always there and Lauren just didn't see it?

8. How does author Diane Zinna use Swedish folklore throughout the book?

9. Why do you think Magnus buries his mother's portraits?

10. What draws Lauren toward Magnus? What do they have in common? Do you think they could have had a relationship if not for Siri?

11. After Magnus draws the portrait of Lauren and Siri sitting back-to-back, Lauren runs away without looking at it. Why do you think she does this?

12. What does the annotated guidebook symbolize? How does what happens to the guidebook mirror Lauren and Siri's friendship?

13. Why do you think Lauren didn't jump out of the van when Karin did?

14. "She was at the age when she was supposed to be reckless," Lauren says of Siri. "I was at an age when I was supposed to be responsible." Do you agree with this statement? Why or why not?

15. Frida, in her essay, accuses Lauren of "[using] her class like her own personal therapy session." Do you agree with this assertion? Overall, do you think Lauren was a good teacher?

16. Just like she lied about her parents, Lauren lies about Siri after her return from Sweden to avoid facing the truth about what happened to her. How do these lies keep Lauren from processing her grief? Have you ever been tempted to lie about something to avoid the truth? Do you think it's possible to both know and not know something?

17. "When you don't share your stories," Lauren says, "you eventually lose their normal starting places." Why is it important to share your stories and memories? What is the balance between dwelling on the past and ignoring and forgetting it?

DIANE ZINNA is originally from Long Island, New York. She received her MFA from the University of Florida and has taught creative writing for over a decade. She formerly worked at AWP, the Association of Writers & Writing Programs, which hosts the largest literary conference in North America each year. In 2014, Diane created the Writer to Writer Mentorship Program, helping to match more than six hundred writers over twelve seasons. Diane lives in Fairfax, Virginia, with her husband and daughter. *The All-Night Sun* is her first novel.

dianezinna.com
Twitter: @DianeZinna
Instagram: @DianeZinna

ABOUT THE TYPE

This book was set in Bembo, a typeface based on an old-style Roman face that was used for Cardinal Pietro Bembo's tract *De Aetna* in 1495. Bembo was cut by Francesco Griffo (1450–1518) in the early sixteenth century for Italian Renaissance printer and publisher Aldus Manutius (1449–1515). The Lanston Monotype Company of Philadelphia brought the well-proportioned letterforms of Bembo to the United States in the 1930s.

RANDOM HOUSE BOOK CLUB

Because Stories Are Better Shared

Discover

Exciting new books that spark conversation every week.

Connect

With authors on tour—or in your living room. (Request an Author Chat for your book club!)

Discuss

Stories that move you with fellow book lovers on Facebook, on Goodreads, or at in-person meet-ups.

Enhance

Your reading experience with discussion prompts, digital book club kits, and more, available on our website.

Join our online book club community!

f g randomhousebookclub.com

Random House Book Club [TM]

Because Stories Are Better Shared

RANDOM HOUSE